Fear flooded through her again as a sense of impending danger squeezed her heart. Her feet seemed frozen to the wooden boards beneath them. The encroaching fog pressed in on her like a smothering animal.

Again she heard the falcon's eerie cry. She sank to her knees, cowering away from the evil around her. Closing her eyes, she prayed for assistance.

Soft footsteps sounded behind her.

She rose and whirled around. A black form loomed through the fog.

Molly screamed as a hand grabbed her arm. She twisted away, part of the sleeve of her gown ripping away. Then two arms wrapped around her and she was pulled forward in a smothering grasp against the dark form. She slipped down and out of the clutching embrace, stumbling backwards in her panic to escape.

Her fingers grasped at a railing where there was no railing and she felt herself falling . . .

MISTRESS OF FALCON COURT

CHARLOTTE LAMMERT

ZEBRA BOOKS
KENSINGTON PUBLISHING CORP.

ZEBRA BOOKS

are published by

Kensington Publishing Corp.
475 Park Avenue South
New York, NY 10016

Copyright © 1989 by Charlotte Lammert

First Printing: May, 1989

Printed in the United States of America

Chapter One

1846

An unearthly shriek brought Molly to her feet, heart pounding in fear. Huk! Was he outside in the storm? Mythical harbinger of doom, but real to her since she was a child. Or was her imagination working overtime? Were the legends of her mother's people truth or fantasy?

"Huk calls when evil is nearby, Molly," her mother had said, eyes fixed on some faroff vision in the flickering flames of the fireplace. "The quills of his feathers carry red poison. When he screeches in the night, someone dies." Her black braids had glistened in the light from the shooting tongues of fire as she turned to look at Molly. The soft doe eyes in the heart-shaped face were solemn and filled with awe.

Then seeing her daughter's fear she smiled reassuringly and picked up the book on the bench beside her. "But let us not think of Huk," she said. "We must concentrate on your reading. Your father wishes you to be knowledgeable."

Molly returned to the present as thoughts of her gentle mother quieted her pounding heart. Huk was just one of the many tales told by the Indians and nothing for her to fear. But she had heard his call the night her mother died. She was twelve at the time. When she told her father of the eerie cry in the night, he brushed her away while his grief-stricken eyes watched the labored breathing of his beloved Amatil.

Her mother was an Indian of a coastal tribe in the territory known as California. She had left her people to take a wild Irish trapper as husband and follow him into the Sierra Nevada to live in the rough log cabin he provided. When her daughter was born, Amatil's happiness was complete.

They were a contented family. The cabin was always a comfortable shelter—warm in winter and cool under the summer sun. They were a happy family until Amatil took sick with mountain fever and wasted away into death. Then Colin O'Bannion's laughter was buried with her and his life became a dreary emptiness. Although five years had passed, even a smile was a rare thing on his face. He chored doggedly and was kind to his daughter, but part of him was dead.

Molly shuddered as a gust of wind cut through a crack in the log cabin chinking. Straining her ears, she wondered if she had mistaken the howling of the wind for the voice of Huk. Where was her father? The snow began about noon and by all good sense he should have been here hours ago. Was the man daft?

A faint halloo sounded over the wailing of the blizzard and Molly leaped to fling the wide door open. A wall of snow fell in on the floor, followed by her father leading a limping horse burdened with a form roped to the saddle.

"What are you thinking of, father?" she shouted, pushing the door closed behind the strange parade.

Turning, she ducked around the restive feet of the black horse as he pranced on three legs on the wooden floor. She shouldered the huge head aside and looked closely at the ashen face of her father. "What . . ." she began, then tried to grasp him as he fell.

"Molly," he said wearily as he sank into a heap before the fireplace. His head touched the floor and the remaining words were muffled in a moan.

Then she saw it! An arrow protruded from his back and blood oozed around the shaft. A cry of terror escaped her. "Pa, you're hurt!" She knelt beside him and gingerly touched the embedded arrow. "Shall I pull it out?" she asked fearfully.

He groaned and pushed her away. "Ye've not the strength, child . . ." A cough nearly strangled him as red-flecked phlegm spewed from his mouth. When the spasm passed, he motioned toward the bundle on the horse. "See to him," he muttered.

With a bewildered glance at the blood on her dress, Molly went to pull the man from the horse. She meant to lay him gently on the floor, but he slipped from her arms with a great thump that roused him to consciousness.

A groan escaped him as he stirred. "*Que pasa?*" he mumbled. "Garanon?"

The black stallion nickered and nuzzled the man with his nose.

Both men were caked with snow that began melting into puddles on the clean floor. The black horse heaped further indignities on the mess, but when Molly grabbed the reins to turn him out into the night, her father intervened.

"Leave him be," he gasped. A spasm of pain crossed his face and he wiped his mouth with the back of his glove, then flung it disgustedly off his hand when he noted the blood.

"Let me help you, father," Molly said, kneeling to remove his boots. "What happened?"

"Indians," he began, but a cough interrupted him, a cough that gurgled with his fluids. He lay helplessly trying to regain his breath while a blue tinge slipped under the skin on his face.

Molly slid her lap beneath his head, raising it so he could breathe. The panic inside her subsided when the dreadful gurgling cough ceased.

The stranger pushed himself erect and looked dazedly around. He said something in Spanish, then shook his head. Slowly, his eyes cleared and his jaw hardened.

Her father took a deep breath, wincing at the pain, and when he spoke his voice was faint. "Can you speak English? *Inglés?*" he asked.

"Of course I speak your barbaric tongue," the man said as he rose. "You brought me here, *senor?*" He shook his head. "I cannot remember what happened. Where is here?"

"You were lying in the snow with your horse standing over you," Colin said tiredly. "This is our cabin in the Sierras."

"But you are hurt, *senor!* What can I do to assist you?" he asked, kneeling beside Colin and examining the arrow. "Ah, it is bad, my friend," he said, shaking his head. His piercing dark eyes turned to Molly. "*Senorita,* will you bring some cloths and hot water, please? We must tend to this wound as soon as is possible."

His glance fell on the indignity his horse had made on the floor and he shook his head again. "Garanon! Thou hast no manners!"

Molly hurried to fetch a pan and fill it from the steaming kettle that was kept at the side of the fireplace, while the stranger slit the bloody coat with a long knife he pulled from his belt. A groan was wrenched from the injured man before he clamped his lips stubbornly shut, gritting his teeth against the agony. "It's no use," he whispered hoarsely. "They've done for me this time."

"Ah, *senor*, do not say such a thing," the stranger protested. "Don Jabal has fixed deeper wounds than this. You must live, my friend. God has no need of you yet."

"Stop!" Colin panted. "Before you go farther, we have things to say." Perspiration broke out on his forehead in spite of the chill in the cabin. His face was bluish gray and his voice only emerged with great effort.

The stranger sank back on his booted heels with a practiced gesture that kept him clear of the rowelled spurs. "What is it, my friend?" he asked.

"My name is Colin O'Bannion," he said faintly. "This is my daughter, Molly."

The stranger rose and bowed. "Conde Jabal del Valle at your service, Senor and Senorita O'Bannion." Then he resumed his squatting position beside Colin.

"Her mother is dead . . . good girl," Colin whispered, then another gurgling cough silenced him. Soon he opened his eyes and fixed them fiercely on Don Jabal. "You . . . owe . . . me!"

"I owe you my life, Senor O'Bannion," Don Jabal said. "I owe you my life."

Colin nodded. "If I die you must take care of her," he said, his voice fading on the last words as he again closed his eyes.

Don Jabal leaned forward to hold his knife blade in the flames. "If I can remove the arrow, perhaps you will not

9

die," he said.

At the first touch of the hot blade, the injured man gave a cry of agony, then fainted.

"Father," Molly pleaded. "Pa, don't die!" Terror-stricken, she looked at the dark man. Huk had called. It hadn't been the storm. Was this Spanish don the devil's emissary? Was Huk lying in wait for her father as he had for her mother?

"Try to stem the flow of blood," Don Jabal commanded. "Use the cloth behind my knife."

His knife darted around the arrow almost too fast for Molly's eyes to follow while she used the cloth to obey his order. At long last Don Jabal drew the missile from the wound and cast it into the flames. He took the cloths from Molly and pressed them against the open gash. "Do you have spirits, Senorita O'Bannion?" he asked.

Dumbly, Molly nodded. With uncertain steps she went to get the jug of whiskey from beneath the bed. Her father was lying on his stomach, unconscious, and she felt a faintness that was a stranger to her usually robust self. Forcing strength back into her body, she carried the demijohn to Don Jabal.

Don Jabal grabbed it impatiently, uncovering the wound as he did. Then he dribbled liquor into the open gap and a groan came weakly from his patient. "A cup?" he prodded Molly.

She hurried to fetch one, then put a pad of clean folded cloth over the gaping wound, and tied it firmly with another strip of cloth around her father's chest.

Don Jabal gently eased the injured man to a sitting position. He poured whiskey in the cup, held it to Colin's mouth, and tipped some of the fiery liquid inside. When it trickled down his throat, Colin's eyes opened and he coughed again. Then Don Jabal raised him to his feet. "Can you stand the pain while I help you to your bed?" he asked.

Molly ran ahead to turn down the covers so he could lower her father into place. With a moan of pain, Colin rolled to his side and closed his eyes. "Thank you," he muttered.

Don Jabal watched her cover the wounded man, then bestirred himself. "A thousand pardons for Garanon, Senorita O'Bannion," he said, gathering the indignity from the floor with one of the bloody rags, then throwing the whole mess into the flames. "I cannot turn him out into this storm to die."

"There is a shed at the back of the cabin where our burro beds," Molly said. "Your horse can stay there tonight."

"Of course, Senorita O'Bannion." He stooped to examine the foot Garanon held carefully just touching the floor. When he rose, he glanced at her. "Can you spare another bandage? He has sprained himself badly and should be wrapped."

With a nod she handed him the remaining rags. He poured whiskey into his cupped hand, spreading it gently on the swollen area before wrapping the leg tightly. The great black horse stood like a statue, then dipped his muzzle to inspect the new appendage. It must have pleased him for he then rubbed his soft nose against his master's cheek.

"There is a door to the shed in my room, Don Jabal," Molly said, staring dubiously at the huge horse. "It isn't so wide as our front door, but if he will fit through it, you needn't go outside in the storm."

"Thank you," he said gravely. "I'm sure Garanon can

11

squeeze through." He shot a rueful glance her way. "Especially now that he's so . . . so empty." He led the horse into the rear and already the limp was not as bad as before.

In a few minutes he returned to look down at his patient. "Perhaps sleep is the best thing for him," Don Jabal said quietly. "For us, also," he added. He motioned to the floor in front of the fireplace. "With your permission, Senorita O'Bannion? I can be most comfortable there on the floor."

"Why don't you use my bed?" she asked, pointing toward the room he'd led Garanon through. "I shall stay here with my father tonight in any case."

"*Gracias,*" he murmured politely. "If I can be of further assistance, please wake me."

She watched him, torn between fear for her father and awe for this tall man. He stood at least six feet tall, lean and aristocratic, with a face that was handsome and proud and cruel as an eagle's. Jet black hair covered his head, although it didn't conceal the angry swelling on his temple.

"Don Jabal . . ."

"Yes, senorita?"

"Do you wish a cloth for your head?"

His hand went to the lump as he smiled ruefully. "*De nada.*" A frown replaced the smile. "For a horse to stumble is bad enough, but for a del Valle to fall from his back! This is an indignity I shall not forget. Perhaps a lump will remind me to keep my attention where it belongs." He went into the small cubby hole and Molly heard the bed creak under his weight.

He must be one of the grandees her father had told her about, she decided, and a sigh came from her soul. What must it be like to own miles of California and hundreds of people, much like a king? Conde Jabal del Valle even looked like a monarch!

A moan brought her attention back to her father. He was watching her through pain-filled eyes. "Molly . . ." he whispered, motioning her toward him with a feeble hand.

"Yes, pa?"

"I'm dyin', daughter."

Tears filled her eyes as she leaned forward to kiss him. "Don't say that, pa," she pleaded. "What am I to do if you leave me?"

"You're seventeen, Molly, and all you've known is a shack in the mountains since you were born. When your mother died I should have taken you back to civilization . . ." A spasm of coughs closed his eyes and he struggled to regain his breath when it was over.

"Hush, father," Molly whispered, hoping to quiet him so the blood wouldn't gush from his wound. "You must rest and sleep so your wound will heal. Don Jabal said so."

"I have to talk to you," he said impatiently. "Lean close, daughter, for I cannot talk overly loud. Is our visitor out of hearing?"

She nodded. Soft snores came from her small room. "He's sound asleep, pa."

"Then mind ye this, daughter," he whispered. "Tell no one your mother was an Indian. Ye are tow-headed and white-skinned like me. Ye show no sign of a breed. No one must ever know you are."

Her eyes widened in astonishment. Breed? The word was new to her. Her mother was an Indian princess! She was beautiful and gentle and never had it occurred to

13

Molly to be ashamed of her.

"But why, father?" she asked indignantly.

Despair showed on his face. "Whites despise half-breeds even more than they hate and fear Indians!"

She stared at him in bewilderment. "You're white," she said accusingly. "You loved my mother, didn't you? You married her!"

"I loved your mother," he whispered. "I still do. Bein' a trapper isn't the best life for a woman. Your mother was better suited to sharin' it with me than most." His eyes closed and for an instant she thought his breathing had stopped. Then his eyelids opened. "Don't tell . . . *ever!* Promise me . . ."

Each breath became more labored as his head strained backward pulling him to lie on his wound. When it touched the bed he grunted in agony. Then a rattle came from his throat and his body grew still as his breathing stopped. Colin O'Bannion was dead.

"Father . . ." Molly said, sobs choking her as she realized he had gone. She put her head on his lifeless chest and let tears soak the bandages she had put on him. Now she was truly an orphan! She had neither father nor mother to comfort her. Huk had taken his toll. Twice his chilling screech had sounded, once each time she lost a parent. Huk was not just a legend—Huk was real! Her sobs filled the room as she mourned her loss.

At last she ceased crying. Rising, she washed her father's face and smoothed his sandy hair. Then she covered him decently with the blanket before she pulled a chair close to the bed. She would sit the wake for Colin O'Bannion until the night had passed.

Memories came as the fire subsided into glowing embers. Life in the Sierra Nevada was all she knew, just

14

as her father had said. She could still hear her mother's voice . . .

"Molly! Molly!" Amatil called, running down the path to where her daughter puddled in the mud beside the bubbling spring. "Naughty girl!" she exclaimed. "Look at your gown! We'll never get it clean again."

Her mother's hair was tied with bright ribbons and her soft eyes regarded her daughter lovingly despite her disreputable state. "Time to do lessons," she said gaily. "Come, we'll get cleaned up."

Colin was gone from morning till night most days checking his traps. Twice each year he disappeared for several weeks, taking his catch to wherever it was he sold the pelts he cared for so tediously. When he returned he always brought supplies in his pack for his wife and child.

And books. He had taught Amatil to read as soon as they married, she had told Molly. After their daughter was born, Colin said it was her mother's job to teach the child to read. By the time Molly was four, she had. The books Colin brought were old and tattered, to be sure, but they were read by both mother and daughter until they knew them by heart.

The only people they saw were occasional wayfarers who happened on their cabin, and her mother always disappeared until they had gone. She pondered this fact as she sat watch over her dead father. She had always thought her mother shy, but after her father's words, perhaps there was something more. Had she disappeared because she was Indian? Was she ashamed she had married a white man? Or was she afraid he would be shamed by her presence?

None of it seemed right to Molly. Her mother was proud, holding her head much as Molly imagined a princess should. Her people were Cheyennes, friends of the white man. She told Molly this friendship was brought about because white men always brought *mok-ta-bo-mah-pe* with them. It was the Cheyenne word for coffee, and the only one she taught her daughter, deeming it best for Molly to speak her father's language. Laughing, Amatil told her her father swapped coffee for her after they met. A great deal of coffee as proof of how much he loved her.

Whatever, Colin O'Bannion had adored his Amatil, always treating her like the princess she was. In the harsh country of Ireland from whence he had come, he said there was no castle good enough for her. Although he provided only the rough shack, it was filled with warmth and love and the best he could provide while she lived.

Colin O'Bannion was a great tall man with a shock of straw-colored hair over flashing blue eyes. Molly had never thought of it consciously before, but her parents were as different as two people could be, for her mother was tiny and dark. Molly was small, but there the resemblance to her mother ended. She had her father's fair hair in which her mother took great pride, brushing it into curls when Molly was small, while she murmured how blue her daughter's eyes, like the skies in springtime.

The chill of the room brought Molly back to conventional things. She rose and fed the embers in the fireplace with logs from the box against the wall. The air was even colder than before, a thing that happened toward morning. Perhaps the storm would leave with dawn's coming. It had lessened its rage outside as she sat pondering her parents. If the sun emerged from behind the clouds, it would warm the cabin. Perhaps it would even chase away the dreary chilliness around her heart.

Her eyes filled with tears as she sat again beside her

16

father. Then she remembered his words when her mother died. "Tears will nay bring her back, daughter. Be ye as much like her as ye can, and her memory will live in ye." Tears would not bring back her father, either, so it was useless to shed them, and she could not become like him, except perhaps in having his courage and stubbornness. About the bravery she yet had to find out, but about the stubbornness . . .

"Sure and ye're the most like a mule of any woman I know!" he had shouted at her, and more than once.

Well, perhaps living so much alone had made her set in her ways, she reflected. But it seemed to her there was a right way of things and a wrong way . . . and then another way that was purely her father's. Now she was sorry they had clashed.

"Is there any change in your father, senorita?" a polite voice asked.

She started, her heart beating wildly, then realized the voice belonged to Don Jabal. Turning as she rose, she faced him. "My father is dead," she answered.

"But . . ." He stepped quickly to look at the man on the bed. "Why didn't you call me?"

"There was the wake to sit," she said quietly.

He frowned in puzzlement but Molly didn't elaborate. It was not necessary that a foreigner understand their ways.

"I'm very sorry he died," he said soberly.

When Molly said nothing, he walked to the door and opened it a crack. "It will soon be daylight," he announced. "The storm has subsided." He closed the door, hesitating before saying, "If you have a shovel I will dig a grave for your father wherever you wish."

She thought for a time, then answered slowly, "It will

be difficult with the ground frozen so deep. Perhaps beneath the straw in the shed?"

"Do you not wish a marker on the grave?"

"No!" she said sharply, then caught herself. This man could not know how they survived in the wilderness. "It is best not to point to a grave," she explained.

He nodded, although she could see he didn't understand. "I will move Garanon and your burro outside," Don Jabal said, turning to leave.

"Thank you," was all she could manage. A lump had risen in her throat again, but she swallowed until it disappeared, for she would not show weakness before this grandee.

He turned to face her, looking at her for some seconds before he spoke. "While I am working, senorita, can you manage your packing and perhaps fix a little hot food for us before we go?"

"Go?" she asked. "Go where?"

"Your father asked me to care for you, senorita. I will see that you get to your people, wherever they are."

"I don't know where they are," she said firmly. "I can stay here in my home."

A thoughtful look crossed his face. "That is impossible, senorita. I will think while I work." With that, he disappeared through her room into the shed.

She heard him speak to Garanon and then came vague noises as he set to work. With a sigh, she busied herself preparing morning coffee and slicing thin pieces of bacon from the side that hung on the wall. When the food was ready she went to the door and summoned him.

Despite the cold, perspiration beaded his forehead when he took his seat at table. He mopped it with his handkerchief, smiling an apology. "It has been a long

18

time since I worked in such a manner. One does not realize one's softness until circumstances point to it."

"When we have eaten I will help you dig," she said.

"Oh no, senorita. That is man's work. It will not take me long to finish. The ground is not frozen where your burro has lived."

They ate in silence until Molly said, "My name is Molly, not senorita. An O'Bannion could not be Spanish."

His eyes widened in surprise while a smile pulled at his mouth. "I realize that, se . . . er, Miss O'Bannion."

"My name is Molly," she said stubbornly.

He took another sip of coffee, studying her. At last he inclined his head. "*Bueno!* We shall be friends. You address me as Jabal and I shall call you Molly. *Si?*"

She nodded.

He rose, looking around the cabin. "You have not packed, Molly?" he asked.

"No."

"I haved decided what to do," he said emphatically. "You shall go home with me to be companion to my mother. Pack only your immediate needs to take along. It will be my pleasure to replenish your wardrobe when we reach my home."

"No."

Friendliness vanished from his face. "Your father gave you to my care and a del Valle fulfills his obligations," he said coldly. "If you do not wish to leave here today, we can stay until tomorrow, but then I must go, and you . . . you will go with me!" He spaced his words carefully as one would talk to a child who had trouble understanding.

Molly clamped her lips shut and glared at him.

With a shrug, he returned to the shed.

19

He meant what he said, of that she was sure. She really didn't want to stay here by herself, but neither did she want to be beholden to a stranger. She looked around the room. Had her father left her ought but alone?

His packsack lay in one corner where he had dropped it on returning from his last trip to sell pelts. When she lifted the flap, at first it appeared empty, but then she thrust her hand into its depths and her fingers encountered coins at the very bottom.

Warmth for her father flooded through her. Even in death he had done what he could for her. And his words to Don Jabal, "You owe me!" echoed in her ears. Very well! She would go with the Conde to his home and meet his mother. If she did not like it there, perhaps her father's coins could pay her passage to civilization. Her father had said he should have sent her to this civilization, whatever it was, so if she left Don Jabal's home it would only be to fulfill Colin O'Bannion's wish.

Leaving the coins where they were, she quickly selected the belongings she would take along and packed them into the remaining space atop the coins. She donned clothing she thought suitable for the trip and when Jabal came in from the shed, he found her waiting.

His face was grim as he glanced at the covered body on the bed. "Are you ready, Molly?" he asked, his voice gentle and concerned.

She nodded, fighting back tears.

Jabal wrapped the blanket tightly around her father, then lifted his lanky form and carried it into the shed. Molly followed with the small Bible listing the marriage of Amatil and Colin O'Bannion and the birth of their child.

Carefully, Jabal laid his bundle in the narrow grave.

Then he pulled himself up beside her. His dark hair was damp from his labors and curled loosely on his forehead, giving him the appearance of a dark angel of death. She shuddered, remembering the cry of Huk in the night, then chided herself for her superstitions.

They stood beside the grave while she read from the psalms. When she reached, "Yea, though I walk through the valley of the shadow of death, I will fear no evil," she paused. She *did* fear Huk! Was her father's God strong enough to overcome the bird of evil her mother believed so powerful? Twice she heard Huk, at the death of each of her parents. Would he follow her all the days of her life? What more could he do to her?

When she glanced up, Jabal was watching her with a puzzled look in his eyes, so she hurriedly resumed reading. "For thou art with me; thy rod and thy staff, they comfort me. Thou preparest a table before me in the presence of mine enemies; thou annointest my head with oil, my cup runneth over. Surely goodness and mercy shall follow me all the days of my life; and I will dwell in the house of the Lord forever. Amen."

"Amen," Jabal echoed. "He was a good man, Molly. Even though badly wounded himself, he saved my life."

"That psalm was his favorite," she said. Would goodness and mercy follow her? Or was it her lot to be dogged by the evil Huk? A shudder shook her.

"Perhaps you'd best prepare for our journey," Jabal said.

She realized he was waiting for her to leave so he could fill in the grave. With a sad heart she left her father to his God.

Chapter Two

When Jabal finished the grave, Molly went into the shed to check his work. He had smoothed the ground to flatness, then respread the used fodder. No trace of a grave could be seen. She nodded, approving the arrangement. One more act would assure the grave's not being disturbed by man or beast and Colin O'Bannion would rest in peace.

Garanon's leg was still bandaged but he placed his weight on it in normal fashion so the sprain must have healed. Jabal had him saddled and he had fashioned a pallet from a blanket that was just behind the saddle. His roll of possessions was atop the burro. Her packsack of belongings hung on one side of the burro and a matching pack of their remaining food dangled from the other side.

"I can ride the burro," Molly said quickly. "I've done it before."

An exasperated sigh stirred the hairs in Jabal's mustache before he said, "It will be more comfortable for you to ride behind me on Garanon while the burro carries our belongings. It is a better arrangement."

"I will be comfortable on the burro," she insisted.

Once again she saw the transformation from friendliness to implacability as his eyes hardened and his head raised haughtily. "Will you be comfortable if an attack forces me to leave the burro behind?" he demanded.

"Attack?" she echoed. "Who will attack us?"

"Perhaps the same enemy who put an arrow into your father's back. There are Indians around, you know, and the American butchers who hire them," he said, glaring at her.

"I don't understand—"

"You are a woman," he said shortly. "If you rebel against every decision we shall be a long time reaching my house. It is not your place to question the orders of one who knows better than you."

She glanced at the animals, then back to Jabal. "Well . . . since the burro is already packed," she conceded. "One moment, please, while I finish my chores."

With emptiness inside her, Molly returned to the cabin for a last look around. Old memories stirred in the shadows bringing tears to her eyes. Amatil . . . Colin . . . good-bye, mother . . . father. She choked back a sob.

Then deliberately she drew a burning brand from the fireplace and went around the room touching it to the bed, then to the rags left on the table. The shelf of old books seemed to cringe, then glow as the flames shot up around it. When the furniture was crackling and she was sure the fire would not flicker out with its work uncompleted, she left the cabin.

"Now I am ready to go, Jabal," she said.

He glanced at the blazing interior, then swung her lightly to the pallet on Garanon. Now that he had gotten

23

his way, his friendly mood was restored. He gave Garanon an affectionate pat, then offered Molly the lead line of the burro. "Will you hold on to this for a moment, Molly?"

At her nod, he stepped to the stirrup, swinging his right leg over Garanon's head to the other side, then settling himself into the saddle.

"Is your horse's leg well enough to carry us both?" Molly asked.

"If Garanon can carry me, he will not notice your added puff of weight," he answered. "Now put both your arms around my waist."

"I can hold to the saddle."

"Molly . . ."

"Oh, all right!" She circled his waist as far as she could while he gathered the reins and relieved her of the burro's lead line.

She did not want to look back, but when they reached the edge of the descent down the mountain, Jabal pulled Garanon to a halt and turned to look at the cabin. It was ablaze in the snow, melting a ring of black around the edges as sharp little points of flame grew from the icy surroundings. While they watched, a portion of the roof fell inside with a great crash. A strangled cry of pain was wrenched from Molly's throat and her grip tightened on Jabal.

With a gruff, "Hold tight," Jabal wheeled the black stallion around and on his way. Garanon picked his way down the mountainside with the burro clattering over the stones behind them. Molly allowed her tears to soak the back of Jabal's coat while she tried to banish the image of her lifelong home suffering in the flames, but she knew it was a sight she would never forget for as long as she lived.

At the bottom of the mountain Jabal pulled Garanon to a halt and jumped lightly from his back. "I must check his leg to see what damage the descent has done," he said. "If it is swelled, I shall have to lead him."

"Shall I get down?"

"It isn't necessary."

He knelt and ran both hands up and down Garanon's bandaged leg. Then he unwrapped the bandage and repeated the process. At last he rewound the rag, nodding his satisfaction.

"The leg is fine," he said, "but I shall leave the wrapping on for another day or two."

He remounted and they were away. Garanon's friskiness made her clutch wildly at Jabal's waist until she forced herself to relax on her side-seated pallet. Then she could enjoy the swift pace that covered so much distance in so little time. They were below the snow line now and the lush California landscape made her wonder where winter had gone.

They nooned on the sunny side of a mountain before resuming their journey. Jabal sprawled lazily against a stray rock while he ate, but Molly walked around to stretch muscles that were cramped from holding herself erect on the sidesaddle pallet.

Soon they were back on Garanon traveling over a land Molly had never before seen. By the time night fell they had reached the flatlands and the air was considerably warmer. Molly wondered about the night ahead, then breathed a sigh of relief when Jabal guided the stallion toward a huge lighted house and gave a halloo as they rode through its wide gate. As they reached the veranda of the house an Indian boy was waiting to take their animals. He kept his eyes lowered, patiently holding the reins and lead line Jabal handed him.

"Ho, Don Jabal!" a hearty voice called from the open door. "What brings you here so late?"

Jabal lifted Molly from the pallet and offered her his arm. With a scornful glance, she walked up the steps alone, lifting her skirts a fraction so she wouldn't step on them. She had never walked up stairs before, but she would show him she was no country bumpkin.

The men greeted each other in a flurry of Spanish too rapid for Molly's small comprehension. They gestured and chattered and then suddenly Jabal remembered her presence. Sweeping his hat off in a courtly gesture, he said, "But I'm forgetting my manners, Don Carlos. This is Senorita Molly O'Bannion. Don Carlos de Cruz y Cuatro, Molly."

"Oh, ho!" their host shouted. "Don Jabal . . . you have captured a rose! Come in, come in! *Mi casa, su casa!*" He caught Molly's hand and planted a damp kiss on it.

A plump little woman came to greet them. In the course of introductions Molly learned she was Dona Rosalinda, Don Carlos's wife. Since her English was as scanty as Molly's Spanish, they contented themselves with friendly smiles.

They were served a bountiful supper and Molly hungrily applied herself. There was more food on the table than Molly had seen—quail, roast venison, a variety of breads, and several dishes of vegetables. One platter passed to her had round breaded objects on it and Molly tasted her first oyster, an experience that made her recoil to take a closer look at the morsel from which she had taken a bite. The men, however, seemed more interested in conversation than food.

"What news of the war, Don Jabal?" Don Carlos asked. "What have you learned since last we met?"

"We will never settle our disputes in American courts, my friend. As more and more settlers come to California, more demand will be made for the Pre-emption Act of '46 to be enforced," Jabal answered.

Don Carlos swelled, much like a pouter pigeon. "Our grants must be recognized! The Treaty of Guadalupe Hidalgo stipulated that property of every kind would be inviolably respected!" he said angrily.

"The only thing these Americans respect is force," Jabal said. "They are bribing the Indians to fight against us and for the Americans."

"My Indians will never turn on me!"

"Nor will mine," Jabal said quietly. "However, there are others not so loyal. Some of our people have joined with the American locos who think their Indians should be free to choose as they please."

Their conversation puzzled Molly, for her father had mentioned nothing of any war to her. His death had so shocked her, the fact it was done by an Indian arrow hadn't entered her mind until now. He had always been friendly with the mountain tribesmen he encountered, and they, in turn, left their cabin and them in peace. Why had an Indian shot him? Why would any of Amatil's people turn on him?

Dona Rosalinda rose, as did the men, so Molly followed suit. Jabal and Don Carlos resumed their seats as Dona Rosalinda led Molly to the second floor and a room so delicately beautiful it took her breath away. Was this the "civilization" of which her father spoke?

Left alone, Molly removed her outer garments and

27

sank into a bed so soft she feared the feather ticking would close over her face to smother her. When she found she could still breathe, she slipped into bone-weary sleep.

A young Indian girl woke Molly next morning with a basin of warm water held ready for her use. She smiled shyly while Molly wondered if all Indians were servants. Could that be the reason Amatil was so shy around whites? Did the rough mountain men who came on their cabin all hate Indians? The Indian who killed her father surely had been nobody's servant. At least it didn't seem likely. So it was not possible that all Indians were servants. Her puzzlement stayed in her mind and she vowed she would solve the enigma at her first opportunity.

Jabal's eyes looked somewhat weary and quite red at the breakfast table. Molly assumed he and Don Carlos spent the night with a bottle and much conversation instead of sleep. The meal was over in a minimum of time and Jabal hastened their departure as quickly as good manners would allow. He seemed relieved to be back on Garanon with Molly behind on the pallet.

"Did you sleep well, Jabal?" she asked innocently. "As soon as my head touched the pillow I drifted off."

"But of course, *senorita*," he said sarcastically.

A giggle came unbidden from her lips, then she tightened her grasp around his waist as a lunge nearly unseated her. They flew through the morning air, nearly losing the burro who was hard put to keep up with Garanon's long legs. Several times the smaller animal stumbled and nearly fell.

"Jabal! Slow down!" Molly gasped. "The burro can't keep up with us."

Reluctantly, he pulled Garanon to an easy lope.

"Thank you," she said demurely, squelching another giggle that threatened to emerge.

"*De nada,*" he growled.

Jabal's suave manners were somewhat ruffled this morning, but he was clean-shaven except for the black mustache, and quite handsome in spite of his red-rimmed eyes. Staring at the nape of his neck before her caused a strange sensation. It looked defenseless and somehow quite tender, different surely from the look of a predator she'd seen on his face. There was a hint of gray flecked here and there. How old was the Conde? Was he married?

It would not be polite to ask him personal questions, Molly knew. Once when she had questioned a guest too closely, her father reprimanded her at once, while her mother waited until the guest had gone to lecture her sternly on the impropriety of such behavior. But she would like to know, she thought wistfully. Perhaps if she got him talking he would speak freely.

"Where is your home, Jabal?" she asked softly in his ear. "Shall we reach it today?"

"Costa Cordillera is near Bodega Bay," he said grudgingly. "If all goes well we shall reach it tonight some time. Can you ride longer than yesterday?"

"I can ride as long as you," she said indignantly. Then curiosity overcame her pique. "Is that the name of your house?"

"Costa Cordillera means seacoast of mountains," he informed her in somewhat better humor. "It is the name of our ranch. Our house is the Casa del Valle."

"It sounds quite grand, Jabal. Is it as big as Don Carlos's home?"

"Somewhat larger," he said casually. "My grandfather

29

received a grant as reward for services rendered. He built a castle for my grandmother to live in. My father decided it was too small for his family, so he built a hacienda to accommodate us."

"And they all still live there?" she prompted.

"No. The males in our family seem to pass on before the females. My grandmother still lives in the castle, but with only servants to tend her. My father is dead. My mother, also. My stepmother still rules the hacienda."

"Stepmother? What is that?" She could not even imagine steps on a mother.

He was quiet for a time. Most likely digesting her ignorance, she thought in despair. Well, she would ask no more questions of him!

"A stepmother is the lady your father marries after your real mother is gone," Jabal said at last. "When my mother died, my father was heartbroken for a while. Then he grew lonesome, I suppose. Dona Espicia became his wife and presented him with a son—my half brother, Michael."

"And this is the mother to whom you referred when you said I would be her companion?" Molly asked, forgetting her resolution. "It seems to me she must have many companions already. Why would she want me?"

"She is crippled," he answered shortly. "Although she never complains, I think she is lonesome. A surrogate daughter should correct that. You can fill that role admirably."

"She has no daughters of her own? Not even a daughter-in-law, perhaps?"

His grumpiness dissolved in laughter. "You're a sly minx, aren't you? Such guileless questions! Soon you will know more about me than I know about myself!"

She flounced angrily on the pallet. Now he was laughing at her!

"I'm tired of riding," she complained, trying to cover her embarrassment.

"Unless we keep going, we'll have to camp out on the ground tonight," he said. "However, if you are too uncomfortable and want to stop, we shall."

Alarm filled her. Of all things she did not want, the one she did not want most was to camp in the cold with Jabal!

"Never mind," she said crossly. "I'd much prefer to sleep inside tonight."

"Good!" He reached into a saddle bag and handed her a piece of beef jerky. "Chew on this so you don't starve before we reach the hacienda."

The tough meat kept her mouth occupied although she had already returned to her resolution to ask no more questions of Jabal.

Night fell while they still traveled the flatlands and Molly wondered if she were to spend the rest of her life on the blanket pallet. Gradually then the land underfoot changed to rolling country and they came to low hills that preceded steep little mountains. Fog drifted wispily around them as Molly smelled a strange odor. She inhaled deeply, trying to place it. "What is that smell, Jabal?" she asked.

He glanced over his shoulder and smiled. "That's the ocean, Molly. Have you not smelled salt water before this? It has a scent like no other."

"The ocean!" she breathed ecstatically. "Oh, Jabal, will I be able to see it soon?"

"You've never seen the sea?"

"I've never been away from the mountains before now, although I read about the many strange places in the world," she said, and found herself chattering on about the many books her father had brought home and of how her mother taught her to read.

Then Jabal asked about her mother and she remembered her father's admonition and answered only that she was very beautiful and kind.

"I can well believe that," Jabal said gallantly. "You are quite beautiful yourself, Molly O'Bannion."

Her face grew warm and she realized she was blushing for the very first time! She laid her cheek against Jabal's rough coat and basked in the pleasure of being admired. Her parents loved her, but never had they told her she was beautiful.

"Are you sleeping?" he asked softly.

"No. Are we almost there?"

The fog was thickening, making it seem as though they floated through an eerie world atop a legless horse. A ghostly form suddenly rose beside Garanon's head and her heart leaped into her throat as she clutched Jabal closer.

"Ho, Chia," he said quietly.

"Don Jabal," the man replied, "I have been waiting for you to return."

"I was delayed."

Molly noted the man was an Indian—another servant?—and he carried a rifle. He turned, and she heard the hooting of an owl in the fog. Then another ghostly shape emerged to join the first.

"Tomas," Jabal acknowledged.

They rode through the fog with Chia beside them. Garanon's hoofbeats were muffled but seemed to echo flatly against barriers hidden by the ghostly curtain.

"We are in the canyon that is the entrance to Costa

Cordillera," Jabal informed her. "There is solid rock on either side."

Suddenly a huge form loomed ahead in the fog. Molly's gasp of fright brought Jabal's glance.

"It's only a statue, Molly." He waited while Chia made obeisance, then urged Garanon to a lope while Chia trotted alongside.

"Statue of who, Jabal?"

"*San Rafael.*"

They rode in silence for a while as she wondered just how far it was from the entrance to the hacienda itself. She was weary in every bone and tired unto death of sitting so cramped on the blanket. Would they never reach the house?

Then she saw lights flickering through the fog ahead and Garanon pranced to a halt before wide steps. Jabal dismounted and held out his arms to catch her as she slid thankfully from the wide rump. Silently, Chia took the lead line and reins and disappeared with the animals into the fog.

"This is home," Jabal said as he led her up the stairs.

Before they reached the door it opened to show an aproned woman standing in the lamplight. "Don Jabal, we've been worrying."

"I was delayed, Maria. We have a guest, as you see. This is Miss Molly O'Bannion." He turned to her and said, "This is our housekeeper, Molly."

Molly mustered a smile as the woman bobbed a brief curtsey of greeting.

"Have the blue room readied for Miss O'Bannion, Maria. I know she is quite tired of Garanon."

Her eyes widened in surprise as she glanced at Molly, then back to Jabal. She turned and uttered a string of

Spanish to an Indian girl behind her before turning back to her master.

"Come in, come in," she said, obviously confused. "May I take your cloak, senorita?"

Her words were directed to Molly, but her black eyes watched Jabal. "You are hungry, Don Jabal?" she asked.

"We are starved, Maria! Bring us a great feast in front of the fire in the main room." He motioned toward an open door. "Shall we warm ourselves while we wait, Molly?"

She walked into a huge high-ceilinged room to stand before a crackling fire that dissolved the chill from her bones in minutes. The fireplace alone was as wide as their entire cabin had been, she noted. A broad couch and deep chairs faced the flickering flames. The thickness of the rug underfoot muffled their footsteps and gave the sensation of floating as she crossed over it. Great pictures adorned the walls between heavy drapes covering wide windows. It was a magnificence of such a scope as Molly had never before seen, and her eyes were wide with excitement.

Jabal went to a small cabinet and removed a bottle and two glasses. He returned to the fireplace with the goblets filled with purple liquid. "Shall we toast our safe arrival, Molly?"

She accepted the one he offered, looking curiously at the contents.

His gaze held a glint of laughter as he held the glass out before him. The liquid seemed to be alive as the firelight sparkled on it and mirrored its color in his eyes. Uncertainly, she imitated his gesture. He touched his glass to hers, then drank deeply, watching her over the rim of the glass. She swallowed and felt a river of warmth

34

go down through her body. It was good!

"You have the most expressive face I have ever seen, Molly," he said softly.

"Have I now. What did it say?"

"You have never been toasted before nor tasted wine. You like the taste and the warmth of the wine inside you."

His face no longer had the harsh look, of a hunter and she marvelled at the changing moods Jabal exhibited. His brown eyes were soft, almost liquid-looking, and at one side of the black mustache a slight dimple showed and disappeared as his lips moved. Her knees grew strangely weak as she felt another blush creep up her face. She turned away from him.

"I shall have to see that my face is more reserved in the future," she said lightly.

She was saved from further embarrassment by Maria and several maids. They entered carrying trays of food of a kind and variety even greater than at Don Carlos's home. A silent Indian girl pulled a low table before the couch and the viands were placed upon it.

"What else do you wish, Don Jabal?" Maria asked.

"Only to know of my mother," he answered. "How is Dona Espicia?"

"She is sleeping now, Don Jabal, but she has been worrying about your late return. Also, she has had some pain in her hip the last two days. A very bad headache plagued her most of yesterday." She paused uncertainly. "You will see her first thing in the morning, Don Jabal?"

"Of course, Maria. I will run up now if she is awake."

"No . . . no, she is sleeping soundly," Maria said hurriedly.

"Did you give her laudanum again?" he demanded.

35

The plump little woman wrung her hands in distraction. "She ordered it, Don Jabal. There was no way to refuse her."

With a curt, "You may go," Jabal came to sit beside Molly. "When I am away everything goes crossways," he grumbled. "My orders are pushed aside and everyone does as they please."

Since Molly's mouth was full of food she did not answer.

He looked at her and grinned. "Let's be gluttons, Molly. We'll make up for our Spartan rations now." While he spoke he filled a plate with various delicacies. "I am starving and this looks good."

After swallowing she answered, "It is good! And before you begin reading my face again, I'll tell you that I don't even know what most of it is."

His handsome face split in a wide smile. "We'll begin your education tomorrow, Molly. You have much to learn, but for tonight just eat and enjoy."

Suddenly his gaze transferred to someone behind Molly as a voice said, "Feliciana! You're back!"

Turning, Molly saw a dark young man rushing toward her. He stopped, obviously confused.

Jabal rose lazily. "Hello, Michael. Will you join us? We have a guest, as you've already noted. This is Miss Molly O'Bannion. She will be staying for a time. This is my brother, Don Michael, Molly," Jabal said.

The young man walked slowly toward her to take her outstretched hand. There was a puzzled look on his face as he studied her, examining every detail. Then he smiled and his handsome face lit up before he bent over her hand.

"Your servant," he murmured, then planted a light kiss on the back of her hand. "We are honored you are here."

Molly felt a blush creep up her cheeks. Don Michael was as handsome as his brother, but there was a kinder look about him than Don Jabal. When he lifted his head, his eyes were full of laughter.

"Sorry I barged in, brother," he said to Jabal. "I mistook your guest's identity. From behind, her blonde hair much resembled Feliciana's." Then his gaze returned to Molly and he smiled as he bowed again. "Your pardon . . ." he said, backing away. Then he turned and strode hastily from the room.

Molly's bewilderment must have showed on her face as she looked at Jabal.

"Who is Feliciana?" she asked curiously. "Why did he think I was she?"

He was silent while his gaze roamed over her head and face. At last he nodded. "You are very different from Feliciana, but your blonde hair would make such a mistake possible. You are quite as petite as she."

"Are you going to tell me who she is?" Molly demanded.

With a sigh, Jabal resumed his seat. "Feliciana is my wife."

Her heart sank at his words. So he was married! And she was a silly goose. He was at least twice her seventeen years and much too handsome to have been left single all this time.

When she said nothing, he glanced at her before his gaze went to the crackling flames before them. "She is not here now," he said quietly. "She returned to Spain six months ago."

"Oh," Molly said lamely. Then, "When will she return?"

A bitter laugh escaped his lips. "Never!" His eyebrows cocked sardonically as he said, "She fled this 'barbaric hole' to return to the exciting courts of our Spanish graciousness and the young grandees who amuse the ladies."

Not knowing what to say, Molly said nothing for a time, then rose and asked awkwardly, "Isn't it time for bed?" Then she felt a blush begin as she realized what she'd said!

Jabal took no notice of her gaucherie, however. He rose and held his arm for her hand. "Of course, Molly. I should have realized you are weary. May I escort you to your room? We can't have you getting lost."

He led her up a curved stairway to an inner balcony that circled the salon below. Numerous doors lined the paneled wall, and before one of them Jabal stopped. "This is where you will stay, my dear. I hope you rest well." He opened the door inward, then stepped back with a bow, murmuring, *"Buenas noches,"* before he turned to continue farther on the circle.

She stared after him until he stopped before a door two rooms away, then hastily ducked inside before he could catch her gaping after him.

The Indian girl that Maria had spoken to stood waiting for her. She smiled and bobbed a curtsey in imitation of the housekeeper. "Senorita," she said shyly.

She was about Molly's age and beautiful in the way Amatil was beautiful. Her black hair was neatly braided around her head and her dark eyes beamed a welcome.

"What's your name?" Molly asked.

She giggled before answering, "Dolores, senorita."

"My name is Molly."

"Senorita Moll-ee," she said.

"No . . . Molly. Just Molly. No senorita."

A dubious look crossed her face before she nodded.

She had turned down the covers on the bed. Now she tried to help Molly undress, but Molly shook her head. "*Buenas noches*, Dolores," she said, then watched her go out the door, closing it behind her.

Chapter Three

Alone, Molly looked around at the luxurious room. Everything in it seemed to be blue—the carpet, the shiny coverlet on the bed, the hangings at the big window. A portrait on the wall.

Against a light blue background a golden-haired, blue-eyed lady, clad in royal blue brocade, serenely gazed at her surroundings. One finger rested lightly against her chin, showing to advantage an elaborate blue-gemmed ring on the finger beside it. A delicate filigree of gold surrounded the large center stone. It was inlaid with smaller gems of the same misty blue color. The ring seemed to come alive as it glowed in the lamplight.

Molly stared at this vision of beauty, then looked down at herself, so drab in comparison. What must Jabal think of the poorly dressed sparrow he had brought to his home? How could anyone have mistaken her for the glamorous woman who was his wife?

"The courts of Spain!" she whispered, conjuring up the magical scene as she imagined it to be. "Feliciana . . ." She tested the name on her tongue, shivering at its grandeur.

A filmy blue garment lay spread on the open bed. Her

curiosity whetted, she picked it up to see that it was a gown, a gossamer creation of fairies, surely, it was that ethereal. She held it against her to determine its fit and it seemed only to be a little long. With a shrug, she shed her drab clothing down to her skin and put the blue gown on.

Ah, the silky feeling as it lay against her! Twirling, she watched the rippling waves of blue swirl around. If it hadn't been so sheer, she would have thought it a ball gown, such as she had read about. However, since she could see the glow of her skin through the material, it would never do to be seen in. What a waste!

Swooping to scoop her discarded clothing from where it lay, she danced around the room looking for a hanger. A closed door caught her eye. A closet, perhaps? Cautiously, she opened the door and peered inside.

She gasped with fright at sight of the young woman inside, then froze. The other woman froze. Molly moved, and the other woman moved also. Cautiously, Molly reached out to touch the other woman even as her hand came to meet Molly's. Molly touched glass, not another hand. She smiled at the image in delight. This was a mirror! She was looking at herself.

There was a smudge of dirt on her face. Her hair was tousled, but rather nicely. Natural curls were a blessing, her mother had said. The nightgown was lovely, but when she stood still, it lay in folds around her feet. Its owner must be taller than she. Since it matched the room it must belong to the owner. She stepped back to take another look at the portrait on the wall.

Feliciana . . . She blushed at the thought of Jabal seeing her in this diaphanous non-covering. Then a twinge of jealousy shot through her. Quickly, she hung her garments on the hooks provided before closing the door on the mirror. Then her weariness overpowered her excitement and she climbed into the invitingly soft bed and pulled the covers up to her chin.

A racket in the hall outside her door brought her to a sitting position with the coverlet clutched tightly under her chin. A thud preceded the bursting open of her door as a small boy charged into the room.

"Mama? Mama?" he sobbed, swiping a small fist at the tears running down his cheeks. He made a dive for the bed and landed atop Molly's legs. "Why didn't you let me know you were here?" Then he jerked erect and stared at her. "You aren't my mama! Chia said you were my mama!"

Molly stared open-mouthed as Maria came running behind the small boy. "Don Jaime, you mustn't!" she exclaimed. "Oh, Miss O'Bannion, I'm so sorry."

"Where is my mama?" the boy demanded. "Where is she?"

"I don't know," Molly answered, glancing at Maria in bewilderment. "Don Jabal said your mother had gone to Spain for a visit."

"Oh, dear," Maria sighed. "Chia must have thought you were Dona Feliciana. You have hair the color of hers, and since you were riding behind Don Jabal . . ."

The pushed-out lower lip on the little boy quivered as his eyes gushed new tears. He pushed himself off her legs and sat cross-legged to think things over.

Molly smiled at him but there was no answering grin. "I am pleased to meet you, Don Jaime, but someone will sit on that lip," she said softly.

He sniffed, drawing the offending lip into its proper place. "What's your name?" he asked belligerently.

"Molly."

While he was thinking this over, Molly glanced at Maria. "Is there a robe I can use, please?"

The housekeeper nodded and went to the closet. In a moment she brought a blue robe, draping it around Molly's shoulders so she could slip her arms into the sleeves while she kept the cover beneath Molly's chin. When the robe was in place, Molly rose and held out her hand to the little boy.

"Shall we sit over here and get acquainted?"

He drew a quivering breath before he took the proffered hand. Molly led him to a couch, smiling over his head at the housekeeper. "May we have a glass of milk, Maria?"

With a nod and curtsey, the housekeeper left.

When they were seated, Molly and Jaime looked at each other. She noted the resemblance he bore to Don Jabal, although at present it was more the look of a slightly ruffled baby eagle and not nearly so fierce as his father.

So your name is Jaime," Molly said gently.

He nodded.

"How old are you, Jaime?"

"I'll have seven years in April," he answered, then, "Where did you come from?"

"I came from a cabin in the Sierra Nevada range. It was very beautiful and quite peaceful most of the time."

"Why did you leave?" he asked, cocking his head to one side.

Molly hesitated before saying, "My father died and there was no one to care for me."

"Where's your mother?"

"She died a long time ago, Jaime."

He climbed on her lap and laid a hand against her

cheek. "Poor Moll-ee. Would you like me to be your mother?"

She took his hand and planted a kiss on the soft part of the palm. "I think there is something just a little crosswise with that, Jaime, but we should be able to work something out. Would you like me to be your aunt? We could be very good friends and perhaps I can read to you when you wish."

He considered this. Then the same elusive dimple she had spied on Jabal winked from his cheek when he smiled.

"*Tia* Moll-ee," he said as though testing it on his tongue. Then a small Don Jabal said, "*Bueno!*" and the matter was settled.

Maria came carrying a tray with two small glasses of milk and two napkins on it. She offered it first to Molly, then Jaime.

Molly raised her glass to Jaime. "A toast to my new and dear nephew!"

Jaime giggled as he imitated her gesture, saying, "A toast to *Tia* Moll-ee!"

Solemnly, they drank their milk.

"Now, Don Jaime, it is time for bed," Maria said sternly.

Before he left Molly's lap his arms went around her neck. "I'm glad you are here," he whispered in her ear.

"Thank you, Jaime," Molly said, kissing the small cheek. "*Buenas noches.*"

He held out his arms to Maria. As she carried him away, he smiled sleepily over her shoulder at Molly until the door closed behind them.

Molly sat for a time mulling the evening's events in her mind. She could not imagine why a woman would leave Don Jabal, but then there were a lot of things grown people did that made little sense. But for a woman to leave an adorable little boy like Jaime?

Rising, she looked up at Feliciana's portrait. "How could you?"

Then she noticed a signature in a lower corner and bent forward to read it. Michael del Valle was the scrawled name. So Jabal's younger brother was also an artist! His smiling face came to mind and caused her to smile in return at the thought. Was the entire family as handsome as these brothers?

With a sigh she laid the blue robe across the bottom of the bed and once again slid into its softness. Her last thought before her eyes closed was that never in her life had she been so weary as she was now . . .

She was still in deep and dreamless sleep when a voice disturbed her, pulling her awake.

"Senorita Mollee! Senorita Mollee!"

Stretching lazily, she opened one eye to see Dolores standing beside the bed. She smiled at the one eye and repeated her name.

A yawn pulled at Molly's face as she sat up. "What is it, Dolores?"

"Dona Espicia wishes to see you, Senorita Mollee. She wishes to see you now," she said.

Molly glanced out the window. The fog was nowhere to be seen and the sun was almost directly overhead. Now fully awake, she scrambled out of bed. "Why didn't you wake me earlier, Dolores?"

A frown crossed her forehead as she tried to understand, and Molly realized she had spoken too rapidly.

"*Que?*" Dolores asked.

Molly shook her head. "You have no *Inglés,* Dolores?" Then she slowed her words. "Do you not speak our language?"

"I have the English," Dolores said indignantly. "Maria is teaching me."

"Of course," Molly soothed. "Wash. I want . . ." She struggled frantically for the word and found it. "I want *agua.*" She made motions to show washing her face.

"Si, senorita," Dolores said, opening the door to the hall.

Two maids carried a tub between them into the room. Two more followed with steaming kettles of water which they poured into the tub after it was put down. One of the smiling girls offered Molly a bar of soap.

Dolores went to the closet and returned carrying a towel and a wash cloth, then pointed to the tub saying, "*Agua caliente!* Hot wa-ter."

When the bevy of maids left, Molly slipped into the tub. The heat of the water brought a surprised cry from her at first, but then she settled into its warmth with a contented sigh. What a lovely feeling . . .

Surely this must be the civilization her father talked about. In summer they had bathed in the water at the spring, its iciness bringing a tinge of blue to her skin if she tarried too long. In winter she had always washed standing before a small basin of water, and that only tepid. Lolling in the smooth tub full of water at this temperature was heavenly!

Dolores regarded her with a worried frown. "Dona Espicia want see you," she repeated.

With a sigh Molly proceeded to wash herself, splashing warm water luxuriously over her back and paddling her toes in the tub. After she had thoroughly soaped and rinsed her body, she rose and let Dolores wrap the towel around her.

Her drab gowns were hardly suitable for her surroundings but they would have to do. She had worn one dress and wrapped the other into the saddlepack and she doubted if Don Jabal had thought to have the pack brought to her. Her gown was probably quite soiled from their trip, but there was no help for it. It would have to do.

She pointed at the closet. "My clothing is in there, Dolores."

"No, Senorita Mollee. Here." She walked to the couch and lifted clean undergarments and a pink dress to bring to her. "Dona Espicia have fix for you today. Maybe not fit but can make," Dolores said anxiously.

Once again Molly was reminded the day was half gone. She quickly donned the garments. Ah but it felt good to be so richly clothed! The undergarments were silky against her skin and the pink wool gown was soft as drifting clouds. It was a bit long but she remedied that by blousing it a bit more over the belt.

Then Molly combed her hair before the closet mirror, smiling back at the pink-clad person before her. The color went well with her blond hair that was even curlier than usual because of the steam from the bath water. A thought came unbidden to her mind—would she see Jabal today?

Turning to Dolores, she said firmly, "Dona Espicia is waiting, Dolores."

The maid led her out the door and around the circular balcony to a flight of stairs leading to a third story. Motioning Molly to follow, she ran lightly up the stairs. At the top Molly paused to look around. She was in a round turret, much like a fairy tale castle. The room was the size of the main salon below. Windows dotted the wall showing the huge basin of the valley with its collar of mountains in every direction. It was a view with such grandeur it took her breath away.

"Do you like my tower?" a dry voice asked.

Then Molly noted two women sitting in an alcove behind the stairwell. The one who spoke was seated in a wheelchair. The other had risen to stand behind her.

"Very much," Molly answered, hurrying to the alcove. "Are you Dona Espicia?"

The woman in the wheelchair nodded.

"I'm very sorry I slept so dreadfully late this morning," Molly said contritely.

Dona Espicia's hand raised to stop her apology. "I gave orders not to disturb you, Miss O'Bannion. Don Jabal reported to me early this morning before he left. You must have had a very tiring journey. I hope your bed and quarters are comfortable and that you rested well." She glanced up at the woman standing behind her. "You may go, Juanita."

She waited until the woman disappeared into the stairwell before she continued. "She sits beside me to see to my wants, but Indians are too silent to be very entertaining. Don Jabal thinks you would make a good companion for me. Would you?"

"I don't know, Dona Espicia," Molly said doubtfully. "I really don't know what a companion is supposed to do."

A laugh came from her that was mixed with a sort of snort. "Honesty is refreshing, my dear. Tell me about yourself. Have you ever worked before?"

"I have worked all my life," Molly said. "My mother

taught me to cook and sew. She also taught me to read and to write. My father showed me how to cure hides and shoot a rifle and ride a burro."

"Well, well," Dona Espicia murmured. "You are quite the accomplished young lady."

Her hair was almost all gray and her face was creased with lines etched by pain and weather. She had bright blue eyes that must make her stand out in a family of brown-eyed people, Molly surmised. Just now those eyes were studying her closely and she began to feel uncomfortable.

"But you are just a child," Dona Espicia finally pronounced. "How old are you, my dear?"

"I am seventeen years old and quite grown, I'm sure," Molly answered.

"Well, sit down, sit down," the older woman said impatiently. "Sit here beside me."

When Molly had seated herself on the chair Juanita had left, Dona Espicia spoke again. "I am very sorry about your father, my dear. Your mother, too, for it is hard to lose one's parents. However, we all must die some time and there's no use letting yourself grieve about it too long. When you lose a loved one, you must get on with your life no matter how much you miss him." There was a faraway look in her eyes and she was quiet as she contemplated her own words.

Molly said nothing. Dona Espicia's voice sounded different than Don Jabal's and the people she had met since coming here. Somehow it was . . . what? More American? More like the trappers she had heard talking to her father? And then she realized it was more like her father's, only without the Irish brogue that crept into his speech. Dona Espicia hadn't the soft Spanish accent of the rest of the family.

"Yes, I am an American," Dona Espicia said.

Startled, Molly stared at her. Was Jabal right about her thoughts being mirrored on her face? Were her private thoughts printed like words on her forehead? She would have to be more careful in future.

The older woman chuckled at Molly's expression. "No, I'm not a mind reader, child. It's just that I know I sound different than my family. Everyone notices it when I first meet them. Since curiosity about one's companions is universal, I always explain my difference."

"Yes, ma'am."

"Before the gossips tell you about me, I may as well. I was the housekeeper to the Conde Pablo del Valle and his Condesa Veronica for many years. Don Pablo adored his wife . . . always. But then she died." She paused to think about the past, then said, "After a time Don Pablo grew lonely and depressed, so depressed I was afraid he would take his own life. It was then I married him."

Her gaze went out the window to the surrounding valley. "I didn't marry him only because he was lonely. Or for his wealth, either," she said, almost to herself. "We both missed Veronica, for she had been a dear companion to us both. It was natural that we console each other. I loved them both so it was easy to combine that love for Pablo. Conde Pablo del Valle was quite a man! He gave me a son . . ."

"I met Don Michael last night," Molly said uncertainly. "He is very handsome."

The keen gaze swung around to her. "Both my sons are handsome like their father," she said. "Jabal is as dear to me as though he were my natural son." She paused, seeming at a loss for words, then continued. "Jabal and Michael do not like each other," she said at last. "They fought as children and now they quarrel as men. They cannot seem to agree on anything."

"Why, Dona Espicia?"

A shrug lifted her thin shoulders. "Who knows why men quarrel? And these two—neither will own Costa Cordillera, although I'm sure both would like to. Don Jabal's son owns everything. He will somehow be the Conde del Valle. My husband saw to that."

Molly didn't want to ask why, although she was greatly puzzled, so she sat silent.

"Jabal angered his father too much," Dona Espicia said. "Women! He cannot get his fill of them, much like the great black stallion he rides. Garanon has sired more colts than any horse in the country, as you will notice by the number of black horses around here." She frowned. "The pity of it all is that there's no telling how many small Jabals are growing up in the quarters," she said darkly. "Women pursue him as though he were the only male on this earth, and no matter how badly he treats them."

Molly's heart sank at her words. Jabal had treated her more like a child than a woman, she remembered. Was his gallant compliment on her looks just a sop thrown to someone he'd been trapped into rescuing? Her father had forced the man he'd saved from death into promising to take care of his daughter. Was Jabal so practiced at smoothly given compliments that they came from his mouth without effort on his part? Then she remembered how her thoughts often were mirrored on her face and forced them back to Dona Espicia.

The older woman seemed to have brought herself back

to the present as she smiled at Molly. "Enough gossip," she said briskly. "Jabal told me how your father saved his life and I cannot thank him, so my gratitude goes to you. You may be our welcome guest for as long as you wish, Miss O'Bannion, and do nothing but amuse yourself if you so desire." Her brows drew together in thought. "Or you may help me and tutor Jaime in his lessons. In that case you will be paid, of course. Knowing how to read and write English well is a rare accomplishment in these parts."

Molly started to answer, but Dona Espicia continued. "If you prefer to speak with my grandson before you decide, we can send for him now."

"I have already met him," Molly said quickly. "He came to my room last night thinking I was his mother."

"Maria told me of Chia's mistake." Dona Espicia sighed. "It is unfortunate for the child that his mother chose to leave, and only natural that he grieve." She glanced at Molly. "Were you able to talk to him last night? Was he too overcome with his disappointment?"

"At first he was angry when he discovered I was not his mother," Molly said. "Then we talked a little and Maria brought us each a glass of milk." She smiled. "Now I am Tia Mollee. Oh, Dona Espicia, how could any woman leave a child as adorable as Jaime?"

"I don't know," she said bitterly. "I understand the Spanish as little as I do the Indians. Dark passions seem to boil inside them, erupting at odd intervals in the most appalling incidents. My sons—my stepson and my natural son—at times both are enigmas to me."

Molly was puzzled but said nothing. Jabal, so imperious and handsome, had helped her when she needed it. The younger man she had met last night was as

52

handsome and had seemed even kinder than Jabal. It hardly seemed possible these two could hate each other.

The blue eyes seemed to drill into her. "Had the trouble come to your mountains yet? Was your father killed because of the brewing war?"

Molly shook her head. "Before I heard Don Jabal and Don Carlos speak of it, I had never heard one word about any war or trouble between people, ma'am."

"Well, there will be war," she said bluntly. "I think it has already begun. Perhaps it isn't so bad for Americans, but there are times when I cringe for my people. My adopted people," she amended. "Perhaps that is why I allow myself to be called Dona Espicia."

Again she retreated into her own thoughts. Then after a time her gaze returned to Molly. "My name is Bridget Shaughnessy, or was before I married the Conde. I was a raw Irish lass when I came to work in this country. The family I worked for decided to come west to make their fortune and brought me along. They were massacred by Indians while I was out in the woods gathering berries for supper. Don Pablo happened on me while I crouched shivering under a bush. I was too frightened to speak so he put me on the horse behind him and brought me to Veronica, much as Jabal treated you." A chuckle shook her. "Perhaps that is the reason I like Molly O'Bannion so much?"

Then her smile vanished. "The Conde said Bridget would never be a Spanish Condesa, so he changed my name to Spice—Espicia." She sighed. "It took a while to get used to my new name and to get rid of my Irish brogue, but I did both. Now I am mistress of this hacienda and on the side of the Spaniards in this war."

"Jabal said my father was probably killed because of

trouble between the Americans and the Spaniards, but I don't understand why the Indians would take to the warpath if it has nothing to do with them," Molly said uncertainly.

"As usual, the Indians are in the middle," Espicia said with a sigh. "The Americans want California and we Spaniards do not want to give it up." A wry smile twisted her lips. "My sons do not fully believe I am a Spaniard, so they tell me very little of what goes on. However, they are both involved in the skirmishes up to their eyebrows and I know more than they think. Today Jabal has gone to meet with his men and cook up some raid or other."

"Don Jabal has gone to fight?" Molly asked, and fear filled her. Would Huk call again? Would he cry in the night because Jabal would die? Oh, no!

"Waste no time on that one, my dear. He is still married to Feliciana, remember. Besides, he would only make you unhappy. Feliciana adored him enough to die for him, but he made her very unhappy most of the time. Only her *manner* of leaving surprised me when she left, for I often wondered how she could stand his dark moods. Do not let Michael annoy you, either. His father loved him, but because he is half American Pablo would never give him Costa Cordillera. It has made him quite bitter and I think causes his bad temper too often." She nodded, almost to herself. "For a long time I was a little bitter myself."

Then she raised her head proudly. "But the Conde was right, as usual. Jaime will make a better Conde than either of them when he comes of age. He is made of the stuff of Spanish grandees and will rule wisely and well if the Americans have left him our land."

She pointed out the window. "Look around us, my

dear. Everything the eye can see belongs to the Conde del Valle. Fifty thousand acres of the best California soil, and well worth fighting for! The buildings alone are worth a fortune. If taken care of, they will last for generations of del Valles. Since the first Conde settled here on a grant from his Majesty, each, in turn, has added to the value by erecting more buildings and accumulating more Indians to care for the estate. The rancho cannot be seen on horseback for a week of riding, it is so huge. Cattle grow fat on the lush grass the year round, for nothing colder than rain falls here in the winter. This climate is God's blessing bestowed on the grandees who first settled here. They opened up the wilderness and made it safe to live here. Now the Americans want to shove them aside and take it as their own. It isn't fair," she said.

Molly had gone to stand by the window as Dona Espicia spoke. She looked at the surrounding lush landscape and the well-tended buildings in the courtyard. Indians hurried to and fro attending to chores. Again she wondered if most Indians were servants now. Amatil certainly had been no servant to anyone and neither had her people. She had told Molly her tribe roamed the land in freedom, taking game to supply the larder, and harvesting berries and fish for variety. Had things changed this much since Amatil died?

A banging on the floor caused her to turn from the view. Dona Espicia had taken the cane that hung on the arm of her wheelchair and was hitting it against the floor.

She gave Molly a mischievous grin. "This is my signal for Jaunita," she said. "She has grown lazy sitting in attendance on me and dozes off quite frequently. Only a noise such as this wakes her to her duties."

"Is there something I can get you or do for you?"

55

Molly asked.

"No, thank you, my dear. And I've been talking so much and so long I didn't give you a chance to answer my question. Do you wish to be guest or employee?"

"I will be happy to help you in any way I can, Dona Espicia. However, it is not necessary that you pay me. My father left money for me." She stood as straight as she could, as befitted the daughter of an Indian princess.

"Nonsense!" the older woman said with a snort. "You have not tried to teach my grandson his lessons yet, so you do not realize what a chore it will be to keep him working. He knows he will some day be Conde. It is difficult to make him remember he is only a little boy and must take orders. It will be a full-time job for you and you shall be paid accordingly."

"I think it will be fun to help Jaime with lessons in English. My mother taught me and I remember how she did it. I will use her methods and he will enjoy learning just as I did," Molly said.

"M-m-m, well, we shall see," Dona Espicia murmured. "After lunch I will arrange for someone to show you around our holdings so you will not get lost in future. Now, run down and tell Maria I'm hungry. You must be, too. And tell that scamp Jaime not to forget to come see me this afternoon."

"Yes, ma'am."

Juanita came silently up the stairs and resumed her seat beside Dona Espicia. With a parting smile, Molly flew down the stairs. She hoped Don Jabal had returned to eat lunch.

Chapter Four

Her hopes were not realized, for only Jaime and Don Michael were at table when Molly entered the dining salon. Both rose courteously until she was seated and she marveled at the good manners Jaime had acquirred so young.

"Tia Mollee, you slept the morning away," he complained. "Maria would not let me wake you."

"It's true I slept very late and I'm sorry," Molly said. "Riding on a wretched blanket pallet for two days made me appreciate the softness of my bed too much, I'm afraid. I hope you will forgive me, Jaime, but I was very, very tired."

Don Michael's dark eyes twinkled as he smiled at his nephew and then at Molly. "The del Valles are the ones who should apologize, Miss Molly. Jabal should not have kept you on that pallet for too long at a time, and I must apologize for breaking in on you so abruptly last night. We do not have visitors often enough to keep my manners polished."

"There is nothing to apologize for, Don Michael," Molly said. "Don Jabal rescued me after my father died. He was most kind and gave of his time to bring me here.

57

The long ride was necessary."

"You are looking very beautiful this morning," Michael said softly. "It was worth the wait to see you again, but duty calls and I must go."

Molly felt a blush begin when Michael's gaze grew more admiring as he rose and folded his napkin. He was clad in vaquero trousers that outlined his trim body and accentuated his manliness to advantage. A trim coat exaggerated his broad shoulders and made his hips look even slimmer than they were. With a slight bow, Michael turned and left.

To cover her pleased embarrassment, Molly brought her thoughts back to the present and looked at Jaime.

"Dona Espicia asked that you come see her this afternoon, Jaime," she said. "Shall we go together to her room? I think she is rather lonely in that tower of hers. I'm to see the ranch after while, so let's go now."

"Yes, let's," Jaime agreed.

He slipped his small hand into Molly's as they climbed the stairs. She was panting by the time they reached the tower and even Jaime sat down on the top step with a sigh of relief, waving a greeting to his grandmother.

Dona Espicia handed the tray that was on her lap to the waiting Juanita when she saw them. "Jaime, you rascal, you didn't come to see me yesterday," she chided. "Is it necessary that I send for you before you think of me?"

"I am here now, *abuelita*," he said diplomatically as he rose from the step and went to her side.

"Grandmother," she corrected. "I'm trying to Americanize my family, Miss O'Bannion, but without much success. It is almost sure that California will be taken by the Americans. I think we will fare better if we can communicate in their language. I hope you will help me in this endeavor. If the future Conde sets a good example, the rest will follow."

Molly nodded, wondering about this war she was hearing about on every side. Why had her father not mentioned it to her? Was war the reason an Indian had shot him? She had always thought of her family as Americans, along with the Indians who inhabited the mountains they lived in. Were these Indians now on the side of the Spanish? Why would they side with such a haughty race against Americans who had befriended them? Then she silently chided herself. Whatever, it was too late to do her father any good.

Dona Espicia had been chatting with her grandson with evident pleasure. She turned to Molly even as she kept a protective arm around Jaime.

"Miss O'Bannion, Don Jaime will have to cope with Americans more than any of the rest. He will have to learn to speak with them, read their writing, and above all, learn the mannerisms that will please them. To survive a conqueror one must know enough diplomacy to manipulate him," Dona Espicia said.

"Please . . . can you just call me Molly? It would truly make me more comfortable."

"Moll-ee!" Jaime shouted gleefully.

"No, Jaime. *Moll*-y," Molly said firmly.

"Moll-y," he said doubtfully. "No *tia?*"

"No *tia*. Aunt Molly, if you wish."

"Aunt . . ." He tasted the word as though it were a new kind of food, then, "Aunt Molly," he said with a smile. "Aunt Molly, Aunt Molly, Aunt Molly. Now I'll remember."

Dona Espicia chuckled. "You will make a fine teacher, Molly. Jaime, will you apply yourself to your books if

59

Aunt Molly teaches you your lessons? Will you learn all that you can about Americans and their ways?"

"*Si, abuelita,*" he said, lapsing into the more familiar Spanish.

"Your work is cut out for you, Molly," Dona Espicia said with a sigh. "Don Jabal and Michael have been with the Americans enough to make English come easy for them, but the balance of the household find it difficult to break from the old ways. However, they will all have to learn to live with the Americans if they take over California."

"Even if they don't, there are so many of each nationality, we should learn to communicate. Perhaps while I am teaching Jaime English, he will teach me the language of his people," Molly said. She paused, then hesitantly added, "Why do you stay so remote up here, Dona Espicia? If you would take a room on the first floor, everyone would be more under your influence and you would surely have more visitors. It would make it so much easier for you to get around the house."

The bright blue eyes focused on Molly while she pondered her suggestion. At last she nodded. "Perhaps you have the solution, Molly. After Conde Pablo died I was very desolate for a time, so when I hurt my hip in a fall, I hid myself up here away from everybody and everything." She straightened in her wheelchair. "Now perhaps it is time I moved myself into the heart of the family again. With Feliciana gone, someone has to be present as mistress. Also, there are dread times ahead, I fear, for there is unrest among the landowners such as I have never before seen. Your suggestion is an excellent one, my dear, and I shall heed it."

Jaime clapped his hands. "I will come to see you much

60

oftener, *abu* . . . grandmother, if you are not so high up."

The older woman smiled, saying, "I should like that, Jaime. Now, why don't you have two horses saddled so you can show your Aunt Molly your holdings this afternoon? Acquaint her with the ranch so she won't get lost when she has no guide."

Leaving a dutiful kiss on his grandmother's cheek, Jaime scampered down the stairway. When he had gone, Dona Espicia turned her attention to Molly, checking her from head to toe.

"There is a riding habit in the closet of your room, Molly. It will probably fit you well enough. Feliciana was a few inches taller than you, but other than that you are both much the same size. I'll have the rest of her clothing shortened to fit you today."

"Why did she leave her clothing behind?" Molly asked timidly. It didn't seem natural for any woman to leave a full closet, especially when she apparently meant to be gone a long time and perhaps forever.

Dona Espicia shook her head, a bewildered look in her eyes. "I wish I knew, child. The entire affair was very mysterious. Jabal and Feliciana were not getting along well at all, as everyone knew. They quarreled at times, most times, or else they didn't speak to each other at all. One morning Jabal announced that Feliciana had left with a guest he'd entertained the night before. After that, he would say no more on the matter unless I forced the issue. When I asked about her clothing, Jabal shrugged and said it probably wasn't good enough for her and she would get what she needed when she reached Spain."

"Didn't she even say goodbye to Jaime?" Molly asked. How could a mother leave her child so abruptly? Especially a child so adorable as Jaime!

"He was heartbroken for a long time," Dona Espicia said soberly. "He probably still is, although he hides it well for one so young." Her thin shoulders straightened. "You had best run along and change, Molly. Instead of spending your time beguiling an old woman, it will be better for you and for Jaime if you are with him."

"Yes, ma'am." Then, like Jaime, Molly brushed a kiss against her cheek before she left. When she glanced over her shoulder there were tears in the blue eyes, but the older woman said nothing.

Molly hastened to her room, or rather Feliciana's, and opened the closet door. Again her own image confronted her. She stopped to admire the pink gown before she began her search through the abundant clothing for the riding habit Dona Espicia said would be there.

An elusive fragrance arose when the clothing was disturbed that made her nose wrinkle. What was it? What did the scent bring to mind? She sniffed, trying to solve the enigma. The odor was sweetish with a faint spicy tang.

Dolores stood waiting, so Molly paused in her search.

"Dona Espicia is having the hems lifted on these gowns, Dolores," Molly said. "While it is being done, will you please air the closet? Perhaps even wash it to remove the smell." She did not want to remind Don Jabal of his wife, although why it was important eluded her.

Then she spied the riding habit and removed it, shaking out the creases gathered from its long sojourn. It consisted of a long full skirt with a matching short jacket of gray wool. Black velvet lapels decorated the jacket and set off the crisp white blouse with its ruffled bosom. When she donned the outfit it fitted nicely save for the length. The skirt must be gathered over her arm before she could move without tripping, but she would manage.

"Boots and hat, too, senorita," Dolores said, bringing them from the closet.

"Thank you, Dolores, but please don't call me senorita. My name is Molly. I'm Molly."

The maid nodded and Molly saw a blush suffuse the dusky cheeks around her embarrassment and pleasure.

The boots were somewhat loose, but would do, Molly decided. However, the hat was too much. She had only worn a scarf on her head when the weather was cold in the mountains, and here the air was mild and sunny despite the fact March was almost upon them.

"No hat," Molly said. She ran a comb through her hair, watching it spring back into curls in the closet mirror. It had grown long during the last months, but she was glad it had. Her judicious gaze decided it was quite attractive curling on her gray-clad shoulders against the black velvet lapels.

Leaving Dolores to her tasks, Molly sped down the stairs and out on the veranda, carrying the folds of the skirt high enough so they would not trip her up. An Indian groom held the reins of two saddled horses while Jaime waited impatiently for her arrival.

The groom cupped his hands for Jaime to step into so he could seat himself on the saddle, then repeated the gesture for Molly to help her to the high-cantled sidesaddle on the black mare beside Jaime's horse.

"Do you wish me to accompany you today, Don Jaime?" the groom asked.

"Not today, Tomas," Jaime answered regally, and Molly realized she was seeing the guard who relieved Chia the night before.

She looked around the courtyard, marveling at the

hum of activity as the servants went about their chores. It was a huge space with a covered well in the center. Barns and sheds of many sizes flanked the hacienda, but across the courtyard was another house that made her gape in wonder.

"That is the Casa Grande, Aunt Molly," Jaime said. "*La Magnifica Condesa, mi bisabuelo,*—that is her abode."

Molly shook her head. "I'm sorry, Jaime. I'm afraid I don't understand."

"That is the home of my great-grandmother," he explained. "Condesa Ana Estrella Luisa del Valle. She is very powerful and likes to be called *La Magnifica*, at least in front of our guests."

Molly stared as Jaime reeled off the string of names, then returned her gaze to Casa Grande. Never had she seen such a mass of turrets and balconies and leaded windows. How many rooms were inside this huge mansion? It reminded her of a fairy-tale castle she'd seen in a book. The stones used in building it were polished to a high sheen, making it somehow seem unreal.

"The small house beside it is where Don Michael lives and keeps the books of Costa Cordillera," Jaime said, pointing a finger at a building of the same polished stones, although this one included some adobe bricks and was dwarfed by the size of its neighbor. "I will take you there when we return and show you the rifles and other guns of Tio Michael. He has a very great collection."

"Your uncle seems to be a busy man," Molly said. "I would not want to get in his way."

"Pooh," Jaime scoffed. "We will go when he is not there to object."

"But you cannot enter another's house without being

invited," she protested.

"The house belongs to me," Jaime said casually, "as does the rest of Costa Cordillera. My *abuelito* . . . my grandfather said it is mine."

He seemed older than his seven years as he sat easily atop the black horse and claimed his monarchy. A small child, perhaps, but one who realized he was a ruler from birth. A miniature of his father, Don Jabal.

"Perhaps you had better show me Costa Cordillera first, before the sun decides to go to bed," Molly suggested.

With a grin, he nudged his heels against the gelding and led the way out of the courtyard. They rode through a long broad valley in grass a foot deep, despite the fact it was still winter. Fat cattle dotted the valley and rolling hills leading out from it, and Molly marveled at a land where grass grew all year round.

Jaime was silent, letting her see for herself the beauty of his domain while he led her farther and farther from the hacienda. Soon they were climbing into steeper hills and the broad valley ducked behind its collar of mountains.

Molly grew worried. "Jaime, don't you think we have come far enough? Isn't it time to turn back?"

"Not yet," he answered. "I want to show you my secret place, Molly. I have shown it to no one since mama left. It is where we went when we wished to escape by ourselves for a time."

"Escape what, Jaime?"

He shrugged. "Oh, if papa was angry, or sometimes when La Magnifica was being unpleasant, or . . . whatever," he concluded lamely.

They reached the summit of a high hill and paused to

65

let the horses catch their breath. Molly looked around her, enchanted with the surroundings. Off in the distance she could see the haze above the ocean, and even this far away the boom of breakers against the sands of the shore sent tom-tom echoes through the clear air. There was an aliveness to this land Molly had not seen before.

Then overhead a huge bird swooped toward them uttering a harsh and raucous cry. Molly's heart missed a beat in fear as she watched his approach. Was she seeing Huk himself after all these years? Had the bird of evil come for her this time?

"*Culebra!*" Jaime called. He drew a leather glove onto one hand and held out his arm even as he whistled a shrill note. "*Culebra,*" he cried again, clear command in his voice.

The bird sailed down to land lightly on the small arm, then regarded them with baleful yellow eyes.

"See, Aunt Molly? It's Culebra—Condesa's falcon." He chortled in delight. "She calls him snake because he is so quick when he strikes." He uttered a string of Spanish, then raised his arm high.

With an ear-shattering shriek, Culebra soared into the sky. Molly watched open-mouthed until he disappeared into the sun and she could stare no longer. Then she closed her eyes with relief that the horrible apparition was gone.

"Why do you look so frightened, Aunt Molly?" Jaime asked. "Culebra will not harm you. He is trained to hunt animals and other birds, not people." He nudged his horse closer so he could put a small hand on her arm. "Your face is very white," he said anxiously. "Are you all right?"

Molly swallowed the lump of fear that had risen in her throat and tried to regain her composure, but her voice trembled when she said, "I thought it was Huk."

"Who is Huk?"

His innocent voice brought her back from the past. She forced a smile. "He is no one of importance, Jaime. The bird just took me by surprise." She glanced toward the lowering sun. "If we don't turn back soon, night will catch us before we get home."

"Then hurry, Aunt Molly. My cave is just ahead."

She followed him through a winding canyon until they reached a sort of cul-de-sac filled with wildflowers. It was a beautiful spot, rampant with shrubbery and grass beneath the towering trees.

Jaime dismounted, dropping the reins to the ground. Then with no hesitation he walked into a dense clump of shrubbery and disappeared!

"Jaime!" Molly called in alarm.

"In here, Aunt Molly," a disembodied voice answered.

Imitating his action, Molly dismounted and pushed through the tall grass. With just a few steps she was inside a narrow cavern. It took a moment or two for her eyes to adjust to the dim light before she could see. Then she saw several blankets on one side and a statue on the other. A small rug lay before it. The spicy sweet odor of Feliciana hung like a miasma in the air.

Jaime stood before the small statue, gazing up at the serene face of a madonna.

"Who is she?" Molly asked softly.

"Madre de Dios," he said simply. "Mama said she would always protect us, so we came here whenever she was afraid for either of us."

Molly said nothing. What had Feliciana feared so badly

to make her need the Madonna's protection? Her fears sounded as real as Molly's fear of Huk. Was it Jabal who frightened his wife? Or was it the great-grandmother who owned the horrible falcon? What?

A small hand slipped inside hers. "You will never leave me, will you, Aunt Molly?"

"No, of course not, Jaime. But hadn't we best go home now? It's getting quite late."

A volley of shots sounded as Molly started to push her way through the screening shrubs. She stepped backward so quickly she trod on Jaime's toes.

"What . . . ?" he began.

"Sh-h." She clamped her hand over his mouth, holding her own breath as long as she could.

More shots sounded, but then she realized they must be quite far away. Cautiously, she loosened her hold on Jaime and parted the shrubbery. Their horses munched on the grass at their feet, peaceful despite voices drifting faintly through the clear air.

"It's only a skirmish," Jaime said calmly.

She looked a question at him.

"The Americanos are trying to take our land, but our *defensarios* will prevent them succeeding." A shrug shook his small shoulders. "They fight."

He marched to his horse and waited until she helped him mount. She had to position her mare close to a rock so she could step on it and reach the saddle.

"Jaime . . ." she said slowly, "is that what Don Jabal is doing today? Is he fighting the Americans?"

"Possibly." His small heels urged his horse onto the path. "Papa commands a company of men."

She followed him, noting the noise of the battle was south of them, away from the hacienda. "Shouldn't we wait until it's quiet?" she asked breathlessly. "What if we get in the way of this fight?"

"Papa does not allow fighting near the hacienda."

She doubted even Don Jabal could dictate the course of a war, if that was what they heard. However, the sun was sinking fast and she did not relish being in the mountains after dark, so they continued on their way.

Suddenly, Jaime's horse leaped as though he'd been stung by a bee. While Jaime clutched his mane with both hands, the gelding raced down the trail in headlong flight, reins lying loosely on his mane.

"Jaime! Wait for me!" Molly called. Then realizing he had nothing to do with the mad flight, she swung her leg in the clumsy skirt so she was riding astride and kicked the mare with frantic heels.

They fled in a mad cavalcade down the twisting path, through the narrow canyon, coming finally into the broad valley. Try as she might, Molly's mare could not reach Jaime's horse. She kicked as hard as she could, flailing at the sweating withers with the ends of the reins, but the black horse and his small rider stayed lengths ahead.

"Hold on, Jaime," she managed to gasp, although she doubted he heard her. His short arms were locked in a death grasp in the long black mane. His knees were clamped in the hollow between saddle horn and shoulder. Oh, Jaime, please don't fall off, she prayed silently.

Then she heard pounding hoofs coming from behind. A glance over her shoulder showed a sombreroed rider overtaking them on a huge roan horse. He passed her as though her mare were standing still, reached the side of Jaime's horse, and slipped smoothly from his saddle to a seat behind the small boy. Gathering the reins in one hand and Jaime in the other, he pulled the black gelding to a halt.

Molly's lathered mare stopped beside them. "Jaime, are you all right?" she gasped.

The sombreroed man stepped to the ground with Jaime in his arms. It was Don Michael and his face was worried as he put the small boy on his feet. "Are you all right, Molly?" he asked.

She nodded and one hand reached to touch Jaime's cheek. Then her knees began to buckle as weakness overcame her at her relief that her small charge was all right.

Michael caught her as she fell and swung her up in his arms against his chest. She felt his strong heartbeat and somehow gathered strength from its beat. She struggled and he set her on her feet much as he had done Jaime.

"You both are lucky to be alive," he said. "Jaime, what possessed you to bring Miss Molly so far from the ranch? It is not safe and you must never again ride this far afield without a guard. Neither are you to gallop the horses in this manner."

He drew a kerchief from his pocket for Jaime who was trying manfully to stifle the tears rolling down his cheeks. The small lips quivered, but Jaime pushed the handkerchief away.

"We were not galloping the horses on purpose, Tio Michael," he said. "My horse ran away when something stung him and Aunt Molly was trying to stop him."

Molly's own eyes had filled with tears of relief when Jaime was safe, but now she straightened. "It was not our fault we went so fast, Don Michael. I rather think the fault was yours."

"Mine?" he asked in amazement. "If I had not caught

70

sight of you and stopped Jaime's horse, I shudder to think what might have happened."

Molly walked to Jaime's horse and examined the broad rump. A half-spent bullet had lodged itself in his side. When she gently removed it, a trickle of blood ran down the shiny haunch.

"Is this a remnant of your skirmish, as Jaime called it, Don Michael?"

He examined the pellet carefully, then dropped it into a pocket. "I see," he said thoughtfully.

The sun dipped behind the hills toward the distant sea and Molly shivered in the suddenly chilly air.

"We had best be getting home, Jaime. Shall we walk the remaining way?" she asked, holding out her hand.

Michael removed his jacket and wrapped it around her shoulders. Then he lifted her into her saddle. "That will help warm you, Miss Molly, but it is best we ride home."

He picked Jaime up and reseated him on the black gelding, then handed him the reins. "We ride," he said firmly.

"But he's just a little boy," Molly protested. "He was frightened very badly."

Michael shook his head and his eyes were pleading as he said, "Jaime must never know fear of a horse, Molly, if he is to be a proper Conde of Costa Cordillera. It is better he not have time to think of this. He is the Conde Jaime Luis del Valle and that is something none of us should forget."

Jaime straightened in his saddle and smiled at Molly, nodding in agreement.

"A del Valle owes you another apology, Miss Molly," Michael continued. "Our recent battle was the first to occur on Costa Cordillera soil. I did not know a bullet

71

would seek out Don Jaime's horse as its target."

The sombrero was replaced as he stepped up on the roan. "It will be best if you both stay closer to the hacienda in future," he added firmly. "These are unsafe times, as you have seen."

They rode through the gathering dusk up the broad valley to the cluster of buildings that was the heart of Costa Cordillera. Lights winked from the windows of the hacienda and Maria waited on the veranda, anxiously wringing her hands.

"Ah, you are here!" she said. "Are you all safe? Dona Espicia must be notified." She turned to go inside, then stopped in the doorway. "Are you sure Don Jaime is all right? He is not hurt?"

"He is just tired," Michael said.

The housekeeper disappeared inside. Jaime slipped from his horse, handing the reins to Tomas who had appeared soundlessly to take charge of the mounts.

"We are late for supper, *Tia* . . . Aunt Molly. Grandmother is sure to be angry. I am going to wash up because I'm hungry and I don't want to miss supper," Jaime said, then ran up the steps and into the house.

Michael handed his reins to Tomas and came to help Molly dismount. She sat tiredly on the side saddle, wondering if she had strength enough left to walk to her room and change to something more suitable for dinner.

"May I assist you in dismounting?" Michael asked, holding out his arms in invitation.

She stared at him, suddenly too weary to speak. Everything seemed unreal, as though in a nightmare. It had been such a lovely day . . . and then to be in the midst of a battlefield without any warning . . . what if the bullet had hit Jaime instead of his horse?

When she didn't move, Don Michael reached up to lift her bodily from the saddle and swing her to the ground.

He brushed a soft kiss across her forehead before he asked, "Can you walk?"

She loosened herself from his arms and gathered the train of her habit so it would not trip her.

"Thank you, Michael. Thank you for everything," she said softly. "Now I will be all right."

She walked up the steps with her chin high. She was weary enough to weep and stiff in every muscle, but she would not allow anyone to see any weakness in her!

Chapter Five

When Molly entered the hacienda, Dona Espicia was there to greet her. "I'm glad you are safely returned, my dear," she said. "I took your advice and changed my quarters to this floor and tonight I dine with my family."

"Good evening, ma'am," Molly stammered, looking with dismay at her bedraggled riding habit and sure her face looked as bad. "I'm sorry . . ."

"Nonsense, child," the older woman interrupted. "We have been waiting supper for your return. We have guests tonight I would like you to meet. Run to your room and change into something more appropriate. On his way through Jaime informed me he was starving."

Her friendliness made Molly less tired. Michael's kiss had given her food for thought—did Spaniards all do things like this so casually? Or did the fact that Michael was half-American contribute to his character to dilute the haughty Spanish blood she found so disconcerting? Whatever, he had rescued Jaime and her from what might have been a terrible accident and she was grateful.

She hurried through a bath that was waiting for her, then allowed Dolores to help her into a fresh gown. It had been shortened to fit, but the elusive scent of Feliciana still came faintly to her nostrils as it was slipped over her head. "Are there scents other than this available, Dolores?" she asked.

The maid looked puzzled. "Ma'am?"

"This perfume offends me," Molly said impatiently.

"Oh . . . yes, ma'am. Dona Espicia uses lilac and I'm sure she will let you use it, but I cannot ask her now. Tomorrow . . . tomorrow I will ask her."

"Please do," Molly said, then, hoping Jabal had returned, she hurried down to the dining salon.

Dona Espicia was surrounded by her sons and two people Molly hadn't met. The older woman spied Molly when she entered and said something to Jabal that made him come offer Molly his arm, albeit somewhat reluctantly.

"Molly, come meet our guests," Dona Espicia said. "Senor y Senora Cazadero, this is Miss O'Bannion." Then she chuckled. "Or shall we be less formal. Don Miguel, Dona Eulalie, this is our friend Molly."

Don Miguel bent gallantly over her hand while his wife stood looking at them with an amused smile. Her glance at Jabal was knowing. "So this is your little charge, Jabal. Perhaps you will learn to keep your seat on Garanon in future." A tinkle of laughter was meant to remove any sting.

Dona Eulalie had black hair to go with sparkling black eyes. She was tall and tiny-waisted, but buxom breasts filled her bodice to the point of bursting. Were her hips as ample under the billowing skirt?

When Jaime had bounded in, they seated themselves around the huge table. Dona Espicia saw to it that Molly was included in the conversation at intervals, but Michael maintained a brooding silence and Jabal's attentions were centered on the beautiful Eulalie. She flirted with him to an outrageous degree, and he lavished gallant compliments upon her until Don Miguel eventually grew tired of their game and glowered angrily at Jabal.

Dona Espicia caught his eyes once and frowned in warning, but Jabal only shrugged and returned his gaze to the dark-haired woman who found him so attractive. Jabal was unusually elated, refilling his own glass oftener than he did any other. Could today's fighting—or rather, today's exchange of shots—have this effect on him?

At long last the meal ended, much to Molly's relief. She was hurt by Jabal's neglect, even though she told herself she was a silly child he could not possibly consider his equal. Jaime was about to fall asleep in his plate, so she asked permission for both of them to be excused and led him up the stairs to his room.

There she turned him over to the maid waiting in his room, then escaped to the blue room where she could nurse her wounded feelings in private. The day had taken its toll and she was weary beyond belief.

Thoughts of Feliciana filled her mind as she sat on the blue-covered bed. Had she been forced to watch her husband flirt with attractive women as Molly had watched Jabal tonight? The twinges of jealousy she had no right to feel would be as nothing if she were his wife.

Then she felt a ridiculous blush start up her cheeks as she thought of being Jabal's wife. Amatil had not mentioned the relationship between a man and his wife, but over the years Molly had heard enough in the small cabin to know it was somehow a joining of bodies. Angrily, she pushed her silly thoughts away, forcing herself to think of other things.

The saddlepack with her clothing inside had been brought to her room, she noted. She rose and put it in the closet, pushing it to the back out of the way. Her mountain clothing was unsuitable in this elegant house, and not needed since Feliciana had left so many garments behind.

The pack was stopped from sliding out of sight. When Molly parted the hanging garments to see why, she saw a small wooden box leaning against the rear wall of the closet. Curious, she pulled it forward to inspect more closely. It was a lap desk, she decided, since the top was slightly slanted to make writing easier.

She returned to the bed with the box in her arms. The top was hinged, and when she lifted it, a small book was revealed inside. Putting the desk aside on the bed, she opened the small volume.

Meticulous penmanship gave a formal look to the contents. Molly read several lines before she realized it was Feliciana's diary. Embarrassed at her intrusion on something so private, she quickly closed the book and returned it to its place inside the desk, then thrust the whole business back to the rear of the closet. It seemed quite strange that Feliciana would leave such a thing behind.

Her thoughts were interrupted by the sound of crying. Listening, she realized it was coming from Jaime's room which was next to hers. Was he hurt?

She hurried into the hall and opened the door to Jaime's room. He was lying on the bed with his head in his arms, sobbing as only a small boy can.

"Jaime, what's the matter?" she asked as she gathered him to her.

His sobs changed to hiccups as he looked dolefully up

77

at her. He sniffed, and the lower lip quivered as it had earlier. "My mother is dead, isn't she?" he asked between hiccups.

"Oh, Jaime, whatever makes you think that?" she asked, dabbing at his tear-swollen face with her kerchief. "Your mother just went away for a while. She'll be back, I'm sure." She tried to make her voice more convincing than her treacherous thoughts.

He leaned against her, sighing. "She wouldn't leave me if they hadn't made her, Aunt Molly. She loved me and I know she wouldn't leave me unless she couldn't help it."

She patted him gently, marveling at such wisdom in one so young. "Now who would make her leave, Jaime?"

A shrug shook his small shoulders. "Oh . . . I don't know," he said vaguely. "I just wish she hadn't taken Mouse along." His voice was wistful.

"Mouse?"

He looked up at her and the elusive dimple flashed for an instant. "Mouse is my pet. He comes whenever I'm lonely . . . or he did before Mama left. I can't seem to find him any more." He thought for a moment, then added, "Mama played with him, too."

"What did this Mouse look like?" she asked softly.

A mischievous grin lit his face. "Like a mouse, of course! That's how he got his name, because he *was* a mouse!" He burst into giggles.

"Well now," Molly said, returning his grin, "Mouse comes from your imagination, doesn't he? There isn't a real mouse, is there?"

He sobered. "Mouse was real enough," he said sadly, "only now it doesn't seem so. He sort of disappeared when Mama disappeared."

Molly knew she was seeing a small boy growing up. She

hugged him to her saying, "We will just have to find some new friends, Jaime. And we will, you just wait and see."

A yawn split his face. "I'm glad you're here, Aunt Molly. You will stay, won't you?" he asked sleepily.

It was an echo of his cry in the night and once again Molly wondered how a mother could leave such a son as this. Why had he said she was dead? It was a mystery that needed unravelling.

Molly tucked Jaime in, then waited until his eyes closed and his breathing showed that he slept before she left. The hall outside his room was quiet, despite the voices and laughter drifting up from the salon below.

Suddenly Jabal's door opened and he emerged, buttoning himself into a different waistcoat than the one he'd been wearing. He saw her and laughed. "Ah, little Molly awaits," he said with a wide swing of his arm. He swaggered toward her with unsteady steps.

When he was close enough to grasp her shoulders, she smelled the strong odor on his breath. It was the odor of alcohol and she realized he was drunk.

"Sweet senorita," he murmured, bending his head toward hers.

His brown eyes were nearly closed but still a roguish glint leered at Molly. Her gaze fastened on the neat black mustache until it became a blur before her eyes. Then his lips covered hers.

Her heartbeats thundered in her ears and her knees grew weak as she felt his warm mouth. His lips opened to allow his tongue to gently probe between her teeth. She gasped as she tried to push away from him, but his strength was like that of iron. Darkness began to swirl over her in huge waves and she fought the rising faintness.

Then suddenly his mouth left hers and he stepped back, grinning like a small boy caught in some mischief. When his grip left her shoulders, she staggered, and he hastily caught her around the waist. "Steady, sweet Molly," he whispered.

He glanced over the railing at the people below before his gaze returned to her. "*Querida*," he murmured, again letting his hands feel her arms inside the sleeves.

She jerked free of his hands and ran to her room, slamming the door behind her to shut him out. Tears filled her eyes and she angrily brushed them away. How dare he! Who did he think she was? A slut to be handled so intimately? How dare he! She was the daughter of a princess!

Then her fingers touched the lips he had kissed and she felt anew the strange sensation that almost caused her treacherous knees to give way. She remembered the waves of faintness and a feeling she had not known before. Jabal . . .

He kissed her! Her first real kiss, other than from her parents. And he was drunk, her mind added. Her face burned with mortification. What must he think of her! That she would allow such a thing! But then, how could she have prevented it?

Her gaze went round the blue room as she wondered wildly if she should leave immediately. Then fear scattered her thoughts as she realized there was a dark face peering in at her from the window!

Without moving her head, her eyes returned to the curtained window and the face staring through it. She could see hooded eyes on the motionless figure, then suddenly it was gone. With a cry, Molly sprang forward to the window.

Peering through the glass, she searched for movement, but there was none. Slowly she opened the window and stuck her head through the opening, trying to see in all directions at once. A narrow veranda circled the house on the second floor, much like the inner balcony. She could see no stairs leading to the ground, but they were most likely on the far side of the veranda and out of her sight.

A moon sailed on high, flickering through vague clouds and wisps of night fog drifting into the courtyard. The smell of the sea came to her nostrils and she breathed deeply of it, savoring its uniqueness. It seemed to have a steadying quality, for her heartbeats slowed and she could think more calmly of recent events.

Had she really seen a face at the window or was it her imagination? Jabal's kiss had so unsettled her, she wasn't sure. Why would anyone want to spy on her? Surely no servant would dare such a thing. Perhaps she was being silly.

Wearily, she readied herself for bed, wondering why Dolores hadn't appeared tonight as she had before. She thought not to sleep, but her head scarce touched the pillow before her eyes closed and darkness claimed her.

Her sleep was a troubled period of dark nightmares wherein hooded eyes hung over her and black mustaches smothered her until she could hardly breathe. Once she was clinging desperately to a black horse, unable to stop his headlong dash toward a high cliff. Despite his speed they seemed to move in a sort of slow motion that was agonizing because she could not stop it. Just as he leaped into the chasm below, she sat up wide-eyed.

"Ah, you are awake, Molly," Dolores said. "Do you wish bath this morning?"

Molly looked dazedly around. Fog swirled around the window, but it had the yellowish cast that meant the sun already tried to burn its way through.

A deep breath steadied her. "No, thank you, Dolores, not this morning. Just the wash basin, please," she said, then added, "Has breakfast been served yet?" This morning she would not wish to be late for breakfast.

"No, ma'am. You have time for wash and dress before," the maid answered.

Molly dreaded seeing Jabal after last night, but there was no escape. However, she would confront him with a cool gaze and her head held high. She would ignore his boorish behavior of the night before. Perhaps he wouldn't even remember the episode. After all, he had been dreadfully drunk.

Her ordeal was postponed when she saw Jabal was not at the breakfast table. Neither were the guests, nor was Dona Espicia. She wondered curiously just how the evening had resolved itself. Had the beautiful Eulalie caused her husband and Jabal to fight?

Don Michael and Jaime were the only ones at table. Both rose as she entered, and after she was seated, Maria continued serving.

"Good morning," Molly said, determined to be pleasant to everyone today.

"Good morning, Miss Molly," Michael said. His smile assured her he was in a much better mood than their company had produced the evening before. "I hope there are no bad effects from your ordeal of yesterday."

"Good morning," she answered with a smile. "Yesterday has become but a bad dream, and I thank you again for rescuing us. Even though you were the cause of our plight," she added mischievously.

There was a speculative look in Michael's dark eyes as he nodded his agreement and returned her smile.

"We have to go see Condesa Magnifica this morning, Aunt Molly," Jaime said glumly. "She has sent word she wants to see us both."

"Oh? Well, I shall enjoy meeting your great-grandmother, Jaime."

Michael snorted in amusement. "No, you won't. She is carnivorous . . . eats little boys and big girls on sight. Or perhaps she will just tear your head off this time."

Jaime giggled. "Tio Michael, you are making jokes. La Condesa makes me wear a tie as though I am in church, and she is very stern when she asks what I have been doing, but she would *never* eat me."

"Maybe not you, Conde," Michael said soberly, "but she will probably dig into Molly in a way she will never forget. You will have to be her guardian today."

"Now why would she attack me?" Molly asked calmly. "I am prepared to like her. Perhaps she will want me to read to her."

Michael sighed, shaking his head. "Miss Molly, you are very naive. You are also very transparent in your worship of my so-charming half brother. He treats women very shabbily and he is much like the Condesa in his cruelty. If La Condesa thinks Don Jabal is the least bit interested in you, there is no telling to what lengths she will go."

"Don Jabal is a married man, Don Michael," Molly said indignantly. "I would never become involved with a married man."

Had this Spaniard read her thoughts? Was she so transparent in her fascination with Jabal? She would have to be more careful in the future not to allow her thoughts to be read by others.

"I am not enamored of Don Jabal, Don Michael," Molly said slowly. "It is just that he helped bury my father and brought me to this house because my father made him promise to do so. I shall always be grateful for his assistance at a time when it was needed."

Michael nodded. "Why don't you call me Michael, Miss Molly. I would like very much for us to be friends while you are here."

"If you will omit the Miss from my name," she answered. "You know I value you already as a friend."

"Bueno," he said, rising. "Now, with your permission, I had best be on my way. Jaime, be careful the Condesa doesn't eat you."

Jaime sat with a spoon held pensively in his mouth. When he removed it, his face was serious. "Condesa *is* very stern, Aunt Molly. She doesn't like many people, you know, so you must not mind anything she says." He dabbled his spoon in the remaining porridge. "She didn't like Mama."

"Why not, Jaime?"

He murmured something she couldn't hear.

"What, Jaime? What did you say?" she asked.

He looked up, shamefaced. "Mama was afraid of Condesa," he said sadly. "If you do not stand up to her, she will strike at you, like Culebra."

"Then I suppose I had better stand up to her, no matter what she says," Molly said lightly. "Are we to visit her right now?"

He sighed. "I will have to put on my Sunday clothing first." His glance was critical as he surveyed her gown. "You had best not wear Mama's frilly dress. Condesa never did like it."

"What should I wear, Jaime?"

He thought for a moment. "Something plain, I think, Aunt Molly. A real skinny sort of gown," he said, making straight up and down lines with his hands. "Then perhaps she will not notice you."

"Well!" Molly sputtered indignantly. "Then why should I go at all? Perhaps you had best go without me."

"I can't, Aunt Molly. Noyo was very definite. He said she wanted to see us both."

"Noyo?"

"Noyo is her manservant. He is always with her unless she sends him on an errand," Jaime said, laying his napkin beside the bowl. "I suppose we had better get ready," he said resignedly. "One must never argue with Condesa."

Molly followed him up the stairs.

"Don't be long, Aunt Molly," he said as he went into his room.

Dolores was straightening the room when Molly entered.

"Something is wrong, Mollee?" she asked.

Molly shook her head. "Not really, Dolores. It's just that I must dress for a visit with a dragon."

When Molly opened the closet the elusive fragrance she had tried to banish drifted out. "Did you get the lilac scent for me?" she asked.

The maid put her hand over her mouth. "I forgot," she said, and the words were muffled. "I'll get now."

"Never mind, Dolores, I don't have much time," Molly said, looking through the garments. "Her majesty probably knows every one of these gowns," she muttered.

Stooping, she pulled her packsack from beneath the

racks and pulled her best dress from it. She shook it, trying to erase the wrinkles, but they were obdurate.

Dolores smiled as she took it from her. "Iron," she said, and hastened out the door.

By the time Molly had the morning dress back on its hanger, Dolores returned with her gown. Molly put it on and looked at herself in the long mirror. The dress was one she had made and it was quite plain. The material was a drab green in color. The long sleeves and high neckline made her look years older, but perhaps it would please the formidable old woman she was going to meet. She sniffed, then smiled. At least she smelled like herself again.

The packsack lay open where she'd left it. She felt the remaining small garments before touching the old Bible and the metal coins. She fingered the gold coins thankfully, knowing she could escape from Costa Cordillera if it became necessary, for her fortune was intact. She carefully closed the pack and pushed it out of sight beneath the hanging garments.

Reluctantly, she went to meet Jaime. Although Casa Grande was just across the courtyard, it seemed to her they were embarking on a very long journey. Jaime must have some of the same feelings, for he slipped his small hand into hers as they walked sedately over the old cobblestones.

Molly noted the scarcity of male Indians that were usually hurrying about their chores. One held a horse for the blacksmith to shoe, but the other servants going about their business were all women. Had the men gone with Jabal to fight again? She shivered, remembering the bullet lodged halfway into the hide of Jaime's horse. War always meant death, she had learned from her reading, although why wars were waged was usually quite vague. Would this war mean the death of someone important to her? Would Huk cry again in the night?

Before they reached the wide front door of Casa Grande, it swung noiselessly open to admit them. Inside, the light was dim, but Molly saw the hooded eyes and dark face of the Indian who held the door for them—the same eyes she had seen outside her window the night before. She hadn't imagined it as possible! Had the fierce old Condesa sent him to spy on her?

"Bring them in here, Noyo," an old voice said impatiently. "Bring them in, bring them in."

The Indian led the way to a raised dais and a throne. On it, crouched like a protective bird on a nest, sat a wizened old woman. A black mantilla covered sparse strands of hair. Her face was like old parchment, but it had the same cruel look of the predator Molly had seen on Jabal when he was angry. Behind her perched Culebra, making warning noises in his throat. He broke into an ear-splitting screech when Molly and Jaime neared his mistress.

"*Silencio, Culebra!*" she ordered.

The bird subsided, grumbling in his throat as he closed his eyes and pulled into himself at her command.

The old woman waited until Jaime had kissed her withered hand before speaking. "Ah, Conde," she said, then added a string of Spanish too quickly for Molly to understand, while Jaime looked gravely into her face.

When the raspy words ceased, Jaime answered her just as rapidly, while Molly wondered what they talked about. At the end of the exchange Jaime bowed his head politely, saying, "Si, Condesa Magnifica."

Then he turned to Molly with a slight smile, and she

marveled at the aplomb of this small child.

"She wishes to meet you," he said in a low voice. "You must kiss her hand, Aunt Molly, and curtsey. And don't forget, she is the Condesa Magnifica."

He again faced his great-grandmother and made the introduction. "Condesa Magnifica, I would like to present to you Senorita Mollee O'Bannion."

Molly accepted the imperious hand held out for her and brushed it with her lips. It felt papery and dry, as though her body were already retreating into the dust it would soon become. Then Molly curtsied, although she wasn't sure what exactly a proper curtsey was, murmuring, "Condesa Magnifica, it is such a pleasure."

The piercing eyes stared at her, examining every inch of her attire and her face. Then the old woman snorted contemptuously. "*Senorita?* Bah. You're nothing but another shanty Irish like that . . . that *woman* who trapped my son into marriage. A marriage that disgraced the family!"

She picked up a *cigarillo* and waited until Noyo held a candle to light it, then puffed clouds of smoke around her head. "How did you trap Don Jabal into bringing you here?" she demanded harshly.

Molly felt an angry flush rise to her face as she stared at this ancient virago. How dare this woman speak to her as she had? Then a small hand tugged at hers and she looked down to see Jaime shake his head in warning.

Molly forced her voice to be calm as she answered, "Don Jabal brought me here to be of assistance to his mother and his son, Condesa. My father had saved Don Jabal at the cost of his own life . . ."

"We are the Condesa Magnifica," the old woman interrupted, "and you will so address us!"

Molly stared at her until once again a small hand tugged at hers. Then she continued, "As I was saying, Condesa Magnifica, my father saved your grandson's life. Since the death of my father left me quite alone, Don Jabal felt honor-bound to make some provision for my future. I don't believe a trap of any kind was involved. Don Jabal's mother seems quite relieved that she now has someone to tutor her grandson."

While the words tumbled out, the look on the old woman's face grew more menacing with a frown that drew the wrinkles even closer together. When Molly had finished, the Condesa snorted contemptuously. "Don Jabal's *mother?* Conde Jaime del Valle's *grandmother?*" she squealed in such a manner as to make Culebra stir on his perch. "The Irisher is neither Don Jabal's mother nor Don Jaime's grandmother. She pleases to think of herself as such, but she is not a member of this family!"

The Condesa seemed on the point of exploding as she held a long breath, then she blew out, spittle mixed with her breath. "Just how do you plan to be of assistance to anybody?" she asked spitefully. "What can you possibly do for us?"

"I can teach Jaime to read and write English," Molly answered.

"You can teach Don Jaime del Valle to read and write English?" the Condesa mimicked. "Why? Why do we need more of these Americano language and ways? They are foreigners who dare usurp our properties. How dare they demand we learn their ways? We were here first!" As Molly tried to speak, the old woman held up a hand for silence as she continued. "We shall be here last, for God is on our side. We shall drive these bastards from this land as though they were animals. And perhaps the

89

Irisher with them," she said in conclusion.

"Your own command of English is quite excellent," Molly observed calmly, although she was far from calm.

"You will address me as Condesa Magnifica when you speak," the old woman screeched.

"Condesa Magnifica, the way you speak English is quite good," Molly said again.

The rheumy eyes reddened with anger. "You are impudent!" she shouted. "When I ruled here, such impudence would have gotten you whipped! Whipped until your impudence was gone."

Molly said nothing. She kept her face impassive, trying to meet the cruel glare without a show of fear, despite the fact her heart was beating so rapidly it made breathing difficult.

"You are not needed here, Americano," the old woman said viciously. "You shall not twist my grandson and my great-grandson into traitors to Spain! They are of the Spanish royalty and that they will remain!"

She swept her gaze up and down Molly's gown while her lips curled into a sneer. "I need not worry you will entice Don Jabal as that woman did Don Pablo. A crow! Dowdy, drab . . . even your straw-colored hair will not be enough. But you will not stay at Costa Cordillera! Do you hear me? You will leave or you will be dealt with!"

Her voice had risen to a shout, cracking as she strained it even more on the last sentence. A prickle of fear ran down Molly's spine as the spittle flew from the Condesa's mouth in her rage. Culebra roused himself to utter a piercing shriek, a sound that echoed against the high ceiling of the throne room.

Molly stood watching her, wondering what would happen if she ran from the room. Then she felt Jaime's hand press reassuringly against hers and steeled herself to stand facing this enemy until her rage subsided.

When the old woman had caught her breath again, she sat measuring Molly with her red and watery eyes.

"May we be excused now, Condesa Magnifica?" Jaime asked politely.

The old woman glanced at him, then turned to Noyo. "Show them out," she rasped.

Her voice followed them to the door. "Mind what I have said, *gringa!*"

Chapter Six

When Molly and Jaime were again outside the castle, she sank to a wooden bench beside the covered well as her knees gave way. The evil eyes stabbing hatred at her had frightened her to the core. What had the old woman meant when she said she would "deal" with her? Had she promised Molly death?

Jaime sat beside her and slipped his hands into hers. "Do not be afraid, Aunt Molly," he said anxiously. "She did not make you cry and that is good. Mama always cried, and then the Condesa grew even angrier."

Molly tried to laugh, but it emerged rather shakily. "How old is your great-grandmother, Jaime?" she asked. "I have never seen a face quite so ancient as hers."

"La Condesa Magnifica celebrated her ninety-first birthday last fall, Aunt Molly," he said, and then with a sigh, "She is quite strong and will likely live forever . . . at least it will seem so."

"Yes," she agreed, remembering the youthful years of her parents when each had died. It seemed like such a waste! Did only the wicked live long lives?

Then Molly remembered the lengthy conversation held in Spanish while she waited. "What were you and your great-grandmother talking about, Jaime? I can not follow Spanish when spoken that fast."

"She was telling me it is time for me to learn to rope the bulls," he said, then looked up at her. "They are quite large bulls, Aunt Molly. They were brought here from Spain and their horns are sharp as razors. They are very fierce and will kill anyone on foot if they can. Everyone but Papa fears to get near them, but of course they must."

Molly stared at him incredulously. "You mean she wants you to rope bulls *now?* That is ridiculous, Jaime. You are just a small boy and your strength not developed as yet. Bulls are gigantic in comparison. You must not do as she wishes."

He picked a splinter from the bench they sat on, not meeting her eyes. "If I am to be Conde, I must know how to do these things. Age does not matter. Condesa Magnifica says a Conde must have heart from the time he is born."

Molly watched him as he sat with eyes meticulously studying the bench they sat on. She was horrified at the idea of one so young doing things only a man should be required to do. Why should he risk death just because an old witch said he must? At every turn she was learning how different Spaniards were from Americans.

With a sigh, she rose. "Shall we begin your lessons this morning, Jaime?"

He stood up. "First I will show you Tio Michael's gun collection," he said firmly. "Tio Michael went with some of the Indians to check the movements of the Americans this morning, so we shall not be interrupted."

"Oh, Jaime, I really do not think we should go in his house when he's away," she protested.

"You forget, **Aunt Molly**. It is my house." The small monarch led her to the rock and adobe house near the castle. The door was unlocked and no one challenged their entry.

Inside, Molly paused to look around the room. It was much smaller than the castle's throne room, but it bespoke of a man who liked his comforts. A desk dominated the room, leather chairs and a large couch flanked the fireplace. Bright serapes draped the walls. A shawl lying on the couch was evidently used as a coverlet during naps. Over the fireplace a portrait of a hawk-faced man stared haughtily down at them.

"Who is that?" Molly asked.

"*Abuelito*," Jaime answered. "That is the grandfather who said I shall be Conde."

She nodded, noting the resemblance of both Jabal and Michael in the proud face.

"Now come see the guns," Jaime urged.

He led her to an elaborate wooden case in one corner of the room. Then he fished around behind it before bringing forth a large iron key. "Tio Michael hides the key where it is hard to find," he said with a grin.

He opened the door to the case and revealed a rack of rifles, polished to such a sheen that the steel glittered almost like jewels. Even the wood stocks shone with the velvety glow of loving care. Pistols in varying sizes hung on the walls beside the rifles. It seemed a monument to war and killing, Molly thought.

Jaime reached for a pistol and held it caressingly. His smallness of size made the weapon seem huge in comparison. "Pow!" he exclaimed, aiming toward a window. "Pow! Pow!"

Molly's uneasiness increased. "Jaime, are you allowed

to play with these guns?" she asked. Somehow the instrument of death he held so carefully seemed obscene in his small hands.

"Tio Michael is teaching me to shoot," he said, evading an answer to her question. "I know all about guns. Would you like to hold this one, Aunt Molly?"

"No, I wouldn't," she said. "I would really like to go now. The gun collection is beautiful, but I don't think we should stay here any longer."

"All right," he said, replacing the pistol and locking the door. When he had placed the key back in its hiding place, they left, much to Molly's relief.

"Now shall we go look at your books, Jaime?" she asked.

The impish grin flashed again. "It is lunchtime, Aunt Molly."

She had to laugh at his wiliness, but went with him to the hacienda. Only Dona Espicia shared their lunch and Molly was relieved that she would not have to spar with her Spanish benefactors. Had her father any notion as to what he had let her in for?

"How did you fare with La Condesa Magnifica?" Dona Espicia asked.

"She was quite fierce, *abuelita*," Jaime said cheerfully. "She was very nasty to Aunt Molly, but she could not make her cry. If Condesa ever hurts her, I will get one of Tio Michael's pistols and shoot her."

"Jaime!" Molly exclaimed, shocked at his calm assumption he could kill.

Dona Espicia's laugh was a dry rasp. "It is as I told you, Molly. Spaniards have fierce and fiery natures—even the small ones." She winced with pain as she shifted in her chair. "My hip pains me more at times than it did," she said, glancing at Maria as she entered with a pitcher of water. "Please prepare a sleeping potion for me this afternoon, Maria."

Molly recalled the anger Jabal had shown when he learned of her taking laudanum again. It surely was not a good thing for her. Molly's mother had taught her other ways to relieve pain and suffering.

"Dona Espicia," she said hesitantly, "a boiling spring would probably help you more than sleeping."

"Now how could *that* help?" the older woman asked doubtfully.

Molly started to tell her of the many cures of her mother's people, then remembered her father's warning never to tell of her heritage, never reveal her mother was an Indian.

"In the mountains when we had sores that would not heal or pain from sprains and bruises, we would go to the mineral springs bubbling from the ground and soak the hurt away. I don't know why it helped, but it always did," she said.

Dona Espicia's gaze was speculative as she searched Molly's face. "I see," she said at last. "Well, I doubt it could do any harm." She glanced at her housekeeper. "Send a wagon with empty barrels to the nearest hot springs. When it returns heat some of the water for my bath."

She propelled her wheelchair backward from the table. "I don't know why I didn't move down to this floor sooner, Molly. It's much more convenient for everybody." She turned to Jaime. "I see my grandson much oftener and that pleases me. As soon as you finish your lunch, young man, I want you to attend to your lessons."

"*Si, abuelita,*" he murmured.

When she had left the room, his mischievous grin appeared. "I am glad you did not tell her I showed you the guns, Aunt Molly. I am really not allowed to touch them when Tio Michael is not there, even though he does live in my house."

"I rather thought that was the case, Jaime. Thank you for telling the truth, although somewhat late. If we are to be friends we should be honest with each other," Molly said. "Now, shall we take a look at your books? We have the afternoon to ourselves."

Jaime led her to a room she hadn't as yet seen, one where the walls were lined with richly bound books. Her eyes feasted on the wealth before her. Reverently, she ran her hands over soft leather bindings and gold-encrusted titles. She remembered her one shelf of books in the cabin in the mountains, marveling that one person could own this many volumes.

Then she began to examine the titles. "Almost all of these books are written in Spanish, Jaime. Will you teach me Spanish even as I teach you English?"

His small-boy grin appeared. "I do not read and write Spanish very well, Aunt Molly. *Abuelita* has always insisted on the English when we do lessons."

"And your mother? Did she prefer English, too?"

A sober look replaced his smile when Jaime thought of his missing mother. "No, she didn't. She said Spanish was a more beautiful language, but American was essential if we were to live in this country. When I was small she taught me Spanish, but after I grew up she explained why I should learn English. Before she left we studied *Inglés*."

Molly smiled at his mixture of languages before the impact of his words reached her mind. Feliciana's diary

97

was written in English! If, as Jaime said, she was planning to stay in this country, why had she suddenly left?

Perhaps the diary would supply an answer, she decided. It would not be polite to look into her private life, perhaps, but in this instance it might be well to do so. Once she had made up her mind to it, she pushed the topic from her thoughts and turned to the matter at hand.

"What books do you study, Jaime?"

He led her to a corner table that held several books and writing materials. She leafed through the books and saw they were compatible to teach as Amatil had taught. Jaime was an apt pupil, eager to learn once he grew interested. The afternoon passed quickly as they made games of spelling words and adding sums. When the sun sank too low to adequately light the room, they closed the books.

"Will your father return today, Jaime?" Molly asked casually.

A shrug lifted the small shoulders. "Perhaps. I do not know of the affairs of the *defensarios*. Papa says they do not concern me yet." He cocked his head to one side, considering the matter. "It concerns Costa Cordillera, however, so I think it must concern me, also. Is it not so?"

Once more the Conde Jaime del Valle looked out of wise brown eyes, and Molly nodded. "It is so, Jaime. I think if our country is at war we must all be concerned, and I, for one, would like to know more of what this war is all about. It has already killed my father and I would hate for it to kill yours, too," she said.

Shouting voices in the courtyard put an end to their idle speculation. Maria's wail of anguish brought them hurrying to the open front door of the hacienda. Tomas was standing at the foot of the steps beside the big roan horse, patiently untying ropes that held Michael in the saddle. When the Indian had loosened the last strand, Michael slipped awkwardly from the saddle into his waiting arms. Holding the lanky form in his arms as though it were just a baby, Tomas slowly mounted the steps.

"Is he dead?" Maria asked fearfully.

"No."

Blood covered one sleeve. Michael's head lay against Tomas's chest, as though he were too tired to hold it upright. Molly saw his eyes open briefly, then close with the infinite weariness of mortality.

"Bring him to my room," a voice behind Molly commanded.

Startled, Molly turned. Dona Espicia had been wheeled to a spot behind them. She looked tired, but her blue eyes were clear as she brought order to her household.

"Maria, send a boy for Doctor Laughlin. Tell him to ride without stopping. You will most likely find the doctor in Santa Rosa, but find him wherever he is, and bring him here," she said.

Without waiting for an answer, she turned to the Indian maid behind her. "Turn down my bed . . . hurry! Then bring hot water and cloths."

"Dona . . ." Maria said uncertainly.

"Well, what is it?" Dona Espicia asked.

"The doctor . . . he is with Americanos?"

"Yes."

"At settlement?"

"Yes, yes!"

"The boy will be afraid," Maria warned.

"The Americans' fight is not with the Indians," Dona Espicia said sharply. "Now go! Tell the boy if the doctor is not here by sunup, he will surely have something to fear, but from me, not the Americanos."

Her glance met Molly's. "My son has been shot, Molly. Will you help me with him?"

"Of course."

Molly wheeled the older woman's chair toward her room. Tomas was inside with Michael. The wounded man groaned when he was laid on the bed.

"As usual, Jabal is away when I need him," Dona Espicia said tartly. "Molly, have you ever removed a bullet from flesh? Your hands are steadier than mine. Do you think you can pry this one out?"

Before Molly could answer Dona Espicia noticed Jaime standing round-eyed as he watched the bustle. "Go to the kitchen, Jaime, and tell cook to give you your supper. There will be no time for a formal meal this night."

When Jaime had started for the kitchen, Dona Espicia looked up at Molly. "Well?" she demanded.

"I have never done such a thing," Molly said faintly. "Don Jabal cut the arrow from my father's back while I watched." A shiver crossed her back. "He did it very fast."

"No matter," Dona Espicia said impatiently. "I will do it myself, if necessary. Come."

Her strong hands propelled her chair toward her waiting son so quickly Molly was hard put to stay close. They entered to see Michael's white face twisted in pain as he lay where Tomas had deposited him. He was more like a small boy now than the imperious man before.

"Remove his coat and boots, Tomas," Dona Espicia ordered. She glanced up as her maid entered with a basin from which steam drifted ceilingward. "Put that on the table beside the bed. Where are the cloths I requested?"

"I get now," the maid said, and hurried on her errand.

Tomas pulled off Michael's boots quite easily, but the blood-soaked jacket was more of a problem. When he touched the sleeve Michael's gasp of agony made him pause and look at Dona Espicia for directions.

"Cut it off," she ordered. "Use a knife and be careful how you do it. Remove the shirt, also. We need to see the wound in order to repair the damage."

Tomas brought a knife from its holster on his belt and slit the coat sleeve up to the shoulder. With an added deft slash he cut through the collar so the pieces were free to be removed without disturbing the injured man. He repeated the process on Michael's shirt to bare the wound.

Dona Espicia sloshed a cloth in the hot water, then twisted it so the excess would be gone. She leaned toward her son.

"Let me do that, ma'am," Molly said quickly.

The older woman relinquished the cloth with a grateful smile, watching while Molly carefully washed Michael's arm and shoulder. The angry wound still oozed blood, but she could see the end of a bullet in the mangled flesh. It must have been partially spent when it entered.

Dona Espicia bent over her son and examined the mangled flesh, then nodded as though agreeing with herself. "Now you can take out the bullet, Molly. With part of it out in the open, you won't have to probe for it. You can cut it out quite easily and then we shall be rid of it."

Molly looked at her fearfully. True, she had helped her father with his bloody hides, and at times had herself skinned a small animal, but never had she probed into living flesh. Sickness rose to her throat at the thought. "Can we not wait for the doctor, Dona Espicia? I'm not sure I can do it."

The older woman shook her head impatiently. "No, we cannot wait, Molly. Michael will get blood poisoning if the lead isn't removed quickly, and then it will be too late." She glanced at Tomas. "Heat your blade in the flames, Tomas, and make sure it is clean."

When he had gone to do her bidding, her blue eyes bored into Molly's. "I can make Tomas dig for the bullet, Molly, but his big hands will be harsher than yours. Will you do this thing for my son?"

Michael groaned, and they saw his eyes were open. "Do I not have anything to say in this matter?" he asked, panting with the effort of speech. "Do not make Molly play doctor, Mama—let Tomas get the bullet."

"I will do it, if you wish me to," Molly said.

"Are you sure it won't make you sick? Bullet wounds are a bloody business."

Tomas returned holding the smoking knife by the bone handle. Molly reached for it but the Indian held up a hand to stop her taking it. "Must cool some," he said.

While the knife was cooling, Molly's gaze locked with Michael's. Even in his pain his face was handsome and a glint of humor lurked in his eyes. One eye closed in a wink and Molly smiled. Only death could still the flirtatiousness in a Spaniard, she decided.

At the first touch of the knife, Michael stiffened, but no sound emerged from his tightly pressed lips. The hot odor of blood came to Molly's nostrils and she felt her stomach heave in rebellion.

Forcing herself to ignore it, Molly probed with the tip

102

of the knife until it was beneath the lead pellet, then turned it slightly and brought the missile out of the wound. Fresh blood gushed from Michael's shoulder. She dropped knife and bullet into the basin, hastily grabbing cloths to catch the welling moisture.

"It should be cauterized now," Dona Espicia directed. "Heat the knife again, Tomas."

Tomas retrieved the knife from the basin of water and took it back to the flames.

A glance at Michael told Molly he had fainted and she was glad. No man should have to endure such torture, especially a man as kind as Michael.

Dona Espicia's eyes were filled with tears, but she smiled when Molly looked her way. "It is well he feels no pain for a time," she said softly.

Tomas returned with the smoking knife. He waited for Molly to lift the cloth so he could touch the tip of the hot steel into the gaping hole left by the bullet. The odor of searing flesh filled the room. Michael gave a cry of pain, then lapsed back into unconsciousness. As soon as she could, Molly hastily lowered the cloths and turned away.

"Now if only the bleeding will stop . . ." Dona Espicia said as in a prayer.

"Spiderwebs," Molly said. "Spiderwebs will stop the bleeding." She had remembered a time when her mother stopped a gash her father made in his leg with an axe.

"What?" Dona Espicia asked.

"I need a handful of spiderwebs," Molly repeated. "Where can I get them?"

She stared at Molly for a moment, then made up her mind. "You can find spiderwebs in the tower. There are always webs in the far corners."

Molly mustered a smile as she handed the older

103

woman the cloths to hold against Michael. A spurt of blood stained the bedclothes as he stirred. With a startled look, Dona Espicia returned the padding to her son's shoulder, pressing on it to stop the flow of blood.

Remembering to gather her gown so she wouldn't trip, Molly flew up the stairs to the balcony, then up the remainder of steps to the tower. It looked strangely bare without Dona Espicia and the furniture that had been removed, but there were still large wardrobes between the windows. It was behind these she found what she sought.

Before she gathered the webs she was careful to blow the spiders from their creations. Her mother had never feared them, but Molly was not so hardy. When her hands were full of the sticky strings, she hurried back to Dona Espicia's room, hoping the wounded man had not bled to extremes during her absence.

Dona Espicia made way for her without comment. She watched while Molly plastered the webs against the blood and ragged flesh on Michael's shoulder. A groan came from his lips as returning consciousness let him feel the pain.

Then Molly stood back to look at her handiwork. Already the flow of blood was just a trickle and soon it began to clot as the webs worked their magic.

"Perhaps some spirits would help, Dona Espicia," she said, remembering Don Jabal's treatment of her father.

Maria had come to stand behind her mistress, and when Dona Espicia turned to nod at her, she went swiftly to do her bidding.

In a short time Maria returned with a bottle and a glass. Pouring some of the golden liquid into the goblet, she handed it to Molly without comment.

Molly raised Michael's head carefully with one hand, holding the glass to his mouth with the other. After she had forced some of the liquid between his lips, he coughed, then moaned as the movement awoke the agony of his wound. The brown eyes opened. *"Venganza,"* he muttered.

Again she held the glass to his lips and this time he swallowed several times, watching her over the rim. His lips closed as he glanced at the matted mess on his shoulder, then looked back at Molly. He opened his mouth, indicating his desire for more liquor. When he had drained the glass, he relaxed into the softness of the bed. His gaze went to his mother, and a slight smile twitched at his lips.

"Bravo, mi madre."

Then with a tired sigh, his eyes closed.

Outside a shriek startled Molly into dropping the empty glass. A shiver of fear ran clammy fingers up her spine. Was Huk calling?

Dona Espicia snorted at sight of her terror. "It is only Culebra, my dear. La Condesa Magnifica of the castle hunts him at night sometimes. However, he usually doesn't fly this close to our hacienda." She frowned. "I detest seeing him descend on a bird with those tearing talons. It's a dreadful way to die, and quite unnecessary."

Then she sighed as her attention returned to her son. "Michael will sleep now. Perhaps it would be best if you did the same, Molly." She glanced at Tomas and the waiting maid. "You may all leave."

Remembering how she had sat with her father, Molly nodded and went to her room. The Irish she could understand. Spaniards she could not. How and why had Michael been shot? He usually stayed close to Costa

Cordillera. Was the war closing in on the del Valles?

Why hadn't Dona Espicia questioned Tomas? Perhaps she was more Spanish than she imagined, Molly thought wearily. Would she, too, become like these secretive people in time?

Dolores was waiting when Molly came in, and Molly sighed with relief. "I am glad you are here tonight, Dolores," she said wearily. "Somehow you make this room more . . . oh, not quite so haunted."

The maid's face flushed and she bowed her head in shame. "Forgive me for last night, senorita. I did not think you would retire early. I was with Chia."

"Chia?"

Her head rose and a proud look came over her face. "*Si.* We are to be married."

"That's fine," Molly said automatically. Evidently other minds than Jabal's had been centered on romance the evening before when he had treated her so cavalierly.

Dolores seemed to be waiting expectantly, so Molly said, "Will you see your Chia again tonight, Dolores?"

"Oh, no, Senorita Mollee. Chia is with Don Jabal. He is his best warrior," she said with pride. "He protects Don Jabal during a battle. He has kept the Conde safe for a great many years now."

"Don Michael was hurt very badly, Dolores. Was he with Chia and Don Jabal today?"

She nodded.

"Where did they fight?"

She hesitated, then said uncertainly, "I am not supposed to say, ma'am."

"Tell me," Molly ordered. "Tell me everything that is going on. I will not repeat anything you tell me."

Her dark eyes looked carefully around the dimly lit

room before they returned to Molly. "They went to burn the settlement of Santa Rosa," she whispered. "If the Americanos have no place to stay, perhaps they will leave. Especially if most of them are dead," she added.

"Santa Rosa! Oh, Dolores, that is terrible!"

"*Que?*"

"Dona Espicia sent a messenger to get the doctor at Santa Rosa," Molly said slowly. "An Indian boy."

The maid shrugged. "The Americanos do not kill boys, I do not think. By now the fighting is over, *si?*"

"I hope so!"

Was Jabal all right? Her eyes ached with a gritty feeling of too much sun, or perhaps too many lessons. She let Dolores help her ready herself for bed, thinking how easy it was to become accustomed to the services of a maid. After living with the del Valles could she ever return happily to the simple life she had known with her parents?

"*Buenas noches,* Dolores," she said.

The maid opened the door as she murmured an answer, then gently closed the door behind her.

Molly burrowed into the pillow, determined to sleep, but it was not so easy as she thought. The harsh voice of Condesa Magnifica echoed in her ears. How could a woman as old as she still be so full of venom? Molly would not leave Costa Cordillera because of her, but she admitted to herself the old woman had instilled a great deal of fear in her.

How did she plan to deal with Molly? Would Culebra descend from the skies to tear at her throat? Or would Noyo come silently in the night? A shudder of revulsion drove her deeper into the covers.

Dona Espicia seemed untroubled when Jaime told her

of the old woman's threats. Perhaps the venomous words were just the Condesa's way of being unpleasant, a form of idle torture to make her victim squirm.

Jaime said his mother always cried when Condesa Magnifica railed at her. Well, she hadn't cried, Molly thought defiantly. An O'Bannion knew how to fight!

Chapter Seven

As sleep continued to elude Molly, she raised her head to listen, wondering about Jaime. No sound came from his room tonight and she hoped he was sleeping peacefully.

How could Feliciana have left him? A thought brought her upright in bed. *Had* she left? Jaime had sobbed out she was dead. Had Jaime the gift of prescience Amatil told her the gods granted to some? If so, was Jaime's feeling correct?

But how could Feliciana be dead without anyone knowing? Goose bumps broke out on her arms as the answer to her last question came to mind. She couldn't! If Feliciana was dead, somebody killed her! But who? And why?

This was silly, she told herself. She was tired to such a degree, her imagination must be working overtime. Her fists pummeled the pillow into fluffiness again before she laid her head on it. Resolutely, she cleared her mind so she could sleep. She would think about riddles tomorrow.

As she had been taught, Molly prayed silently to the God of her father. For Dona Espicia's sake she asked that Michael's wounds would heal quickly and that Jabal would come home safely. Jabal . . . what kind of man was he? The considerate and gentle stranger who had buried her father and brought Molly to his home? The flirtatious roue who infuriated the beautiful Eulalie's husband? Or the amorous drunk who had accosted her in the hall? As she pondered these ideas, sleep mercifully came to claim her.

Rain cascaded in torrents from the eaves outside her window when Molly woke to a gray and dreary day. It poured in a thick curtain that hid the courtyard as effectively as a blanket of fog. It must be very early, she thought, for Dolores had not yet come to wake her.

Then she remembered Michael. She thought of Dona Espicia on her lonely vigil through the night. Now fully awake, Molly scrambled from bed and hastily dressed. She hurried from her room, wondering at the lack of servants or anyone else in the halls and rooms below.

When she reached Dona Espicia's room, a bearded man was bending over Michael examining the wound. Dona Espicia still watched anxiously through sleepless eyes, her face lined with weariness and worry.

"Good morning, ma'am," Molly murmured. "Have you not slept at all?"

She patted the hand Molly laid on the arm of her chair and gave her a wan smile. "I will sleep when I know my son is resting well."

The bearded man glanced their way. "Then you may go to sleep immediately, Condesa. Your son has surprisingly little fever, considering the nature of his wound. I don't know what that . . ." He indicated the gory mass of webs he had removed from Michael's shoulder. "That . . . *mess* is, but evidently it has helped a great deal."

"Dr. Laughlin, this is Molly O'Bannion. She is staying

with us, and it is she who prescribed spiderwebs for Michael's shoulder," Dona Espicia said mildly.

"Ah," he said, inspecting Molly minutely, "so I have a rival! Miss O'Bannion, it is a pleasure to meet you. Wherever did you learn to use webs in this manner?"

"I am happy to meet you, also, Dr. Laughlin," Molly said in reply. "I hope your being here means the small boy who was sent to find you is back home safely." She deliberately left his question unanswered, hoping he would forget he asked it.

"Oh yes," he said cheerfully. "My small guide is now probably sleeping. It was fortunate for both of us that I was in my office when he came looking."

Molly had stayed behind Dona Espicia instead of going to present her hand when she was introduced. Dr. Laughlin was a huge man, even taller than Jabal. His hair and beard were flaming red, making his bright blue eyes even brighter in comparison. His shoulders were broad, seeming to fill the room, but his hands, although covered with fine red hairs on the back, were long. His fingers were narrow as a woman's. It was difficult to determine his age, although it seemed likely his was an age close to Dona Espicia's.

The doctor turned his attention back to his patient for a last inspection, then snapped a black bag shut and handed Dona Espicia a small vial. When he moved away from the bed, Molly saw that Michael's eyes were open.

"Give Don Michael a spoonful of this, if the pain becomes unbearable," Dr. Laughlin said. "His bandage should be changed daily, of course. If mortification appears even slightly, send for me immediately." His eyes met Molly's in an amused stare. "Spiderwebs!" Then he grew serious. "However, the wound is unusually

111

clean, so they must work. You are to be congratulated on saving this man's life, Miss O'Bannion."

Molly stirred uncomfortably. This doctor was not easily dismissed from his prying.

When Molly said nothing, the doctor glanced down at his feet. He had left a puddle of water beside the bed. The cuffs of his jacket were dark with moisture as were his boots. He glanced out the window and drew his mouth into a grimace of distaste. "When it rains in this country, someone must hold a giant bucket tiptilted in the sky! Will you look at that downpour? That is the way it rained on us for the entire journey here. My small guide was drenched to the skin. Were it not for the more rugged quality of my apparel, I would be entirely soaked also," he said.

"Why not stay here for a few days until the rain stops, Dr. Laughlin?" Dona Espicia asked. "You are more than welcome, as you know."

"Thank you, Condesa, but I have patients waiting for my return, and we do not have much of a hospital for them to wait in since yesterday's fire," he added wryly.

"You had a fire at Santa Rosa, doctor? How very dreadful!" Dona Espicia exclaimed. "Fires are rather unusual in the wet season, aren't they?"

"Humph!" The doctor's red eyebrows came together. "Not when they are purposefully set, Condesa. Your son is evidently one of those wounded in the skirmish, so you must know about it." He shook his head. "I try to remain neutral, but it isn't easy when friends are hurt by your hot-headed, death-dealing *defensarios*, madam!"

"I am sorry, Dr. Laughlin, but I did not know! Since I am an American myself, my sons do not always confide in me about the course this war is taking," Dona Espicia said, and there was regret in her voice. Then her head raised and the muscles in her jaw tightened. "However," she continued, "I am a Spaniard in my convictions as to who owns the land our family was granted and has held for generations."

"Ah, of course," he said, sighing. "Well, let's not bring the war in here to our patient, Condesa. He seems to have had a full share of it already."

"Will you have breakfast with us, Dr. Laughlin?" Dona Espicia asked, changing the subject. "Your clothing is still wet from the rain and you will be more comfortable if you start your return journey with a full stomach, at least."

"Now that is something I will enjoy, Condesa, and I thank you for your invitation," he said. Then his glance returned to Michael. "Is there anything else I can do for you, sir?"

"I think not, doctor," Michael said coolly. "Your probing into my nice quiet shoulder has waked it to enough ferociousness to punish me sufficiently. However, I thank you for coming all this distance. Any bill you render will be paid in full, you can be assured."

With a grunt of anger, Dr. Laughlin followed Molly and the older woman from the room. When they were in the hall, he took Molly's place behind the wheelchair. "If I did not value your friendship so much, Condesa, I would not attend your son," he grumbled. "Snobbish don! The Spaniards are all that way. You cannot reason with them."

"Now, doctor, you must have patience," Dona Espicia said pleasantly. "All young people are high-tempered and disagreeable at times."

Seeing the doctor and Dona Espicia were engrossed in

their conversation, Molly returned to Michael in order to see if there were anything he needed.

"Did you sleep well, Michael?" she asked softly. "Would you like something to eat this morning? Food will help you regain your strength," she coaxed.

"No," he said grumpily.

"No you didn't sleep, or no you aren't hungry?" she asked.

Reluctantly, he grinned, then winced as his shoulder protested his move. "Sorry, Molly. I'm just grumpy because I was shot. Will you send Tomas to me? I want to get out of this bed!"

"So soon? You will start your wound bleeding again," she said. "Perhaps if you ate something . . ."

"Please don't fuss over me, Molly," Michael said wearily. "Fuss over Jabal when he returns."

"And when will your brother return, Michael?"

"At the moment I don't feel very brotherly to Jabal," he growled. "How can you still moon over my so-handsome brother after seeing him wag his tail at the lady Eulalie? Oh, Molly, this is no place for you to be. Why don't you leave while you still can?"

Molly frowned in frustration as she wondered if Jabal, too, had been hurt. How could one brother not care for the other? It was a puzzlement.

"I will tell Maria you wish to see Tomas," she said, turning on her heels to leave.

She slipped into her chair at the breakfast table, hardly noticed by Dona Espicia and Dr. Laughlin. They were still carrying on a spirited discussion about the pros and cons of who was right or wrong in the land dispute.

Jaime was eating porridge. He grinned at her while a trickle of milk ran down his chin. "What shall we do while it is raining, Aunt Molly?" he asked.

"We will catch up on our lessons," she said, then laughed at the face he made.

When Maria came to serve her, Molly gave her Michael's message and the maid returned to the kitchen. Shortly thereafter Molly saw Tomas pass the open door on his way to Don Michael.

"Does it rain like this where you lived, Miss O'Bannion?" Dr. Laughlin asked, interrupting her thoughts of Michael.

She smiled at him in gratitude. "Only in the spring, Dr. Laughlin. Our winters were always very white . . . very *deeply* white!"

He chuckled at her feeble joke, then sobered. "I am told you lost your father in this stupid controversy. May I offer my condolences and say I am very sorry?"

"Thank you," she said. Tears came to her eyes at his words, but she raised her head, forcing them back. "However, I didn't know a war was going on when my father came home with an arrow in his back. I doubt he did either. He brought a wounded Spaniard home with him to care for, so there was no enmity between them, at least so far as my father was concerned."

The red head bowed in acknowledgement. "Why would a trapper take sides in this, or even care?" he asked, almost to himself. "Only those who wish to control the land and those who wish to own it fight each other." Then his voice grew louder. "No one can or should claim title to the soil! It belongs to all the people, not just a few."

"It belongs to those who are strong enough to hold it," Dona Espicia said quietly. "Costa Cordillera will always belong to a Conde del Valle."

As she spoke, over her shoulder Molly saw Tomas supporting Michael in a walk down the hall. The rain still teemed down, making her wonder where the stubborn Michael was going. Dr. Laughlin saw them also.

"What the . . . !" he exclaimed. He rose from the table and strode into the hall where they could hear his voice demanding to know where Don Michael thought he was going.

Dona Espicia followed on his heels, as did Molly, leaving Jaime to his porridge.

Tomas was lowering an enormous poncho over Michael's head, completely covering his body. When the poncho settled on his wound, Michael winced, trying to cover his face with the wide sombrero Tomas placed on his head.

Then he looked at his mother, ignoring the doctor's angry questions. "Mama Condesa, I will not take your bed any longer," he said. "I have a house of my own and until this . . . abomination heals, I can recuperate just as well in my house. Tomas can bring my meals to me."

She sighed. "Very well, my son. If you are stubborn enough to do this, you are probably not mortally wounded. In any case, I know you will do as you please." Her gaze went to the Indian. "Take care of your master, Tomas, and report to me on his progress."

The two men went out on the veranda, but when Michael started down the steps, he wavered, and Tomas scooped him up in his arms. He carried Michael into the curtain of water and then the door between them was closed.

"Well, it is time I should leave, Condesa," Dr. Laughlin said. "You are not to worry about that young man. He's a tough one. Now about your hip . . . is it

116

improving at all?"

"I am trying a new course of treatment, Doctor," Dona Espicia answered. "Hot mineral baths every day." A smile tugged at her lips. "I do not know if it can make me walk again, but it feels delightful."

He looked startled, then glanced at Molly. "Another remedy of yours, Miss O'Bannion? Perhaps one day you will be the doctor and I the patient."

"In the mountains where I was raised, we learned to take care of our own hurts," Molly said. Again she was careful not to mention her mother's people.

He nodded. "Folk remedies do as well as anything for some ailments. Arthritis settled in the Condesa's hip after it was sprained. Mineral baths should help. Heated pads are very often used for this ailment."

"Do you wish a guide to accompany you on your return trip, Dr. Laughlin?" Dona Espicia asked.

The red-haired doctor shook his head, smiling. "If I could not find my way home, Condesa, I would be shamed indeed." He stooped to brush a kiss across her hand. "Take care of yourself, my dear, and send someone to fetch me anytime you're in need." With a nod toward Molly, he bundled his oilskins closer and made a dash to the stable where his horse waited.

"Now I shall sleep," Dona Espicia said wearily. She looked toward the dining room. "Please see that Jaime keeps busy at his books, my dear. This wretched rain is liable to endure for weeks."

Her prediction was correct. The downpour lasted so long, it seemed to Molly to be a permanent feature of the weather. She kept herself and Jaime busy with learning, trying to make the time pass faster, but still it dragged. They grew weary of the same books and selected others to study. Meals were made to last as long as possible in order to take up more time. Bedtime was moved to an earlier hour because of general boredom, and still the rain came steadily down in a never-ending stream.

Don Jabal failed to appear. When at last Molly ventured a timid inquiry, Dona Espicia said he had sent word he was staying with friends. The Indians of Costa Cordillera who had gone with him returned quietly to the ranch to dry out in their quarters and heal any wounds they had received. Only the necessary feeding of livestock in the barns and chores that could be done indoors occupied the servants of the Costa Cordillera.

Michael stayed inside his house. Tomas passed back and forth through the rain to fetch meals for his master and to report to Dona Espicia how her son fared.

The days passed with drearying sameness while Molly occupied herself as best she could. She was filled with a vague restlessness she was hard put to account for. She had spent many solitary winters in her father's cabin, happily occupied with her few chores and her books. Why was this so much worse when she had Jaime and Dona Espicia for company? Was she such a goose that she mourned Don Jabal's absence?

Then the rain at last ceased to fall. Dona Espicia said she hoped it was the last winter rain they would have to endure this year. Molly echoed her sentiments, but tried to remain outwardly cheerful as she had been doing. The sun came from behind the clouds to lift the spirits of all as the warmth of its rays drew some of the water out of the sodden earth.

Jabal returned to the ranch with Chia, giving Dolores a reason to smile again. Don Jabal was much his imperious self, however, and gave scant attention to either Molly or

Jaime. He seemed full of himself and still elated by the last skirmish at Santa Rosa.

"Papa is planning future actions, Aunt Molly," Jaime said. His wise eyes surveyed his immediate kingdon. "He will make sure this will remain my property."

"Perhaps the war is over," Molly said hopefully. "With most of Santa Rosa burned to the ground, maybe the Americans will go back to their country."

"I doubt they are beaten yet," the small monarch observed. "Papa has not yet disbanded the *defensarios*. But then, perhaps he never will. Always there is someone who covets the property of others."

The weeks passed and talk of war lessened while the family, guest, and servants of Costa Cordillera settled into a routine of sleep, meals, work. An occasional outing was Molly's delight when Jaime demanded they go afield, but they kept close to home. The outing when Jaime's horse had taken a bullet was still fresh in their minds.

Then Jaime informed Molly it was time to prepare for his birthday fiesta. The party was scheduled for the first Sunday in April, since his birth date was the second of April. It was unthinkable for ranch work to be laid aside any day but Sunday, so the custom was kept.

Maria supervised cook and the maids as they baked sweets for the event. They tried to keep the results from Jaime, but he seemed to be everywhere, grinning in delight as he spied first one delicacy, then another.

The men killed a steer to barbecue over the immense pit in the courtyard that was covered with heavy planking the rest of the year. They had penned the steer weeks before so it would be tender and fat for the occasion. Indians had even ground the corn the steer ate in order to coax him to consume more. Because of the size

119

of the animal, it took several Indians to kill and skin, but there would be enough meat for all.

There would be games of skill and daring for the young men. They would compete for the prizes Don Jabal would supply. They would also try to outdo each other to gain the attention of the ladies. Music and dancing would fill the day, as would the feasting that was planned.

One should have presents from everybody on his birthday, Molly decided, and found she had nothing to give Jaime. She grumbled of her predicament to Dolores one evening and she thoughtfully considered the problem.

"Chia's dog had puppies that are now ready to wean," she said doubtfully. "Do you think Don Jaime would like to have one of them?"

"I suppose he would, Dolores," Molly said slowly, "but I doubt Dona Espicia would wish a big shaggy dog in her home. Think of the mess it would make."

Dolores giggled, then said conspiratorially, "These are very small dogs, Mollee. They have hardly any hair at all. Would you like to see them?"

"All puppies are small, Dolores. How big will they be when they are grown?"

"Just like so," she said, holding her hands cupped to form about a six-inch oblong. "That is the size of their mother and father."

"So small? I've never seen dogs that small," Molly said. "All right, let's go look, but let's not say anything about this to Jaime yet."

They slipped down the stairway and into the kitchen.

"Where are these puppies, Dolores?"

"In the horse barn, senorita."

The maid led the way out the back door, skirting the

courtyard so they could stay in the shadows. Outside the big horse barn she paused, taking hold of Molly's hand to lead her into the dim interior. They hurried down the aisle between the stalls to the rear of the barn. There the maid dropped Molly's hand and opened a stall door.

"In here, Mollee," she said.

Inside, she stooped to peer under the wide manger, then reached her hand into the dark space. When she withdrew her hand it held a wriggling little animal she held out to Molly, watching her expectantly.

Gingerly, Molly accepted her offering, wondering what it was. Then she held it cupped in her hands and saw the tiny creature. It resembled a deer, somewhat, save for its size. Pointed ears flanked an apple-shaped head. Big bright brown eyes that took up almost half the space on the wee head looked trustingly into her face. A soft, smooth little body was attached to the head. Four of the tiniest feet imaginable curled under the body in her hands. As Dolores had said, it was hairless.

"It is Mouse!" Molly said in surprise.

"What, senorita?"

Molly laughed. "It looks just like a mouse Jaime described to me."

"But, no . . . it is a dog."

Dolores stooped to slip her hand again into the dark space beneath the manger. This time when she rose she held a somewhat larger animal, but still one not much bigger than a teacup. It stuck out a small red tongue to lick her nose as it wriggled in ecstasy.

"This one is the mother, Mollee. This is Chia's dog. The puppy will not grow bigger than this." She stroked the little dog briefly, then replaced it in the nest.

"You think Don Jaime will like?"

121

"Oh, *yes!*" Molly breathed. "*His* mouse was only in his imagination. This one is real! He will have a companion to sleep with so he will not get lonesome in the night." She brushed her lips against the smooth little head and the puppy tasted her finger with the tip of his pink tongue. "Oh, Dolores, may I have him, please?"

"Of course, Mollee," she said softly. "I will tell Chia. Do you want him now?"

"Let's leave him with his mother until the day of Jaime's birthday. A present seems more special when it's received on your birthday, don't you think?"

"*Si.*"

She returned the tiny creature to the nest before she hurried back to the hacienda. Jaime would adore his present, of that Molly was sure. It was only two days until April 2nd, and then Sunday the fiesta would be held. He would have a companion to share his delight at the party.

She sniffed the smell of spring on the air—a delightful pine scent mixed with the smell of the fog that drifted into the courtyard. It was the season Molly loved most. New growths came from the earth, the cares of winter were behind, and life had always seemed at its very best. The whole world seemed to be born anew, offering hope where there had been gloom.

Always before her father had been with her to enjoy this new blooming, she thought sadly. Then she brightened as she remembered Colin O'Bannion's great good humor when spring arrived. When Molly was small, he would swing her on high and hold her while he danced a wild Irish jig to music that was only in his head. With her arms tightly around his neck, Molly felt the thrill of motion that took her breath away. Then Amatil would join them and the three held hands while they pranced over bright green grass and under towering pine trees.

Once Molly had asked her mother what kind of dancing her people did in celebration, but Amatil smiled and said it was no match for the Irish. Molly had never posed the question again, and now she realized Amatil had been protecting her from the Indian part of her heritage so that Molly would never be hurt when she went into the world of the white man.

Since Molly had arrived at Costa Cordillera she had seen how Indians were treated. The del Valles were kind to their servants, but Indians were considered to be the property of the Conde del Valle, much like the horses and cattle that were owned by him. Why this was so eluded her.

Once she ventured a question to Dolores as to why the household staff and the workers on the ranch were Indians, and her maid's answer was simple.

"Here we have houses better than tepees, warmth in winter when the cold rains come, and always enough food." Dolores paused to think, then added, "Much better than before, I think."

"Can you leave Costa Cordillera if you wish?" Molly asked.

Dolores stared at her. "Why would we want to do that?" she asked slowly. "Here we are happy. Conde Jabal provides for us in every way. Before the white man came to this land, my people were hunters. Game was here but their weapons were primitive, so often they went hungry."

"Did you live with them then?"

The maid shook her head. "No, Mollee. That was long ago. I was born here. Most of the Indians here now were also born here. The old Conde del Valle came a long time ago. He needed people to build the castle and serve the old Condesa. There were other white men with him and together they captured Indians and made them slaves. If they did not do good work they were beaten or killed. Some were even burned."

Molly frowned, saying, "And yet you all still stay here?"

"*Si*," Dolores answered cheerfully. "Now there is never such punishment. The old Condesa stays in her castle where she does no harm. We are much better off here than the Indians who live in the forest."

Molly had let the subject drop, knowing she would only sadden Dolores if she pointed out the fact that the Indians of Costa Cordillera were still slaves. They were treated well because it made them easier to control, but the del Valles considered them theirs, and any defection would not be allowed.

Then as a soft spring breeze stirred her hair, Molly's thoughts turned to pleasanter memories.

It seemed only yesterday her mother had performed what she called her "spring rites." When the snow had melted and new sprouts pushed from the earth, Amatil would gather strange herbs and certain barks. These she brewed to make a strong tea with a terrible odor. Neither Colin O'Bannion nor his daughter had cared for the taste, but they drank the tea to please Amatil, only grimacing when her eyes could not see them.

Amatil had other rites during this season. She would don a special ritual gown made from soft doe hides and go stand in the sun with her eyes closed and her face upward. She would permit no one to distract her while she meditated for more than an hour in this position. To her daughter she had looked like a beautiful statue worshipping the sun god of her people, as she probably was doing. Despite their differences, Molly's parents had always seemed to her to be of one people—Americans.

They were lusty Americans, too, as Molly learned when she grew into young adulthood. While she was small she slept soundly in her small room, not hearing anything. Then as she matured she knew there were times when her parents somehow joined themselves together in love. There were whisperings in their bed, small giggles from her mother, then silence until she heard her father panting from his exertions. When her parents again slept, as Molly could tell from her father's snores, then she, too, would drift back to sleep. She never questioned her mother about these things and Amatil never volunteered anything concerning her marriage, so Molly remained ignorant of what marriage meant. A sigh accompanied her wistful wish that her parents were as happy now as they had been together in life.

Suddenly Molly realized Dolores had come into her room and was watching her.

"You are lonesome, Mollee, *si?*" the maid asked.

Molly laughed, realizing her face had betrayed her again. "*Si*, Dolores," she agreed.

"Do not worry. You will fall in love and then you will never be lonesome again," she said with a shy smile.

"Ah, but you are still lonesome when Chia is away with Don Jabal, Dolores."

"Not lonesome, Mollee . . . worried for his safety," she said. "Whether Chia is here or away, his spirit is always with mine." She smiled. "When you are truly in love, you can never be lonesome," she repeated.

Molly nodded. Perhaps she was right, but if you fell in love with someone who did not return your love, that was the most lonesome feeling of all.

Chapter Eight

On the morning of Jaime's birthday, Dolores brought a squirming bundle of warmth to Molly in the pocket of her apron. Molly smiled, thinking of Jaime's delight when he saw the tiny puppy.

"It should have a ribbon," Molly decided.

"*El*," Dolores corrected. "*Perro* is a little boy."

"Well, *he* shall have a ribbon then."

She removed a satiny blue ribbon from one of Feliciana's gowns and tied it in a bow around the small neck.

"Now you look like a birthday present," Molly told the small creature. His ears perked proudly while he wagged his tail furiously.

"Si," Dolores agreed.

"I wish I had something to put it . . . him in," Molly fretted. "A gift should be wrapped."

"A small basket? That should be agreeable?"

"Of course! Dolores, that would be perfect. The basket can be his bed in future." Then she frowned. "Can you make one quickly?"

She laughed, clapping her hands. "The basket-maker has many sizes already made, Mollee. *Uno momento*." She ran out the door while the puppy squeaked excited barks at her hand-clapping and tried to squirm from Molly's grasp and follow.

"Sh-h-h," Molly cautioned, gently stroking the small head with a careful finger. "Jaime will hear you, if you aren't quiet. You are to be a surprise, you know."

In a short time Dolores returned with a small basket about a hand's breadth wide, complete with a woven lid fitting over the top rim.

"Perfect, Dolores!" Molly said. She folded a soft handkerchief into the bottom before placing the puppy inside. "Sh-h-h," she repeated. "You are to be very quiet, Senor Mouse, until I give you to your master." Then she fastened the lid.

With the basket nestled in one arm, she descended to breakfast. Both Michael and Jabal were waiting. Jaime chattered to his father and uncle with all the assurance of an adult. He smiled when Molly entered, but didn't interrupt the conversation they were carrying on.

Then abruptly the three men froze at the sight of something behind her. She turned to see Dona Espicia *standing* in the doorway!

"Dona . . ." Molly said, springing to offer her support. "What are you doing?"

The older woman held up her hand. "Never mind, Molly. I am very much all right."

With the aid of a light cane she walked slowly to the head of the table and waited while Jabal arranged her chair. When she was seated, she glanced around.

"Come sit down," she bade them. "Good morning, everyone. I believe Don Jaime has a birthday today, so happy birthday, my dear."

"*Abuelita*, you can walk!" Jaime exclaimed.

127

"Grandmother," she corrected automatically, then, "Yes, I can walk . . . thanks to the hot mineral baths Molly prescribed." Her blue eyes twinkled mischievously. "I have been practicing just for your birthday, young man. I may even dance a little at your fiesta Sunday."

Excited questions and answers flew back and forth as Jabal and Michael expressed their happiness at her well-being. One might be only a stepson, Molly reflected, but both seemed genuinely devoted to Dona Espicia.

She was strong on discipline, but warmly fond of her family. No matter they were grown, when either of her sons stepped out of her line of proper behavior, she would draw him up sharply. Both Michael and Jabal obeyed her instructions, at least when they were in her company. Jaime, of course, adored her.

Molly put the basket beside her feet, waiting a better opportunity to give Jaime his present. During the meal, however, her tiny gift set up a protest at being shut in such a container. Sharp squeaks preceded a yapping it was hard to believe came from such a tiny mouth.

"What in the world is that?" Dona Espicia asked.

"*Que pasa?*" Jaime inquired, round-eyed.

Don Michael sat next to Molly at the table. He raised the cloth and stared down at the moving basket. Stooping, he brought it up.

"It would seem we have a noisy basket," he observed. "Now where could this have come from?"

"It is mine," Molly said, reaching for it. "Or rather, it is Jaime's birthday present."

With a crow of delight, Jaime came around the table to take the little basket. "What is in there, Aunt Molly?" he asked.

128

"Perhaps you had better open it and see, Jaime."

He raised the lid, then dropped it in astonishment. "It is Mouse!" he exclaimed, and his voice was filled with awe. "You made Mouse come to life, Aunt Molly!"

The ribboned puppy pushed the lid open with his head and raised his forelegs to the edge of the basket. Then he licked furiously at Jaime's nose. "Oh, Mouse," Jaime said, then lifted the little animal from the basket and cuddled him in his hands. "Oh, Mouse," he repeated.

Dona Espicia cleared her throat. "Well, Molly, it seems as though you hit on the right present for my grandson. Where in the world did you find such a thing?"

"Is it all right that Jaime have it?" Molly asked. "It . . . *he* will never be bigger than a teacup."

"Of course he can have it, Molly," Dona Espicia said, her eyes sparkling. "Is it a *dog*? I don't believe I have ever seen one so small before."

"It's a puppy," Molly assured her. "Chia's dog is the mother."

Jabal's eyes were full of amusement. "Chia is fonder of that dog than he is of Dolores," he said. "He bought it . . . her, that is, three months ago from a tribe that came up from Chihuahua. I suppose she had already been bred at the time or she wouldn't now have pups, would she?"

"No, I don't suppose she would," Dona Espicia said drily. "How many pups did she have?"

"Chia is the proud owner of two puppies and a bitch," Don Jabal said. "Or he was before Dolores gave one of the puppies to Molly."

Jaime kneeled on the floor and began gently teasing the tiny dog with one small finger held just beyond reach, while he drew the little creature in circles with its magnetism. When he tired of the game he picked him up.

"I wish Mama could see him," he said wistfully. "Do you think she will come for the fiesta, Papa?"

Jabal's brows came together. "No, I do not, Jaime. Your mother preferred to leave us in favor of the courts of Spain, so let us hear no more on the matter."

He rose, leaving his half-eaten meal. "My congratulations on your recovery, Mama Condesa. I hope it continues to progress," he said. With a formal little nod, he was gone.

Dona Espicia led the conversation to other matters, but Jaime's question lingered in Molly's mind. If Feliciana *had* left, as Jabal said, surely she would have sent some token of remembrance to her son on his birthday, wouldn't she? No mother, no matter how lightly she took her motherhood, would forget her child's birthday.

The diary Molly had dismissed from her mind returned as she sat pondering. When she could speak to Dona Espicia alone, perhaps she would mention it. A close member of the family such as a mother-in-law, perhaps, might not think it ill-mannered to read such a personal book.

Michael followed Jabal's example, rising from his seat. "I must go, Mama Condesa. I will be glad when this fiesta is over," he said. "It makes a great deal of extra work for the hands and for you."

Then he bent over his nephew and tickled the soft underbelly of the puppy. "However, for the Conde del Valle, it must be done, eh, Jaime?"

"*Si*, Tio Michael," Jaime said absentmindedly, perhaps because his thoughts were still of his mother.

"Do you have your costume ready for the event,

130

Molly?" Dona Espicia asked.

"No, and I had better get busy on it."

The women wore bright-colored swirling skirts at the yearly fiesta, Molly had been told. Dona Espicia had helped her obtain the materials needed, and Molly had been working on her costume whenever she had the time. The blouses had to be snow white, although the reason eluded her. She had found one in the assortment of clothing in Feliciana's closet that was perfect for the occasion. The men blossomed out in wild colors, too, and she wondered if the gaiety of attire would lift the glumness from Jabal and Michael for a while.

Michael's wound had healed without further trouble, and Jabal returned from his lengthy visit after the attempted burning of the settlement, but there was a pall still hanging over Costa Cordillera. There seemed to be some mysterious conspiracy to keep all knowledge of the war from the women of the house, but rumors came to them of the brewing conflict, although nothing concrete.

The Spanish were loathe to give up their grants and holdings, naturally enough, but the Americans were determined to add California to the United States. Word of clashes occurring here and there drifted in, and Molly knew the *defensarios* still held frequent meetings and practice drills, but news was scanty. They depended on visitors to spread tidings, but as travel grew more perilous by the day, few people braved the dangers of the long trip they were forced to make in order to see their friends. Some settlers had been slain in the raid on Santa Rosa, Dona Espicia had learned much to her dismay, but to date no retaliatory raid had been aimed at Costa Cordillera. But since Don Jabal led the slaughter, it was only a matter of time.

Molly busily plyed her needle while thoughts swirled through her mind. She no longer had to wear Feliciana's gowns since Dona Espicia had her sewing woman making a wardrobe for her, but it was the custom for everyone to make their own fiesta costume. The yards of material in the skirt required hemming. It was slow going, especially when Molly preferred other occupations.

When Sunday morning arrived, Molly hurried from her room earlier than usual to see if Dona Espicia needed her. She was in conversation with a round little man in a brown robe cinched around his ample girth by a tasseled braided belt.

"Ah, come in, Molly," Dona Espicia said with a smile. "This is Padre Rodriguez. He comes from his mission on fiesta day to give us his blessing. Miss O'Bannion, Padre. She is my companion as well as Jaime's teacher."

"Good morning, Miss O'Bannion," the Padre said. "Perhaps you can assist me in bringing these good people to services once in a while."

"Good morning, sir," Molly murmured, eyeing him curiously. Her father had told her of priests, of course, but this was the first she had seen.

Padre Rodriguez was bald with a fringe of hair just above his ears that encircled his head like a slightly slipped halo. Laugh wrinkles crinkled the corners of his eyes, giving him the look of a man at ease in his surroundings. A brown robe covered him from neck to feet, and these were clad in open sandals that exposed some rather dirty toes.

"The Condesa has told me of the loss of your father, my child," the Padre said. "God's will seems harsh at times, but there is always a purpose in what He does." He turned pious eyes toward the ceiling.

"Yes, Padre," Molly said, glancing toward Dona Espicia.

"I shall add my prayers to yours for your father's soul," the Padre continued unctuously. "We are all sinners in need of divine forgiveness before and after our deaths."

Molly stared at him. How could her father be a sinner when he had done nothing but work for his beloved Amatil and his daughter? Amatil was no sinner either, of that she was sure. Her parents had worked hard all their lives and did what they could to help the people who came in contact with them.

Without answering the Padre, Molly turned to Dona Espicia, saying, "May I be of help to you this morning, ma'am? Is there anything I can do?"

"You can join us for coffee, Molly. The Padre and I were discussing the problem of where services can be held, since the chapel is no more."

"By now I thought the church would have been rebuilt," the priest said reproachfully.

Molly's face must have mirrored her curiosity, for Dona Espicia handed her a cup of steaming liquid while she explained.

"Our chapel burned to the ground, Molly. It stood behind the statue of San Rafael, just inside the entrance to Costa Cordillera since the first Conde del Valle built it after settling here on his grant. No one knows what started the fire. Despite the efforts of every man on the place, it was completely destroyed. Now the Indians have only the statue and the open fields in which to pray." She glanced at the priest. "We planned to rebuild the chapel, Padre Rodriguez, but then the battle for our lands began. Since the men are away so much in this war as to

133

who owns our lands, there has been no time to build another chapel."

The priest's face was sad as he said, "When men war on one another, everyone suffers. It is against God's law to kill a fellow man, but in this lawless land might seems to rule over right. Don Jaime will have to receive his blessing beneath the skies today, and my dark-skinned children as well. Perhaps by the next fiesta God's work of building a chapel will have been accomplished."

He rose from the table. "With your permission, Condesa, I shall go prepare an altar."

Dona Espicia nodded. "I have already sent Tomas to see what can be done, Padre. He will assist you in any way you wish. If you need more hands, ask him to get them for you."

She watched the priest leave before turning back to Molly. "You look like a butterfly, my dear. Your costume is most becoming. Bright colors make your eyes sparkle."

"Thank you," Molly said. "Is your hip hurting you this morning?" Dona Espicia was in her wheelchair again, and Molly had thought it banished.

"Not especially, Molly. Today will be a long one, though, so I thought to utilize my old means of getting around until there is a reason for me to walk." She frowned as her gaze went to the window. "The matter of the chapel had almost slipped my mind until Padre Rodriguez appeared. It was still here for last year's fiesta. But then, so was Feliciana."

"When did the chapel burn?" Molly asked curiously.

Her question brought a sigh from Dona Espicia. "It happened the morning after Feliciana left Costa Cordillera. It added to the general confusion, of course." She shook her head. "Nothing seems to go right any more. It is as though there is a curse on the family since Feliciana returned to Spain. Don Jabal has dark moods more often than before, but perhaps it is natural for a man so attractive to all women to become depressed when his wife runs from him. Then there is the matter of Michael being shot. I see no reason for my sons to be harmed because others covet our holdings."

"If a thing is yours, then it should remain so," Molly said, wondering if she were more Spanish than American after her stay at the hacienda.

The older woman smiled. "You are right, my dear, and I should not be so gloomy on fiesta day. Perhaps the Padre's blessing today will bring a more auspicious wind to the del Valles. Perhaps our troubles are all behind us."

Jaime's arrival brought Maria hurrying to bring his breakfast and an end to the women's conversation. He was dressed in finery such as Molly had never seen. Silver embroidery in intricate patterns adorned his bright blue shirt. A silver buckle with an eagle hammered out on its surface held a carved leather belt around his small waist. Elegant black trousers flared over boots that matched his belt. Silver spurs adorned his heels.

"Jaime, you look so handsome!" Molly exclaimed.

His dimple flashed in a shy smile. "And you look beautiful, Aunt Molly. You will put the other senoritas to shame when you dance beside them."

Then he held Mouse up for her inspection. "Senor Mouse received a new ribbon for fiesta, Aunt Molly. Doesn't he look nice, *abuelita?*"

Dona Espicia smiled at her grandson. "You both look very grand, Jaime. However, I am afraid Mouse is too small to attend the fiesta." As his face fell, she added, "You wouldn't want to see him hurt, would you?"

While Jaime sat thinking about it, Dona Espicia said briskly. "Besides, you will be riding in the games, won't you? Now where can Mouse fit on a horse?"

A grin brightened his face. "I have not taught Senor Mouse to ride as yet. Perhaps he would be better off staying in our room." He scrambled from his chair and left with Mouse securely in his hands.

"Will your sons eat breakfast this morning, Dona Espicia?" Molly asked.

"Michael ate very early today so he could start arrangements for the fiesta. On fiesta days Don Jabal always goes to see his grandmother at Casa Grande," she answered.

She waited until Maria had left, then continued. "Jabal is too much under her influence, I'm afraid. The Condesa Magnifica, as she likes to be called, has a streak of cruelty in her that I have never understood. When she and Conde Luis settled here, they built a chapel, and that was good. Then they also built a whipping post and a small sweatbox for recalcitrant servants. From what I have heard, they used them frequently," she said sadly. "There are also rumors of terrible things that were done in the cellars of the castle that I find very difficult to believe, but at times when I see the Condesa Magnifica abuse her servants, then I believe."

"She really frightened me when we met," Molly said. "I thought for a moment of leaving Costa Cordillera, but then my Irish blood arose, and I decided I would not allow such a person to scare me away."

"You must not mind her, child," Dona Espicia said. "She does not have the power she once had. When Don Pablo became Conde after Luis died, he changed things. He married Dona Veronica, even though his mother never approved the match. The old witch hates all women, I suppose, and especially me."

She paused in thought and then a snortlike laugh came from her lips. "Condesa Magnifica has never really approved of anyone other than her grandson, Jabal. Don Pablo was too gentle for her taste. He and Veronica abolished the whipping post and confinement box by tearing them down and burning them." A sadness came over her face. "Jabal is a throwback to Conde Luis in many ways. When the mood strikes him, he is as barbaric as his grandparents. Cruelty seems to run in the line much as cancerous disease is passed down in some families. The old woman forces him to dance attendance on her so she can fill his head with her own ideas. After he has been with her, his behaviour can be deplorable. Since he was a young lad, I have looked after his welfare, and I am as fond of him as though he were my own son, but my influence over him has always been tempered by his grandmother."

Her eyes met Molly's. "I believe that is the main reason his father willed Costa Cordillera to Jaime instead of Jabal, although Jabal's immorality was a contributing factor. Don Pablo never approved of Jabal's conduct with women or with servants. He wanted no more cruelty or torture to occur on this beautiful soil."

Molly wanted to cry out in defense of Jabal, but held her tongue. Jabal was proud and perhaps ruthless, but not cruel, not like the venomous old woman in Casa Grande. She remembered the look on his face when he was angry, but she also had seen his brown eyes soft and teasing as the dimple flashed in his cheek. His mouth could be stern, but his lips were warm and exciting, as she well knew. Jabal . . . Jabal . . .

137

Jaime returned to the salon, announcing, "Mouse is going to stay in my room during the fiesta. Now I shall eat."

The rattle of wheels rolling over the cobblestones in the courtyard interrupted Dona Espicia's memories. She called to Maria and went to meet her guests.

Carriages arrived in a steady stream as neighboring Spaniards brought their families to celebrate the young Conde's birthday. Jaime gulped a hasty meal, then went to greet the younger members and become a happy small boy playing with friends. He changed from the adultlike Conde to just another child, and for a while confusion and gaiety mingled in happy harmony. Even the pending war seemed forgotten for a time.

The courtyard was filled with hurrying Indians looking like brightly colored birds in their holiday garb. Smells of roasting meat filled the air causing Molly to feel hungry although she had just eaten. The sweets from the kitchen were lined in mouth-watering splendor on long tables in the fresh morning air. No one had to go hungry today.

This was the one day in the year when Spanish royalty would mingle with the Indians of Costa Cordillera in games, dancing, and feasting, at least during the early part of the day. Toward evening the Spaniards withdrew to the hacienda to continue the celebration in their own way, while the Indians parted from them to do likewise.

The strumming of a guitar came to Molly's ears, making her crane her head to locate it. Near the covered well in the center of the courtyard, musicians had gathered to tune their instruments. The scraping sound of a bow drawn over untuned strings puckered her lips like a sour pickle. In the background a tom-tom sounded a rhythmic beat as one of the Indians softly patted his hands against the skin.

Then the clarion call of a trumpet brought all eyes to the entrance of Casa Grande. Noyo had appeared with the instrument at his lips, blowing a call that could be heard for miles. It announced the entrance of Condesa Magnifica with all the pageantry of a medieval queen. Her throne chair had been placed on a platform carried by four servants. She sat as straight as her age-rounded shoulders allowed. Her old eyes darted over the assemblage like a preying hawk.

She was dressed in black, as usual, but silver had been added in great abundance. The black mantilla that covered her sparse hair was topped by a silver tiara sparkling with diamonds. Silver chains hung round her wrinkled throat and rings covered her withered fingers. In one hand she clutched a silver-knobbed cane that caught the rays of the sun and sent them flashing hither and yon as it moved with her trembling.

Don Jabal strode beside the platform, more handsome than Molly had ever seen. He, too, was dressed from head to toe in black, although he had removed the black sombrero to escort his grandmother to the hacienda. Silver embroidery covered his short black jacket and long flared trousers. A crisp white shirt under the jacket had the same pattern of silver etched across it with a silver neckerchief fluttering in the breeze. Huge silver-rowelled spurs jingled at the heels of shiny black boots.

Molly's heart skipped a beat as he approached the veranda where they waited. Jabal . . . so handsome! A conqueror of all he surveyed, if he so wanted. His black hair had formed curls after he removed his hat. They formed a halo around his head that made him look like a very stern cherub, only so human and so very desirable. Feliciana, oh, Feliciana, how could you leave him?

The procession mounted the steps of the veranda and then the old lady and her throne were deposited in the midst of the guests assembled there. The women dropped hasty curtseys when the imperious gaze fell on them, and Molly followed suit when the rheumy eyes passed over her. Conversation had ceased, and even the servants in the courtyard had stopped their chores to watch this ancient ruler emerge from her castle into the world of reality.

When Condesa Magnifica was settled, Jabal dismissed the carriers and bowed to kiss the withered hand she presented. Then he turned to Dona Espicia and repeated the salute before asking, "Do we have your permission to start the fiesta, Condesa Mama?"

"Let the fiesta begin," she answered.

"Conde Jaime del Valle to the front," his father said in a loud voice.

Jaime excused himself from his guests to answer his father's call. Together they strode from the courtyard while all eyes turned their way. In a few minutes they returned, this time on prancing black stallions, magnificent in their strength, but much too full of themselves. Don Jabal rode with elegant ease as he fully controlled the animal beneath him. Jaime, however, was not so much in command. He pulled frantically on the reins as the spirited animal tried to break into a gallop and pass Don Jabal. The older man merely reined his steed's head in front of the other stallion, effectively causing them to remain abreast of each other until they reached the veranda. Both father and son then swept the sombreros from their heads in an elegant bow as clapping hands broke into wild applause for the performance. Don Jabal raised his hand and the clapping died into silence.

Jaime sat proudly erect on the fidgeting animal as he said, "Papa gave me a stallion for my birthday, *abuelita*. Now I can ride beside him."

Dona Espicia glanced at Jabal, frowning. "Is not your son a little young to be given such a willful mount, Don Jabal? Are you not afraid for his safety?"

Before Jabal could answer, his grandmother interrupted, cackling in delight. "It is surely a more fitting mount for the Conde del Valle than the milk cow he has been riding," she said spitefully. "It is a sorry sight to see one of his station on a nag not even good enough for servants."

Don Jabal bowed to both women. "Condesa Magnifica, your great-grandson is a del Valle and deserves only the best of everything. Condesa Mama, your grandson is more capable than you imagine. A stallion of such beauty is only his due."

The horse was more than Jaime could handle, Molly was sure. The gelding he had been unable to halt in its flight was older and a great deal more gentle than the animal he was now astride. What was Jabal thinking of? Did he not know of their mishap? Perhaps neither Jaime nor Michael had told him. She had been fearful at the time that Jabal would hear of it, but now she wished he had, for Jaime's sake.

The black stallion reared, pawing the air, while Jaime clung desperately to his mane. He struggled manfully to control his fright, but Molly glimpsed the fear in his eyes. She covered her mouth with her hands so she would not cry out.

The old Condesa clapped her clawlike hands in delight.

"Bravo, Conde! Show the beast who is ruler of this rancho. Costa Cordillera needs both men and stallions to create more wealth for the del Valles."

Don Jabal at last reached for the reins Jaime had dropped and brought the stallion under control. He frowned as he handed the reins to his son. "You must not allow this to happen again, Don Jaime. You must learn to be master of animals and men if you are to be Conde."

Shamefaced, Jaime grasped the reins and straightened himself in the saddle. His sombrero had fallen from his head when he was almost unseated. Noyo now left his mistress to come solemnly down the steps, pick up the hat, and hand it to the young master. Then he returned to his post beside her throne, his face expressionless throughout.

Don Jabal again faced the guests gathered on the veranda. "The fiesta will begin! The first event will be the games. If you will all come to the arena we have constructed, the action will commence," he announced.

With that, he wheeled his horse. Jaime followed suit, the black stallion fighting the reins as the two riders galloped from the courtyard.

If you are to be Conde! The words echoed in Molly's ears. How often had Jaime been forced to feats beyond his strength because of his destiny? He was just a little boy, a fact his father and his great-grandmother seemed to ignore. They seemed determined to treat the little boy as an adult, no matter the consequences. With a sigh, she followed the crowd to the arena.

Chapter Nine

With Condesa Magnifica and her throne again being carried by servants with Noyo leading the procession, the guests followed across the courtyard onto a wide level meadow outside the circle of buildings. A large oval part of the field had been fenced with stout planking for the games. A narrow lane led from the largest barn to the arena to allow animals to pass from building to game field. A wide gate at the opposite end opened to let mounted riders either in or out.

Beside the large game area tiers of plank seats had been constructed behind an enclosed box the size of a small room. Condesa Magnifica was carried there and her throne gently deposited on the floor of the box. Then Dona Espicia's chair was lifted inside so the two Condesas could watch the festivities from seats of honor, but when Dona Espicia entered, the older woman curled her lips in scorn.

"Put the Irisher's chair as far from mine as possible," she ordered the hovering Noyo, "and back from mine so I will not have to see her. She does not belong at a Spanish fiesta. Especially not in a chair beside mine."

Noyo did as his mistress bade, placing the chair back in

one corner. Dona Espicia entered with Molly at her side and smiled pleasantly at the older woman. When Molly noticed the placing of the chair, she quietly carried it from the corner to a place beside the old Condesa and held it until Dona Espicia had taken her seat.

"Get another chair, Noyo," Dona Espicia said, "and place it beside mine."

Reluctantly, Noyo glanced at the stony face of his mistress, then went to obey the order.

When the chair was in place, Dona Espicia smiled at Molly. "Come sit here beside me, my dear."

Molly did as she was bid, looking first at Condesa Magnifica and then Noyo, but neither gave Molly so much as a scowl. Their attention was on the men and their activities in the arena.

Bright pennants flew from poles placed at the outer edge of the enclosure. Gay serapes with the colors of a rainbow were draped at the front of the box of honor. Together with the colorful attire of both guests and Indians, it made a festive appearance under the day's bright sunshine.

Guests had filled the plank seating behind the two Condesas. Their chatter filled the air, and at intervals cheers arose as one rider or another passed before them going about the chore of arranging for the games.

Jaime came running from the barn, where Molly presumed he had left his birthday stallion, much to her relief.

"Did I do all right, *abuelita?*" he asked anxiously.

"You did fine, Don Jaime," Dona Espicia assured him. "You and your father looked quite handsome on your matching mounts."

"Why are you not with the other contestants?"

144

Condesa Magnifica demanded. "The Conde will be looking for you and you will not be there."

"He *is* the Conde, Condesa," Dona Espicia said before Jaime could answer.

The old woman seemed to swell in size. "Don Jabal is the Conde del Valle until his son comes of age," she said spitefully. "If something happens to the boy meantime, Don Jabal will be Conde forever!" Her baleful glance settled on Jaime. "A Conde del Valle is not a sniveling coward who is afraid of a horse! A Conde del Valle fears nothing!"

"I am not afraid of Gato, Condesa Magnifica," Jaime said, straightening his shoulders and holding his head high. "He is just a little young and needs training. Papa will help me when we are riding and soon Gato will behave as he should."

"Bah!" the old woman snorted. "Don Jabal can rope a wild mustang and ride him instantly. He knows how to rule animals and the people of Costa Cordillera. He was born to rule! What do you know of such things?"

Jaime slipped a small hand into Molly's, much as he had when Molly was the target for Condesa Magnifica's spleen. It seemed to give him courage, for when he spoke, it was much as an adult. "I know as much as I have to know, madam, and I am learning the rest. When I am Conde, I shall rule as well as Papa does now."

The old woman seemed on the verge of apoplexy, so Molly changed the subject.

"Is Gato the name of your birthday horse, Jaime?" she asked. "What does his name mean?"

"It means cat," he answered, smiling gratefully at her. "Papa said he is quick and light on his feet and can jump great barriers, so it is fitting." He looked around as his

145

father came close to the fence on Garanon.

"Come ride behind me in the grand entry, small Conde," Don Jabal invited. His face had the mischievous look Molly loved when he glanced at her and said, "It is a seat that is infinitely safe, is that not so, Miss O'Bannion?"

Her face grew uncomfortably warm, but she was saved from answering when Jaime scrambled to the top rail of the fence and settled himself on Garanon's broad back behind his father, wrapping his arms as far as he could around his father's waist.

Instead, Molly turned to Dona Espicia. "Isn't a stallion too dangerous for Jaime to handle?"

"*I* think so," she said with a sigh. "However, he is Jabal's son and a father has authority over his children. I tried to talk him out of giving Jaime this dangerous gift, but he was adamant."

"If his mother were here, things would be different," Molly said softly.

Dona Espicia nodded. "I wish Feliciana were here, Molly. It is strange we have had no word from her. I was sure she would write as soon as she reached Spain."

"Bah!" Condesa Magnifica said with a snort. "It is well the pasty milksop is gone. My great-grandson needs no coddling. Spanish royalty does not know fear, unless they are as inbred as Feliciana. Cousins marry cousins until there is no spine left in the line."

"Don Pablo approved his daughter-in-law. It was one of the few things he did approve in his son's actions," Dona Espicia said.

"My son!" the old woman sneered. "How he ever sired a child such as Jabal is beyond my comprehension. He and my daughter-in-law were both soft-headed ninnies.

146

Jabal is a true del Valle as our ancestors were in the days of old. How a mating between Pablo and Veronica produced him is a miracle! So far as I am concerned, Don Jabal will be the Conde of Costa Cordillera for all time."

Her baleful eyes were aimed at Dona Espicia, much like Culebra's eyes before he swooped on his prey. "At least Veronica came from a line of grandees, so Don Jabal is a grandee from head to toe. Crossbreeding is as dire as inbreeding, or perhaps much worse. Mongrels come from such a match."

Molly gasped when the words were said. This vengeful old woman had called Don Michael a mongrel to his mother's face! If anyone had so maligned a child of hers, she would make them repent the words!

Dona Espicia's face remained impassive. "It is well to renew worn-out bloodlines with an infusion of new juice at intervals," she said calmly. "As you yourself remarked, Condesa Magnifica, intermingling the same blood for too long a time causes a lessening of vitality."

The old woman reddened with repressed anger. The heavy cane shook in her trembling hands and Molly feared she meant to use it. Hastily, she sought to change the subject.

"Dona Feliciana left her diary behind," she blurted. "Perhaps something in it would explain why she left so abruptly. And if she plans to return," she added, somewhat lamely.

Silence greeted her outburst and she felt herself the cynosure of all eyes. Condesa Magnifica stiffened, then relaxed into her throne, pretending interest in the riders passing before them. At least she had quelled the old woman's anger at her daughter-in-law, Molly thought comfortably.

147

Dona Espicia's startled gaze met Molly's. "That is very odd," she mused. "Feliciana must have been very angry, indeed, to leave such a thing behind." Her thoughts turned inward for a time, then she said, "Tomorrow you must bring the book to me, Molly. I do not like to pry, but in this case perhaps it would be a good thing to do."

They were diverted by the start of the grand cavalcade of all the contestants riding and walking into the arena. Many of the male guests had brought decked-out horses so they could ride in the event. Chia and Tomas were mounted, as were some of the other Indians. Those without mounts ran beside their companions. All were dressed in colors like the rainbow to celebrate the day, and there was enough gold and silver sparkling in the bright sunlight to almost blind the spectators.

Jaime rode proudly behind his father on Garanon, making Molly remember her two-day ride in the same position when Don Jabal brought her to his home. She could still see in her mind the back of his neck and how vulnerable and endearing it had looked.

Much had happened since Colin O'Bannion died, not the least being that Molly loved both the men now mounted on the prancing Garanon. Jabal was as changeable in his moods as the weather, but although sometimes he made her tremble in fear, he also drew her like a magnet does a piece of metal. She was in love with a married man and that was a sin. Then Molly pushed her thoughts aside as the parade passed from the arena and the men scattered either to watch or participate in the next event.

It was a ring catch, wherein a silver ring about the size of a water glass was dangled from a ribbon on an overhead arch. One by one the riders flashed down the arena at full tilt with a spear in hand to take the coveted prize. Since the ring would just allow the passage of the spear, it was quite difficult to hold the weapon at the exact angle to let it slide through the ring. The fact that spears were used only occasionally for such games as this made the user's task doubly difficult. Several times the ring was torn down but not captured. Then it was replaced because the required insertion of the spear had not been made. Despite their failure, each rider was applauded for his gallant attempt.

When each of the waiting riders had tried, Don Jabal rode into the arena on Garanon. He bowed to the audience as the wave of their applause swelled to a roar. With superb confidence, he poised his spear. A hush fell as the audience held its breath. Then Garanon dug into the turf and sped down the field at full tilt. The weapon seemed aimed at the exact center of the ring, but instead of passing through its target, it was deflected and the ring left swinging in the breeze. Don Jabal scowled in anger as he pulled Garanon to a halt.

Before he could leave the field, however, another rider appeared, entering the open gate at full gallop. He thundered down the field bent low over the neck of the big roan horse beneath him. Under the arch his flashing spear slid smoothly through the ring. He took it with him like a bright trophy as he raised the spear so the ring would slide down into his hand.

Without pausing where Don Jabal sat on Garanon, the rider came galloping to the area before the seats and pulled his horse to a prancing halt. It was Michael who leaped from the roan and brought the silver ring triumphantly to Dona Espicia, but it was a Michael Molly had not seen before. He was laughing and his eyes sparkled with mischief as he glanced at Molly, then back to his mother. He was much handsomer than Molly had noted before, but very different from Jabal, for there was not a trace of cruelty in his face. His muscular body moved with such grace, it was almost as though he danced rather than walked as he approached his mother.

"Condesa," he murmured, bowing as he handed her the trophy. *"Por favor . . ."*

Dona Espicia had risen from her chair to walk to the arena fence and accept the prize. Now she smiled and stooped to kiss her son as she answered, *"Gracias, caballero."*

Then she stepped back and said so everyone could hear, "You have done well, Don Michael del Valle. *Vaya con Dios."*

With a sparkle of mischief in her eyes, Dona Espicia returned to her seat. Then she bent closer to Condesa Magnifica and said, "Mongrels often surprise everyone with their intelligence and skill, is it not so?"

The old woman scowled but did not answer. Instead she thumped her heavy cane loudly to get attention. "Let the fiesta continue," she called.

Jaime returned to sit between his grandmother and Molly as event followed event. He cheered each contestant as he passed the stand, but his eyes were mostly on Don Jabal and Garanon. Jabal had regained his good humor, brushing aside his half brother's triumph as though it were of no consequence. Jaime looked at Molly and squeezed her hand and they smiled at each other like conspirators when Don Jabal caused Garanon to prance on his hind legs as he marshalled the contestants for each game. The senior Conde del Valle came into his own while he reigned over the fiesta and the many guests assembled on Costa Cordillera.

The old Condesa sneered at such mild games as the roping of calves or the milking of wild cows brought in from the range. She said they were for *afeminados*, which Jaime explained to Molly meant sissies.

"Come here to me, great-grandson," she said to Jaime.

Reluctantly, Jaime left his seat and went to stand by the old woman's side.

She nudged him in the ribs with her elbow, saying, "Your great-grandfather, Don Luis del Valle, was a very great man, Don Jaime. He began his training with the bulls as soon as he learned to walk. He was afraid of nothing!"

Then came the perilous game of fighting the black cows that had originally come from Spain. They had long dangerous horns with deadly sharp points. Unlike bulls, the cows charged with their eyes open, aiming for their tormentors in a wild dash that could follow any twist or turn man contrived in his effort to escape them.

"The men fight the cows, Aunt Molly, because they are more dangerous than the bulls. Besides, it ruins a bull to fight him more than once," Jaime said. He laughed, saying, "Bulls close their eyes and lower their heads to charge. They don't even know where they are heading, but a cow watches where she is going." His eyes twinkled. "Females are smarter than males, is that not so?" He had leaned in front of Condesa Magnifica so he could better see Molly, and now the old woman nudged him back to stand beside her.

She leaned close to Jaime, but her cracked voice drifted over to Molly as she said, "You must be brave like your ancestors, Don Jaime. You must show the world a del Valle is afraid of nothing." She removed a red serape

151

from the wall and handed it to him. "Climb over the wall, great-grandson. Use the red cape to attract an animal's attention, then fight them as Don Luis fought. Go!"

Jaime stared at her, then craned his neck to see Molly. His face showed his fright as he appealed to her with his eyes.

Dona Espicia pushed herself to her feet. "I believe I have been too long in the sun," she remarked. "Don Jaime, will you be kind enough to escort me to the hacienda where I can rest a bit in the shade?"

There was a look of relief on Jaime's face as he offered her his arm. "Of course, *abuelita*. It will be my honor." Then the dimple flashed as he glanced at Molly. "Aunt Molly, will you lend the Condesa your arm on the other side? Together we can give you more support, *abuelita*."

Dona Espicia took the red cape from Jaime and tossed it back to its place on the wall before saying, "You will excuse us, I trust, Condesa Magnifica. I fear my stamina is not nearly so great as yours."

"Go! Go!" the old woman said angrily, motioning them away with her wrinkled hand. "Noyo! Noyo! Get the servants to carry me back to the castle. Quickly, now. These games are beginning to bore me."

The three rebels left the stand with Dona Espicia bowing to the guests as she walked slowly between Jaime and Molly. When they were back in the courtyard, she withdrew her hands from their supporting arms and stood erect. "I do believe I feel stronger already," she observed.

Jaime looked up at her. "I am really not afraid of the cows, grandmother. I am waiting to fight them, but only when I have grown more to their size."

"Of course you aren't afraid, Jaime. I was fearful they

wouldn't see you if you went into the ring. If they fell over you they might break those beautiful horns they are so proud of." Her eyes sparkled as she bent to kiss him.

Then she walked over to the pit where two Indians were attending a slowly turning carcass of a steer. They constantly dipped sauce from a large pot to pour over the browning meat. The smell was delicious and made Molly's mouth water in anticipation of a feast. Jaime closed his eyes and rubbed his stomach, complaining, "I am *hungry*, Aunt Molly."

Dona Espicia spoke briefly to the cooks in Spanish, then came back to her companions. "The meat is ready, children, and it would seem the games are about over." She smiled at some of the guests as they returned to the courtyard in straggling little groups.

The three returned to the veranda out of the hot sunshine to watch the festivities continue. A group of Indian musicians gathered by the well and began to play merry tunes, the like of which Molly had not heard before.

"May I be excused, *abuelita*?" Jaime asked. His eyes were on his former playmates as they returned to partake of the sweets on the tables.

"Of course, Jaime," his grandmother answered. "Go get something to eat." When he had scampered away, she turned to Molly. "You go, too, my dear."

Molly was watching the Condesa Magnifica's procession as the servants carried her and her throne on the platform to Casa Grande. Noyo glanced back over his shoulder at the women on the veranda as he and Condesa Magnifica disappeared inside and the door closed between them. A chill raced across the nape of her neck and Molly shuddered.

"Aren't you hungry, Molly?"

Dona Espicia's voice chased away the cloud of fear that enveloped her. Molly's smile was one of gratitude. "I believe I shall eat a little later, ma'am. Would you like me to bring you something?"

"Not yet."

They watched a pair of dancers swaying in rhythm with the music. Then another duo joined them, feet swirling blithely over the cobblestones in intricate steps and patterns. Molly wondered wistfully if she could learn to dance. It seemed like such a happy thing to do.

"Ah, the little rose is in fine bloom today," a voice boomed, and Molly turned to see Don Carlos standing before the veranda. "May I have the pleasure of a dance, senorita?" He came up the steps to offer her his hand.

"I'm afraid I don't know how," Molly said uncomfortably. "I have never danced before."

"Besides, this is *my* dance, Don Carlos," Michael announced, coming from the hacienda behind them. "You will have to wait your turn." His brown eyes regarded Molly gravely. "Am I mistaken, senorita?"

She accepted his proffered hand gratefully, "No, you are not mistaken," Molly said. She smiled at Don Carlos. "Perhaps after Don Michael has taught me to dance you will ask again, Don Carlos?"

With a sigh and a shrug, he philosophically returned to the courtyard and to one of the other ladies.

As Molly walked toward the dancers with her hand on Michael's arm, she said, "I really don't know how to dance, you know, but I am very grateful you rescued me from showing my ignorance."

Michael looked at her in surprise. "You mean you really *are* the little isolated mountain dweller Jabal told us you were? You have never been to a dance before?"

"I am a country bumpkin, Michael," she said cheerfully.

"You certainly don't look it," he said gallantly. "You look very beautiful, as always."

"Thank you, Michael," she said softly.

He smiled and patted her hand. "Dancing is quite easy, my little rose," he said, imitating Don Carlos. "Come, let me show you."

He led her to the area where the dancers spun and galloped and Molly watched their maneuvers doubtfully. It surely must take a great deal of practice to master the art of dancing.

Then Michael turned her so she was facing him. He clasped her right hand with his left, then put his right hand on her waist. "Put your free hand on my shoulder, Molly, and hold on."

Michael started slowly, and after the first few steps Molly's feet seemed to take over on their own as they followed Michael's over the smooth cobblestones. Then he stepped up the tempo and they circled and swooped in time to the music. This was no sedate posturing as dancing was shown in the books she had read. This was a wild romp with skirts flying as she was swirled around in the ever faster circlings to the pagan beat of the music. Michael's strength became hers as he led her expertly through the intricate maneuvers.

When her heartbeats threatened to strangle her and she was gasping for air, Michael maneuvered them to the outer edge of the dancing area, then deftly drew her away between two outbuildings to a grove of gnarled oak trees behind.

"Now you know how to dance, Molly," he said, laughing at her efforts to catch her breath. "In fact, you are now a very excellent dancer."

Molly leaned against the trunk of one of the trees and forced herself to breathe normally, but her heart still throbbed in too fast a beat for her to succeed. She fanned her face with her hand as she said, "Thank you, Michael, for showing me. You are very expert. I'm afraid I am not an excellent dancer as yet."

He stooped and brushed a kiss across her lips that was as light as the touch of a butterfly. "That is my fee for teaching you, little one," he said softly. Then before she could answer, his lips met hers in a kiss so gentle it startled her with its warmth.

"Don't look so surprised, little one," he said. He smiled as he sank to the ground in the shade. "Perhaps it is better if we sit here for a time so you can properly catch your breath." He tsked between his teeth and tongue. "Poor physical condition," he said gravely.

"Poor phys—" she started to say indignantly, then clamped her lips shut as he grinned up at her. Then mirth rose inside her. Giggling, she sank to the ground beside him. "At least I haven't fainted lately," she said smugly.

"So! You bring up my weakness under your knife!" He leaned against the rough bark of the tree. "Have you ever felt your little knife, my sweet rose?"

"Will you please stop calling me that? Don Carlos must think he is a great lover, the way he acts, and I am no more his 'little rose' than I am yours. And no, I have never felt my knife," she mocked. "However, I thought all del Valles were able to stand anything."

Michael considered her statement with his head held to one side. "M-m-m, perhaps torture by savage Indians, or burning at the stake, or being dragged through cactus by a wild horse," he conceded. "But the knife of a *gringa* woman? No!"

"Your mother ordered me to remove the bullet in your shoulder," she said primly, "or I would never have considered such a thing. She said it was a matter of life and death—*your* life or death, I believe."

His face grew serious. "Clod that I am, I have never thanked you properly for saving my life, have I?"

"It isn't necessary, Michael. I thought we were friends, and friends do what is needed to help one another," she said.

"Friends?" he asked gently. "I would like to be more than just your friend, Molly."

Again he drew her to him and covered her lips with his, but this time his touch was not so light. Molly felt herself responding to his kiss and drew back in confusion.

"Please . . ." she said hesitatingly.

"All right, my fair mountain lady, don't be alarmed," he said with a grin. "I will not take liberties with you, if you do not wish me to. I do not wish to resemble my brother."

Molly blushed and smiled her forgiveness for she did not know what to say.

Michael changed the subject as he said, "I do want to thank you. You did me a great service when you removed the bullet from my shoulder and I appreciate it. Your knife didn't hurt nearly so much as the red-haired doctor's probing the next morning."

"You are very welcome, Michael."

"One thing I have been meaning to ask is, where did you learn that trick with the pack of spiderwebs?"

"On my isolated mountain," she mimicked.

He nodded. "They surely did the trick of keeping my wound from mortifying, and that, in turn, kept my fever down. It is something I shall remember in case of future need." He paused, watching her face, then continued. "I would like to thank you for your help with my mother. From the day you arrived, you have influenced her all to the good. I wanted her closer to us, but she seemed to want loneliness up in her tower. Now she has taken her rightful place again where she can rule the hacienda as she did before Papa died."

"Your mother is a magnificent woman, Michael. She is all goodness and deserves her place of honor in the family. How she stands that . . ." She motioned toward the castle as she found herself at a loss for words.

Michael nodded. "The old battleaxe is all the words you cannot say, Molly. She is evil personified. It has always been a great wonder to me that she did not find a way to kill me when I was born, she hates me so much."

"But you are her grandson as much as Jabal is her grandson," Molly said. "Why should she hate you so much?"

"Condesa Magnifica hates everyone but Jabal," Michael answered. "She is a sadist. She would like the world to be as it was during the Inquisition. Don Luis was not an evil man at heart, but he married an evil woman. It was she who urged him on to torture chambers and whipping posts here in a new land where all was pure and good."

"Surely Jabal is not evil. He is high-tempered, true, but there is underlying goodness in him. My father saved his life and he tried to repay him, but when my father died, Jabal was kindness itself in the way he helped me bury him and then brought me to his home so I would be safe."

Michael sighed, saying, "Jabal is Jabal and all women fall in love with him, at least for a time. Are you still enamored with him, Molly?"

She felt a flush warm her cheeks and turned away so Michael would not see. "Of course not," she said, trying to make her voice indignant. "Don Jabal is a married man and it would be a great sin for any woman other than Feliciana to covet him. I am not so silly as you think, Don Michael, for I am not in love with anyone!"

"You needn't get so mad, you know," Michael said mildly. "I am not married. If you would stop pulling away when I kiss you, you might even fall in love with me."

"Why do all Spaniards think they are so irresistible?" she asked. "And why should a woman fall in love at all? The only men I've seen since my father died are peacocks who preen their feathers while they wait for a silly hen to come along."

"Why you little . . ." Michael sputtered. He rose and tried to catch hold of her, but she was away before he could reach her. With a derisive laugh aimed over her shoulder, she sped back to the courtyard.

The music had changed to a seductive murmur of love, giving the guests a choice of dancing slowly as they regained their breaths or partaking of the repast spread for their pleasure.

Deciding she was hungry, Molly filled a plate and walked to the veranda with it. After she was seated, the panorama of the fiesta was spread before her eyes. She had never seen so many beautifully dressed people in one place or so many servants hurrying to wait on them. She tasted the food she had taken and found she was ravenous. The veranda was deserted so she could eat every bite without wondering what anyone thought of her.

Laughter and chatter drifted through the air. A kaleidoscope of bright colors swirled in ever-changing patterns before her. Her heart skipped a beat as she spied Jabal's tall form swaying to the music, then resumed its normal pattern when she saw Dona Eulalie held close to him, smiling at something he had said.

Would God forgive her for the lies she told Michael? And even worse, would He forgive her for loving a married man? She resolved to do penance in some way to erase her many sins.

Chapter Ten

Don Carlos interrupted her reverie when he came to claim her for the dance she had promised. Since her appetite had vanished, Molly allowed him to lead her to the cobblestones.

"You are the prettiest little rose I have ever seen," he said, still playing the gallant. "You are an excellent dancer, Senorita O'Bannion," he said as he led her through a slow waltz.

She smiled her thanks, trying to keep her eyes from Don Jabal and his partner. Then the music grew faster and Molly had trouble keeping up with the small man's steps.

"Don Carlos, may we stop? I am still a novice at this occupation, as you can tell. Besides, I have been away from Dona Espicia for too long a time. I really must go tend to my duties with her."

"Ah, my little rose, you are still shy," he said. "If you dance closer to your partner it is easier to follow his steps. But it is as you wish, my dear. I shall escort you back to the veranda for safety, and then you can attend the Condesa."

At the foot of the steps he bowed to kiss Molly's hand,

then said, "Thank you for the dance, my dear," and left.

She flew up the stairs and into the hacienda, but no one was in sight. Then she went to Dona Espicia's room and discovered her lying on the bed with her eyes closed. She started to leave, but the Condesa's eyes opened and she said, "What is it, Molly? Am I needed somewhere?"

"No, ma'am," Molly answered. "It's just that I've been away dancing and wondered if you needed me."

The older woman smiled, saying, "Ah, I see. Did Michael teach you to dance? He must have led you through a wild reel, for your cheeks are quite pink."

"Well, he tried," Molly said with an answering smile. "Then I had to dance with Don Carlos. He . . . well . . ."

"Isn't he a pompous ass?" Dona Espicia asked. "He means well, however, and he is a friend of Jabal's, so be as pleasant to him as you can." She yawned, then excused herself. "Now why don't you go back to the fiesta and have a little fun? If I take a short nap now, I'll be able to get through the rest of the day without trouble."

Molly nodded and went back to the veranda. The festivities continued while the heaps of food disappeared and the steer carcass was carved down to the bones. Wine circulated freely and faces grew rosy under the warm sunshine. The women brought small fans into play, using them either to cool themselves or to flirt with their partners.

Don Jabal and Eulalie disappeared from the dancing area for a time, then appeared again to partake of the food. Dona Eulalie seemed even more vivacious than usual as she clung to Jabal's arm. Her husband occupied himself with the other ladies, occasionally sending a glowering glance their way. He filled his glass at least twice for every time he filled the glasses of the ladies with whom he chatted, and soon his eyes grew reddened in his glowing face.

Molly looked for Michael but he was nowhere to be seen. He had probably gone off to help Tomas and Padre Rodriguez improvise a chapel for the sunset services that were planned. A blush came as she thought about his kisses—was kissing this common in civilization?

Another guest came to claim her for partner and she danced again, first with one and then another. She soon grew weary of the feel of the cobblestones beneath her feet and escaped to oversee Jaime at play with his small guests. He had become a child again, laughing as he joined in the games most children played. Molly did not interrupt for she knew he would soon have to become the Conde of Costa Cordillera again. Wistfully, she wondered why he was not allowed to play with the Indian children that lived on the ranch, although she already knew the answer. A Conde does not play with the children of his servants.

When Dona Espicia emerged on the veranda the musicians laid down their instruments and looked to her for instructions.

"It is siesta time, dear ladies. May I invite you into our hacienda to rest and refresh yourselves before this evening's gala begins? The sun is becoming almost unbearable." Then she raised her voice to carry where the children played. "Don Jaime, will you bring your guests inside also? We have cold lemonade for your thirst, and a siesta will be beneficial to you all."

The women and children straggled into the hacienda and the men were left to their cigars and the shade under the twisted oaks. Molly had taken a last look around the veranda to see if anything was left behind and was entering the hacienda when it happened.

Angry voices drew her attention to the courtyard. Don Jabal and Eulalie's husband, Don Miguel, faced each other. An insult had apparently been given, for Don Miguel's hand rose as he delivered a stinging slap across Jabal's face.

"I demand satisfaction for your disgraceful conduct with my wife, sir!" he said icily. "And although I do not consider you a gentleman, your seconds may call on me in the morning to arrange a time and place."

"Seconds, hell!" Jabal said, recoiling from the blow. "Chia, bring the *espadas!*" His face was white with rage and his fists were clenched. "We shall settle this now, sir. No one strikes a del Valle . . . not if he wishes to continue living. You are dead, Don Miguel!"

A shocked silence fell over the group around the angry men. Protests came from some who tried to reason with Don Jabal, but to no avail. Slowly, he divested himself of his jacket, handing it to a servant who had come up behind him.

Don Miguel did the same, protesting, "This is barbaric, sir! Gentlemen do not fight in the presence of ladies. Can we not settle this in the morning?"

"The ladies have retired, Don Miguel," Jabal answered, "and I consider you no gentleman either, so we may as well get this brawl under way." His voice had grown cold as steel and his words were measured, much as a judge delivering a verdict.

Chia came swiftly with two swords lying across his outstretched arms. He stopped beside Don Jabal, but his master motioned him toward Don Miguel.

"You have the choice, Don Miguel," Jabal said.

Molly had been drawn to the railing of the veranda as

though by a magnet. Jabal's face again had the look of a predator. She noticed how much he resembled Condesa Magnifica and even Culebra. He was much like an eagle waiting for a smaller bird to come within range. She shrank back against the door jamb, wanting to leave, but held fascinated by the scene in the courtyard.

Several of the men again protested the impending duel, but Don Jabal ignored their words and them, his eyes fixed on Don Miguel. With a shrug, Don Miguel accepted the choice of weapons as he selected one of the blades.

A movement at a window of Casa Grande caught Molly's eye. Condesa Magnifica was peering from the second floor with Noyo standing closely behind her. The window had been opened so she could better see the spectacle.

Molly heard Culebra's shrill scream from somewhere in the near vicinity, but no one's attention was diverted from the duelers. A momentary chill shook her. Had she heard Culebra or the cry of Huk that came only to her ears?

The clash of steel on steel brought fear to her heart while Jabal and Don Miguel slashed at each other in savage anger. Sunlight bounced against the flashing blades as the two men thrust and parried, each seeking an opening to plunge his blade into his opponent. A glint of light made Molly blink, but she could not tear her eyes away. She found herself silently praying that Jabal not be harmed.

Don Miguel drew first blood with a lunge that pinked Jabal's side with the tip of his blade. It seemed only to spur Jabal to even faster slashing as he danced away from Don Miguel's sword. Then he drove in harder and a bloody streak appeared across Don Miguel's white shirt.

"This must stop!"

Dona Espicia's voice broke the magnet between the duel and Molly. She looked around to see the ladies crowding the door and lined at the windows overlooking the courtyard. With a cry of fear, Dona Eulalie pushed her way to the fore, then sped down the steps toward the fighting.

It was too late. When Molly looked again, Don Miguel lay writhing on the ground. Jabal's dripping sword was held carelessly in his hand while he stared down at his fallen foe. Then with a shrug, he turned away.

Condesa Magnifica had leaned far out the window and now she cried, "Bravo! Bravo, Conde del Valle! Bring me his ears!" She raised a wrinkled fist in salute, cackling her delight at the slaughter.

Don Jabal turned to face her and solemnly raised the bloody sword to his forehead as he bowed, then continued on his way.

By the time Dona Eulalie reached her husband, he was no longer moving. She knelt beside him, speaking urgently to the non-hearing man. Then she looked up, bewildered. "He is unconscious. Jabal has hurt him. Oh dear, the wretch has hurt him badly!"

Dona Espicia motioned to a group of servants. "Bring Don Miguel into the hacienda," she ordered.

Don Miguel was carried in on an improvised stretcher made from a tightly held blanket. He was deposited on the bed in one of the guest rooms as Dona Espicia ordered a runner sent to fetch Dr. Laughlin. Then she shooed everyone out, leaving a maid to help Dona Eulalie attend her husband until the doctor arrived. The guests gathered in the hall expressing their shock at such an outrageous thing.

166

Soon Don Jabal approached with all traces of the recent battle gone. He glanced into the injured man's room for a moment, then closed the door and turned to the waiting assembly.

"You will forgive us, I trust, dear ladies," he said suavely. "In the heat of the day we forgot ourselves for a moment. If you will all continue to your siesta, when you have rested, we shall go receive Padre Rodriguez's blessing as well as his forgiveness for our sins."

Molly stared at him, for the predator was gone. Now Jabal was the gracious host reassuring his guests. Then she spied a red spot on his clean white shirt. As she watched, the spot grew larger and she knew Jabal had been wounded.

She raised herself on tiptoe so she could whisper in his ear. "You have been wounded and you are bleeding."

He pulled away from her and his head rose haughtily. "*De nada,* madam," he said carelessly.

Then he bent over Dona Espicia's hand and kissed it. "Until later, Mama Condesa."

The ladies exchanged anxious whispers and speculations until Dona Espicia brought order to her house by saying, "Shall we retire, ladies? We can do nothing to help Don Miguel now. Perhaps Don Jabal's suggestion has merit."

Wearily, Molly went to her room. The day that had begun with such gaiety and happiness now had a pall over it. Would Don Miguel recover? Dona Eulalie's words puzzled her. If she loved Jabal as much as her behavior had shown, why had she called him a wretch as though the blame were all his?

The bed was tempting, and Molly stretched out full length on the shiny blue coverlet. Condesa Magnifica's behavior was another enigma. Why would she prod Jaime into such danger as fighting the cows? Was she trying to get rid of him so Jabal would remain Conde? How could she be so cruel to a great-grandson as sweet as Jaime? If she wanted the del Valle name continued, her grandson was the best candidate, surely.

She idly contemplated the portrait on the wall. "Feliciana," she whispered, then stopped. If she were here to protect Jaime, she would also be here to claim Jabal. Shame filled her as she pushed away the unworthy thought. Thou shalt not covet, she thought sadly . . . especially another woman's husband . . .

When she woke from her nap, the sun was dipping toward the ocean. She rose and freshened herself before returning to the courtyard. Many of the guests had risen before her and others were just coming from their temporary quarters. The ladies still chattered about the duel, wondering aloud how Don Miguel fared and how Dona Eulalie felt. In the way of ladies, the blame for the unfortunate event was mostly placed on Eulalie's shoulders for her disgraceful flirtatious behavior.

Since it was a fair distance to the entrance of Costa Cordillera and the statue of San Rafael, carriages waited to take them to Padre Rodriguez. Don Jabal assisted Dona Espicia into one of the vehicles, then looked around until he spied Molly. He said something to Jaime that made him come escort her to their carriage. After Jabal lifted Jaime to the seat beside his grandmother, he helped Molly inside. Then climbing in with them, he gave the signal for the cortege to move out.

He had changed shirts again and resumed wearing his jacket, but his face was still quite pale. He answered Jaime's chatter as briefly as possible. Since Dona Espicia remained silent, Molly followed her lead.

When they neared the statue of San Rafael, Molly saw Padre Rodriguez. He stood on a makeshift dais before a crude altar, looking more like a mischievous imp than a stern representative of God.

Behind him lay charred black stones that must have held the chapel before it burned, but there was nothing left of the timbers to mark where it stood. It would take a fierce fire, indeed, to erase a building of such size completely, Molly thought. One perhaps like the one she had set to make her parents' cabin disappear.

The service was briefer than most. The priest seemed troubled and his attention elsewhere. Probably because of the duel, about which Molly was sure he must have been told. However, he didn't mention it.

Padre Rodriguez blessed Don Jaime del Valle first as befitted his place of honor. Then he included the entire family, even though Condesa Magnifica was not in attendance. Then the Indians were admonished to keep to their Christian ways, and blessed in the priest's sure belief that they would. In his final summation the good Padre blessed the guests who had come to the fiesta and the world in general.

Chill night fog was drifting in when the assemblage dispersed. They re-entered the carriages for the return to the hacienda while the Indians followed on foot to continue the fiesta in their own way without their white masters.

Inside the hacienda a meal awaited their return. The crackling fireplace gave welcome as light chatter and tinkling laughter signalled their arrival. Wine was passed around to dispel any discomfort from the outside air, then glasses were refilled to sip with dinner.

Brandy circulated freely, making men's cheeks glow with unnatural ruddiness and the glances from the women became more abandoned. The uncomfortable feeling produced by the afternoon's duel seemed to dissolve as the flow of liquor washed it away. Conversation was turned to subjects other than that of Don Miguel and Dona Eulalie.

Don Jabal was all cordiality. He flirted with first one woman than another, even tossing a few gallantries toward Molly. His mother eyed him warily as his glass was refilled much too often.

Don Michael joined the assemblage, unusually urbane as he complimented first one guest and then others as he circulated through the room. He bowed over Molly's hand and his lips touched its back, but his smile was not as intimate as it had been after their dance. Had he been offended by Molly's teasing?

When it came time for the children to go to bed, Jaime rose to the occasion manfully. He thanked the assembled guests for the many gifts they had brought, then like a small monarch, concluded, *"Mi casa, su casa.* Please return often. *Buenas noches."*

"Bravo!" Don Jabal exclaimed. He raised his glass. "To the Conde Jaime Luis del Valle!"

The guests followed Jabal's lead, toasting their small host and wishing him well.

Molly rose to follow the maids escorting the visiting children up the stairs to bedrooms. Glasses clinked and the sound of voices followed them as Molly led the sleepy Conde to his room.

"Now may I have Mouse?" he asked sleepily.

"Of course, Jaime."

A puppy was a much better gift than a stallion, Molly

thought. In the short time Jaime had the tiny animal, the two had become almost inseparable companions.

Mouse waited expectantly in Jaime's bed, held there by the maid who attended the small master of Costa Cordillera.

"Senor Mouse is waiting, Don Jaime," she said in greeting.

With a sigh of relief, Jaime allowed her to undress him while he clutched the puppy as best he could. Then he settled into the pillows with a murmured, "I wish Mama could see you, Mouse," before his eyes closed in sleep.

Molly tiptoed out on her way to her own room, but she was not to be allowed solitude yet. Michael waited in the hall.

"Poor Molly," he said, brushing the hair back from her forehead. "You look so tired, but I am afraid you must go back. Mama sent me to get you, for your many admirers are looking for you. Can you stand a little more tonight?"

"I suppose so," she said with a sigh. "I hardly know those people, and I hoped I wouldn't be missed."

Michael shook his head, his disapproval showing on his handsome face. "The lovely Eulalie has apparently left the field and Don Jabal expressly asked for your presence with his guests. You will be careful, won't you? He is drinking much too much tonight."

"Oh, dear," she said, but accepted his arm as he escorted her down the stairs.

Don Carlos spied her descending the staircase and came to meet her. "Ah, the little rose returns," he said.

She noticed his unsteady walk, but since he was not the only one with a too-flushed face, no one seemed to mind. Molly dodged around him to where Dona Espicia

171

sat with some of the other ladies.

"You wanted me, Dona Espicia?" she asked.

The older woman looked up with a tired smile. "It is fiesta night, Molly, when only children go to bed early. The musicians are getting ready to play again. Don't you want to dance some more?"

Molly looked toward where the musicians tuned their instruments, then slipped into a seat beside Dona Espicia. "If you don't mind, ma'am, I would rather sit here with you," she said.

Jabal huddled with several men over glasses and cigars and had noticed neither her absence nor her arrival, she was sure.

The salon furniture had been moved away from the center of the room, leaving watchers the comfort of couches and chairs if they didn't care to dance. Guests came to talk with Dona Espicia and she smiled and spoke, but there was a drawn look around her eyes that bespoke inner pain. Molly noticed the cane lying on the floor beside her chair.

"Do you feel all right, ma'am?" she whispered when she had the chance.

"I am only tired," she said with a sigh. "I wish Dr. Laughlin would get here. When I looked in on Don Miguel, he was still unconscious. The bleeding has stopped, but Dona Eulalie was very upset, and rightly so." Her head moved slowly from side to side. "I knew Jabal would go too far one day."

Then she raised her chin. "Well, what is done is done. Now we shall have to make what reparation we can. When the dancing begins, I shall excuse myself and go wait with Dona Eulalie."

"I'll go with you," Molly said.

172

"No, Molly. Enjoy life while you are young." She glanced up as Jabal approached.

"May I have the honor of the first dance with you, Condesa?" he asked with a gallant bow.

"My dancing days are past, my son, as well you know. My remark was made in jest." She glanced at Molly. "Molly will be my substitute, I hope. She is a safer choice then your too-constant companion of this morning." Ignoring Jabal's angry frown at her reference to Eulalie, she rose, supporting herself with the cane until her maid offered an arm for her to lean on.

Then she addressed her guests. "Ladies and gentlemen, I want you all to enjoy yourselves," she said. "Your rooms are ready whenever you wish to retire, but on fiesta night the music continues so long as there are dancers." She glanced around the room. "And now, goodnight, and God be with you."

"Goodnight, Condesa," Jabal said. His face was bland as he kissed her hand.

Then he turned to Molly. "Miss O'Bannion, will you do me the honor?"

He swept her into a dance, leading the way for the other guests to join in. Her feet ached from her day on cobblestones, but the soft rug made it possible to forget them. As always, her heartbeats increased to a tempo she could hardly bear when she was close to Jabal.

His mood was slightly ironic. Molly decided he was likely worried about Dona Eulalie's reaction to his wounding her husband. Also, he was somewhat drunk.

"Please don't hold me so tightly, Don Jabal," she said.

The dimple showed for an instant, then was gone. "*Don* Jabal? What happened to the pact we made in the mountains?" His arm around her tightened.

173

"Your guests are watching us, Jabal," she murmured, pushing against the confining arm.

He whirled her down the center of the room, laughing as a path was cleared for them. "Of course they are looking, my dear. You are quite beautiful to look at."

She caught a glimpse of Michael's glowering face before she succeeded in freeing herself from Jabal's embrace. His laughter sounded in her ears as she ran from the room and up the stairs. Tears filled her eyes, but whether from rage or disappointment she didn't know.

Oh, why do I love Jabal, she thought miserably. A smile from him made the whole world shine brightly, while a frown had the opposite effect. He usually treated her carelessly with the same kindness and disinterest he showed his son. His word of honor to her father would be meticulously kept, she was sure, but he was too wrapped in the charms of Dona Eulalie to see anyone else. And there was always Feliciana to reckon with.

Inside her room, she threw herself across the bed with a sob of pain. She would not take what Dona Eulalie left! More than anything she wanted Jabal's arms around her. She wanted to feel the crisp mustache and the warm lips while he kissed her again. But she wanted him to see *her* while he was doing it—not be treated like a silly child playing grownup!

She wept until she was drained and worn, then sat up as she decided to prepare for bed. Perhaps tomorrow things would look better.

Dolores was not here tonight, since she had told her to enjoy the fiesta as long as she liked. With leaden hands she started to unbutton her gown, then noticed the closet door standing ajar, held open by the saddlepack.

Her curiosity aroused, she went to investigate. Some

174

of her clothing protruded from the opening. Her heart lurched. Had someone stolen the coins her father had left her?

She knelt and ran her hands around the bottom of the pack until she felt the cool metal coins where she had left them. Relief filled her. Then she noticed one of her possessions that was missing. The Bible. The Bible—all she had left of her parents—was gone! Why would anyone steal a Bible and leave valuable money behind?

Then she noticed the wooden writing desk no longer was propped against the wall. It was lying flat on the floor. When she raised the top, she discovered the desk was empty. Feliciana's diary was gone!

She sat back on her heels to puzzle over the missing items. Why would anyone steal a Bible and the diary of Don Jabal's wife? No one knew the items were there except Dona Espicia and herself. Then she stopped in mid-thought. She had blurted the information that Feliciana had kept a diary at the fiesta! Almost anyone could have overheard her outburst. Oh, why hadn't she given the book to Dona Espicia!

Then another thought took precedence. Why would anyone steal her Bible?

She looked around the shadowy room and a shiver ran over her back. She must have interrupted whoever was rifling her room when she returned half-blinded by tears. Then the curtains moved as a breeze billowed them inward. The window was always closed at night, but now it was open!

Even though she knew it was too late, she ran to poke her head out the window so she could see the balcony. Fog closed in like densely packed, liquid cotton, making visibility more than a foot away impossible. She strained

175

her eyes in all directions but could see nothing.

Forgetting dignity, she gathered her skirts and climbed through the opening to the balcony outside. The fog was like a thick wall, giving way reluctantly as she pushed through it. Her groping fingers found the outer railing on one side the redwood siding of the hacienda on the other. Slowly, she walked through the night, straining her ears to hear the slightest noise. All she heard were the thudding beats of her own heart. She paused to pull herself together, waiting until her heart resumed its normal beat. She was afraid, but an O'Bannion did not give way to fear.

Although she could detect no movement nor sound around her, faintly in the distance she could hear the music from the revelling Indians still at fiesta. Using the railing as a guide, she resumed her walk around the veranda. When her hand felt an opening in the railing, she knew she had found the steps leading to the ground. Had the intruder retreated in this direction? If it had been a guest, he could have entered her room this way and gone out the door to rejoin the revelers. But then he would have been carrying the books, an oddity that surely would not have gone unnoticed. Therefore, whoever it was had escaped outside. Would she be able to see him if she went down the steps to the courtyard?

While she mulled the question, the harsh shriek of a bird filled her ears. Was it Culebra? Staring upward, she realized no bird would fly in such a blanket. Was Huk calling his sinister warning again?

Fear flooded through her again as a sense of impending danger squeezed her heart. Her feet seemed frozen to the wooden boards beneath them. The encrouching fog pressed in on her like a smothering animal. Again she

FREE

BOOK CERTIFICATE

ZEBRA HOME SUBSCRIPTION SERVICE, INC.

YES! Please start my subscription to Zebra Historical Romances and send me my free Zebra Novel along with my first month's Romances. I understand that I may preview these four new Zebra Historical Romances Free for 10 days. If I'm not satisfied with them I may return the four books within 10 days and owe nothing. Otherwise I will pay just $3.50 each; a total of $14.00 (a $15.80 value—I save $1.80). Then each month I will receive the 4 newest titles as soon as they come off the press for the same 10 day Free preview and low price. I may return any shipment and I may cancel this arrangement at any time. There is no minimum number of books to buy and there are no shipping, handling or postage charges. **Regardless of what I do, the FREE book is mine to keep.**

Name _____
(Please Print)

Address _____ Apt. # _____

City _____ State _____ Zip _____

Telephone ( ) _____

Signature _____
(if under 18, parent or guardian must sign)

Terms and offer subject to change without notice.

MAIL IN THE COUPON
BELOW TODAY

GET FREE FREE GIFT

To get your Free ZEBRA HISTORICAL ROMANCE fill out the coupon below and send it in today. As soon as we receive the coupon, we'll send your first month's books to preview Free for 10 days along with your FREE NOVEL.

heard Huk's eerie cry. She sank to her knees, cowering away from the evil around her. Closing her eyes, she prayed for assistance.

Soft footsteps sounded behind her. No mythical bird was threatening her. At least if he were, he had a human counterpart, she realized. Therefore this was something that could be dealt with.

She rose and whirled to confront whoever stalked her. A black form loomed through the fog. Molly screamed as a hand grabbed her arm. She twisted away, part of the sleeve of her gown ripping away. Then two arms wrapped around her and she was pulled forward in a smothering grasp against the dark form. She slipped down and out of the clutching embrace, stumbling backwards in her panic to escape. Her fingers grasped at a railing where there was no railing and she felt herself falling.

Her arm crashed against something in a numbing blow. Then her head hit wood and darkness replaced the covering fog while she plummeted ever downward into a bottomless abyss.

Chapter Eleven

"Molly! Molly! Molly!" a voice called.

It was her father, and his voice was urgent, but she couldn't answer him! She tried, but no words would come when she opened her mouth. Searing pain filled her head and throat, pain that made her dumb and blind. Neither could she move a muscle, although she strained with all her might. Pa? Oh, Pa, where are you?

She wanted to feel her eyes and touch her throat but her arms refused to raise. Mother? Mother, are you here? Oh, please! Mother, please help me. Mother, what's wrong with me?

Her father's voice faded away as blackness erased feeling and carried her away on a sea of unconsciousness.

After an eternity of nothing, pain returned to Molly. This time her eyelids could open. She saw a hazy figure moving as it bent over her. Had the killer returned? Was he now going to finish what he had begun?

She opened her mouth to scream, but no sound emerged. Fear was a lump in her throat that almost strangled her. Weak tears flooded her eyes.

"Molly, it's all right. Dr. Laughlin will be here soon," a soothing voice said.

"Is she awake, Michael? Dolores, freshen that wet cloth on her head. Maria, see that broth is hot and ready. Oh, drat that doctor! Why did we let him leave last night?"

Reality returned gradually as Dona Espicia's steady stream of orders penetrated Molly's nightmare.

"I think she's coming back to her senses," Dona Espicia said. "All of you . . . leave us. I will sit with her. Bring the doctor as soon as he arrives."

Molly lay quiet, trying to sort the events that had brought her here. She remembered her terror, first of Huk as he screamed in the night, then of the black form looming through the fog, and her fight to get away from him. A shudder of revulsion shook a whimper of pain from her throat.

"Molly?"

Dona Espicia leaned forward in her chair to peer into Molly's face.

When Molly tried to speak, only a croak came from her throat as tears strangled her words.

"Well, what else is going to happen here?" an impatient voice boomed. The red beard of Dr. Laughlin waggled as he spoke and his huge body seemed to fill the room.

"She is bruised from head to toe," Dona Espicia said. "She fell down the flight of steps from the balcony outside to the ground below. When we put her to bed I could find no broken bones, but we tried to touch her as little as possible. She was unconscious for some time, I think."

"How long, Condesa?"

"She could have been lying there when you left last night, Dr. Laughlin," she said slowly. "Dolores looked in

179

when she returned from the fiesta and saw her room was empty. The window was open, which was unusual, so she came running to tell Don Jabal. He was still entertaining some of our guests. The men went to search the courtyard and Don Jabal found her in a heap at the foot of the stairs."

Dr. Laughlin nodded, then went to examine Molly. His fingers probed gently at her arms and legs as he tried to determine the extent of her injuries. His touch was light but still brought moans of pain, although Molly tried to stifle them.

At last he straightened. "Thanks to the resiliency of a youthful body, I doubt anything is broken. She is terribly bruised, however. Her body must have struck with great violence." The long fingers touched her head, carefully feeling their way over it until they reached the angry lump over one ear. "Ah . . . that is a bad one," he said, almost to himself. Then he smiled encouragingly at Molly. "Why were you out on the balcony, Molly? Were you sleepwalking?"

"No," she said, her voice a hoarse rasp. Then she pushed more after it. "Someone . . . in . . . room."

Dr. Laughlin shook his head. "Don't try to talk any more for a while. Sleep is the best remedy for you."

He drew a vial from his black bag and poured a spoon full of cloudy liquid. "Swallow," he ordered, pouring the medicine into her mouth.

It was vile-tasting and nearly gagged her, but she did as he ordered. Then her eyes closed of their own accord while he was talking to Dona Espicia.

"Give her a spoonful again when she wakes, Condesa. When she is strong enough to be moved, perhaps a hot mineral bath such as she prescribed for you would soak

180

some of the soreness away. Her body will ache for a long time. I only hope the clout on her head has not caused a concussion."

Molly heard his voice as though it came from faraway as it continued.

"A fall such as that would kill either you or me, Condesa. Wouldn't it be nice to be that young again?"

A river of darkness pulled Molly into its current as the pain in her body diminished. The voice she had thought was her father's must have been Jabal's, she thought fuzzily, then let the dark current pull her into its depths.

Returning pain brought her to the surface. She looked at the room through bleary eyes before she felt a spoon touch her lips, then tasted again of the potion Dr. Laughlin prescribed for her. Then the embracing river drew her to its breast once again in a world of painless sleep.

Several times this happened until one morning she swam to the surface with only vague aches accompanying her return to consciousness.

"Don't give her any more of that abomination," a voice said impatiently. "Go get her something to eat, Dolores."

Molly's bleary eyes focused on Jabal as he leaned against a post at the foot of the bed watching her. She forced a smile that hurt her dry lips.

"I'm thirsty," she whispered.

He left his post and poured a glass of water from the bedside carafe. Then he sat on the side of the bed, raised her head with one hand, and held the glass to her lips.

"It is time you woke up," he said crisply. "Does an O'Bannion give up because of a tumble?"

She gulped the cool water until he removed the glass.

"Not too much all at once," he said.

"A tumble!" she croaked indignantly. "Someone pushed me! Or rather, someone grabbed me in the fog, and when I fought to get away, I fell."

"Nonsense! More than likely you just drank too much fiesta wine," he said briskly. He rose and strode to the open door and looked into the hall. "Where is that girl? The servants in this hacienda have been spoiled by too much kindness. They will have to move faster in future."

His glance flicked over his shoulder to her. "When your breakfast arrives you will eat something," he ordered. "Then you will dress and begin living again. The longer you cower in bed, the longer it will take for you to face the world."

Weak rage stirred inside Molly. This Spanish don—who did he think he was? She struggled to sit up, biting her lips to suppress the groans as her battered body protested. At last she sat panting against the headboard, remembering to pull the coverlet up to her chin.

"I didn't drink too much wine," she croaked angrily. "I seem to remember you having difficulty keeping on your feet when I left." Her effort of talking brought a coughing spell that made her eyes water.

Jabal was back at the foot of the bed when she recovered. The brown eyes held laughter as the elusive dimple appeared for an instant. "I was able to walk well enough to pick you up and dump you into your bed," he said. His face grew thoughtful. "In fact, I more than likely saved your life. Therefore, my debt to your father has been paid."

Dolores came in carrying a napkin-covered tray. Jabal took it from her and placed it on Molly's lap. "Now you shall eat," he said firmly. "Eat every bite on this tray. I

182

will have a hot bath sent up for you to soak in and then you will dress. After you have dressed, you will rejoin the family. Jaime has been very anxious about you."

He strode to the doorway, then paused. "Today I am not busy. We shall all go to the beach for some sea air and sunshine." Then he was gone.

Dolores tsked consolingly as she propped pillows behind Molly for more support, then as she noticed Molly's shaking hands, held a spoonful of steaming broth to her mouth. Molly sipped at the soup and the first swallow burned its way to her stomach. It brought tears to her eyes again, but then the emptiness inside her began to fill as she swallowed spoonful after spoonful. When the broth was eaten, Molly relaxed.

Soon Dona Espicia came in followed by a bevy of maids bringing a tub and water. "Now you shall have the remedy that did me so much good, Molly," she said with a smile. She stooped to press a kiss against Molly's forehead. "I am so glad you are recovering, my dear."

With the help of her maid, Molly lowered herself into the steaming tub. As she sat there she felt the warmth of the mineral water seep into her sore body and felt more at ease and well than she had since her fall.

Her thoughts returned to the night of the fiesta and the rifling of her room. Jabal had brushed away her claim that she had fought with someone on the balcony. Too much wine, indeed! Indignation brought strength as she recalled his words. Did he mean what he said or was he merely teasing? Would Dona Espicia believe her, if she told her what had happened?

It would not do to speak of it before the servants. She wanted her parents' Bible back. Who would steal a thing such as that? And Feliciana's diary . . . why would anyone want it? Now she almost wished she had read it when it was discovered, or at least have taken it to Dona Espicia. It was not mannerly to read another person's private thoughts, but in this case . . .

"Do you feel well enough to come downstairs, Molly?" Dona Espicia asked.

"Perhaps I had better, Dona Espicia. Don Jabal has ordered me to go to the beach with him and Jaime today," she answered ruefully. Her voice was still scratchy, but the broth and hot bath had helped a great deal.

"Ah, yes," the older woman mused. "Jabal . . ."

She seemed to make up her mind to something. "Don Miguel died of his wounds, Molly. Dr. Laughlin arrived too late, but it probably would not have helped had he gotten here earlier. The cuts were too severe."

"That is terrible," Molly said slowly. "What will his wife do now?"

"Dona Eulalie will be a widow," she said drily. "And all because of a nonsensical flirtation! It was all so needless . . . but Jabal was warned. He knew he was making Don Miguel angry, but he persisted in the flirtation, and so did Dona Eulalie. Both are to blame, of course, but Jabal will be criticized most."

"He didn't mention it to me . . ." Molly began.

"Jabal does not care!" Dona Espicia interrupted angrily. "He is my son and I love him, but the streak of cruelty in him has always appalled me. Dona Eulalie has one to match, apparently. She seemed not so sorrowful about losing Don Miguel as about the fact of her becoming a widow. Before she left she confronted Jabal. She screamed at him like a fishwife. She said he had better divorce Feliciana so he can marry her!"

Molly stared at her, then closed her mouth when she

184

realized it was open. It had never occurred to her such a thing was possible. Such a thing as divorce was almost unheard of, and for Jabal to marry another woman . . . oh, no!

"Will he?" she whispered.

Dona Espicia gave an angry snort. "Of course he will not! He laughed at her!"

Somewhere in her secret heart Molly was glad when she heard the older woman's words, although ashamed of herself at the same time.

Dona Espicia's gaze lingered on Molly's face while a trace of pity showed in her eyes. Molly flushed, wondering if her thoughts were again so plain on her face.

"Now about today," Dona Espicia said thoughtfully. "Perhaps sea air would be beneficial to everyone. I think I will have a picnic prepared and accompany you and Jaime. Chia can bring my chair in the wagon in the event my hip protests too much." She nodded emphatically. "We shall all go to the beach today."

Molly glanced at the maids still working in the room. "I must speak with you alone, Dona Espicia. There is something I must tell you that is very important. Perhaps at the beach we shall have an opportunity."

Her eyes locked with Molly's. "Of course, my dear," she said. Then she glanced at the Indian girls. "When you have dressed, they will help you down the stairs. I will go order our lunch made ready."

When she emerged from the bath, Molly was pleasantly aware of the disappearance of many of her aches. Weakness from lying so long abed made her steps unsteady, but with a maid at either side, she negotiated the stairs without a stumble. At the bottom she dismissed the maids and walked by herself.

Jaime squealed with delight on seeing her. Tiny Mouse raced wildly around his feet, barking at the excitement.

"Aunt Molly, I have missed you," he said, "and I was not allowed to come to your room. Why did you fall?"

"It was an accident," she said reassuringly. There was no need to worry a small boy. "I'm all right now, except for being just a little tottery."

He held out his arm in imitation of his father. "Let me escort you, Aunt Molly."

"Thank you, Jaime."

Instead of only Jabal and Jaime, an entourage of servants accompanied them on their outing. Dona Espicia claimed Jabal's arm while Chia carried her wheelchair outside.

A wagon waited in the courtyard. When they had settled themselves amid baskets of food and bright serapes, Chia secured the wheelchair at the back. Then he took his place up front with the team of horses. The rest of the servants came behind on foot.

Chia drove slowly across the courtyard, passing Casa Grande on the way to the entrance of Costa Cordillera. Bright sunshine sparkled against the shiny stones, but again a movement at one of the windows caught Molly's eye.

A cold breeze touched the nape of her neck when she saw Condesa Magnifica staring down at them. Her baleful eyes seemed to bore into Molly before she vanished from her post. Did the old woman always watch at a window? Or was she watching only when Molly was around?

The warm day suddenly grew chill until Molly silently chided herself for her silliness. She returned to Jaime's contented chattering. He had Mouse in his cupped hands, pointing out the various ways the little animal had changed since Molly's fall, and how much he had grown.

The wagon rolled slowly through the stone canyon after they passed the statue of San Rafael, then meandered through a meadow of strange stunted oak trees, bent away from the coast like stoop-shouldered travelers forever chained in one place. Jaime explained they were victims of the constant wind and salt air that kept them from growing and bent them in such a way.

They emerged from the forest to a wide sloping stretch of coarse grass that blended with the sandy beach it met some distance ahead. Beyond the sand was the Pacific Ocean. Molly's first sight of it brought a gasp of awe.

White-capped waves raced shoreward, arching high in the air before they came crashing down on the sand. While they performed their strange ritual, a booming accompanied them that was deep and eerie and without echoes. Foam left behind when the breakers scampered back to the depths sank silently into the beach. The strong smell of fish pervaded the atmosphere. It was not unpleasant to Molly, just very different from anything she had encountered.

"Let's gather shells, Aunt Molly," Jaime said, grabbing her hand to pull her toward the water.

The servants were spreading serapes as protection against the sand and unloading the baskets of food for later consumption. Dona Espicia was talking earnestly to Jabal. He had his head bowed in her direction as though concentrating on what she was saying.

Molly pulled Jaime to a walk, saying, "Slowly, Jaime." Mouse raced ahead enjoying the magic of freedom.

Jaime freed himself from her hand. "Mouse! Mouse!" he called urgently. "There is an undertow that can pull him out to sea, Aunt Molly. I'd better go after him." He raced after the tiny dog.

A shadow crossed Molly's face. She looked skyward to see a bird sailing overhead. Then she noticed there were other birds drifting on the currents of wind and turned her attention back to the ocean. With a sigh of pleasure, she sank to a dune to watch the magnificent sea.

A wave washed ashore, curling up to where Mouse dashed madly forward. When it touched his feet, he yelped. Abruptly, he whirled to retrace his steps. Jaime tried to catch him as he flew past, but the little creature eluded his grasp as he headed for the dune where Molly sat.

Just as Mouse reached Molly, a swooping shape came down on them, talons extended as it uttered a hoarse scream. Molly covered the tiny dog with her body as she fell forward with a shriek of terror. The dangling talons meshed with her hair while wings beat madly against her cheeks. She screamed again, unable to fight against the onslaught as she held the frantic puppy with both hands.

"Culebra! Culebra, come here!" Jaime cried. His peremptory voice penetrated Molly's awareness before Jabal and Chia reached her. A string of Spanish emerged from three throats, almost in unison.

Abruptly, the talons left Molly's hair, taking several strands with them. Then the wings ceased beating against her cheeks and the awful bird left her. Sobbing with relief, she turned on her back still clutching Mouse.

She was lifted from the sand, too terrified to do more than whimper as Jabal held her, making soft shushing sounds as he would to a child. Jaime grabbed Mouse and imitated his father as he calmed the frantic little dog.

"That damned bird has got to go!" Jabal said angrily.

"Condesa Magnifica knows better than to fly him when we are on the beach."

"Sh-she's trying to k-kill me!" Molly said.

Jabal placed her on her feet and stared at her. "What are you saying? The bird was after the dog! Probably thought it was a small game animal. You just got in the way!"

She took a deep breath, forcing her knees to hold her erect. "Condesa Magnifica threatened to deal with me, whatever that means. Perhaps this is her way of doing it."

"What do you mean by 'deal' with you?" Jabal asked.

"She told me to leave Costa Cordillera."

Jaime's voice joined their conversation. "She did say that, Papa, the day she made us come see her. She was very mean to Aunt Molly."

"Why would someone try to grab me, then let me fall down the stairs if they weren't trying to kill me?" Molly demanded. "You brush me away when I try to tell you things you do not wish to hear!"

"What are you talking about?" Jabal demanded, frowning first at her, then at Jaime.

"The night of the fiesta there was someone in my room when I returned," Molly began.

"Who?" Jabal interrupted.

"I didn't see who. He must have heard me coming and left by the window. Whoever it was took my Bible and Feliciana's diary."

Dona Espicia had reached them, and the servants crowded around, but Molly didn't care.

"Feliciana's diary?" Jabal asked slowly. "I didn't know she kept one."

He looked at Molly and the haughty look of a preying

189

eagle had returned. "What were you doing with Feliciana's diary?" he asked coldly. "What right have you to pry into my wife's personal things?"

"Jabal . . . she told me she had found it," Dona Espicia interjected. She glanced at the Indians. "Shall we continue this discussion later?" Then her attention turned to Molly. "Are you hurt, my dear?"

Anger had flooded through Molly at Jabal's words. She glared at him, prepared to answer as coldly as he had asked, but Dona Espicia's voice brought her to her senses.

"No, I am not hurt," she said wearily.

"Then suppose we all have our lunch and enjoy this fresh air," Dona Espicia suggested. "Come, Jaime. Bring Mouse with you. It will be safer if you keep him on a leash in future when we are away from the hacienda."

They moved up the beach accompanied by the servants and Molly was left face to face with Jabal.

"I did not read your wife's diary," she said, still furious at his assumption she would.

Amazingly, the anger left his face. He threw back his head and laughed.

She stared at him, wondering if he had taken leave of his senses, but then his laughter ceased. He cocked one eyebrow in a quizzical stare and his eyes were mocking.

"What's the matter with y-you?" she asked, stuttering a little in her indignation.

"You are the matter with me, Molly O'Bannion," he said softly. "This morning I realized you are now a grown woman. You are a very beautiful woman, my dear." The dimple appeared, then winked out.

"I don't understand . . ."

He sighed, raising his eyes to the skies. "Ah, fate," he

said, "you have sent me a woman who does not yet realize the fact she is one." When his glance returned to her, it was full of mischief. "I planned a delightful day on the beach, my dear, thinking Jaime would tire and take a nap. It was my intention to make love to you while you were under the spell of the bright sunshine and the deep mysterious ocean."

Molly realized she was gaping at him and closed her mouth with a snap.

A rueful shake of his head accompanied his next words. "Instead, our rendezvous turned into a parade of chaperones, servants, horses . . . and Condesa Magnifica's ravenous old falcon!"

"I assure you, sir, things would not have been different had we been on the beach alone!" Molly said. "Although you brought me to your home out of kindness, I will not be treated like some child to be handled at will."

He chuckled as he extended his arm. "May I escort you to lunch, Miss O'Bannion? The sea air always gives me a very great appetite," he said, then added, "for many things."

She placed her hand on his arm and allowed him to escort her to the picnic area to a seat on a serape. A maid passed a tray of sandwiches and Molly took one, her mind still on Jabal. She mulled his words while she ate, impervious to the conversation around her. Had Jabal meant what he said? Did he consider her a woman grown and candidate for a romance?

Jabal seemed to have forgotten his brief anger and their conversation as he ate heartily. He chatted amiably with Dona Espicia and Jaime, carelessly giving Mouse a pat at times. His glance passed casually over Molly from time to time, but it seemed merely to include her in a general view of the entire group.

Molly's face began to burn as she recalled that his mention of making love included no proposal of marriage, but then he was already married. Only Dona Eulalie had mentioned divorce—not Jabal. Although his wife had left him, perhaps Jabal still hoped for her return.

She raised her chin defiantly. Did he think her a country wench who would raise her skirts at his first proposal? Despite her love for Jabal, or perhaps because of it, she would be no easy prey for a casual dalliance!

"You look quite flushed, child," Dona Espicia remarked. "Are you getting feverish from the sun?"

"Perhaps I am just tired, Dona Espicia. May I return to the hacienda now?"

"It is time we all went home, Molly," Dona Espicia said. "Even Jaime is much too tired from all the excitement."

She gave orders to the servants and once again they were stowed securely in the wagon for the trip back to the hacienda.

Molly glanced at the sky at intervals, but there was no sign of Culebra. Now that she was calm, her terror began to seem somewhat ridiculous. Jabal was probably right. The falcon had seen Mouse, and how was he to know it was Jaime's pet? And she had gotten in the way by covering the tiny dog with her own body.

But why had the awful bird been turned loose to hunt? The old woman had seen the procession as the family headed toward the beach past her castle. Molly had seen her at the window. If she had ordered Culebra to hunt them, it was not the tiny dog she hoped he would attack. Could a falcon kill a human being if he were so ordered?

The procession reached the courtyard, passing Casa Grande as it had earlier. Molly's fearful gaze went to the windows, but there was neither movement nor sign of Condesa Magnifica. If she were watching, she was careful to stay well behind the curtains.

When Molly glanced away, she saw Jabal watching her with his hunting eagle look. Then he smiled and turned to Dona Espicia. A cold shiver flicked up and down Molly's spine.

At the hacienda Jabal leaped lightly from the wagon while Chia untied the wheelchair. Then Jabal lifted first Dona Espicia, then Molly from the vehicle. He seated his stepmother in her chair and handed her over to the attention of a maid. Then he offered Molly his arm once again to escort her up to the veranda and into the hacienda.

"I hope you did not let Culebra spoil your first day at the beach," he said. "Tomorrow I shall ask my grandmother to be more careful about turning him loose, although I am sure she did not realize we were having a family picnic on the beach."

"Your grandmother watched us when we left this morning," Molly said wearily.

"You must be mistaken," he said carelessly. "Perhaps Noyo let his curiosity get the better of his manners."

They had reached the hacienda and Molly removed her hand from his arm. "Thank you for the picnic, Jabal," she said, then made her shaky knees behave as she walked up the stairs to her room.

Inside, she peered fearfully into the shadowy corners, then chided herself for such foolishness. Perhaps she hadn't recovered from her fall quite so completely as she'd thought. She was shying at shadows, imagining attacks, looking for ogres and witches.

And Jabal . . . what of him? He was indifferent and cold one minute, teasingly romantic the next. The cruel hunter's speculation she had caught on his face for just a brief moment returned to haunt her.

She toyed with the idea of Jabal as a predator, but no, it could not be. Her father had saved his life. In turn, Colin O'Bannion demanded Jabal's protection for her when he died. Jabal had a Spanish don's sense of honor and would fulfill his obligation to her father. Then his words echoed in her ears. "I probably saved your life, so my debt to your father has now been paid."

A feeling of impending danger came to her. Jabal also had Spanish cruelty in his makeup. Would he kill her if she were to get in his way? And how could she get in his way? Was there something in Feliciana's diary she was not supposed to see? Had Feliciana really returned to Spain? Or was there something sinister in her sudden departure?

Questions, questions, questions, she thought with disgust. If she had more answers, perhaps she wouldn't be so confused.

Tomorrow she would make Dona Espicia listen to her, she resolved. If she could help Molly discover who took Feliciana's diary, perhaps they could get it back and find some answers.

And her parents' Bible . . . that was a mystery! Why would anyone want it?

Chapter Twelve

The next morning Dona Espicia sent her maid to fetch Molly to her room. She smiled from her bed where she was having early tea. "How are the aches and bruises this morning, Molly? Are you feeling better?"

"The aches are about gone, I think, and the bruises are fading away. My head still feels somewhat groggy, but I suppose that is from the many sleeping draughts that were given to me," she answered.

"Sit here beside me, my dear, and join me for before-breakfast tea. I have a cup before I put a foot out of bed," Dona Espicia said, indicating a chair her maid had placed by her bed. She made a moue. "It gives me the strength to face the problems of the hacienda."

Molly accepted a cup of tea from the maid with a smile. "I think it's a nice custom, ma'am."

"You wanted a private talk with me, Molly, and I thought this would be a good time for it." She glanced at her maid. "You may leave," she said, and the Indian girl silently left.

"Now," she said, putting her cup on the bedside table, "what really happened the night of the fiesta? How did you happen to fall?"

"I fell down the steps after struggling with someone who grabbed me in the fog," Molly said. "I hadn't taken too much wine as Don Jabal seems to think."

"Oh, Molly, you were fine when I went to see about Don Miguel, and since you went to your room shortly after, I know you didn't drink too much. Now begin at the beginning, and tell me about Feliciana's diary and how you came to have such a nasty fall."

Molly's gaze dropped to the cup in her hand. "I danced with Jabal as you asked, but then I left the party to go to my room." She omitted the fact of Jabal's drunkenness and how he held her shockingly tight in front of everyone. "When I reached my room, I saw it had been disturbed, so I checked my saddle pack to see if anything had been taken." She looked at Dona Espicia. "My father left me money when he died, but it hadn't been touched. However, my family Bible was gone . . ."

"Oh, my dear, you should have told me about this before. Why would anyone steal a Bible? There are Bibles in the library and in the servants' quarters. Padre Rodriguez has seen to that," Dona Espicia said. "Now what is this about Feliciana's diary? I didn't know she kept one and neither did Jabal."

"I came across it accidentally right after I came here," Molly said. "There was a wooden writing desk in the back of the closet. When I opened it, I saw a small book that turned out to be a diary—Feliciana's diary. I only read the first page when I realized what it was, and then I put it back in the desk, and put the desk at the back of the closet. I was going to tell you, but with all the to-do around the festival and other things, I didn't have the opportunity."

"I wish I had known," Dona Espicia said. "Despite the

fact of bad manners to read another person's diary, I do believe I would have read it. There are many things about her leaving so abruptly that are difficult to understand." She smiled at Molly. "You have very good manners instilled in you, my dear. Your parents would be proud of you."

"Thank you," Molly said shyly.

"Now, let's get on with it," Dona Espicia said. "Why were you out on the balcony in all that fog the night of the fiesta?"

"When I realized things had been taken, I noticed the window was open and went out after whoever had been in my room," Molly answered. "I felt my way around by using the railing. When I came to the gap I stopped. It was then a huge black man tried to grab me. When I freed myself, I stepped backward and went crashing down the steps.

"A black man? We have no Negroes at Casa Cordillera," Dona Espicia said.

"He was covered in black, even his face," Molly explained.

The older woman shook her head. "You are much too brave for your own safety, my dear. We shall really have to get to the bottom of this . . . for all our sakes."

"Perhaps it was Noyo," Molly said slowly. "Once before I saw him at my window, but at the time I didn't know who he was."

Dona Espicia sighed. "Condesa Magnifica uses Noyo as her eyes and ears to let her know what is going on in the hacienda. I have asked Jabal to speak to her about it, but he says it is her right to know what goes on in the family."

"I am not her family!" Molly said indignantly.

197

"Neither am I, according to her way of thinking," she said drily, "but she keeps her eye on me just the same. Noyo sneaks around, mostly at night, but I didn't think she would put him up to stealing from a guest."

Molly said nothing, but now as she remembered the night of her fall, she was almost positive her attacker had been the big servant. She hadn't told Dona Espicia how she had cried over Jabal that night, nor had she mentioned Huk's warning cry. She was ashamed of her first actions and wary of mentioning the beliefs of Amatil's people. From the way Indians were treated by some members of this proud Spanish family, she knew her father's warning was one she should heed. She must never let anyone know her mother was an Indian.

Dona Espicia had been deep in thought, but now she looked at Molly. "Condesa Magnifica was there when you first mentioned the diary, wasn't she?"

"Yes, but perhaps some of the other guests heard me, too," Molly said. "Oh, I wish I hadn't blurted it out that way."

"I don't believe our guests would be interested in such a thing, other than idle gossip if they knew what was in Feliciana's diary. But Condesa Magnifica . . . she probably grew curious," Dona Espicia said slowly. "Noyo is her messenger, of course, but I cannot see why he would wish to harm you."

"Her threats . . ." Molly began, but Dona Espicia interrupted her.

"She says dreadful things to everybody these days! When Conde Luis was alive, she was the one who drove him to do the cruel things he did to the Indians." She snorted in anger. "You heard her try to persuade her

198

great-grandson to fight the cows! Her sadistic nature is a disgusting thing, but so far I have not known her to actually carry out the threats she makes."

"Perhaps you have now," Molly said quietly. "At least, an attempt was made to dispose of me."

Her sharp eyes examined Molly's face. "Perhaps Noyo just didn't want to be caught in his thievery."

"He had time to get away," Molly said. "I didn't notice the theft when I first entered my room." She paused, but the other woman said nothing. "Why would he take my parents' Bible, Dona Espicia?"

The gray head moved from side to side. "Now that is very peculiar. Perhaps he could not distinguish between the diary and your Bible, so he just took both."

"I want it back."

"Of course you do, Molly. It is disgraceful that a guest in our house should be robbed."

Once again she sat in thought, but finally her eyes met Molly's. "We cannot accuse the old woman, of course, nor her manservant. However, I shall find a way to return your property to you, my dear. Although Jabal is her grandson, he is also my son. I shall see if he will reason with the Condesa. Perhaps he can get your property returned as well as the diary of his wife."

Dona Espicia reached for her cane and thumped it on the floor. "Now I had best dress, my dear, and attend to my many duties. We shall see what can be done."

Molly left as the maid hurried in. Relief filled her as she realized she had an ally in Dona Espicia. After all, she was the mistress of Costa Cordillera. As such, she could surely restore order in her domain.

As day followed day, traces of the fiesta were cleared

199

away and the rancho returned to its normal routines. Since his declaration at the beach, Don Jabal was different in his manner toward Molly. Instead of treating her with offhanded kindness, he flirted with her much as he had with Dona Eulalie.

At first Molly was angry, feeling he had turned to her only after he lost Dona Eulalie, but gradually her love for him pushed any hurts into the background to be forgotten. He became a dashing caballero courting his love. Jabal teased as he treated her with the utmost respect, while his eyes danced mischievously and the dimple appeared and disappeared as he broke into amused laughter.

With Jaime along, they rode the lush valleys and steep little hills. Garanon and the young stallion fought when they were together, so Jabal returned Jaime to the black gelding more suited to him. It was a period of beautiful calm, but it was interrupted.

"Our rides must cease for a time," Jabal announced one morning as they walked their horses toward the rancho. "I must return to the *defensarios*."

"Why, Papa?" Jaime asked. "Is there to be fighting again?"

Jabal's brows drew together. "There will always be fighting until the Americanos realize the futility of trying to usurp our land."

"Now that I have seven years, should not I be told what is happening, Papa?" Jaime asked. "If I am to be Conde, the affairs of Costa Cordillera are of concern to me."

Jabal's amused eyes met Molly's, then his gaze went to his son. "Yes," he gravely agreed, "the affairs of the

200

country are also your concern, my son, even though the beginning occurred before your birth."

"Well, then tell me, Papa."

In Molly's heart she echoed his demand, for she had never understood the mysterious happenings around her.

"It all began with the end of Spanish rule in California back in 1822," Jabal said. "Our royal officials turned *putas* and took the oath of allegiance to Mexico that made California a Mexican province."

"I did not know we belonged to Mexico," Jaime exclaimed.

"We do not!" Jabal thundered. "We *hidalgos* belong only to ourselves. We do not even recognize this . . ." He searched for a word, but after a glance at Molly seemed to swallow the one he found. "This Micheltorena who was sent to be governor four years ago."

"Is he not a good governor, Papa?"

"Hah! He was supposed to keep this country for his government, but what did he do?"

Before Jaime could answer, Jabal answered himself.

"His *cholos*—his so-called troops—clashed with the Americanos near San Jose in 1844 and they were beaten! Beaten like dogs! Behaved like dogs! Micheltorena signed the Treaty of Santa Teresa and agreed to remove his troops from California," Jabal said, his face red with anger.

Then he got himself under control and continued more calmly. "The *cholos* dispersed, but they did not leave. They looted and stole from good citizens! It was necessary to control them, so our young *hidalgos* organized into companies of *defensarios* to protect our

201

homes and women. Now the Americanos think to push us from our ranchos, but they will not do it!"

"You were coming from the direction of Fort Sutter when my father found you in the snow, Don Jabal," Molly said when Jabal seemed to forget them. "Were your men waiting for you somewhere?"

He glared at her, but then a grin appeared on his face.

"No, my dear. My men were nowhere near me when Garanon tossed me into the snow. I had gone alone to have a look at the army John Sutter organized last year." He chuckled and shook his head. "I have never before seen the like of it!"

"What kind of army is it, Papa?"

Jabal pushed his sombrero back on his head. "My son, it was hard to believe what my eyes beheld. A company of Indians were trained to goose-step their way into battle!" He looked at Jaime, waiting for him to laugh.

"Goose-step?" Jaime asked uncertainly.

"*Si,*" Jabal said patiently. "Raise first one leg straight ahead, then the other, strutting like demented peacocks! Sutter brought German and Swiss drill sergeants to train them. They instructed the Indians well."

He chuckled again, and this time Jaime giggled with him.

"That would be very funny, Papa."

"What is not so funny now is the United States declaring ownership of California," Jabal said gloomily. "Because they are so big, they think to grow bigger by pushing us all off the lands of our ancestors."

They had reached the courtyard and the end of their ride, but Molly had been given much to think about. California was so vast, it seemed to her there was room for everyone. Why did the pride of men force them to fight for its title? Why could not everyone who wished live here? Absently, she smiled at Jabal as he helped her dismount.

Jabal's attention left Molly and returned to his *defensarios*. He brought his entire company to Costa Cordillera. They were housed in the guest rooms of the hacienda between their patrols of the ranchos in Sonoma and northern Marin. At any time the halls seemed filled with booted *hidalgos* going about their affairs. When they met one of the women, they bowed or kissed their hands, but then hurried on their way. They talked of nothing save this raid or that, or of how they were gaining ground against their enemy.

Dona Espicia treated the young men as honored guests even though her patience was often sorely tried. Their boots were usually dusty when they returned and their laundry caused the Indian laundresses to work longer hours than usual. The kitchen was continually a beehive of activity. Large quantities of food had to be brought in at regular intervals. Meals were served at all hours, for patrols were always either coming or going and the members always hungry.

Another aspect of the *defensarios* that Dona Espicia had to address was their lust after the young Indian girls. Don Jabal had issued orders to his men to leave the servants alone, but this was no band of well-trained soldiers. These young *hidalgos* had been raised with their every wish granted. They were loathe to take orders in other than military affairs. However, Dona Espicia paired the young Indians with older women wherever their chores took them, so they were protected from the aggressors in most of the confrontations.

When Jabal was home in the evenings, he was engrossed with his lieutenants in long discussions about tactics and the maneuvers of the Americanos. They studied maps and marked them with various additions indicating trails or ambush spots and whether an area was wooded or open meadow. They plotted raids on American settlements, especially those where members of the Americano army were stationed.

Days were spent in drilling and practicing marksmanship in the courtyard. Indians were kept busy making new ammunition as the young men used their supply with increasing rapidity. The noise of their firing at first made Molly flinch, but she soon grew accustomed to it, scarcely hearing it as she and Jaime attended to lessons.

The war horses of these young men were subjected to continual grooming, as though a shiny coat made them better able to keep their masters away from flying bullets. The Indian blacksmith worked the day through and then some at times, for the *hidalgos* made sure their mounts were well shod at all times. The rocks in the California soil were hard on horses being ridden at full gallop.

Don Michael stayed aloof from these activities. He said someone had to keep the rancho running smoothly and that job was a full-time one. He stayed in his house a great deal, only emerging for meals or to give orders about ranch jobs that needed doing. Occasionally he went to inspect a mended fence or some other project he had ordered, but he never stayed for long.

Several times Michael mentioned the ever-growing number of bills that were presented to him because of the *defensarios*, eventually the matter came to a head one morning at the breakfast table.

"Mama Condesa, the grocer in Santa Rosa has been cheating us," he said. "It is time we called him to account."

Dona Espicia looked surprised. "We have dealt with him for years, Michael. Are you sure?"

"I am sure," he answered.

She looked out the window at the deserted courtyard. "Our guests have gone for the day, but they will return tonight and be hungrier than ever, you can be sure."

"I have taken into account the increase in provisions," Michael said. "*El comerciante* is a cheat!"

"May I see the bills he has given you?" Dona Espicia asked.

He nodded. "As soon as I finish eating, I will get them for you. You will see I am right. The bills are stacked on my desk corrupting the air in my house."

"Would you like me to get them, Michael?" Molly asked. "I am quite finished with my meal."

"Would you, please, Molly?" he answered, his voice gentle as though he were speaking to a child. Then hurt showed in his dark eyes as he added, "You are not so very busy since soldiering is now the order of the day."

Molly paused, then decided to ignore the remark. "Jaime would you like to go with me?" she asked. It was not her fault Jabal and Jaime took up so much of her time, was it?

"I cannot, Aunt Molly," he answered. "I must feed Mouse, that is, after I feed myself."

The June morning was one of nature's better efforts, Molly thought as she reached the courtyard. The sullen fog had stayed out at sea the night before. Idly, she wondered what dictated its actions. Was it the God of her father or one of Amatil's mysterious forces? Whatever,

205

the skies were blue and a gentle breeze pushed fleecy white clouds around overhead. With peace such as this, how could a war be raging somewhere nearby? The *defensarios* had left before dawn, all of them, so there must be something important happening.

Her thoughts vanished as she opened the door to Michael's house. Tomas must have gone with the other men, for she hadn't seen him during the morning. Michael's house looked much as she had seen it with Jaime, save that the gun cabinet stood ajar. There didn't seem to be many guns as she remembered, but then, all guns were in demand these days. Tomas probably took one or more with him as any soldier would.

The big desk was cluttered with an open ledger and a pile of papers beside the usual things. She walked to it to get the bills for Dona Espicia to see, then an open drawer caught her eye. When she looked into the drawer, Feliciana's face stared up from it. Her curiosity aroused, she pulled the drawer farther out, then gasped with surprise. Feliciana was wearing only the diaphanous blue nightgown! The portrait realistically showed the warm tints of her skin glowing through the gown.

Molly felt the heat of a blush as she stared at the picture. Across part of the gown was inscribed, "I love you. Feliciana." Stunned, she sank into the chair beside the desk. Was this the reason Jabal and Michael were at odds with each other? Was this why Feliciana had left her family so abruptly?

The diary! If only she had read it when she had the chance! Dona Espicia had said no more about its theft, nor had Molly's Bible been returned, and she had been too engrossed with Jabal and Jaime to think much about it. Like some silly schoolgirl, she had thought of nothing but her love for a married man.

Condesa Magnifica must still have the books in her possession. It was time—past time—that she return the stolen property. Perhaps one couldn't accuse a member of Spanish nobility of a theft, but then neither could such a member accuse one when the property was retrieved, Molly decided.

With this resolution, she closed the drawer and gathered the bills from beside the ledger. Michael surely hadn't remembered leaving the drawer open or he would never have allowed Molly to get papers for him to show his mother.

The open gun cabinet drew her attention and she paused. If she were going to Casa Grande to retrieve her property, perhaps she should take some protection against Noyo. He had tried to kill her once, of that she was sure. It would be foolish to give him another opportunity.

As she examined the guns, she remembered her father teaching her to shoot. "Never point a gun at anyone you aren't aiming to kill, girl," he had said, "and if you are aiming to kill, don't let him get close enough to grab your gun." He had taught her to hold a pistol with both hands so her aim would be truer and the recoil not knock her off balance. She stood thinking of all the things he had taught her while he was alive. Tears filled her eyes as she wondered what kind of God would let him die while still in his prime.

Then she brought her thoughts back to the present as she lifted first one gun, then another. At last she chose one of the smaller pistols. One look told her it was loaded. She slipped it into a pocket of her gown, concealed in the folds of the skirt. No one would notice it there, so no explanations would be required. With a fast-beating heart, she returned to the hacienda.

Michael paused in his conversation with his mother as Molly entered. "You have been gone quite long, Molly. Did you have difficulty finding the bills on my crowded desk?"

"Of course not, Michael. They were just where you said they would be. It is such a lovely morning, I paused to admire it," she said, then smiled at him so he would smile back. Michael was kind and she would not hurt his feelings if it could be helped.

She handed the papers to Dona Espicia, then looked at Jaime. "If you are ready, shall we get to our lessons?"

"*Si*, Aunt Molly," he said. "Come on, Mouse." He slipped his hand into hers as they left the dining salon.

It was difficult for Molly to keep her mind on lessons as she worried the question of when she would venture into Casa Grande. How many servants were in attendance on Condesa Magnifica? When did they sleep? Where did they sleep? At the thought of the hood-eyed Noyo her courage faltered. Then she remembered the bravery of Colin O'Bannion and was ashamed of herself. However, she would try to find out if he had a room of his own and where it was located. Noyo had come to her room in the small hours before dawn arrived. She would take a lesson from his example and go to Casa Grande before anyone was up.

When it was time for the evening meal, Molly went down the stairs and into the dining salon. Only Dona Espicia, Michael, and Jaime were there.

"It seems we are denied the company of the gallant *defensarios* tonight, Molly," she said drily. "Don Jabal sent word they will not return until late this evening, so for one meal we can dispense with talk of war."

"That's really all it is, isn't it? Talk, I mean," Molly answered as she took her chair. "I think war is a game men like to play, hoping there will be enough danger involved to amuse themselves."

Michael's laugh startled her. "You amaze me with your perspicacity at times, Molly," he drawled.

"Well, I do not think war is a game," Dona Espicia said bluntly. "I doubt very much that it is fun to be shot."

"You are right, *Mamacita*," Michael said, "but so is Molly. It is no fun being gored by a bull or a ferocious cow, but men keep testing fate by fighting them." His eyes were full of mischief when they met hers. "Even women venture into areas where angels fear to tread. Is it not so?"

Molly squirmed uncomfortably, wondering if he had missed the pistol she took . . . or noticed the closed drawer that had been open.

The conversation turned to other things and Molly composed herself, waiting an opportunity to bring up the subject she most wanted to discuss. When there was a pause she had her chance.

"Dona Espicia, has my Bible been returned?" she asked.

The older woman frowned. "I am afraid it hasn't, Molly," she said. "I tried to speak to Jabal about his grandmother, but these days he is interested only in his men and what they are doing."

"Can you confront Noyo at a time when Condesa Magnifica is not with him? I'm sure he is the one who rifled my room and almost killed me."

Dona Espicia sighed. "I'm afraid not, my dear. He is responsible only to his mistress. You have yet to learn about Spanish royalty and their ways. There would be a frightful row if I questioned Noyo about his actions. The proper way is to ask his mistress, but I cannot help there because she regards me as an intruder and always will."

Michael had been listening to the exchange and now he asked, "Mama Condesa, would it be proper if I confronted the old hag about this matter?"

"It would be proper, but it would do no good. She thinks the same of you as she does of me. I doubt she would even acknowledge your presence if you were to go to Casa Grande," Dona Espicia answered.

"Is Noyo her only servant?" Molly asked.

"No, of course not, my dear," Dona Espicia answered. "He is the major domo of her house and it is he who relays her orders to the maids and other servants."

"Does the castle have a servant's quarters like the hacienda?" Molly asked.

"Of course . . . and you are very full of questions this evening, Molly. Casa Grande is the entire world to Condesa Magnifica and she rules with an iron fist, according to the gossip of the servants. I hope she will not summon you to come before her again, for Casa Grande is dangerous ground to outsiders," Dona Espicia said.

Michael snorted, much as his mother did when exasperated. "The old hag doesn't frighten me, nor does her creepy servant. Noyo knows better than to approach me, for he knows I would not hesitate to kill him if he steps out of line," he said.

Molly realized there was a lot of Spanish royal blood in him, for his tone was one of arrogance. No matter that his grandmother thought of him as a mongrel, he was of her blood and no commoner.

"There is war enough around here, my son, without

our fighting with each other," Dona Espicia said. "Leave Noyo and his mistress to your brother. When Jabal has time I am sure he will talk to her and retrieve both Molly's Bible and Feliciana's diary. She is nosy. Or perhaps I should be more diplomatic and say she is curious about her family. When she has examined the books, perhaps she will even have Noyo return them."

Maria entered with coffee and desert and the conversation was not resumed. The evening went its interminable way until at last Molly was in her room, alone with her thoughts.

She tried to relax on her bed, but sleep would not come. But then, she hadn't expected to sleep. In the dark she listened to the sounds of the house as its occupants settled in for the night. She went over her conversation with Dona Espicia about Casa Grande and its mistress, realizing she still didn't know where Noyo would be at any time.

At times she rose to peer out the window at the castle on the opposite side of the courtyard. Condesa Magnifica retired quite late, apparently. It was well past midnight before the flickering lights were doused and the windows grew dark. It was another fogless night that made every object plain in the bright moonlight. Fog made her uneasy, but she would have welcomed its cover for the venture ahead.

Since the courtyard was brightly lit, she would have to become invisible. She remembered a black dress in Feliciana's wardrobe, and although she was glad she didn't have to wear her clothing any longer, she would again borrow one of her gowns. With black cloth around her body and a black mantilla draped over her blonde hair, she could slip through the shadows of the outbuildings to Casa Grande.

Was the big front door left unlocked? The doors of the hacienda were seldom bolted, but perhaps the old woman was not so trusting. However, it was a warm night, so perhaps she could find an open window if she could not get in the door. Fear drew chill fingers up her spine, but she tried to ignore them. She was an O'Bannion!

Tiptoeing from her room, she fled noiselessly down the stairs and out the front door. The shadows from the sheds drew her into their cover as she hurried around the courtyard to the old castle.

Chapter Thirteen

The castle stood like a shining beacon in the moonlight. It had a look of innocence, but Molly knew its chief occupant was like a sinister spider, lying in wait for whatever prey came her way. Was she like a black widow spider that killed her mate after breeding? How *had* Don Luis died? Perhaps she would ask Dona Espicia one day.

The wide front door was in shadow under the overhanging veranda roof. She scanned the many windows, but saw no trace of movement or light. Molly tiptoed up the steps, holding her breath even though she knew it was silly. The thundering of her heart nearly deafened her. She paused in the darkness before the door to force calm with long deep breaths and a silent chiding for her foolishness.

When her breathing was again normal, Molly tested the door, relieved when it pushed open the necessary crack to allow her entry. Inside, she eased the door closed and stood listening for any sound. The castle seemed to press down in an attempt to smother her in quiet like that of a grave. There was a musty odor much like that in a tomb, that added to her unease.

Then to her right she heard soft breathing. As her eyes

grew accustomed to the gloom, she saw an Indian servant lying on a rug. He had evidently been stationed there to greet any night callers.

Molly patted the pocket wherein the pistol nestled, more to reassure herself than in the expectation of making use of it. The throne room beckoned straight ahead, still dimly lit from the embers of the night's flames in the fireplace. Softly, she moved past the sleeping servant into the high-ceilinged stone headquarters of Condesa Magnifica.

The throne was unoccupied, of course, but her imagination filled it with the baleful figure of the wizened crone. Chill fingers of fear returned as she looked over her shoulder at the dimly lit room behind her. Shadowy corners offered no hint of their contents, nor did the room invite hospitality.

The lump of terror in her throat brought tears to her eyes. She wanted to run from the castle as fast as she could and return to the safety of her room, but she would not. An O'Bannion was no coward and neither was the daughter of a Cheyenne princess!

She waited until her heart slowed to its normal beat again, then began her examination of the throne. There was no space in its base where books would fit, nor was there a table nearby on which they could be placed. Silently, she made her way around the huge room, searching for her Bible and Feliciana's diary, but they were nowhere to be found. Evidently the old woman had taken them to a safer place, most probably in the room where she slept. Where was it?

A sound like a pistol shot made her jump a foot, but when she whirled around she saw it was only a dying ember in the fireplace giving a last protest before it crumbled into ashes and died.

Molly returned to the hall where the gloom was almost impenetrable. There she felt a newel post and touched stairs going upward. Her hand found the railing and she went up a curving staircase to the second floor. Moonlight coming in the windows illuminated the area so Molly could see around her. She was on a circular balcony, much like the one in the hacienda. Doors were spaced at intervals around, but which one sheltered Condesa Magnifica? Her room would be the most likely place to find the books she had Noyo steal.

In the dim light Molly saw a slumped figure in a chair before one of the doors. It must be another servant on call lest the old matriarch need anything during the night. To get past her and into the old woman's quarters—that was the problem.

As Molly walked nearer, she saw that the woman was very old. Small snores issued from the open mouth under a shawl-draped head. Wisps of hair straggled over the wrinkled face. Could Molly open the door behind without awakening the aged sentry?

Holding her breath, Molly turned the doorknob, pushing inward and praying that the hinges were well oiled. The door swung silently ajar and Molly slipped into the pitch blackness of Condesa Magnifica's room.

She waited for her eyes to adjust, but this time they could not. No trace of moonlight filtered through the heavy window coverings. Nothing relieved the total darkness. She stood with straining ears, wondering if she had chosen the right room.

Then she heard sounds. Breathing and raspy snuffling as only the very ancient use in sleep. Cautiously, she slid one foot forward, then the other. Her hands groped before her as she tried to avoid objects that would trip her up.

Her fingers tangled in a netted curtain, then felt the curves of a bedpost. Carefully, she eased around the huge bed, feeling for the table she was sure was beside it. She touched wood, then a candle, a carafe of cool metal, a glass—but no book. Disappointment made her heart sink. Had she come this far and been frightened almost out of her wits for nothing?

She stood thinking, listening to the wheezy breaths coming from the curtained bed. An image of the parchment face came to mind as the old woman had taunted Molly at their first meeting and her resolve hardened. She would not give up yet!

Feeling her way around the room, the next object Molly encountered was a chest of drawers. Dare she open the drawers and feel inside? Only a doily of some kind lay atop the piece, so with her heart trip-hammering, she opened first one drawer, then another, hastily running her hands through the clothing inside until she was sure no book was concealed therein.

Molly made her way around the room, passing the door she had entered, reaching the draped windows. Despair filled her. Had the diary and her Bible been destroyed? But then she mentally shook herself. Condesa Magnifica had not enough time to read everything thoroughly, and why would she go to so much trouble to obtain the books if she hadn't meant to keep them? For what purpose was an enigma, but such craftiness as the old woman possessed was not used on a mere whim. Molly decided to continue her search.

She took a step and her foot encountered wood. She froze as the slight noise seemed to magnify to the proportion of thunder. Had it waked the old woman?

A thrashing in the bed held her breath stopped in her throat. Then the resumption of regular snufflings allowed her to breathe again. Her fingers confirmed another table beside the bed. On this one there were two books. Wild joy filled her as she slowly raised them to clasp to her chest. Her mission was fulfilled!

Hoofbeats sounded in the courtyard. Shouted commands seemed to fill the quiet room with resounding echoes. Molly stood in a corner, frozen again, waiting to see if the noise had roused Condesa Magnifica.

The wheezy sounds ceased. The bed creaked. A cracked voice spewed forth a stream of Spanish Molly could not follow. The door opened and a figure came from the hall to merge with the blackness. Soon light from a candle on the table illuminated the room. Molly shrank into the window hangings, praying she would not be discovered.

The old Indian woman she had seen outside the door carefully helped the old woman into a robe. Spanish words now came from Condesa Magnifica's withered mouth in an unceasing mixture of spleen and saliva. The maid kept nodding while she tied a sash around the Condesa's waist, even though her mistress hit her at intervals with a feeble fist.

Then to Molly's horror, Condesa Magnifica shoved the old Indian with a motion toward the windows, evidently ordering her to open the drapes. She must want to see her grandson as he brought his *defensarios* to the hacienda, Molly thought.

Panic filled her as she realized she could no longer stay in the folds of the curtains. Just as the old Indian reached her place of hiding, Molly lunged forward, running toward the door.

"Stop! Thief! Thief!" Condesa Magnifica screeched.

The outraged scream reminded Molly of Culebra's shriek. A hand grasped her skirt, but she jerked free. It spurred her to greater effort as she reached the hall and raced for the stairs.

"Noyo! Noyo!" The shriek echoed against the ceiling as Condesa Magnifica's anger soared.

Molly flew down the steps, praying the servant below would not stop her at the door. Then a dark shape materialized at the foot of the stairway and she recognized the hulking Noyo taking stance to stop her at the bottom. Molly stopped in mid-flight so suddenly she sat on the step behind with a grunt of surprise, staring at her enemy below.

Slowly, he came up one step, then another, while Molly sat petrified with terror. Then she remembered the gun in her pocket. Laying the books aside, she scrabbled in the folds of her gown until she found the gun. The feel of it gave her confidence as she rose to face Noyo.

"Stop right there," she said.

He halted, the hooded eyes in his impassive face staring up at her.

"Down!" she ordered.

She gave the command as she would to a dog, marveling how steady her voice was as it came from a stomach of quaking jelly. Now, if she could force her trembling knees to hold her erect while she finished her descent . . .

Slowly, Noyo retreated backward down the stairs until he was again at floor level.

Molly gathered the two books with her free hand, keeping the gun pointed as near the center of Noyo's chest as she could aim. Then carefully, she walked down the steps toward the man who had tried to murder her.

Condesa Magnifica's voice sounded overhead. "Stop her, Noyo! Kill! Kill!" she shrieked.

Molly kept her eyes on the Indian below her while Noyo shifted his gaze from Molly to his mistress, then back again.

The noise in the courtyard had increased to a roar, and evidently the *defensarios* were in high spirits from whatever mission they had been on. Noyo had his back against the door. At his mistress's command, he folded his arms across his chest as he held his ground.

"Get away from the door," Molly ordered, using the gun to motion him aside.

He stood unmoving, staring at her from beneath his half-lowered lids.

Molly motioned again, determined she would not be stopped now. She would not! Her enemy did not move. With a convulsive sob, she pulled the trigger.

Noise as loud as cannon shot deafened her as she was flung backward against the newel post. The dark man lunged forward. Drawing breath into her lungs, Molly screamed . . . and kept on screaming.

The door burst open as Michael came charging in first. Jabal was close on his heels and several other of the *defensarios* crowded in beside them.

"Molly, are you all right?" Michael asked, sinking beside her where she sprawled.

"What is going on here?" Jabal demanded over the babble of sound.

His gaze rose to where his grandmother stood at the top of the stairs. "Your pardon, Condesa Magnifica. What is this disturbance?"

219

"*La gringa! Ladron!*" the old woman screamed.

"A thief?" Jabal asked, turning to look at Molly. Then he looked again at his grandmother. "No, *abuelita.* She is our guest."

"She came sneaking in the night into my boudoir! Is that not the action of a thief? Or murderer? Perhaps she meant to kill me!" she said, spitting the words from her mouth.

"Noyo . . ." Molly gasped, pointing a finger. "She told him to kill me!"

"Bah!" The old woman turned away. "Take your *gringa* from my house. I want no more of her!"

Don Jabal herded the men from the castle, reassuring them as to the cause of the fracas. Michael lifted Molly to her feet and retrieved the pistol that had dropped from her hand. While he was occupied, Molly hastily gathered the two small books and thrust them under the folds of her gown into the capacious pocket. She was still shaken from the recoil of the gun, but she kept her wits about her.

"Can you walk?" Michael asked, offering her his arm.

She raised her chin. "Of course I can walk!"

However, her knees were not so brave. She staggered. Michael picked her up as he would Jaime and carried her into the courtyard. He made his way through the army of men, ignoring their questions. Some of the young men were already in the hacienda and the rest seemed headed that way. Don Jabal glanced once in their direction, then went with his men.

"Perhaps it will be best if I take you to my house," Michael said quietly.

He walked in the open door Tomas was holding ready, then put Molly on the couch in front of the fireplace.

Dying embers were all that was left of the evening's fire, but the warmth felt wonderful as the shock of the evening's events sent cold chills through her body.

"Bring brandy, Tomas," Michael ordered.

He brought one of the bright serapes to spread over her as she lay shivering, then sat beside her. Tears welled up in her eyes and then she began to cry. Great tearing sobs wracked her body as both fists were held before her eyes.

Gently, Michael pulled her to him, patting her on the back and shushing in her ear. Gradually, her fists relaxed and then her sobbing turned into silent tears that rolled from her eyes onto Michael's shoulder. He pulled a kerchief from his pocket and dabbed at her eyes, then pressed the kerchief into her hand so she could use it herself.

Molly sat back, hiccuping a little as she swiped at her eyes and blew her nose. Soon a weak smile rewarded the man who had comforted her.

"That is much better," Michael said. "You are safe now, Molly, so stop being afraid."

Tomas appeared with a bottle of amber liquid and two goblets. He placed them on a small table, then moved it close to the couch.

"Thank you, Tomas," his master said. "I will take it from here. Go get some rest. I will not need you before morning."

The Indian nodded and left the room. Michael filled both goblets half full, then handed one to Molly. "Try some of this, Molly. We can both use a little bottled courage this night."

Molly took a sip and swallowed. She coughed as the fiery liquor burned all the way to her stomach.

221

Michael laughed at her, then downed the liquor in his glass in one swallow. "That is the way you drink this, Molly."

She closed her eyes and took another larger sip from her glass. The warmth in her stomach spread to the rest of her body and she drank until the glass was empty. Her shivering stopped and she handed the glass to Michael.

He placed it on the table, then asked, "Why, Molly? Why would you try to beard the old lioness in her den? Don't you know how dangerous she and her Indian can be?"

Molly's departed bravery returned and she pushed herself upright on the couch. "Nothing would have happened if your silly army hadn't awakened her!"

He shook his head. "I am only glad we returned when we did. If the old witch and Noyo had grabbed you when no one was around, you might have disappeared forever."

"Pooh!" she said defiantly. "I took a pistol along and I know how to use it."

He grinned at the memory. "Oh, yes, you pulled the trigger, at least. When you steal one of my guns again you had better allow me to teach you how to use it so you won't be knocked on your . . . er . . . back."

Her chin rose defiantly. "How was I to know it hadn't been loaded properly? It not only knocked me down, it pulled to the right and I missed! My father showed me how to use a gun and he always loaded them with a correct charge."

Michael suppressed another grin as he said, "It is well that you did miss, my little Irish rebel. If you had killed Condesa Magnifica's manservant, or even wounded him, there would be the devil to pay."

"I wish I had killed him," Molly said. "He tried to kill me the night of the fiesta. Tonight the Condesa ordered him to kill me. She screamed the order! Once you know who your enemies are, the better chance you have to deal with them."

"Oh, Molly, you are so wrong," Michael said with a sigh. "My mother can do nothing with her and neither can I. The old Spanish grandees had absolute power over their domain and Condesa Magnifica still lives in the past. If Noyo had taken you to the cellars of the castle, you would never have been heard from again."

Molly clamped her lips stubbornly and glared at him, so he continued.

"Mama has tried to speak to Jabal about your Bible, but he is busy with this damnable war. However, I shall talk to him tomorrow and we will retrieve your Bible one way or another."

"You needn't bother," she said. "I found it in the Condesa's room tonight and brought it with me."

Michael stared at her and there was awe in his eyes. Then he grinned and reached for the bottle. "Now that requires another toast to the evening, O'Bannion." This time he filled both glasses before handing her one.

"To the O'Bannions of this world!" he said, raising his glass.

She nodded, then drank as he drank, only coughing a little this time as her throat burned and the liquor passed into her body. When she handed Michael the empty glass, exultation filled her. No matter the consequences, she had her stolen property back in her pocket. No Spaniard could trample on an O'Bannion!

"If we had you fighting on our side, this war would end at once," Michael said. He leaned over her and kissed her

223

on the mouth, lingering until she pushed him away.

"Why do you Spaniards think you can take advantage of every woman you meet?" Molly said angrily. "I told Jabal and now I tell you . . . I am not to be handled as though I were a child!"

"Ah, yes, there is always Jabal, isn't there?" he said with a shake of his head.

His face became a blur in front of Molly as the liquor took effect. Her eyelids grew heavy as sleep threatened to claim her. She felt Michael's hands as he placed her head on a pillow and straightened her limbs on the couch. Tucking the serape around her, he rose and left her alone. Her eyelids closed.

Despite her great weariness and her desire for sleep, it eluded her for a time. Fuzzy thoughts kept circling in her mind denying her the rest she so needed. She had retrieved her Bible and Feliciana's diary, but the exultation that had filled her before had now changed to depression. What would the old Condesa do next?

But she had Feliciana's diary. If she were not so sleepy she would read it now, but perhaps in the morning . . . Then the mysteries that so bemused her would surely be solved. Jaime's mother . . . she would know why Feliciana left, and if she would return. Return to Jabal?

Jabal . . . would he be angry with her because of her going to Casa Grande? Her heart sank. Jabal would be furious! Would he side with his grandmother against her?

Sleep drew Molly into its depths, but her dreams were nightmares in which huge angry Indians chased her around shadowy rooms while an old woman screeched at them to kill her. Molly moaned in her sleep while her feet twitched as she ran and ran and ran . . .

The sun was high in the sky when Molly woke with a raging headache. It took a few moments before she realized she was still in Michael's house, alone on the couch. The bright serape had slipped to the floor.

The events in Casa Grande flashed into her mind. Hastily, she felt for the books that had caused the uproar. The Bible and the diary were still safely hidden in the pocket of her skirt. Her hand explored the surfaces to assure her they were really there, then returned to her head as she tried to stop its ache. Cautiously, she sat up, groaning when the throbbing in her head increased. What was it Michael had given her to drink? And why, oh why had she drank so much of it?

Shouts from the courtyard drew her to the window. The *defensarios* were even more numerous today, it seemed to her, and their noise excruciatingly loud. Evidently enforcements had been added to make the company larger. Was the war becoming more dangerous and closer to Costa Cordillera? She held her head with both hands as the war inside threatened to make it split.

Then she saw Jabal. He was packing something into Garanon's saddlebags while Michael talked urgently into his ear. Perhaps he was trying to excuse her behavior of the night before. This morning it seemed foolish even to her, but she *had* gotten what she went after.

"*Los Osos* will disappear before we arrive!" a young man shouted while his horse capered and pranced against the restraint of the tightly held reins. "Don Jabal, let us go! Let us be on our way!"

"*Uno momento*, Senor Padilla," Jabal shouted above the din in the courtyard. He finished packing the bag and strapped the lid closed. Then he turned to his half brother and said something Molly could not hear before he mounted Garanon and reined him to stand on his hind legs. "*Compadres!*" he shouted.

The noise in the courtyard gradually faded away as all eyes focused on Jabal, their leader.

"We ride!" he roared.

Immediately there was a scramble, the *defensarios* formed columns behind Don Jabal as he galloped from the courtyard toward the entrance of Costa Cordillera. The earth shook as the many hooves descended and rose while the small army cheered themselves onward.

Michael watched the men leave, then strode angrily toward his house. There was a frown on his handsome face when he entered that disappeared when he looked around the room and saw Molly at the window.

"Ah, you are up, Molly," he said, forcing a smile. "Did you rest well?"

She nodded. "Is Don Jabal very angry with me?" she asked hesitantly.

He shook his head and his deep voice was gentle when he said, "I am afraid Jabal has forgotten you for the moment, Molly. He is now totally engrossed with the game of war. He did not even mention the events of last night."

A feeling of relief filled Molly. She dreaded Jabal's cold anger. Then hurt pushed relief aside as the import of Michael's words sank in. How can you totally forget someone you love?

Perhaps Jabal didn't love her—although he had certainly acted the part lately. On their many rides with Jaime he had acted more the courting lover than a guardian fulfilling his promise to her father. He had given her his full attention and paid her many compliments, both by mouth and with his eyes, and she had basked in the warmth.

Now the scene at Casa Grande flashed into her mind. Don Jabal's concern had been for his grandmother more than Molly. He had practically ignored her! It was Michael who had thought first of Molly as he barged into the castle.

"I haven't properly thanked you for last night, Michael," she said.

He grinned at her. "Shall I apologize for claiming my reward as I did?"

"No, of course not," she answered. "However, you should apologize for giving me this tremendous headache. What was it we drank last night?"

He laughed, saying, "That was a form of brandy our Indians brew, so I will apologize for your headache. Wait here a moment and I will try to find a cure."

He went into another room and when he returned he carried a glass filled with some sort of liquid. "Here, Molly. Drink this down as you did the brandy, and your headache will be gone."

She accepted the glass, looking at it doubtfully. When she sniffed the contents the smell made her wrinkle her nose. "It smells dreadful," she said.

"It is a hair of the dog that bit you and guaranteed to cure your hangover," Michael said cheerfully. "Now drink it."

She took a sip. It tasted as awful as it smelled, but she did as Michael ordered and drank until the glass was empty. For a moment her stomach threatened to relieve itself of its contents, but then the concoction settled down. Molly sighed with relief.

"Better?" Michael asked.

She returned to the couch and settled herself against

the cushions. "Perhaps . . . I'm not sure yet," she answered.

Michael went to the gun cabinet, glancing at Molly as he took the hidden key and opened it. He selected a rifle and checked to see if it was loaded.

"I hope this one has a proper charge," he said, then grinned impishly at her. "I would hate to be knocked from my saddle when I pull the trigger."

Molly's headache was disappearing so she ignored his jibe. She watched as he gathered a few possessions. With a bundle in one hand and his rifle and sombrero in the other, he came to stand before her.

"I must go now, Molly," he said. "Are you feeling better than before?"

"I am all right," Molly said impatiently. "Where are you going? Are you going after Jabal? What is happening? Please tell me, Michael."

A tinge of irony twisted his smile. "The game is becoming more exciting, senorita. When fools grow violent, death joins the play."

"What are you talking about, Michael? I don't understand what you are saying."

"Early this morning the American settlers surrounded the Mexican army barracks in Sonoma and took General Vallejo prisoner. They call themselves the Bear Flag Army—*Los Osos*—and have declared the territory the California Republic," Michael said with a shrug. "Spain, Mexico, the British, Russians, and Americans—all have tried to take California for themselves. We have survived through all of them, keeping our lands and our possessions despite covetous strangers. Now the Americanos have organized themselves and declared themselves owners of California."

"What has all that to do with Costa Cordillera? When something belongs to you, isn't it yours?" Molly asked, a frown drawing her brows together as she tried to understand.

Michael grinned, much as Molly had seen a wolf draw back his lips before a kill.

"It means, my dear, that now the Americanos will take from the Spaniards the land they stole from the Indians," he said. And there was irony in his voice as he added, "If they can."

"But Costa Cordillera belongs to the del Valles," Molly said uncertainly. "How can anyone take it?"

A shrug answered her question.

"Will there be fighting again?" she asked fearfully.

His eyebrows rose quizzically.

"Well, answer me, Michael!" she demanded.

"Yes, there will be fighting, and yes, someone can appropriate Costa Cordillera if we lose." Then anger showed on his face. "I believe, like Dr. Laughlin, that the land should belong to all! Yet I must go fight to preserve fifty thousand acres of it for a handful of Spanish royalty." His voice lowered. "If it were not for my mother, I would leave the del Valles to their fate."

"But you are a del Valle," she pointed out.

Bitterness pulled the corners of his mouth down. "No! Even my father realized I was not a true del Valle, and were it not that he loved my mother, most likely I would have been drowned at birth. You see, senorita, I am a half-breed!"

She stared at him. When her father used the word, she had thought it meant only half white, half Indian.

"You don't understand?" he asked. "Dona Espicia is an Irish lass, not a Spanish grandee. Therefore, I am half

229

Irish, half Spanish. Condesa Magnifica christened me at birth—a mongrel, I believe she said."

He placed the sombrero jauntily atop his head. "However, even we serfs must do our duty, my dear. I shall join Jabal in his mad battle. I shall even try to keep him from being killed." He saluted her with his rifle. "Adios, O'Bannion."

Molly watched him go through the door, then ran after him. "Go with God, Michael," she said as he mounted his big roan. As he rode from the courtyard she added, "And please come back," even though she knew he could not hear her.

Chapter Fourteen

Molly drew a deep breath. Now she would have to return to the hacienda and face Dona Espicia. Nervously, she tried to smooth the wrinkles out of her skirt. Sleeping in your clothing did not make it neat. Her efforts were fruitless, but after she straightened her hair, she decided to try to get to her room where she could better tidy herself. She crossed the courtyard and mounted the steps to the hacienda.

Inside, only Maria came to greet her. "Miss Molly, are you all right? Dolores told me you had not slept in your bed last night and we were worried."

"I'm fine, Maria. Was Dona Espicia worried?" Molly asked.

"We did not tell her you were not here, Miss Molly. She had trouble enough getting to sleep," the housekeeper said.

"Thank you."

"Will you have breakfast now?"

"I would like to go freshen up first, Maria. Is Jaime up yet?"

"He, too, was up late last night. Don Jabal and Don Jaime were together until very late. I think they were discussing the war and the plans to fight. Sometimes Don Jabal forgets his son is only seven years old."

"Then I will go to my room," Molly said. "Will you have a bath brought as soon as possible?"

"Yes, ma'am."

Molly went to her room, relieved she could tidy up before Jaime and Dona Espicia saw her. Her gown was grimy from the fray of the night before, and somehow she felt as rumpled as her dress. She removed her clothing and when maids brought a tub of hot water, she stepped into its warmth to soak.

Dolores had come with the bath and she now shooed the other maids out of the room.

"Mollee . . ." she said hesitantly. "Are you all right?"

"I am now, Dolores," Molly said. Her headache had fled and the warm water was easing the aches in her body.

"Where did you sleep?" her maid asked. "I was so worried when I heard shots and such a commotion! What happened? The *defensarios* were talking about you, but I could not make out what they said."

"Didn't Chia tell you?"

Dolores shook her head. "Don Jabal sent him to groom his horse and I had no chance to talk to him."

Maria knocked, then entered. "Miss Molly, Dona Espicia has had her tea and would like to see you at breakfast. Will you be ready soon?"

"I will dress right away and come down, Maria," Molly said, rising to allow Dolores to wrap her in a towel.

"I will tell Dona Espicia," the housekeeper said, and left the room.

"Hurry, Dolores. Help me get dressed," Molly said.

While she was dressing, Molly answered the question Dolores had asked before Maria appeared.

"I slept on Don Michael's couch last night, Dolores. I am probably in a great deal of trouble because I went to Casa Grande last night, but I'll tell you all about it later."

Dolores looked alarmed as she fastened the last button on Molly's gown. "Oh, Mollee . . ."

"I must go," Molly interrupted, then hurriedly left her room and ran down the stairs to the dining salon.

"Good morning, Molly," Dona Espicia said as she came in.

"Good morning, Aunt Molly," Jaime echoed.

Molly answered their greetings and seated herself at the table.

"Did you sleep well?" Dona Espicia asked.

"Yes, ma'am," Molly answered and her heart sank. The older woman's tone was cooler than usual. How much did she know?

Maria served their meal. It was eaten in unaccustomed silence, even Jaime seemed subdued.

When they were through, Dona Espicia said, "Jaime, it is time you took Mouse outside for a while. You are excused."

"*Si, abuelita,*" he said, and left to do her bidding.

Dona Espicia looked thoughtfully at Molly. "You are a guest in this hacienda, my dear, and I am responsible for your welfare. Is that not so?"

Molly nodded.

"Perhaps we had better discuss the happenings of last night," Dona Espicia said. "Why did you go to Casa Grande?"

"I went to get the books that were taken from my room," Molly answered.

"Oh, Molly, how could you be so foolish? Didn't I

233

warn you how dangerous Condesa Magnifica and her servant can be?"

"Well, yes, but . . ."

Dona Espicia interrupted. "I told you I would have Jabal speak to the Condesa about your Bible and Feliciana's diary. Why didn't you wait?"

"Because Jabal is only interested in his silly war," Molly said. "Besides, I am not afraid of that old lady. I am an O'Bannion, not a Feliciana who leaves her possessions behind!"

"Please do not malign my daughter-in-law, especially now she is not here to defend herself," Dona Espicia said. "You are not like Feliciana at all, I'm sorry to say. Feliciana is a gentle lady." She shook her head. "Although at times she is like a child who fears darkness and mysterious things known only to her." Then she looked at Molly and smiled. "How did you ever find the nerve to do such a thing, child?"

"Because I am not a child, as I keep telling everybody," Molly answered.

"No, you are not," the older woman conceded. "However, it is well that you missed Noyo when you shot at him. By the way, where did you get the gun?"

"I took it from Don Michael's cabinet in order to protect myself."

"Hm-m-m, it did not protect you much, did it? If my sons hadn't returned in time to hear the shot, you might not have fared so well," Dona Espicia said.

"I would not have been caught if your sons hadn't arrived to make so much noise," Molly retorted. "I had already found the books and would have left without discovery if they hadn't waked the old woman."

Dona Espicia looked startled, and then she laughed.

"Oh, Molly, you are a true Irisher. I should be angry because you might have gotten hurt quite badly, but I cannot. Did you really find your Bible and the diary?"

"Yes, I did."

The older woman sighed. "This will make a tale to tell for years to come. Every hacienda in the county will buzz with such a scandal."

"Perhaps everyone is too concerned with the war to even tell about it."

"You do not know Spaniards if you think that, Molly," Dona Espicia said. "The young men in Jabal's army thrive on gossip and this is a choice bit they will not soon forget. They saw Michael carry you to his house, you know."

Molly felt a blush cover her face as she said, "I had been knocked down and Don Michael picked me up as though I were a child," she said indignantly. "He gave me something to drink that made me drunk and I slept on his couch. I thought my head would split when I woke this morning, but then he gave me something else to drink that almost made me sick." She paused, then added, "However, it did cure my headache."

"Michael went with Jabal and his army this morning," Dona Espicia said. "I had hoped he would remain out of this war as much as possible."

"I know," Molly said. "I saw him leave."

The older woman looked thoughtful, then changed the subject. "Did you bring Feliciana's diary with you?"

"Yes, I did . . . oh, dear! It is still in the pocket of the gown I was wearing. My Bible, too. I had better tell Dolores to remove them before she launders the dress," Molly said as she started to rise.

"Stay where you are, my dear," Dona Espicia said. She

called Maria and asked her to get the books from the pocket of Molly's gown.

While they waited, Molly asked, "Was Jabal very angry at me?"

"I'm afraid Jabal was furious. I told you he was totally under the influence of his grandmother. If the news of General Vallejo's surrender to the Americans hadn't arrived, I tremble to think what might have happened."

"Perhaps I had best leave, Dona Espicia," Molly said slowly. "I am very sorry I caused so much trouble."

"You must not think of leaving, Molly, at least until this war has ended. The country is in such an upheaval, anything can happen. Besides, Jaime would miss you terribly and so would I. You have become much like a daughter to me, or didn't you know that?"

"I didn't," Molly answered. "Thank you very much, Dona Espicia. I shall try to be not so headstrong in future."

The older woman patted her hand and they sat silently until Molly asked, "How could you send your son to fight? Aren't you afraid he'll be killed?"

"Of course I am!" she answered. "But Michael hasn't gone to join the *defensarios*, at least not right away. Don Jabal asked him to go to Sutter's Fort to see how the General is faring with his captors. By the time he reaches Jabal, I hope the fighting will be over."

A frown wrinkled her brow as she rose from the table. "I wanted Michael to stay here and guard the compound. There are only Indians left, and not many of them. Don Jabal bought a supply of gunpowder for the army that entirely fills one of the sheds in the courtyard." She winced at a twinge of pain in her hip, then went to sit on a couch. "Have you any idea what the Americans would do

236

to get it if they knew it was here?"

Their eyes locked as they examined the possibility.

"Will the men return tonight, Dona Espicia?"

A snort emerged from Dona Espicia's mouth. *"Quien sabe?* They may return soon, or they may be gone for days. Don Jabal thinks no one would dare invade his property, but he is wrong! Already there have been Americanos sneaking in—as witness the skirmish when Jaime's horse bolted. The del Valles think they are held in awe by everyone. Perhaps the Indians feel that way, but the Amercians do not."

Maria entered carrying the books which she handed to Dona Espicia.

"Here is your Bible, Molly," the older woman said as she handed it to her. "I shall take a look at Feliciana's diary when I am feeling better. Maria, will you help me to my room? I do believe a nap will help."

Molly thought about her words as she went to find Jaime, then dismissed them from her mind as she and her charge began lessons.

"I am getting very good at American, yes, Aunt Molly?" Jaime asked after writing a letter to his grandmother for practice.

"You are indeed, Jaime. Your spelling has greatly improved," Molly answered.

"I would like to show you what Papa and I have read," he said, selecting a book from the shelf.

"Alexander the Great and His War Strategies," she read. "My goodness, Jaime, this is deep stuff."

"Papa has learned much from this book, Aunt Molly, and so have I. Papa and I talked of these strategies last night. I have not the size to accompany him as yet, but if I am to be Conde, I must know how to defend

237

my property."

Once again Molly saw a small monarch preparing for his future. Why would they not let him be a child until he was of an age to assume his responsibilities? She said nothing, however, and the day wore on in its usual fashion.

After supper when night had fallen, Molly went to her room. She allowed Dolores to help her prepare for bed, but when the maid had gone, Molly lay awake. Dona Espicia's words returned to haunt her. Would an invasion come to Costa Cordillera? What did soldiers do when they invaded enemy property? Had Jabal and his men been successful in their mission? Was Jabal safe? Michael had said he would try to protect his brother, but what if he hadn't arrived soon enough? What if Jabal were dead? Her heart seemed to miss a beat as the thought of Jabal dead came to her. But no, he couldn't be dead—she would know if he were. Huk hadn't cried in the night and he always gave warning, didn't he? At last she fell asleep.

Her first thought on waking was to peer out the window, but the courtyard was quiet. When the *defensarios* were around there was always noise and shouting, and today only Indian women passed to and fro. The day passed as usual, with meals and lessons with Jaime the only interruptions. Dona Espicia elected to stay in bed for the day. She said without the *defensarios* around she would just enjoy the peace and quiet.

Don Jabal and a small band of men returned in time for supper. Dona Espicia had dressed in order to dine with Molly and Jaime, so she was ready for company. Maria and the maids hastily prepared a meal, for they knew without asking that the *defensarios* were always hungry.

Molly stayed behind Dona Espicia as she greeted Jabal, wondering if the stern look would return to his face at sight of her.

He greeted them with a smile, however, kissing Dona Espicia's hand as he said, "Mama Condesa, we come home in victory."

She looked at the milling men and asked, "Is Michael with you, Jabal?"

"Michael?" he asked as though he had never heard the name. Then he relented. "Mama Condesa, your son is probably still at Fort Sutter. I did not see him arrive in Sonoma."

Relief showed on her face, but she merely asked, "Where are your other men, Jabal?"

He shrugged, saying, "Some went home to care for their wounds and some just went home."

"Were there any casualties?"

He laughed. "No, madam, there were none. We hardly fired a shot before the Americanos surrendered themselves to our mercy." He frowned. "The cowards fired on us, inflicting wounds on our men, then surrendered before we could repay their generosity. Such people can never last in this land—I shall see to that," he said angrily, but then his mood changed as he said, "Shall we eat, gentlemen?" and escorted Dona Espicia to her seat.

There was jubilance in the air as the Spaniards toasted each other and the Spanish flag. Then they fell to and filled their stomachs from the abundance on the table. When they had finished, Jabal arose.

"We shall have brandy in the salon, ladies and gentlemen." He helped Dona Espicia to rise and escorted her to the main salon where he seated her on one of the many couches.

239

Jaime scampered ahead while one of the gallants offered Molly his arm. They all acted like a bunch of strutting peacocks, Molly thought. Jabal, in particular, had an exhilaration she had never before seen.

When all glasses were filled, Jabal held up his hand for silence. "I wish to make a toast," he said, raising his glass. "To Molly!" he exclaimed, turning all eyes in her direction. "Let us all drink to the rose of the Sierra."

Molly was embarrassed by so much attention, especially since she had refused the glass offered to her. She smiled and went to sit beside Dona Espicia, but Jabal came to claim her, escorting her to a place of honor beside him in front of the fireplace.

He offered Molly a goblet of wine in a way she could not refuse, but she was careful to merely sip at its contents. She would not drink whatever was handed her as she had with Michael, for she would remember the dreadful headache for a long time to come.

Still elated by the excitement of battle, perhaps Jabal had forgotten the ruckus at Casa Grande. The talk was all on how they had chased the Americans away from Sonoma. Glasses were filled again and again as toasts were made first to this victory, then to others in the past. Faces grew ruddy and speech slurred, but the party continued. Jaime went to bed of his own accord when the time came, apparently still tired from his late night with his father.

Jabal kept Molly close to his side while he bandied words with his lieutenants. Then he again called for silence.

"We shall get General Vallejo and return him to the fort, gentlemen," he declared. "Thirty-three settlers! That is what composes *Los Osos!* That is the American

240

army that thinks it will take California away from me!"

Molly gasped with surprise as Jabal claimed the vast territory as his own. Then she decided it was probably just a figure of speech. No one commented about it.

When cigars were brought out, Dona Espicia rose and motioned for a maid. She pleaded weariness and excused herself. Molly tried to leave at the same time but Jabal would have none of it.

"Fresh air, my dear. That is what you need," he said. "I prefer it to a cigar." He offered his arm, leading her to the door. "Tonight I want to savor the taste of victory. One day I shall rule all California, either as its governor or its king!"

Since his mood seemed to require no answer, Molly said nothing. The night was cool and clear with the same mellow moon she had avoided on her way to the castle. Thousands of winking stars studded the sky above while Jabal expanded on the subject of his future power.

"A country as grand as this deserves a king," he said. "I was born to rule just as Don Luis ruled, only I want a larger domain than Costa Cordillera. Don Jaime del Valle will become Conde of Costa Cordillera, but I shall become the king of California!"

He was in a very strange mood tonight, Molly decided, and only smiled her encouragement. They strolled along until they reached the crouching oaks outside the circle of buildings, then Jabal drew her to a halt beside him.

"A king needs a queen," he said softly.

He bent to kiss her and for the second time she saw the crisp black mustache blot out everything else as it drew close and his mouth covered hers. This time there was no question in his manner. His lips demanded surrender with a rough eagerness that frightened her.

She struggled against his grasp, but his arms held her as though in a vise. When he loosened his hold so one hand could explore her bosom, she broke loose.

"Stop it, Jabal," she said angrily.

With a triumphant laugh, he gathered her to him again and kissed her, forcing her lips apart with his tongue. Her knees grew rubbery and her heartbeats threatened to strangle her.

The laughter was gone from his face when he picked her up and carried her to a dark spot beneath the twisted old branches.

She beat at him with her fists, saying, "Put me down, Jabal! Put me down this minute!"

His breath came in ragged gasps, more like the panting of an animal, as he placed her on the grass and knelt over her. She tried to wriggle away from him but he held her down with both hands.

"You will be mine tonight, little Molly," he muttered.

Putting all her weight into a push, Molly shoved him from her and sprang to her feet.

"You are already married, Jabal—have you forgotten? I am no country wench to be taken at your pleasure, despite what you may think!"

Surprise showed on his face, erasing some of the cruelty she had seen a moment before. Then he threw back his head and laughed while she gaped in amazement.

"Spitfire!" he gasped, when he had caught his breath. "Stubborn little *gringa*. Molly, Molly, you must grow up some time—why not tonight? Under the wide California sky with the future king of all he surveys, you can be queen! You and I together could rule the world!"

He caught her to him again and kissed her, but this

time more gently. Then his mouth left hers and his lips traced a warm line to her ear.

"I want you, Molly. I need you," he whispered.

Molly wrenched herself away from his grasp. "My love will belong only to my husband, Don Jabal. He will speak of marriage, not of rutting."

"Oh, ho!" he exclaimed. He put his hands on his hips and grinned at her. "The O'Bannion temper has come to the fore! Very well, Miss O'Bannion, will you marry me? Will you be my queen? I love you!"

"Oh, Don Jabal?" Molly asked. "And what of Feliciana? Do you just pretend she does not exist? She is still your wife. Perhaps she will return."

He shrugged. "She deserted me and I shall divorce her." He reached for Molly. "That will not take long, and then we can be married, *querida mia.*"

One hand pulled Molly to him while the other began to unbutton her gown. Her bodice ripped when she whirled and ran toward the courtyard.

Then Jabal's arm encircled her waist as he flung her to the ground. He lay atop her, his weight crushing the breath from her body.

"Do not run, little rabbit," he said coaxingly. "Have I not said I will marry you? What more can you want? You have been offered the world!"

Wordlessly, she struggled against him. When she had freed her hands, she beat his shoulders with her fists, then tried to hit his face. "You are crushing me, Don Jabal. Get off!"

With a laugh, he eased his weight to his hands and knees, ignoring her futile blows as he crouched over her. "You will have to get used to my weight, *querida,* for you shall feel it often." His eyes were exultant.

Molly stopped hitting him and lay exhausted on the ground. "I will not have to get used to your weight until we are married," she said wearily. "Have you forgotten your promise to my father? Is this how you care for his daughter after he saved you from freezing in the snow?"

A look of surprise crossed his face as he sat back on his heels, freeing her. "I thought you loved me, Molly. I thought you wanted me as much as I do you."

The moonlight illuminated his face, showing first his amazement at her resistance, then his hurt, as though a small boy had been denied a plaything. She saw his dimple flash before he spoke.

"I love you, *querida*. I think I have loved you from our first encounter. I remember your bravery when your father died and you were left alone. I remember your arms around me and your body close to mine while we rode Garanon to Costa Cordillera. You are everything I have always wanted—fire and ice, hardness and softness. Perhaps I did not realize it right away, but now I know it is you I desire." His smile was tender and coaxing. "You will marry me, won't you, Molly?"

Her breath caught in her throat. He had proposed to her, but was this the man she loved? Was this the man she wanted to live with for the rest of her life? How had she gotten into this ridiculous situation? She rose to her feet.

"It is time we returned to the hacienda, Jabal," she said, then turned on her heel and walked toward the porch.

Jabal scrambled to his feet and hurried to catch up with her. When he reached Molly he grabbed her arm and turned her to face him.

"What is the matter with you?" he asked indignantly. "Why are you so stubborn about keeping your virginity? It is a thing of which most women are glad to be freed."

"I am not most women, Jabal," Molly said. "I am Molly O'Bannion, as you surely know by now. I do not roll around under the trees with any man, especially a married one."

Her insides were churning as she remembered the look on Jabal's face when he tried to make love to her. There were so many sides to him: lord of creation, small boy, charming gentleman, some kind of predator—which was really Jabal? Did she really love him or was it just infatuation?

Amatil had said, "When a man and a woman marry, they become one person, Molly. A woman must accept only one man into her body, my daughter, so be sure it is the man you will love for the rest of your life. You know how you feel, but the one sure way to know how the man feels is when he offers you marriage. Accept nothing less."

Don Jabal del Valle had offered marriage, but he was still married to Feliciana. Does an honorable man do such a thing?

Jabal stood before her, frowning. "You are stubborn as a mule, Molly. Why are you so unreasonable? When we have said our intentions, is that not the same as marriage?"

"Nothing is the same as marriage, Jabal, and I have not said I will marry you. You are not yet a free man to make such a proposal, are you?"

"Bah!" he said angrily. "A priest babbling words does

245

neither make nor undo a marriage. Only a man and a woman who want each other enough to complete their union physically makes a real marriage."

"Oh, really!" Molly said. "Then how often have you been married, Don Jabal? Did you marry Dona Eulalie? Was that why her husband wanted to kill you?"

"Don Miguel may have wanted to kill me, but he did not. I killed him, which proves me in the right!" Jabal answered, and again the haughty look of predator was on his face. "Besides, little *gringa*, that was before I realized I was in love with you." Then his face became again that of a coaxing lover. "My philandering days are over, Molly, and you must believe me. But I am a man—a man in need of a woman. One who loves you desperately. Let us begin our marriage now, for tomorrow I may die. Americanos shoot first, then surrender, which is no consolation if you are dead. Do you want me to die without knowing you completely?"

Molly shook her head. "I do not want you to die at all, Jabal, and I am not sure we will ever be married. In any event, I will not become an easy woman."

With that, Molly turned and walked away from him through the moonlit night. She crossed the courtyard and went around to the rear of the hacienda where she could slip through the kitchen and up the stairs without showing her dishevelment or seeing anyone who might question her about the tears in her eyes.

Jabal had frightened her tonight. She had seen a part of him she did not like. What had happened to the handsome Spanish gentlemen who had been so kind to her while her father died and was buried? What had happened to the gentle lover who teased her just to make her smile? What had happened to her dream?

246

As she hurried to her room she was crying. Crying because she was confused. She readied herself for bed, tears still streaming down her cheeks.

Did she love Jabal? Did he really love her or was he only lusting as she had seen him lust before? *Amatil . . . mother, please help me . . . help me . . .*

Chapter Fifteen

There was little sleep for Molly during the night. She tossed and turned, trying to forget for a time, at least, her contretemps with Jabal. When the sky began to lighten with the coming day, she donned her riding habit and slipped down to the stables. An Indian groom rubbed sleepy eyes at her approach, looking askance at this white woman out so early by herself.

"Saddle my mare, please," Molly said shortly.

Her tone was enough, for he scrambled to do her bidding. He returned with the mare and silently helped her onto the saddle. Even as Molly rode from the courtyard she heard morning sounds of the *defensarios* beginning the day's activities. Would Jabal leave this day to war again? And Michael. It was strange he hadn't caught up with his brother at Sonoma. Dona Espicia would be worried if he didn't return soon.

Approaching hoofbeats caused her to rein the mare hastily aside into concealing shrubbery. She watched as a night patrol galloped homeward, usually squared shoulders slumped with utter weariness.

Then she returned to the open valley and let the black mare canter. The morning was cool and brisk and

248

bracing. Cool breezes smelling of the ocean blew hair into her eyes, then swirled it out again. Gradually, her mind cleared of the muddle it was in. New spirit filled her while the sun sent warm fingers to explore the world.

She rode through the waving grass, then guided her mount upward on the steep tree-dotted hills guarding the valley. Her actions were more instinctive than planned. She wanted to draw nearer to the purity of the sky, the promise of a haven to come. More than anything, she wanted her parents!

At the thought, she pulled the mare to a halt. Since the deaths of Amatil and Colin O'Bannion she had thought of them frequently, but never with such intensity as now. Mother . . . Amatil . . . guide me, she prayed. What shall I do about Jabal? What *can* I do?

As she waited for an answer, she looked around the small bowl she had reached. Wild roses and sweet peas tangled together in the overgrown clumps of brush. Flowers she couldn't identify flourished under the trees. Then suddenly she realized she was in front of Jaime's cave!

She dismounted and pushed her way into the narrow opening. In the dim light inside, the Virgin Mary looked gravely down as Molly sank to the small rug at her feet. She was the mother of her father's God—what magic was in her power? Could she help Molly solve the problem with which she wrestled? Could she grant her peace of mind?

Peace gradually filled her as she lay there. It was as though Amatil's gentle hand stroked her back in commiseration of her sorrow. Her eyelids grew heavy as the sleep she had been denied through the long night now came to comfort her. Molly drifted into dreamless sleep to find the respite she sought.

When Molly woke, she lay trying to remember where she was, then saw the statue above her. The air had grown quite chill in the sheltered cavern and the light that filtered through the growth outside was much less. The statue wavered in the half light like a ghostly spirit until a rub at Molly's eyes made it settle again into the stone figure it was. Stiffly, she sat up and rubbed her numb arms to restore the circulation. How long had she slept?

She rose and walked through the brush to the twilight world of evening. Her mare cropped grass a short distance away, patiently dragging the reins as she moved. Leading the mare again to the rock Molly had used on her first visit with Jaime, she mounted and began her descent through the darkening hills leading to the valley.

Peace filled her soul. Jabal loved her, she was sure. His haste was only the urge of virility that most males felt. If they were married, she would make him be gentle with her.

The harsh cry of a bird brought her eyes up to search the sky. She wondered fearfully if Condesa Magnifica had turned Culebra out for his night's hunting. The thought of his tearing talons in her hair filled her with dread, but she could see no sign of any winged creature.

Chiding herself for being so jumpy, she urged the mare to a faster pace. Just before they reached the broad valley trail, Molly heard a noise in the brush and pulled her mount to a halt. A faint groan came through the clear air and then a weak cry. A shiver crossed her back. Was someone there or was her imagination playing tricks?

She was undecided until a long drawn moan of pain came from the shrubbery. Hurriedly, Molly dismounted and pushed through the brush to the source of the sound.

Her gasp of dismay opened the eyes of one of the men lying on the ground.

"Help," he whispered.

Sickness rose inside her as Molly knelt beside him. Great burns covered his face and the upper part of his body. Blood oozed from gashes in his forehead and cuts on his arms. He looked more dead than alive.

"What happened to you?" Molly asked, swallowing the gorge that rose in her throat.

He moaned as he tried to speak. "Partner . . ." he gasped. One arm twitched as he tried to motion. "Over there."

Molly looked toward where another man lay, then rose and walked over to him. His body was even more tortured than the other's—so horribly mutilated that this time Molly could not control her sickness. She leaned against a tree and emptied her stomach into the brush, gasping until the waves of nausea slowed. When she could again stand erect, she returned to the man and felt for a pulse, but there was none. The man was dead. Quickly, she returned to the first man.

"Who did this?" she demanded.

"The dons . . ." came raspily from his throat.

"What did you say?" Molly asked, for she wasn't sure what she had heard. "Did Indians do this to you?"

"No . . ." His voice was so weak Molly had to lean close to hear him. "Spanish dons . . ."

Her mind refused to believe her ears at first. Spanish dons? Don Jabal and the *defensarios*? Surely, not Jabal! Not those nice young men who were so polite!

"Oh, no!" she said, shocked.

Then she looked at the wounded man again. This was the work of soulless men—savages or perhaps wild animals, but not anyone she knew! Oh, please, Mother of God, make it not anyone she knew!

"Love of God . . . water," he whimpered weakly.

The despair in his halting words brought Molly back to reality. Here was a human being in need of help, and only she was here to give it.

"I have no water with me," she said. "Can you help me get you up on my horse? I will take you to Dona Espicia—she will dress your wounds and take care of you."

It would be impossible for Molly to load him on the mare without assistance, she knew. Her mind raced as she mopped at his cuts with her kerchief, looking first in one direction, then another, for a way to help him.

"No," he muttered as a swollen tongue licked weakly at parched lips. "Span . . . kill . . . Water . . ." Then his eyes closed.

Was he dead? Molly searched for and found a weak pulse in his wrist. He must have fainted. Then she looked around her. Where was the nearest water?

She remembered a rocky crevasse where water trickled in a never-ending drip. It was off the trail, but not far from where she was. She crashed through the underbrush toward it, wishing the moon would rise to light her way.

When at last she stumbled on the damp rocks, Molly searched frantically for something to catch the water in, but without success. Could she soak the heavy material in her habit and then wring it out into the wounded man's mouth? Then a better thought struck her. She removed a boot and let the water trickle inside until it was filled. Inelegant, she decided, but it would do.

Wincing at each twig and rock she stepped on, Molly hobbled back to her patient. There were no more moans, no movement of any kind. When she sank beside him she saw he was dead, staring from eyes still filled with horror.

With a sob of pity, Molly closed the sightless eyes and tenderly bathed the grimy face with a kerchief soaked in water. The other man's nose had been smashed into his face and she couldn't bring herself to perform the same ministrations for him. Instead, she emptied the boot and put it back on, then sat staring into space, wondering what she should do.

Dr. Laughlin! He would know what to do next. She would go tell him where the men lay and then he could take over. Could she find her way to Santa Rosa? She knew it was eastward from the hacienda. Surely a settlement would not be difficult to find, but could she find it in the darkness that was fast covering the land?

She would have to, she decided. If she returned to the hacienda she would probably not be allowed out by herself again. By now Jabal would be furious at her absence—that is, if he and his men were still at the hacienda. If the *defensarios* had done this . . . this *horror* . . . they would want no report of it made.

The black mare stood docilely beside her reins and Molly blessed the training that kept her tied where they were dropped. With a heavy heart, she pulled herself into the saddle and turned her mount toward Santa Rosa.

The moon had risen, but fog drifted over the hills like small puffs of low-hanging clouds. The night was full of the croaking of cicadas and sleepy twitterings of birds going to nest. It was a beautiful California night, but Molly was in no mood to appreciate it.

The tortured faces of the two men she had found stayed in her mind, filling her with sickness and disgust. If this was war, she wanted no part of it. How could Dona

Espicia condone behavior that could result in something so horrible. But then, perhaps she knew nothing of this aspect of war.

The soft hooting of an owl sounded as Molly rode past a clump of oaks. It brought her up short when she remembered the cry of another bird that night—a bird she hadn't seen. Huk had warned her again of death, but she had been too engrossed with her feelings for Jabal to heed his cry.

Shivering, she urged the mare to a faster pace, keeping her eyes on the star she had decided was the one that shone over Santa Rosa. Twice during the long journey she saw ghostly shapes riding purposefully through the hills. Between puffs of fog, the metal on their guns glittered menacingly in the moonlight. Each time she pulled the mare into the shelter of the nearest trees and sat motionless until they were gone. Once her mare had nickered, making her heart miss a beat as she pulled on the reins, but it went unnoticed and the men kept on their way. Her back hurt and her knees grew stiff as she rode on her seemingly endless journey.

When dawn dimmed the moon, Molly saw a cluster of rude buildings ahead. Mounted men milled around the settlement. One of them saw her and came galloping forward on a vicious-looking mustang that constantly fought the bit. When he drew near, he pulled the animal to a plunging halt, gaping in astonishment.

"Gawd, it's a woman!" he exclaimed, then glanced over his shoulder toward his companions. "Hey . . . there's a lady over here!" he shouted.

Then he turned back to Molly, spitting a stream of tobacco juice before he asked, "What you doin' out here, ma'am?"

"I wish to see Dr. Laughlin," she answered.

His eyes took inventory of her mare and the saddle. "Are you Spanish, miss?"

"I am an American," Molly said coolly. "Is Dr. Laughlin here?"

He nodded. "I'll show you his shack."

She followed his lead, holding her head high as the curious stares of the rough men passed over her. Some made catcalls and other rude noises, but these Molly ignored. Her guide soon reined the mustang to another halt before a small building.

"Doc is in there, miss."

"Thank you."

Dismounting, she wrapped the reins around the hitching rack in front of the shack. She doubted ground-tying would hold where so many strange horses were present. And so much noise from the men. Her wet boot squished uncomfortably as she walked to the door and knocked.

"Come in," an impatient voice ordered.

When Molly opened the door she saw the red-haired man sitting at a desk lit by an old lamp. He looked up, then hastily rose and came toward her.

"Miss O'Bannion! What in the world are you doing out at night? Are you alone?" He craned his neck to see over her shoulder before his attention returned to her.

"Dr. Laughlin, there has been terrible trouble," she said.

"There is always trouble now," he answered. "Is someone hurt at the hacienda? Why did they send you? It isn't safe for a woman to travel alone, as everyone well knows."

"No one sent me, Dr. Laughlin, and no one at the

hacienda is hurt, at least that I know about." Molly paused, then added, "I must tell you something privately since I'm not sure I should tell you at all."

He closed the door and led her to a chair beside the desk. "Are you ill? Your face is as white as a ghost's!"

"I'm just tired," she said impatiently. "I have been riding most of the night." She sneezed and groped for a handkerchief that was nonexistent.

The doctor took a clean square of cloth from a drawer and handed it to her.

"You are taking cold, missy. Night air will do it!"

"My boot is wet," she explained.

"Your boot . . . ?"

Then Molly told him of finding the two Americans on Costa Cordillera, omitting the accusation one had made before dying—and the extent of their wounds. She merely said one was dead when she found them and the other died soon after.

"I thought you would want to bury them before they become prey for California buzzards," she concluded.

He sat in thought when she finished, his bright blue eyes focused on her face. After several minutes, he spoke.

"There is more, isn't there? Why didn't you return to the hacienda to report this? One of the Indians could have brought the message."

"They are Americans," she said uncomfortably.

"And they are the first men to be killed in this stupid war," he said bitterly. "Now there will be hell to pay!" He rose to pace the floor, then said, "Excuse me, Miss O'Bannion. I didn't mean to swear in front of you."

She sneezed again.

"I'm letting you sit there with a soaked boot on your

foot," Dr. Laughlin said, shaking his head at his stupidity. "Take it off at once and I'll try to dry it out."

Molly stuck out the offending boot and the doctor pulled it off. He wiped it out with soft rags, then laid it where the heat from the fire could penetrate.

"That should be enough, Dr. Laughlin," Molly said wearily. "I had best get back to the hacienda. Dona Espicia is probably worrying about me."

"But you need rest . . ." the doctor began.

"I shall sleep when I reach home," she interrupted. "I am all right, but I could use a hot drink, if you have it." She sneezed again.

"What am I thinking about! I'll get some food for you right away, Miss O'Bannion," he said. "Please forgive my bad manners." He hurried out.

Molly stood up, leaning against the desk. It felt better to stand, even with only one boot on. She rubbed her back as she wondered if it would ever stop aching. A sidesaddle became an instrument of torture if stayed on too long.

Dr. Laughlin returned shortly with a napkin-covered tray from which delicious smells emerged. He put it on the desk and held his own chair for her to sit in, then removed the napkin to reveal a hearty breakfast.

"While you are eating, Miss O'Bannion, I'll get two men ready to go with us," he said.

With her mouth full, she looked a question.

"Now you don't think I would let you return alone, do you? I told you it wasn't safe. Besides, you will have to show us the location of the bodies."

Before she could answer, he was gone. Thoughtfully, she chewed, listening to shouted orders and the attendant noise of departure. During the night her

257

coming here seemed perfectly logical, but now she was not so sure. When Jabal found out she had led his enemies to the fallen men, what would he say? What would he do to her?

Anger filled her. It was only decent to bury the dead, as Jabal well knew. Then another thought occurred. If Jabal had killed them, he would have seen to their burial. Perhaps some of the *defensarios*—without Jabal's sense of honor—had committed the outrage. Perhaps Jabal knew nothing about it. It was a comforting thought to hold on the long ride back. It was a comforting thought if only some nagging doubts stopped eating on her.

When Molly finished eating she hobbled to her boot and brought it back to the chair so she could put it on. It was still wet, but this time it was warm wet which wasn't so bad. Then she opened the door and looked out.

Dr. Laughlin and two bearded Americans were waiting to leave with her. Her mare had been fed and watered, so although she was tired, she would carry Molly back. It would be better than trying to ride one of the shaggy bad-tempered brutes her companions rode.

They left the settlement, only now there were no smiles or good-natured jibes. Now the men scowled as they huddled in bunches and discussed the news she had brought. Molly shivered, wondering if she had done the right thing. Of course she had! Any Christian would have done the same thing given the same circumstances, wouldn't he?

Their journey was made mostly in silence. The men seemed engrossed in their own thoughts, especially Dr. Laughlin. He seemed to have grown a permanent frown as he contemplated the dire consequences of a killing. Since Molly was wearier than she had thought, it suited her well to doze in the saddle as the mare nodded along.

Instead of entering Costa Cordillera through its formal entrance, they retraced Molly's path across the hills and valleys until they reached a point near where the bodies lay.

"You'll find them in those bushes," Molly said, pointing. "Now if you will excuse me, I'll continue on to the hacienda."

"Wait a moment, Missy," Dr. Laughlin said. "I'll get these men under way first, then go with you."

Molly waited while the men vanished into the bushes. Her pulse raced with fear of what they would do when they saw the condition of their comrades. When Dr. Laughlin again appeared, rage was in his eyes and his jaw was clamped in anger.

He mounted his horse, then waited until Molly's eyes met his. "You left out quite a few details, Miss O'Bannion," he said. "What I just saw was not the work of decent white men. It was more as though wild animals had been at work."

"I'm sorry," she whispered fearfully.

"Humph!" was all he answered.

"Perhaps it would be best if I went on to the hacienda alone, Dr. Laughlin," she ventured.

"No, it wouldn't," he said shortly. "I want to see Dona Espicia to see if she is well, and if you have made yourself unwelcome by this act of charity, I will see you safely to a place of refuge." He paused, then said thoughtfully, "I also wish to find out if hostile Indians have gone on the warpath in this area."

The courtyard was alive with activity when they rode in. It looked as though most of the *defensarios* had gathered again. Don Jabal broke off his conversation with one of the men to meet them in front of the veranda.

"Molly, where have you been?" he asked angrily. "I have had men out all night looking for you. Are you all right?"

"Yes, Jabal . . ." she began.

He interrupted before she could answer his questions, saying, "We are leaving *now*. You have delayed our mission too long with whatever foolishness has occupied you."

The company had mounted, milling in wait. All eyes were turned to where Jabal and Molly stood.

"We shall discuss this matter when I return," Jabal continued. His calculating gaze flicked to Dr. Laughlin. "There will be time then to inquire with whom you spent the night, my dear."

"Don Jabal," Dr. Laughlin said. "I have time to discuss many things with you now."

"Well, I do not," Jabal said. He mounted Garanon and waved for his men to follow as he galloped toward the entrance to Costa Cordillera.

Molly felt the heat of anger at Jabal's words and his abrupt dismissal of her, but there was nothing for it but to await his return to discuss the matter.

Dr. Laughlin dismounted and came to help Molly out of the saddle. "That is a dangerous man, Miss O'Bannion," he said.

She sighed. "He is angry only because he was worried. Don Jabal has asked me to be his wife, doctor."

Surprise showed on his face. "Don Jabal is already married, child. Don't you know that?" he asked.

"His wife deserted him, Dr. Laughlin, which I believe is grounds for divorce," Molly said wearily. "Do you

260

wish to come in with me?"

His hand on her arm stopped her from leaving.

"You don't know what you are saying," he said, and there was incredulity on his face. "Madness is in del Valle blood. Can't you tell from the way the old woman acts at times? It shows elsewhere, too."

"Please, Dr. Laughlin," Molly said, breaking from his grasp. "I am really too tired to discuss this with you now. You are not here often enough to know everything about the del Valles." She walked quickly up the steps into the hacienda.

"Molly, you're here!" Dona Espicia exclaimed. Her eyes were haggard with anxiety. "My dear, I have been so worried! Where have you been all this time?"

"I went to Santa Rosa."

"Santa Rosa? Whatever for?" she asked, then her gaze went beyond Molly to the man coming in the door.

"Dr. Laughlin! What are you doing here?" she asked, confused. "What is going on?"

"Good morning, Condesa," Dr. Laughlin said. "May we have some tea? We have had a long ride."

"But, of course," Dona Espicia said. "Please forgive my manners."

She gave Maria an order to bring refreshments, then shook her head as she said, "This is all too much for me. Perhaps I should have stayed in my tower. Please sit down, Molly . . . Dr. Laughlin." She passed a trembling hand over her eyes. "Don Michael has been taken prisoner at Sutter's Fort. Tomas arrived with the news just before you came. I have asked Don Jabal and his men to go rescue him."

"This idiotic war will be the death of us all," the doctor

261

muttered. "I am sorry, Condesa, but I really don't think the Americans have harmed your son as yet."

Dona Espicia raised her head defiantly. "Perhaps not, Dr. Laughlin, but he is a prisoner and I will not have one of my sons treated in such a manner!" She rose and walked to the window. "Has the whole world gone mad?" she asked fretfully, then turned to face her guests.

"It would seem so, Condesa," the doctor answered. "Two Americans have been killed on Costa Cordillera soil."

"What?"

"Miss O'Bannion was kind enough to ride with the news so we can at least bury them. I hope Don Michael is released before news of this reaches Fort Sutter," he said. "If he is still in custody when the manner of their comrades' death is explained to them, madam, I tremble for your son's safety."

The color left her face. "Killed?" she gasped. "What do you mean by the *manner* of their death?"

"The men were horribly mutilated, Condesa. It looked as though they had been tortured before being killed."

She stared at him, then rallied. "What makes you think Spaniards did such a thing? Perhaps your Indians grew tired of your arrogance and retaliated as animals do."

"Condesa, please . . ." The doctor shook his head. "You know well what this means. Killing has begun, so killing will continue. Before this, the war was mostly talk and wild firing and a few wounds, but now . . ."

"Why don't you find out who killed these men before there are more deaths, Dr. Laughlin?" Dona Espicia asked.

"We shall try, Condesa. We shall try," he said. Then his eyes rested on Molly. "Is Miss O'Bannion still welcome here?"

Bewilderment showed on her face. "Of course Molly is welcome here! Why wouldn't she be?"

Maria entered with a pot of steaming tea, cups, and a plate of biscuits. She placed cups before them and filled them to the brim. "Will there be anything else, ma'am?"

"That will be all, Maria, and thank you," Dona Espicia said.

Dr. Laughlin ate and drank heartily, but Molly and Dona Espicia sipped their tea and refused the biscuits. Molly was weary unto death and wanted only to escape to her room and go to bed.

When Dr. Laughlin had finished his meal, he rose. "Now I must go, Condesa. Thank you for the refreshment."

"Why don't you stay the night?" Dona Espicia asked. "I can have a room prepared for you."

"Thank you, but no, Condesa," he said. "I want to catch up with the men who came with me for the bodies. There will be an uprising when they reach Santa Rosa, and I want to be there to hold it down as much as possible." He glanced at Molly. "You will be all right, Miss Molly?"

"Of course."

"Then I bid you good day, ladies," he said with a slight bow, then left them alone.

"Dona Espicia, there is something I must tell you," Molly said hesitantly.

The older woman held up her hand. "Not now, child. I do not wish to hear more. Perhaps by morning I will be able to sort everything out. Michael's capture . . . two men dead on Costa Cordillera . . ." She sighed. "Not to mention my concern as to your whereabouts. At least your safe return has relieved my mind of one of its worries."

"I am sorry . . ." Molly began, but Dona Espicia waved her apology aside.

"Perhaps we both need sleep, so let's go to bed," Dona Espicia said. She looked up as Maria entered the room. "Ah, Maria, tonight I will have a sleeping potion, no matter Don Jabal's displeasure. It's the only way I will get any rest."

Molly watched her limp out with Maria's support, then walked to the window to stare at the empty courtyard.

Dr. Laughlin's words returned to haunt her while she looked at the castle across the way. Condesa Magnifica seemed mad at times, that was true, but she had assumed that anyone who lives beyond ninety years was bound to be a little eccentric. Only the doctor's anger made him include Jabal in his claim of madness in del Valle blood.

And Jabal . . . so angry! But as she had told the doctor, it was more than likely because he had been worried about her safety. By the time he returned, he would have realized how ridiculous it was to think there was anything between her and Dr. Laughlin. More to the point might be his anger when she told him of her Indian blood. Despite her father's warning, Molly would tell her future husband about her mother before their marriage plans progressed farther.

That was what she wanted to discuss with Dona Espicia tonight, but, as usual, she had been put off, this time because of the older woman's fatigue.

Her own weariness suddenly washed over her. She left

the window and climbed the stairs to her room. It felt good to get out of the garments she had worn for so long, especially the soggy boot that had chafed her foot to rawness.

It brought back the sight of the tortured Americans. The settlers would seek revenge once they saw the bodies. Who would they call to account?

Chapter Sixteen

Despite the bright sunshine when Dolores woke Molly, the maid's face was sober. She helped her mistress dress with none of the usual chatter, until Molly was finally driven to ask her what was wrong.

"I must go to San Rafael and pray this morning, Senorita Mollee," Dolores said sadly. "May I be excused from serving you this morning?"

"Of course, Dolores," Molly said. "Are you in some sort of trouble?"

The Indian girl shook her head. "It is Chia I will pray for. Many bad things are happening and I do not want him to suffer because of *incidentes* over which he has no control. I do not want him to suffer at all!"

"Bad things?" Molly asked. "What bad things are you talking about?"

Her eyes avoided Molly's and she twisted her hands nervously. "Oh . . . the war, and Don Michael's capture . . . and other things . . . you know."

"What are you afraid of, Dolores?" Molly asked gently.

The maid's head rose defiantly. "I do not wish Chia to attend Don Jabal any more. I shall pray to San Rafael and

266

all the saints that he be free."

"Free?" Molly asked, puzzled. "Can Chia not leave if he no longer wishes to serve Don Jabal?"

"Oh, Mollee, we *belong* to the Conde del Valle. We belong to him just as the horses and cattle are his. If we were to run away, we would be brought back and whipped!" she said bitterly. "We are his slaves."

Molly frowned and shook her head. "How can that be? Dona Espicia said Don Pablo had abolished the whipping post, Dolores. Surely such primitive punishment is no longer used. And how can you be slaves? Indians are a free people, aren't they?"

"Indians are not free once a Spaniard takes them in," the maid said. "No one sold us, that is true, but Spaniards just take possession and no one is ever allowed to leave, except when death takes us. Those of us who were born on Costa Cordillera, especially, are considered the property of the del Valles. As for punishment—Dona Espicia does not know everything that goes on. The dungeons of Casa Grande are still there, and the old woman still rules over many things on this rancho."

"I can hardly believe all this," Molly said. "Why haven't you told Dona Espicia what is going on?"

"Because she cannot talk to Condesa Magnifica," Dolores answered. "She would only tell Don Jabal . . ." She paused.

"Would that be so bad, Dolores? Don Jabal can talk to his grandmother and keep her from doing harm. After all, he is Conde until Jaime comes of age."

Dolores stared at her and her eyes were frightened. "You must not say anything about this to anyone, Mollee. Indians who complained in the past have disappeared forever."

Molly tried to find out more, but Dolores would say nothing save to extract a promise from Molly to say nothing to Dona Espicia about the Indians. Molly went down to breakfast, mulling over the conversation in her mind.

Only Jaime and his little dog were in the dining salon when Molly entered.

"Aunt Molly, you are back!" Jaime exclaimed. "Where did you go for so long? Why did you not take me with you? I was afraid you had left, like Mama."

"I'm sorry I was away so long, Jaime, but it couldn't be helped. I went for a ride in the hills to clear my head before you were awake, but something happened that kept me away for the rest of the day," Molly said. "However, since I promised you I would not leave you, you needn't have worried. You should have known I would return."

Maria entered with Jaime's breakfast and saw Molly. "Good morning, ma'am. I'll get your meal in a moment."

"Will Dona Espicia join us this morning?" Molly asked.

"No, ma'am. She gave orders last night she was not to be wakened until teatime," Maria said. She left, then returned in minutes with hot coffee and cereal for Molly.

When at last Jaime laid down his spoon, he wriggled restlessly. "Can we go on a picnic, Aunt Molly?" he asked. "Everyone is gone and *abuelita* wishes to sleep, so we could take our lunch to the beach."

Molly smiled at his eagerness. "I am afraid the beach is too far away, Jaime, especially with a war going on." His face fell, so she hastened to add, "However, we can go with Dolores to the statue of San Rafael and take our lunch with us. You can tell me how the chapel looked before it burned. It must have been very lovely."

"It was . . . and the cemetery, Aunt Molly! I will show you the old stones marking Conde Luis's grave and *abuelita's*, too. They are very elegant," he said with pride, then added, "May I take Mouse with us?"

"Will Culebra try to eat him again?"

"Pooh!" he said disdainfully. "Culebra has had his breakfast by now and is back with Condesa Magnifica. Besides, I have told Culebra my dog is not for him, so he will not make that mistake again."

When Dolores passed the open door, Molly called out to her. She stopped, looking in at us, her face still grave and worried.

"Yes, Senorita Mollee?"

"May Jaime and I go with you to the statue? We wish to picnic. You are invited to join us when you finish your prayers," Molly said.

"Of course," she answered. "While you are finishing your breakfast I will prepare a basket of food."

Shortly, they were on their way. Jaime was full of high spirits. Molly envied him, since no thought of dead men or the course of the war worried a seven-year-old boy for long. He didn't have to worry about his heritage, either, since it was an open book of Spanish royalty for all to read.

Mouse shared his master's glee, running first to one spot, then another, returning to them with his findings. He brought a leaf to Jaime, then a twig for Molly to take from his mouth. He was so tiny Molly was afraid he would get lost, but Jaime assured her Mouse always knew where his master was. Even Dolores joined in their laughter when Mouse returned with a stone held between his jaws. It was so heavy his back legs kept raising from the ground

269

as the weight lowered his head.

"He is a mighty hunter," Jaime bragged. Then he giggled. "Perhaps there is gold in the stone and Mouse has brought us a huge treasure." But the stone was just a stone and nothing more.

Since Molly had a night's sleep, she was quite recovered from her long horseback ride, but not anxious for another. Walking felt wonderful. The sun was warm but a cool breeze made them comfortable. Somehow her vague anxieties were dispelled. If Jabal truly loved her, what difference would it make to him who her parents were? After all, she could forgive him Condesa Magnifica!

It was nearing noon when they reached the site of the old chapel. Dolores put the basket of food on a tombstone under the twisted oaks where it would stay cool.

"I will go to San Rafael before eating," she murmured, her mind on her prayers for Chia.

Jaime and Molly sat down in the shade to let the cool breeze whisper around them, but Mouse was still full of energy. He raced around the tombstones before he spied the ashes on the charred site of the chapel. With a running start and a mighty jump, he cleared the foundation row of stones and landed in the rubble and ashes.

"Was the chapel very beautiful, Jaime?" Molly asked.

"*Si*, Aunt Molly. Conde Luis had it built with heavy rafters. Carved benches and beautiful statues filled the inside. The windows were of stained glass picturing many of the saints. The chapel was always lit with rows of candles when Padre Rodriguez came to bless us."

"What a shame that it burned," Molly said sadly. "I have never seen a church except in books. I would have

270

liked to see this one."

Mouse carried a shard of pottery to Jaime and laid it at his feet, then raced back to hunt for other treasures.

"For so small a puppy, Mouse certainly has a lot of energy," Molly remarked.

Jaime grinned, saying, "He carries less weight than we do, Aunt Molly. That makes it easier for him to go fast and stay longer."

Dolores had covered her hair with a small scarf before she knelt in front of San Rafael. She prayed for a long time, and Molly hoped she would find the answer to whatever was troubling her.

What had made Dolores change from being so proud of Chia's position beside Jabal to wishing he no longer held this place of honor? What had Jabal done and where was Chia now? It was all a mystery.

Since Mouse was nothing if not democratic, his next offering was laid at Molly's feet before he raced back to continue his game. She bent to pick it up, then froze. Twisted with heat, but still recognizable, the elaborate blue-stoned ring Molly had seen in the portrait of Feliciana lay where Mouse had dropped it. Before Jaime could investigate, Molly scooped the ring from the ground and slipped it into her pocket.

"Perhaps I had better help Mouse," Jaime said. He joined his pet and they were soon scratching together in the rubble left by the fire.

Molly sat trembling at the implication of her find. Had Feliciana perished in the fire? Death in such a manner must be horrible indeed! No woman would throw herself into such a conflagration, that was sure. Had Feliciana been trapped inside when the fire consumed the building? Had someone pushed her into the flames? But

271

who? Who would want Feliciana dead?

Jabal said she left with his friends the night before. Had she? Had she left with them and then been brought back to die in the fire? Or was she dead before she left Costa Cordillera?

A shiver of fear crossed her back. Had Jabal killed her? No! It could not be! Jabal would not kill the mother of his son, even if they disagreed as Dona Espicia said they had. Feliciana came from Spanish royalty and Jabal had a great deal of respect for that.

Perhaps Don Michael loved Feliciana to a point where he would kill her rather than allow her to leave? Molly thought of the painting in his desk drawer and the inscription Feliciana had written across it. Were they lovers? Could Michael kill a woman he had loved? Molly rather doubted it.

And there was always Condesa Magnifica. She had thought Feliciana a milksop and worse. Had she hated her enough to have Noyo make sure she was gone forever? A shudder of revulsion shook Molly. The old woman was capable of doing such a thing. She had ordered Noyo to kill Molly in front of everybody!

"Are you ready for lunch, Mollee?" Dolores asked.

She had returned from her prayers while Molly sat deep in thought and was standing beside her mistress.

"Sit here beside me, Dolores," Molly said, noting that Jaime and Mouse were still playing in the ruins. "Have you seen this before, Dolores?" she asked, drawing the ring from her pocket.

Dolores examined it curiously, then handed it back. "Si, Mollee. Dona Feliciana was never without it. She even wore it when she slept. Where did you find it?"

"Mouse brought it from the rubble," Molly said

272

slowly. "Do you suppose she died in that fire? Would it have been possible?"

Dolores looked dumbfounded. "I do not know, Mollee. Dona Feliciana never removed the ring while she was staying at the hacienda. I was her maid." Tears welled up in her eyes. "Oh, Mollee, what is happening here? No one has disappeared in a long time and now people are being killed or hurt or captured or . . . whatever," she ended lamely.

"Please don't cry or you'll have me doing it," Molly said, concealing the ring in her pocket again. "Let us say nothing of this to Jaime. There might just be some simple explanation. Dona Espicia has Feliciana's diary. Perhaps it will shed some light on the matter. By the time we return to the hacienda, Dona Espicia should be up."

The day suddenly seemed sinister, and to Molly it seemed as though much of the warmth had gone. "Dona Espicia said there was a shadow over Costa Cordillera since Feliciana left," Molly said. "The Irish have premonitions of many things . . ." She wondered if Huk would soon cry his warning again.

Soon Jaime returned, starving as usual, and they ate their lunch with Mouse getting tidbits from everyone. Jaime's cheerful chatter seemed to return things to normal, but Molly saw fear in Dolores's eyes, although she tried to smile and join in. Her own thoughts were of things she would like to forget, but she knew that was impossible.

It was mid-afternoon before they returned to the hacienda. Dona Espicia was sitting on the veranda and welcomed their return. She smiled and joined in their conversation, but her eyes turned often to the direction from which the *defensarios* would return. Molly knew her

273

thoughts were mostly on her sons.

Then Molly saw the small book in her lap. Had she read Dona Feliciana's diary? She waited until Dolores and Jaime had gone for their siestas and she and Dona Espicia were alone on the shady veranda, then removed the ring from her pocket and handed it to the older woman.

"Mouse found this in the rubble of the old chapel," Molly said.

Dona Espicia's face blanched when she recognized the intricate gold lacework and the blue gems. "It is Feliciana's," she whispered. "Oh, Molly, this is terrible!" Then her stricken eyes rose. "Did Jaime see this?"

"No, ma'am," Molly answered, glancing at the book in the other woman's lap.

"I read it," she said dully. Her eyes went round the courtyard before she laid her head back against the chair and closed her eyes. After a time, her eyelids opened and Molly saw tears glisten in her eyes. She made a helpless gesture with her hands, then shook her head.

When Dona Espicia spoke, her voice was a monotone. "Feliciana was a child. I knew that even before I read her diary. Jabal brought her with him on his return from Spain, much as a hunter brings home a trophy. She was beautiful and fragile and giddy as a little girl. Jabal played with her as though she were a toy, and at first she was happy. Jaime was born within the year, but then Feliciana could have no more children."

She sighed. "At least, that's what Dr. Laughlin told Jabal. He warned Jabal another pregnancy would kill her." The bitter laugh-snort sounded. "I imagine he said other things to Jabal, which is why Jabal has such a dislike for him. Jabal permits no one to criticize him."

"But wasn't one son enough?" Molly asked.

Dona Espicia rose and walked to the railing. "Not for the Spanish. Spanish men must prove their manhood by siring many children."

When she turned back to Molly her face was sad. "That is why Jabal turned his attentions to the young Indian girls. I have watched the children in the quarters, trying to see his stamp on them, but evidently his likeness does not appear in his Indian offspring."

Molly choked on her emotions, then cleared her throat. "Dona Espicia, perhaps you have misjudged Don Jabal. Perhaps he has done nothing in the quarters."

She put a hand on each of Molly's arms and peered into her face. "Ah, Molly, I warned you not to love Jabal. He was very cruel to Feliciana."

"Was it perhaps because she fell in love with Don Michael?" Molly asked.

Surprise registered on the older woman's face. "You have read the diary, child?"

Molly shook her head. "I saw a portrait of her in Michael's desk drawer on which she had inscribed her love for him, and she was wearing only a very sheer nightgown."

"Ah," Dona Espicia sighed. "Feliciana was in love with Michael as a child loves someone who is kind when she is being abused. They were not lovers, Molly. Michael has too much honor in him to steal another man's wife."

She picked up the diary, holding it thoughtfully. "Besides, the act of love must have hurt Feliciana dreadfully, if this is to be believed. I rather think she avoided wifely duties whenever possible, which is most likely the reason she and Jabal quarreled."

"Was she planning to leave?"

"No-o-o . . . she would not leave Jaime of her own accord. I know that now," Dona Espicia said sadly. "I'm afraid your finding her ring is proof of her death."

"Did Jabal kill her?" Molly whispered.

"I don't know . . ."

The clatter of approaching hoofs drew their eyes to the entrance of the courtyard. Molly's heart beat in anticipation as she waited for Jabal to appear on Garanon. Now that he had returned he could tell them what really happened the night Feliciana disappeared. He would explain everything.

But when the riders entered the courtyard, Molly's heart sank. It was a band of Americans and not the *defensarios*. Dona Espicia's indrawn breath was her only acknowledgement of their presence. Then she and Molly sat waiting.

The leader of the band—a rough, bearded man—rode to the foot of the steps to stare up at them. "Where are your men, ma'am?" he asked.

"They will return shortly," Dona Espicia said curtly. "What do you want?"

"Where's the gunpowder kept?" he asked.

"There is no gunpowder here," Dona Espicia answered. "Be on your way!"

"Ma'am, we know there is gunpowder stored here," he said. "We'll just load that while we're waiting for your men to return. Then we'll deal with the skunks who did what they did to our men."

"Are you thieves then?" she asked.

While they argued, Molly backed into the hacienda, unnoticed by the bearded American. Once inside, she whirled and ran to the kitchen.

"Maria, go warn Dolores the Americans are here. Is

there a place you can hide Jaime where they cannot find him?" Molly asked. Fear filled her at what they might do after seeing how their own men were tortured to death.

"Si, senorita. Do you come with us?"

"No, Maria. Dona Espicia needs me."

Molly flew out the kitchen door, taking the back route to Michael's house. There was no rear door, but an open window provided her entrance. Inside, she groped for the gun cabinet key, then opened it. Perhaps she was not adept at shooting a pistol, but Colin O'Bannion's daughter had learned about rifles. Selecting two, she loaded them, then returned to the hacienda in the same manner she had come.

The kitchen was empty when she entered. Gruff words came from the big salon, mixed with interspersions by Dona Espicia. Molly paused in the hall to listen.

"We should kill every one of you," the gruff voice said, "but we don't fight women. You can say your gibberish prayers for your men, though, for they'll be the ones that need them! You just stay quiet in here, ma'am, and you won't get hurt."

Shots sounded in the courtyard, drawing his attention. Molly stepped inside with one of the rifles leveled at him.

"Get out of here!" she ordered.

His head swiveled around to show the surprise on his face. "Put that rifle down," he said sharply. "Ain't you the lady came to tell about the bodies?"

"Get out of here," Molly repeated.

More shots sounded that made up his mind. With a shake of his head, he ran out the open door to his comrades. Quickly, Molly slammed and bolted the heavy front door.

"The windows, Molly! We need to close them," Dona

Espicia said. She set an example by drawing heavy shutters from behind the hangings and bolting them shut over the windows. "Don Pablo insisted the house be made into a fortress, so we can thank him for this protection."

They went around the house securing the windows and bolting doors while the shooting in the courtyard increased in intensity. Angry shouts could be heard over the noisy commotion. Dona Espicia limped to the front window Molly was securing. "Have the *defensarios* returned?" she asked.

Molly put her eye to the gun slit in the shutter and tried to see around the courtyard. "I think the shots must be coming from Casa Grande, Dona," she said. "At least the castle seems to be the target of the Americans."

"Ah, yes," the older woman said grimly. "Condesa Magnifica would welcome the opportunity to exhibit her prowess. She brags of the number of men she killed in her youth, when she and Don Luis first came to the wilderness."

She looked around, spying the other rifle in the hall. "Get the other gun, Molly, and hide them both. If we do nothing, I doubt we will be hurt."

Molly retrieved the other rifle and hid both beneath the window hangings, then returned to the gun slit.

The courtyard was filled with men on horseback—the rough men on the shaggy horses she had seen at the settlement, only more than she remembered. They were firing at Casa Grande, reloading, then firing again. Bullets came from two of the many windows on the second floor of the building, and Molly wondered if the old Condesa was still able to fire a gun. Or perhaps Noyo had recruited one of the other servants to help him against the Americans. At least they were doing something about this invasion, she thought rebelliously.

"Somehow they have found out about the gunpowder Jabal brought in," Dona Espicia said. "I questioned his wisdom in doing this, for I was afraid this would happen. Secrets cannot be kept when so many are involved, especially during a war."

"They are searching the buildings," Molly said, her eye still at the slit.

The laugh-snort sounded. "They won't find what they are looking for!"

Molly turned to look at her. "Where is it hidden?" she asked.

"It is better for you not to know, Molly. Just pray that Jabal and the men return soon."

The noise in the courtyard dimmed as shots were spaced at greater intervals. When Molly again peered out, she saw that the windows in the castle were now covered like the windows in the hacienda. Condesa Magnifica and her manservant must have decided discretion was the better part of valor.

Then the same bearded man broke from the crowd and came charging up the steps to the veranda. Steady cursing came through the wooden door while he kicked at it.

"Open up!" he shouted.

Molly could not see him through the slit, but she could see the other men who had heard his shout. Another joined the first on the veranda and the blows on the door doubled. Soon another joined them and concerted thuds made the door shake.

It was not long before the door splintered around its bolts and locks and was forced open. Molly shrank into the draperies beside the rifles she had stashed there.

Dona Espicia drew herself to her full height and stared disdainfully at the men who came in. "You are intruding into my home and I will not have it!" she said. "Get out!"

The man who had first questioned her asked again, "Where is the gunpowder, ma'am?"

"I don't know what you are talking about," she answered.

"We know it is somewhere here at ranch headquarters and you might as well tell us where," he said.

Dona Espicia kept her mouth stubbornly shut.

"Start searching the sheds again," the bearded man said to his companions. "Maybe we missed it. I'll look here in the house."

The men left and the bearded man studied the room.

If he searches the house, he will find Jaime, Molly thought desperately. She stepped from the draperies with a rifle held ready. "Get out of here right now!" she ordered.

He turned to face her with a frown on his face. "Put that gun down before you get hurt," he growled. When Molly made no move to do as he ordered, he walked toward her.

When he reached to take the gun from her hand, Molly pulled the trigger. An astonished look appeared on his face while a large hole gushed blood from his stomach.

Molly stared, horrified at her handiwork.

The bearded man stared as though he couldn't believe what he saw on himself. Then with both hands clutched to his middle in a vain attempt to stop the flow of blood, he bent forward in a grotesque bow that ended on the floor.

Dona Espicia took the gun from Molly's hands. "Now

the fat is in the fire for sure," she said. "Oh, Molly, why did you kill him?"

"Because of Jaime," Molly answered dully. "Do you suppose they would spare him? He is a Spanish don, no matter his age, so they would have no pity. I saw the Americans our men tortured to death."

They stared at each other in dismay. The noise in the courtyard increased and fresh volleys of shots rang out over the shouting bedlam.

"The door!" Dona Espicia exclaimed. She dropped the rifle and hurried to close it.

Molly's eyes returned to the body on the floor. She had killed a man! She felt sick and dizzy as the realization came home to her.

Then a sharp cry came from Dona Espicia. She staggered back from the open door, one hand held to her neck. Before Molly could reach her, she crumpled to the floor.

With the sound of war as accompaniment, Molly sank down beside the fallen woman. Blood gushed over her hand from a black hole in her neck. It spread in an ever-wider stain on her clothing and into the deep pile of the carpet.

Numbly, Molly felt the limp wrist. There was no pulse. She put her ear to Dona Espicia's chest, straining to hear a heartbeat. There was none. She sat back on her heels, unable to comprehend what she knew. Dona Espicia was dead!

The battle raged in the courtyard while Molly knelt again beside the still form. A flood of grief washed over her. A torrent of tears blinded her. They ran down her cheeks to soak the unmoving bosom of her friend and she cried as she had cried when she was a child and her mother died. Great tearing sobs shook her body and in between she keened as only an Irishman can mourn when death appears.

When at last her wild grief had abated somewhat, it penetrated her consciousness that the tumult in the courtyard had ceased. She raised her head and wiped her eyes with her skirt, sniffling unevenly.

Michael stood looking down at his mother's body, his face distorted with shock and disbelief at what he saw.

"Mama . . ." he said brokenly.

Molly rose, saying, "Michael, you are back!"

Elbowing her aside, he picked his mother up in his arms, cradling her as though she were a baby.

"Oh, Michael," Molly said, and her tears welled afresh.

As though in a trance, he walked with his burden to Dona Espicia's room and laid her body on the bed. Her eyes were closed, but he brushed his hand over them as though sealing the lids, then crossed himself, and knelt by her side.

He stayed in that position for a long time as he silently prayed for his mother's soul. At last he crossed himself again and rose to his feet.

"Michael, please . . ." Molly said uncertainly.

His eyes were full of tears when he turned.

"Oh, Michael, I am so sorry . . ." Molly's arms went around him and she held him through a spasm of grief that seemed never to end.

Chapter Seventeen

At last Michael took a deep breath and stood away from Molly. He picked up a blanket and covered his mother's body. "Mamacita, mamacita," he murmured, "I shall miss you terribly." He bent his head for a moment before he turned back to Molly.

"Where are the others?" he asked.

She stared at him for a few seconds before the question penetrated her mind.

"Oh . . . I sent Maria to hide Dolores and Jaime," she said. "I don't know where they are . . ." Then she mentally shook herself. "Are the Americans gone, Michael?"

"For now," he said absently. "The cellar! Perhaps they are in the cellar."

He hurried from the room so fast Molly had to run to keep up. In the kitchen he pushed an oval rug aside to reveal the outlines of a trap door. Kneeling, he pulled the door open. Below them Maria and Dolores hovered protectively over Jaime and Mouse.

"Come out," Michael said, extending a hand to help them climb the steps.

Jaime came up first. "Los Americanos! Tio Michael, I

was not afraid of them. Maria made me hide," Jaime said indignantly. "I would rather have fought them!"

"I'm sure you would," his uncle said tactfully. "However, the Americans are on the run now with our *defensarios* close on their heels."

He waited until Jaime scampered out of hearing before adding, "But they will be back."

"Did they find the gunpowder?" Molly asked.

"No."

"Is that the reason they will return?"

He scowled and his voice was bitter as he answered her. "It might be *one* of the reasons for their return, but Don Jabal has seen to another. Killing two of their men was bad enough, but to torture them in such a manner . . . that was abominable. Now they will not rest until he is destroyed."

"But they are so few," Molly protested.

A laugh-snort much like his mother's came from his mouth. "Few!" he exclaimed. "The soldiers of the United States are coming! I heard the news at Fort Sutter before the so-brave *defensarios* rescued me from my prison. The number of *soldados* will make Jabal's army seem as the fingers on one hand! There are hundreds, perhaps thousands of them."

Hundreds? Thousands of enemies? Molly quaked at the thought. How could Jabal overcome an army of that size? Perhaps he might think he was a god, but he was not. He was only a man.

Maria and Dolores had followed Jaime out of the cellar and were listening to Michael's words.

Now Maria said, "I had better go see to Dona Espicia. All this commotion is bad for her."

Michael put out his hand to stop her. "The Condesa

has been shot, Maria."

A wail of fright came from the housekeeper. "Where is she, Don Michael? Have you sent for the doctor?"

He shook his head. "A doctor is not necessary, Maria. The Condesa is dead."

Molly marveled at the steadiness of his voice so short a time after his grief had overwhelmed him.

Then Michael continued in the same dispassionate way. "You will prepare the body for burial, Maria. I will go to fetch Padre Rodriquez when Don Jabal and the *defensarios* return from their chase."

"What about the American?" Molly asked. "He should be buried, too. If the Americans find another of their men dead, their wrath will be even worse, Michael."

"What American?"

Molly took a deep breath and her voice wavered as she said, "The one I shot."

He studied her for a moment, then shrugged. "Others are dead, so one more will not matter. However, he should be buried, so I will take care of it."

He thought for a moment, then apparently made up his mind about something, for he said, "Molly, I want you to take Jaime to his secret cave in the hills. Take enough supplies so you can stay there until I come for you."

"You know about the cave, Michael?" Molly asked. "Jaime told me no one else knew about it."

"Feliciana told me."

"Michael, she is dead!" Molly blurted out.

"How do you know?" he asked.

Molly told him how Mouse found the ring in the rubble and brought it to her. Michael's brown eyes hardened, but he said not a word. When she had finished, he resumed his instructions as though her words had not been said.

"Take Dolores with you and Jaime when you go to the cave," he said. "She can help amuse Jaime. Keep Jaime and Mouse quiet as you can."

"But why do we have to leave?" Molly asked rebelliously.

"You must leave and take Jaime with you because the Americans will return," he said patiently. "I do not know when this will happen, but in their present mood even a very young Spanish don will not be safe."

He walked to the big salon with Molly at his heels. The rifles lay on the carpet near the dead American. He glanced at the body, then stooped to pick up the guns.

"These will do you no good at close range, Molly. Get Jaime and Dolores ready to leave while I get you a pistol that won't knock you down if you have to use it."

By the time Michael returned, Molly had Dolores, Jaime, and herself laden with the few necessities they would need for a short stay in the cave.

"Where is *abuelita?*" Jaime asked. "If there will be danger, should she not accompany us?"

"Your grandmother is dead, Jaime," Michael said. "Come now, you must be on your way."

Jaime stared at his uncle while tears filled his eyes. "No! *Abuelita* cannot be dead. She cannot . . . she cannot! You are telling me an untruth, is it not so?" he asked hopefully.

Michael sighed as he gathered his small nephew into his arms. "I am not lying, Jaime, although I wish I were. Your grandmother was shot by the Americans, although it was more than likely just an accident."

Jaime struggled free and stood with his fists clenched and rage on his face. "*Los Americanos!* If I had not been put in the cellar, I could have protected *abuelita!*" He glared at Michael and Molly and Dolores, then aimed his words at the maid. "See what you made happen?"

"No, Jaime, there was nothing you could have done," Michael said. "There were too many of them. Don Jabal should have left some of his men here to guard you."

"Papa did not know they were coming," Jaime said. "If I am to be Conde, I should have been allowed to defend the hacienda and *abuelita.*" There was a look of defiance on his face as he added, "I will not go hide again in a cave. If the Americanos return, I want to be here to shoot them!" Then a sob came from his throat and he said, "They cannot kill *abuelita* and not be punished for it."

Molly handed the small monarch her kerchief, saying, "Wipe your eyes, Jaime, and blow your nose."

"I am not crying!" he said angrily, although tears rolled down his cheeks. "And I will not go hide."

"Dona Espicia would not want the remaining Conde del Valle to so endanger himself," Michael said gently. "Nor would Don Jabal. If your Papa were here, he would tell you to go to the cave with Aunt Molly."

"Condesa Magnifica says I should fight beside Papa," Jaime retorted. "She says Don Luis was a man from birth and that I have taken too long to grow up."

"Condesa Magnifica has strange ideas, Jaime," Molly said. "Your uncle knows more of what should be done."

Jaime looked uncertainly from Michael to Molly.

"Mouse will be much safer in the cave," Michael said. "Your little dog is so small he could be trampled under a horse's hoof with the rider never knowing it happened."

Jaime stood uncertain as he mulled their words, but the mention of Mouse must have tipped the scales in favor of the cave. He nodded. "*Correcto,*" he said with a sigh. "Why does it take so long to grow big?" He picked up one of the bundles. "Are the horses ready?"

"The horses were run off," Michael said. "The Americans opened the stalls and gates and drove the horses out. Now you will have to travel afoot. It is probably better that way, for you will not be so noticeable as riders would be."

Jaime nodded, then returned the bundle to the floor. "Can I go see *abuelita* before we leave, Tio Michael? I wish to kiss her good-bye."

"No, Jaime, it is better that you don't see her now," Michael said. "She would want you to remember her as she was when alive and smiled at you."

"She is now with God, *si?*" Jaime asked.

Michael nodded, then looked at Molly. "Do you remember how to get to the cave?" he asked. "It will be dark by the time you get there."

"I know how to get to the cave," Jaime said. "Mama and I went there often."

"Then we had better go," Molly said.

"Go quickly and stay hidden in the trees as much as possible," Michael ordered. "No telling what patrols will be out." He handed Molly the pistol he had gotten for her and some ammunition, showed her how to load the gun, then turned away.

The gun was not as heavy as the pistol Molly had taken before, but it still made an awkward weight concealed in a pocket of her skirt. However, it gave her a sense of security that would help bolster her spirits, so Molly ignored its bumping against her leg. Dolores had taken the largest bundle, so Molly picked up the one that remained.

The three of them slipped out of the back entrance and

crept through the trees until they were away from the courtyard and in the broad valley. Molly could see no one in sight, but she was determined to keep hidden as much as possible.

Mouse let out a yip. "Sh-h!" Jaime said to the squirming puppy under one arm. "Wait a minute, Aunt Molly," he whispered, then handed her the puppy while he shifted the bundle he carried to his back so he would have both hands free. Then he took the little dog from her and cuddled him in both hands. "Sh-h," he whispered again.

"Would you like me to carry the gun, Mollee?" Dolores asked when Molly missed her footing on a rock.

"No, thanks, I am all right, but we all must be quiet," she said, again in a whisper.

The twilight air was growing cooler as they worked their way upward from the valley. Molly stumbled several times, but kept her eyes roving over the countryside. If the Americans returned, she wanted warning of their approach. They must not get their hands on Jaime.

Night was upon them by the time they reached the flower-filled cul-de-sac. Tonight the fog rolled in from the sea in a webby covering that would turn into a thick blanket before long.

Jaime dove through the brush-covered entrance with Mouse. Molly followed more sedately, drawing Dolores inside the cave with her.

They fell panting on the blankets inside, exhausted from the long walk. Jaime turned Mouse loose, curled up with a sigh of relief, and was soon fast asleep. Mouse sniffed at his surroundings, ran back a way into the cave, then returned to curl up next to his master.

Dolores picked up a blanket and laid it on the rug in front of the statue of Mary. "Come, Senorita Mollee," she whispered. "You will be comfortable here."

Molly settled herself while the maid lay on a blanket between Jaime and the entrance to the cave. The Madonna towered over her, although it was too dark in the cave to see her head. Her serene image came to mind, successfully blotting out the horrors of the day for a while, but then they returned in full force. Molly was left sleepless when her mind refused to relinquish thoughts of Dona Espicia and the vengeful Americans through the unending night.

Gentle breathing told Molly the others slept. She tossed restlessly on her hard bed, wondering why she had allowed Michael to send her here. She was not afraid of Americans, despite being guilty of shooting one of them. Why should Colin O'Bannion's daughter cower here? By morning rebellion had replaced her grief over Dona Espicia's death, and she decided to return to the hacienda.

They had brought a modest supply of food which would last longer if only two were eating from it. Before Jaime woke, Molly told Dolores to stay in the cave with him until she returned.

"But why are you going back, Mollee?" the maid asked. "Don Michael will be very angry with you. He would not have sent us here if he had not thought it was the best thing to do."

"I am going back because I must, Dolores. Dona Espicia will be buried today and I shall be there. Besides, I must see Don Jabal when he returns. I have waited too long as it is to tell him something of importance."

Dolores looked doubtful, so Molly repeated her

admonition. "Keep Jaime occupied, Dolores, and stay inside the cave as much as you can. Rather, stay inside the cave and don't go outside *at all*. To keep Jaime safe, the Americans must not know he is here. Do you understand?"

"*Si.*"

Molly walked out into the fog-shrouded morning and started on her way. The black mare would have been very welcome, for the long walk of the day before had made her feet tender, and today an hour's walk rubbed a blister on one heel. When she reached the spot where she had heard the groans of the settlers, a feeling of revulsion crept over her.

There was much to be discussed between Jabal and her. On Molly's part she would tell him of her Indian heritage. On his part there would have to be explanations of many things.

The fog grew yellow as the sun probed delicately into its depths. Reluctantly, the fog gave ground, inching slowly back to the sea from which it had come. While Molly plodded onward, perspiration trickled under her arms and down the back of her gown. She glanced up at the sun, wishing it would be covered by clouds, but none were in sight.

It was long past noon when Molly drew near enough to the hacienda to hear men's voices in the courtyard. She took to the cover of the trees until she was sure they were Spanish voices, then walked into the courtyard.

Men and horses milled in seeming confusion, but then Molly saw that Indians and white men alike were caring for their mounts and equipment. Both were necessary for their survival. Don Jabal was deep in conversation with several of his men, so Molly slipped into the hacienda without being discovered.

No one was in sight so Molly went to Dona Espicia's room and found Maria weeping beside the bed. She looked up when Molly entered and wiped at her eyes with her apron.

"Senorita O'Bannion! Why have you come back so soon? Is Don Jaime with you?" she asked.

"Jaime is safe, Maria," Molly said. "I came back because I wish to attend Dona Espicia's funeral. Where is Michael?"

"Don Michael went to fetch Padre Rodriguez," the housekeeper answered. She looked around nervously. "Don Jabal has returned and is very angry. He asked where you and Jaime were and I told him I did not know. Oh, Miss Molly, Don Michael ordered me to tell *no* one where you were, so I did not, but now I am very frightened."

"You need not be frightened of Don Jabal," Molly said. "His mind is on this war going on. He was very likely only worried about his son and me. I will talk to him."

Maria had washed the body of Dona Espicia and dressed her in a black gown with ruching around the neck to cover the hole the bullet had made. She looked quite peaceful and without the anxious frown she had worn lately. Molly closed her eyes and stood beside the bed. Should she pray to the God of her father or to the Great Spirit of Amatil's people?

Soon an Indian maid knocked timidly on the door jamb. Maria went to the open doorway and asked, "What is it?"

"The coffin is finished, ma'am. The men wish to know where to place it."

"Tell them to bring it here," the housekeeper said.

Molly turned away from the bed. "We must wait for Don Michael before we get on with the funeral, Maria."

"Yes, ma'am, I know. But when Padre Rodriguez and Don Michael arrive, we must have everything prepared so the funeral can be held quickly." Tears welled up in her eyes as she added, "Dona Espicia must not be left too long before burial. She would be humiliated if her body gave her shame."

"Yes, of course," Molly murmured. She sighed. Death was a bitter enemy, but one that could not be bested by combat. She left the room, only to meet Jabal in the hall.

"Where have you been?" he demanded. "Where is my son? Again I have wasted the energy of my men in a search for you. Where have you been and where is Don Jaime?"

"We went into the hills in case the Americans returned before you," Molly said. "Jaime is quite safe. I wanted to be here for Dona Espicia's funeral."

Grief replaced the anger on his face. "Mama Condesa died in battle," he said. "It was not her way, but now she will be at peace." Then he added, "And I shall kill the Americanos who did this," and the anger had returned.

Two Indian men carried a wooden coffin past them into Dona Espicia's room. Soon they returned and Jabal ordered them back to the grooming of mounts.

"I must go," he said. "The Americanos scattered like quail when we drew near. They disappeared into the brush and trees as though they had left the face of the earth, but we shall catch the cowardly knaves!"

"You will stay for the funeral, won't you?" Molly asked. "I would like to talk to you about many things, Jabal. Can we do this now?"

"Yes, I will stay for the funeral," he said, "although

the more time we give the Americanos to regain their courage, the harder we shall have to fight. I have no time for talk just now, my dear. Later, perhaps." Then he turned and went out the door.

Later? Molly thought indignantly. Why was the man who said he loved her and wanted her to marry him too busy to talk to her when she asked him? If he were waiting for the Padre to arrive, he could certainly make time for Molly. She hurried after him, pausing on the veranda to see where he had gone.

Across the courtyard Condesa Magnifica was emerging from the castle holding on to Noyo's arm instead of being carried in her chair. Her back had a stooped look and her footsteps were uneven, but with her cane in one hand and Noyo's arm in the other, the old woman hobbled along.

When she reached the steps to the hacienda, Jabal saw her and came to offer assistance. "Condesa Magnifica, you must not exert yourself in this heat," he said.

"The Irisher is dead!" she said triumphantly. "She should have perished long ago." She looked up at Molly and added, "Why did you not die with her?"

Anger rose in Molly and she looked to Jabal for support.

"Condesa Magnifica, you must not excite yourself like this," he said soothingly.

The noise in the courtyard had died to silence as the men looked at Don Jabal and his grandmother.

"Los Americanos did this!" the old woman shouted, pointing to the splintered doors in the buildings where the Americans had searched for gunpowder. "Noyo and I drove them away!" Her glare defied contradiction. "Don Luis and I took care of what was ours! Nobody . . . *nobody* took it from us!"

294

"Yes, *abuelita*," Jabal said. "You have more spirit than any woman I know. We have chased the Americans away, and after the funeral we ride to give them another lesson."

The old woman looked around at the tired mounts and the haggard men. "Your army will do you no good in the shape it is in," she said. "Men today are not as they were in Don Luis's time. Let them rest until morning, Don Jabal." A sneer twisted her mouth. "Today bury the Irisher and make sure the body is well covered so she will not return to haunt us."

"It will be as you say, Condesa Magnifica," Jabal said.

The old woman's eyes rose to where Molly stood on the veranda. "Why do you allow this . . . this *Americano* to remain in your midst? She is a spy for the enemy!" she screeched. "Look how she reported the bodies of the *estiercal* in the woods to the officials at Santa Rosa."

Jabal glanced up at Molly with eyes that made her shiver. What would he exact as a price for her kindness to the Americans? Then her chin rose. Whatever he thought, Jabal had much to answer for also.

Then Jabal offered his arm to his grandmother. "I do not think the senorita a spy, *abuelita*. She is my fiancee."

"*Fiancee?*" The malevolence in her voice brought a gasp from Molly's lips. "You fool! I hoped she had been killed, but instead, she shows up brazen as brass!"

"Now, Condesa . . ." Jabal began, but the old woman continued her tirade.

"She is worse than the Irisher! This one is a breed! A dirty half Indian who pretends to belong with white people." Venom overcame her while a fit of coughing nearly strangled her as her face grew red.

Jabal gently patted the stooped back until the fit

subsided. His eyes went to the group of men who stood mesmerized by the scene.

Condesa Magnifica stamped her cane against the cobblestones. "Hah!" she said pettishly. "Now you know. Take me back to Casa Grande. I will not associate with breeds!"

Her muttering continued while Jabal and Noyo supported the shaking body back to her abode.

Molly's heart plummeted at her words, but then she raised her chin. She was not ashamed of her heritage, but she would have liked to tell Jabal herself. The manner in which the old woman had screeched it out made it a shameful thing.

Then she saw Padre Rodriguez and Don Michael ride into the courtyard and she waited to greet them. They rode to the steps of the hacienda, then dismounted and turned their horses over to an Indian who came to take them.

"This is a sad day for the world," the priest said. "Dona Espicia was such a woman as we cannot afford to lose."

"She is in her room awaiting your blessing, Father," Molly said.

The priest disappeared inside and Molly was left facing Michael.

"What are you doing here, Molly?" he asked. "I told you to stay in the cave until I came for you. Is Jaime here, too?"

"Jaime is with Dolores in the cave, Michael," she said. "I came back so I could attend Dona Espicia's funeral. She was my friend."

Michael nodded, saying, "Then perhaps we had best get at it," before he followed the priest into the house.

The funeral cortege was a sad one. The coffin was placed in the same wagon that had carried them to the picnic on the beach. Family members and Molly walked close behind and the servants and men of Jabal's army trailed after them. Padre Rodriguez pleaded weariness from his long ride and sat beside the driver on the wagon.

The procession passed Casa Grande on its way out. Molly glanced up at the windows as they passed, but this time she saw no one watching. Condesa Magnifica had spread her poison and now she could relax. Jabal had showed the same courtesy to Molly after the old woman's news as he had before, but there was a distant look in his eyes that made Molly uneasy.

The late condesa del Valle was buried in a grave beside Don Pablo, as befitted the mistress of Costa Cordillera. Dona Veronica lay on the other side of Don Pablo, so both of his wives were given the same honor. Before the dirt was shoveled atop the casket, however, Padre Rodriguez preached a long account of Dona Espicia's goodness that influenced her family for so many years. Then he piled blessing after blessing on the dead woman in the hope it would help her to the heaven she deserved. By the time he finished, all the mourners were fidgeting.

As the mourners straggled back to the courtyard in small groups, Molly stayed for a moment at the grave. The headstones for Don Pablo and Dona Veronica were identical, and she wondered bitterly if the "Irisher" would be given one as grand. Then she remembered the look on Michael's face and her bitterness left. He would see that his mother had the honor due her.

Although it was the custom to go to the cemetery on foot, Molly noticed Chia had three horses waiting in the shade of the trees. Now that the service was finished,

Michael and Jabal mounted two of them and galloped toward the hacienda. Chia looked after them, then walked to where Molly stood.

"Senorita," he said uncertainly. "Where is Dolores?"

"She is with Jaime in the hills," Molly said. "She is safe, Chia."

"*Gracias,*" he said, backing away. Then he mounted and galloped after the men.

"He is a loyal servant," a quiet voice said behind her, "but his love for Dolores is stronger."

Molly turned to see Padre Rodriguez.

"May I walk with you, child?" he asked.

"Of course, Padre."

They walked in sober silence, but Molly felt his eyes on her several times, and at last he spoke. "You look very tired, my child."

"I have had very little sleep lately, Padre."

"Shall we rest for a little?" he asked. "I fear I am not a good walker."

A boulder beside the path served as resting place. Molly sat at one side, leaving a space for the priest. He sat with a grunt, puffing from his labors.

"Dona Espicia will be greatly missed," he said softly. "It would be well to send word to Dona Feliciana to return. The hacienda needs a mistress."

"Dona Feliciana is dead," Molly said flatly.

"How do you know this, my child?"

With as few words as possible, she told him of finding Feliciana's ring in the rubble, and of how Dolores had assured her Feliciana never removed the ring from her finger.

When she had finished, he was quiet for a while, then sighed, saying, "It was too much to believe the burning of

298

the chapel shortly after her supposed departure merely a coincidence, but I did. It is well Dona Espicia did not live to learn the full extent of Don Jabal's sinfulness."

"But she knew about my finding the ring, Padre, for I told her," Molly said. "Perhaps it was not Don Jabal who killed Feliciana. Condesa Magnifica might have sent Noyo on the errand."

"Why do you say that, child?"

"Because she has sent Noyo to rob my room and then ordered him to kill me when I went to retrieve the things he took," Molly said.

He rose, saying, "We had better be on our way," and they walked again toward the hacienda.

"Will you stay the night, Padre?" Molly asked.

"Michael has already offered the hospitality of his house. I believe it will be more restful there than in the hacienda this night. The Indians are devastated over the death of their mistress," Padre Rodriguez said.

Molly nodded, bidding him goodnight as he left her when they reached Michael's house.

Chapter Eighteen

Although Maria and some of the Indian maids were in the hacienda, it seemed strangely empty to Molly. Without the cheery presence of Dona Espicia, the heart of the hacienda was gone. The maids went about their chores with sad faces and general gloom filled the house.

Suddenly Molly was overcome with such a weariness as she had never known. Her sleepless night and the screeching tirade she had been through left her tired enough to die. The blister on her heel stung like fire and her clothing was still damp from her perspiring trip from cave to hacienda. She wanted nothing more than to soak in a hot bath and then go to sleep.

Slowly, Molly climbed the stairs to her room. Her sore heel throbbed at each step. An empty hacienda inhabited only by sadness. Dona Espicia dead, Jaime and Dolores in hiding . . . and Jabal. How would he react to his grandmother's words?

Oh, why was everything going so badly, Molly wondered. She had delayed too long in telling Jabal of her mother, and now Condesa Magnifica had shouted it out to everyone as though it were a sin Molly had committed. Her Bible that she treasured so much must have given the old woman the weapon to use against Molly. Amatil was an Indian name, a fact the old woman would know well. Molly sighed. Perhaps if she could sleep for a while . . .

Her room echoed the hollow house when she walked to look at the portrait of Feliciana. There was a haunting sadness around the eyes she hadn't noticed before. Despondently, she kicked the shoe from her aching heel, then sent the other after it. The rest of her clothing soon lay in a heap beside them.

It felt good to get out of the sweaty garments she had worn for so long, and it was too much trouble to replace them. Without Dolores to organize the maids into bringing a bath, Molly decided it was too much trouble to bother. Naked, she snuggled into the soft covers, groaning with relief that at last her body could rest.

The screech of a bird in distress sounded somewhere in the distance. Her thoughts flew to Jaime and Dolores. She hoped they were safe inside the cave. Had the Condesa turned Culebra out for his nightly hunt? Was it his call she had heard? Or was it Huk with a warning about the evil to befall Dona Espicia? If so, he was much too late. Culebra . . . Huk . . . the two became muddled in her mind. Condesa Magnifica's evil face appeared in the mixture as Molly escaped into deep and dreamless sleep.

It was still dark outside when Molly woke. Drowsily, she listened to the night noises coming from the trees nearby. What had wakened her? She thought she had heard a voice. Then it came again.

"*Querida,*" a husky voice breathed into her ear. Bristly hairs tickled around it.

Molly put out a hand, startled, and then she felt a body—a naked body! Stretched out on the bed beside

301

her! She sat up, her heart in her throat.

"What . . . ?" she gasped, then realized it was Jabal. "What are you doing here?" she demanded.

His arm went around her as he pulled her back on the pillow beside him. "Now we shall not wait for marriage," he said, almost gloating.

"Get out of here, Jabal!" she said, struggling against his arm. "I'll scream!"

A hand clamped over her mouth while another explored her body. "Mama Condesa can no longer hear, little Indian. My precious stepbrother and his priest are sound asleep. You don't want to disturb them, do you?" His mouth replaced the hand on her lips and he kissed her until she could no longer breathe.

Molly wriggled from under him, gasping for air, and more afraid than she had ever been. He grabbed her again and dread filled her as she struggled against Jabal's strength. The more she fought, the more exultant Jabal became.

"Little wildcat," he muttered, cuffing her after she drew three long scratches down his cheek.

Her ears buzzed from the blow and her vision blurred, but still she fought on. "Is this how you keep your word to my father?" she gasped.

He held both her hands in one of his, the other raised to clamp over her mouth if necessary. "I gave my word to a white man, *querida*. He did not tell me his daughter was a breed."

Molly ducked her head forward and sank her teeth into the soft flesh just below his shoulder. A grunt of pain came from him as his grip loosened on her hands. Before he could tighten his grasp again, Molly slipped from the opposite side of the bed and ran toward the door.

Before she reached it, his arm came around her waist and she was lifted kicking. A resounding smack of his hand on each of her buttocks left smarting burns where they landed, but she had presence of mind enough to snatch a sharp scissors from the bureau as he carried her back to the bed and flung her on it.

In his mania he did not notice the weapon she carried, but as he tried to mount her, one blade penetrated his flesh and a roar of pain almost deafened her. He scrambled to pull the blade out and when he did, the other blade ripped the soft flesh of Molly's stomach. She gasped and watched in horror as the blood from their bodies puddled on her body.

Jabal rose, his eyes incredulous as he tried to keep his blood from spurting forth with both hands.

"You little bitch!" he snarled. "You'll pay for this!"

With both hands clutching his wound, he faded into the darkness and Molly heard the door open and close after him. She yanked a pillowcase from one of the pillows and held it against her, sobbing as she wondered if she would die.

Sickness filled Molly when he had gone. Leaning over the side of the bed while she still clutched the cloth to her cut, she let the contents of her stomach empty onto the carpet, retching when there was no more to be ejected. Perspiration covered her body as she hung there. Then shame engulfed her. It was a new emotion for her—one that puzzled her.

Wearily, she pulled herself back to the pillow and lay panting. The cut was a superficial one, she decided when she lifted the cloth, for it had stopped oozing blood and now just smarted dreadfully. Every bone in her body seemed to ache and her bruised flesh throbbed as the nerves beneath protested their treatment.

Why was she so ashamed? She felt dirty in a way she had never known, abased to a depth she could hardly believe. A man had pawed over her naked body and forced brutal kisses onto her mouth. She had been powerless to stop what had happened, so why was the shame on *her* head?

She drew the covers up to her chin. Perhaps it was because she had loved the man she thought Jabal was. Her stubbornness had made her cling to him despite all the warnings she had been given. Tonight there was not even the smell of liquor on his breath to give the excuse of drunkenness for what he had done! Was the fact that she was half Indian excuse enough?

Her physical pain was immense, but her tears dried up. She lay pondering the night's events while within her grew a steeliness of purpose she had not known she could attain. Jabal would never touch her again! Perhaps he would not try now that she had shown her metal by driving a blade into his body. But if he did, she would keep him from her somehow.

Maria's quiet entrance interrupted her thoughts. The housekeeper opened the draperies, saying, "Are you awake, senorita? It is time for breakfast."

She noticed the mess beside the bed and stopped short. "You have been ill?" she asked. "What has happened?"

Molly just shook her head, unable to speak.

Maria looked at Molly's white face, then drew the covers back and moved the pillowcase. When she saw the cut, she put the cloth back and quickly replaced the covers while her shock showed on her face.

Molly closed her eyes. There were various sounds, then the door closed and silence reigned. She waited a moment, then cautiously opened her eyes.

The room was empty and Molly alone again. Would the housekeeper reject her because of what happened? Perhaps the whole world would blame her instead of Jabal, especially if Jabal were badly injured. She had never felt so alone in her life as she was now.

Then the door opened and Maria entered. She had a bucket of steaming water and an armful of cloths. Setting the bucket beside the bed, she gently turned back the covers and shook her head indignantly at the bruises on Molly's body before she set to work. With one of the cloths dipped in the water, she carefully bathed the area around the cut, then took a bottle from her pocket and poured disinfectant that brought a cry of pain from her patient. Then she carefully washed Molly from head to toe, much as though she were a baby. When she had finished the bath, she drew a soft nightgown over Molly's head and over her body.

With efficient movements that jarred Molly as little as possible, Maria changed the bedding and plumped the clean pillows beneath her head. When she was satisfied that Molly was as comfortable as possible, the housekeeper went to work scrubbing the carpet beside the bed. It was terribly stained, but the spots gradually disappeared as Maria scrubbed and scrubbed.

When the room was neat, she gathered the soiled bedclothing and her supplies and left, only to return shortly with a tray. She placed the tray on the bedside table, then propped pillows behind Molly until she was sitting up. She filled a cup from the teapot and held it to Molly's mouth.

"Drink, Miss Molly," she said. "Tea is good for you."

Obediently, Molly swallowed. Then she took the cup

from the housekeeper and drank until it was empty.

"Don Jabal has abused you this way," Maria said angrily. "If Dona Espicia were not already dead, she would die of shame that a guest at Costa Cordillera could thus be treated. Oh, I wish the mistress was here! This would not have happened."

"We just fought," she said wearily. "He did not have his way with me." Then she added, "I stabbed him with the scissors and when he pulled it out, the other blade cut me."

One of Maria's hands brushed across her face as though trying to erase something. "Dios mio, it is good you escaped! He does far worse to the Indian girls after he has been in some kind of excitement," she said. "The ones who have returned all hid last night when they heard how he had killed two Americans. They were relieved when he did not come looking."

"Don Jabal tortured those men?"

Maria nodded. "You saw them, senorita?"

"One wasn't quite dead when I found them, Maria. He said the dons had done the torture and killing, but I couldn't believe it of Jabal," Molly said bleakly. "However, now I can believe anything." She handed the empty cup to the housekeeper, then took a deep breath. "How long has he . . . mistreated the Indian girls?"

"Since he was a boy," she answered. "I did not think such a young boy was capable, but he was."

"Why did no one stop him?"

"Who stops a conde from doing anything, senorita? Condesa Magnifica tells him he can do as he pleases. She sends Noyo to kill the babies when they are born."

Molly stared at her, aghast. "Maria! Whatever do you mean?" she asked.

"Whenever Don Jabal has bedded a girl, her baby is born dead, if there is one," she said simply. "Noyo sees that it is so."

"Dona Espicia said she kept looking for his likeness in the children, but could not find any. Did she know of this?"

"She knew of Don Jabal's actions, but not of Noyo's," the housekeeper answered. Her eyes filled with tears. "She would never have permitted such murder had she known."

"Why didn't you tell her?"

Maria twisted her hands nervously. "We are all afraid of Noyo," she whispered. "He obeys Condesa Magnifica's orders much as Culebra does."

"Did Noyo kill Dona Feliciana?"

Her eyes widened in amazement. "Is Dona Feliciana dead, senorita?"

Molly nodded, wincing when she swung her feet to the floor. "I think so, Maria. Will you get my clothing please?" Then a thought occurred. "Or perhaps I had better get things myself, now that you know I am half Indian."

A sad smile was her answer. She went to the closet and selected clean clothing for Molly. "You are still Senorita O'Bannion," she said softly. "I, too, have Indian blood mixed with Spanish. Even the Indians abuse any who are born half white, although it is not their fault, is it?"

"No, it isn't, Maria. My mother was a Cheyenne princess and I am not ashamed of her. The only reason I hadn't told Dona Espicia right away was because my father warned me not to. However, I shall not be so foolish in future."

Ignoring the agony movement caused, Molly dressed

with Maria's help while thoughts churned through her mind. If this was the civilization her father regretted not taking her to, she was through with it. Memories of the peaceful life she had led before Colin O'Bannion died returned and she sighed. There were things she must do before she left this world she did not understand, so she had better be about them.

"Was Don Jabal able to leave on his mission, Maria?" she asked.

She shrugged. "He came from Casa Grande, so Noyo must have treated his wound. Word has arrived that the Americans are preparing to attack us here at the compound. Don Jabal and his men are making ready to defend it. They had planned a mission, but when the messenger arrived with the news, their plans were changed."

"I see," Molly said, stooping to retrieve Michael's pistol from the gown on the floor. She kept her back to Maria, hoping she would not notice, then slipped the gun into the pocket in the folds of the clean gown.

Feeling it was reassuring, but it was a very small gun. Condesa Magnifica had sent Noyo to kill her once, then ordered her death a second time when Molly entered Casa Grande for her property. If she knew of Jabal's desire for Molly, she would make sure Noyo performed his execution next time he was ordered.

Without Dona Espicia to protect her, a feeling of helplessness made Molly uneasy. The pistol in her skirt was no sure protection, but Molly O'Bannion was not dead yet! Her shoulders straightened as she and Maria left the room.

Only Padre Rodriguez was at the table when Molly entered the dining salon. He rose to greet her, then stopped when he saw her colorless face.

"You are not feeling well, Miss Molly?" he asked.

"Good morning, Padre," Molly said. "I am just weary from the happenings of late."

He held a chair for her, noticing the care with which she sat on it, but said nothing until they finished eating.

"Will you go for a walk with me, child?" the priest asked. "It is good to take a morning constitutional to settle one's breakfast."

The last thing Molly felt like doing was walking, but then perhaps the fresh air would lift her spirits, she thought. She nodded and went with Padre Rodriguez. From the veranda they could see the men and horses milling in the courtyard as they prepared to meet the enemy on home ground.

"Let's get away from all this noise," the priest said.

They descended the stairs and skirted the assemblage until they were clear of the courtyard and under the trees. Then Padre Rodriguez found a big rock and sat down.

"Come sit beside me, my child," he said, smiling at Molly. "My feet do not permit too long a constitutional."

Molly sat down, observing, "It is a nice morning."

He sighed. "It would be, indeed, my child, if you were not so distressed." He looked around him, then at Molly. "Tell me, child, was it the funeral or something else that has you so shaken?"

"It was not the funeral, Father," she said. "There have been so many things happening . . ."

"Costa Cordillera is now a ship without a rudder," he said. When Molly said nothing, he asked, "Now that Dona Espicia is gone, would it not be a good idea to send for Dona Feliciana?"

Molly shook her head. "I think she is dead, Father," and she told him of Mouse finding Feliciana's ring in the rubble and how her maid said it was never taken off.

"Perhaps it was not Don Jabal who killed Feliciana," Molly said. "Condesa Magnifica might have sent Noyo to kill her."

"Why do you say that, child?"

"She ordered Noyo to kill me when I displeased her. Now that she has found out I am half Indian, perhaps she will make sure he obeys the next time, especially now she knows I wounded Don Jabal last night."

"What happened last night, my child?" he asked, frowning. "What do you mean, you are half Indian?"

She told him of her heritage and how the old woman had learned of it. Then she told him of her fight with Jabal and how he had tried to rape her after learning she was breed.

"Now I know what that word means," she said bitterly. "Condesa Magnifica will probably send Noyo to kill me as revenge for my stabbing her precious grandson."

"We cannot allow that," he said. "The Indians are all terrified of Noyo, but none will tell me why."

"You do not know of how Don Jabal's . . . *droppings* are disposed of, Padre?"

"Tell me."

Molly repeated Maria's words and saw Padre Rodriguez's face turn from puzzled to stern.

"My poor children," he said, shaking his head. "Even my sturdy faith shakes at times when I wonder what my God is thinking of to allow such monstrosities to occur on His earth." He rose, offering her his arm. "Perhaps we had better continue, my daughter. I must think on this matter and decide what is to be done."

They reached the outer perimeter of the courtyard when they heard shots and the beat of a great many hoofs. Shouts from the *defensarios* told them they were preparing for the attack. The Americans had arrived!

Casa Grande was just ahead of them. The windows were shuttered and the solid rear door closed, turning the castle into a fortress.

"Quickly, child," Padre Rodriguez urged, pulling Molly toward the door.

A quick rap and the sound of his voice demanding admittance brought the door ajar enough for them to slip inside. Then the Indian servant slipped the heavy bar in place, her eyes wide and frightened.

The priest pulled Molly behind him through the long hall to the front vestibule. Noyo stood at the heavy door with his back toward them, a rifle aimed through a narrow slit beside the door. On the balcony above, Condesa Magnifica screeched horrible profanities at the Americans and urged Noyo on, shouting, "Kill them, Noyo! Shoot the Americano bastards and bring me their balls!"

Padre Rodriguez looked up at her with a steady stare. The old woman's shriekings gradually diminished before dying away completely.

The priest bowed. "Madam, we have taken refuge in your house," he said formally.

The old woman noted Molly's presence with a sneer of her lips. Then she turned toward her room. "Stay with the Indios, priest," she said harshly. "I have no need of the likes of you, as you well know."

Molly walked to one of the slotted shutters to see what was happening in the courtyard. A troop of uniformed cavalrymen galloped into the melee, fighting hand-to-hand with the enraged *defensarios*. Wild shots flew through the air and bodies dropped, first here, then there, some to writhe in agony while others lay terribly still. Gunsmoke filled the air like some grimy fog escaped from hell.

Jabal was in the midst, wielding a sword with savage confidence, cutting a swath through the Americans as he worked his way toward a building near the hacienda. Chia and a band of *defensarios* accompanied him, beating back the mounted men that poured into the courtyard in a never-ending stream.

The Spaniards were greatly outnumbered and Molly wondered why they were not trying to reach the stouter Casa Grande. Then Jabal disappeared for a moment inside a shed while his companions kept the Americans at bay. He reappeared with a shout of encouragement for his men and a slash with his sword that unseated one of the mounted cavalrymen and left him bleeding on the ground. Then slowly the *defensarios* beat their way toward Casa Grande, desperately wielding their swords as they retreated.

The confusion in the courtyard was compounded by the smoke of gunpowder. Guns fired, were re-loaded and fired again. Flashing swords stabbed through the air in accompaniment to the barking guns. Cavalrymen left rearing horses to fight on foot, many to fall beneath the savage swords.

Molly spied Michael in the crowd, fighting as energetically as the rest. It seemed as though the Americans would demolish the Spaniards as one after another of the young men was left lying on the cobblestones.

When it looked as though Jabal and his men could not

312

live to reach the castle, an explosion from hell saved them. With a mighty roar, the shed Jabal had entered and quickly left, blew up. The store of gunpowder in its cellar raised the building high in the air and spread devastation awesome to behold.

A sheet of flame covered the area, devouring the sheds and barns like a hungry giant. The hacienda caught fire, seemed haughtily to resist for a moment, then succumbed to the onslaught of the flames. Flaring tongues ate at the ground floor, then raced each other upward to poke inquisitive feelers through the roof. The redwood covering glowed like a huge lantern before it fell to the ravishing foe. When the roof crashed inward with a crack of doom, Molly tore her gaze from the holocaust. Had the whole world gone mad?

The diversion gave Jabal the opportunity to rally his men and reach Casa Grande. "Open up!" he shouted, leading the remnants of his army onto the veranda of the castle.

Noyo slid the bolt free and admitted the panting men, then calmly shot a cavalryman who tried to follow. Then he closed the door and replaced the bolt. With only a glance at the *defensarios,* Noyo returned to his post and fired whenever he had a target.

Molly backed into a corner of the shadowy room and hoped she would be overlooked in the confusion. Padre Rodriguez joined her, shaking his head at the blood that dripped from Jabal's sword.

"Don Jabal seems to go mad in the heat of battle," he said into Molly's ear. "I have seen it happen before."

Jabal had thrown back his head, laughing triumphantly as he waved the bloody weapon. "We have won!" he shouted. "Even the entire American cavalry cannot

313

take our gunpowder. We have used it to send them to hell!"

"Perhaps we sent some of the Americans to the great beyond," Michael said as he made his way to Jabal, "but there are some of us who need wounds cared for before we can fight again, Don Jabal. Shall we set up an aid station?"

"Aid station?" Jabal thundered. "What Spaniard worries about a little blood?" Several of the young men began agreeing with Michael, so Jabal said, "Get some of the maids to doctor our brothers. They are probably hiding in the cellar in fear of our gunpowder."

"I will go ask the Indian maidens to come to your assistance," Padre Rodriguez said as he emerged from their corner. "They will know where to get bandages and disinfectant medicines, I'm sure."

Jabal shrugged, then turned his attention back to his men who were whole. He stationed them through the ground floor at the gunslits, hitting them on the back in encouragement. He looked more like a giant preying eagle than ever before. His eyes flamed with madness that Molly assumed was caused by the bloodletting in the courtyard. How could she ever have thought him gentle and kind? Perhaps the knock on his head had tamed him momentarily when he was so considerate of her welfare when her father died. Perhaps he needed an even greater blow to bring him to his senses now.

Don Jabal bowed elaborately to his grandmother when she appeared on the balcony. "Condesa Magnifica, we shall guard your castle to the death," he said dramatically.

"You fool!" she retorted. Her ire built, burning her

face into a red mask of such incredible ugliness, it brought a stab of fear to Molly's heart. "You idiot! You have destroyed most of your empire," she screeched. "The hacienda and the sheds and barns are destroyed! Only *my* house is left, and that because Don Luis built it of unburnable stone. Perhaps he knew he would have an idiot grandson!"

Padre Rodriguez returned with two maids carrying cloths and basins of water. The wounded men crowded around to have their slashes and bullet holes cleaned and wrapped in strips of cloth to keep the blood inside them.

Condesa Magnifica's eyes bulged while she stomped her cane up and down and apoplexy blurred the tirade that spewed from her mouth.

Jabal stared at his grandmother in amazement. Always before she had applauded his deeds and bolstered his confidence in himself. Then his eyes grew steely and he stood with his legs apart and his sword tip on the floor.

"We can rebuild the hacienda and the sheds, Condesa Magnifica," he shouted. "When we have killed the last American, I will build an empire such as Don Luis never dreamed could exist!"

Suddenly, the old woman caught at her throat, clawing as though to open a passage for air. Her face turned purple while she slowly strangled. Then her knees buckled and she sank to the floor, a strange rasping issuing from her mouth mixed with the foam of her former anger.

Jabal sprang for the stairs and raced to where the Condesa lay. "Condesa Magnifica! *Abuelita!*" he exclaimed, trying to bring her to consciousness. "Get water!" he shouted to no one in particular. "Get Dr. Laughlin.

315

One of you men—ride fast and bring him back. Where is that water?"

Padre Rodriguez toiled up the stairs behind Don Jabal at a slower pace. When he reached the fallen woman, he felt first at her wrist for a pulse, then at her throat, but found none. He shook his head. "The Condesa is dead, Don Jabal," he said. He closed the staring eyes and made the sign of a cross over her head.

"No!" Jabal said harshly. "It cannot be so. Condesa Magnifica will never die! Never!" He shook the black-clad shoulders. "*Abuelita!* Open your eyes!"

"Let her go, Don Jabal. Condesa Magnifica is dead," the priest repeated.

Jabal shoved the priest aside and came running down the steps. "Go tend your mistress, Noyo," he ordered. "She has need of you."

Noyo nodded. He handed his rifle to one of the Spaniards and started for the stairs. Then he stopped and glanced around the room. His half-closed eyes paused when they reached Molly. His gaze was as a cold cloud rising from a grave. A prickle of fear raced up her spine. Then slowly, Noyo turned and walked up the stairs to the balcony.

Padre Rodriguez backed away from the Condesa as Noyo knelt beside her. Noyo lowered his head to the Condesa's mouth as though receiving instructions from her even in death.

Don Jabal rallied his men, raving and frothing much as his grandmother had done just before she died. The young men looked at him strangely, but stationed themselves as he ordered.

Before Noyo rose from Condesa Magnifica's side, he scooped her into his arms, then carried her to the balcony overlooking the room below. He stood there until the men below noticed him and their talk faded away.

"Condesa Magnifica welcomes you to her home," he said in a monotone. "She must rest now, but she will speak to you in the morning." Then he turned and carried his burden into the room from which she came.

Chapter Nineteen

The great blast and the resulting fires sent the Americans scrambling out of harm's way with men and horses fleeing panic-stricken into the valley. There, however, cooler heads called them to a halt and they reorganized into an orderly troop. When the flames died down, the cavalrymen returned to assault Casa Grande. They used one of the hitching racks they had torn apart as a battering ram to break the huge door. Thud after thud was heard as they repeatedly struck the heavy wood.

Inside, the fiery Don Carillo confronted Don Jabal. "They will be inside soon, sir! Let us retreat to my rancho and there regroup."

"Retreat?" Don Jabal asked incredulously. "Retreat? I never run from any enemy, sir."

"We will not be running from them, Don Jabal," Don Carillo said. "The Americanos left the courtyard to reorganize themselves. It seems wise that we do the same."

Don Jabal's extended pupils seemed almost on the point of bursting from his eyes, but then his face changed. A crafty smile brought the flash of a dimple as he said, "Yes . . . why not?" He raised his sword high over his head, shouting, "Gentlemen, shall we go?"

"What about Condesa Magnifica?" Molly asked in a loud voice.

Her question brought Jabal's attention, but he looked at her as though she were a stranger.

"Who?" he asked.

"Your grandmother," she answered.

A frown beetled his eyebrows. "Women have no place in the affairs of men! What are you doing here?" Then he ignored her and again waved his sword with a shouted, "Gentlemen!"

Jabal had dismissed his grandmother as though she had never been, Molly thought wonderingly. How could his men still follow him, when he was obviously mad? Then her attention was pulled elsewhere.

The front door of Casa Grande cracked under the repeated blows and Molly cringed back into the draperies. What would the Americans do when the door gave way? She was saved from her speculations when Michael grasped her arm.

"Come, Molly, we must get out of here," he said.

They fled with the *defensarios* and Jabal through the hall to a small door. Jabal produced a key that unlocked it. Behind the door was a dark steep stairway leading downward. He tossed Michael the key saying, "Lock it behind you, brother dear," then led the small band down the steps.

The castle door cracked with a splintering of wood, and Molly knew the Americans had entered. Their shouts echoed in the big front hall as they began the search for the Spaniards.

When the last of Jabal's men had entered the passage, Michael pushed Molly through, squeezing her between the man and himself while he pulled the door closed and locked it.

Molly stumbled down the steps until her feet felt cobblestones. A light flickered up ahead. Jabal swung a lantern on high, motioning the men onward to another narrow hall at the other side of the room.

Molly gasped when she saw the surroundings. They were in a damp dungeon holding every instrument of torture she had ever read about. Chains hung from the ceiling and a rack stood in the middle. Whips and branding irons lined the walls. Then the light vanished.

Again Michael's hand was on her arm and he said, "Hurry, Molly. We had better keep up with the men."

"This is a terrible place," Molly said with a shudder.

"I hope the Americans tear this place down piece by piece," Michael said.

In her heart Molly echoed his wish, for this . . . this *horror* was the secret power that ruled Costa Cordillera. She wished she had never seen it.

They entered a narrow tunnel and trod on each other's heels as they fled from the enemy upstairs. The nightmare seemed endless to Molly as she speculated on just how far the passage extended. When she was panting for air and about to drop from exhaustion, she smelled the sea. A patch of dim light showed above where the men scrambled up a ladder. They were at last emerging from the tunnel!

Michael pushed Molly upward over the edge and she tumbled onto grass. When her eyes grew accustomed to the light, she saw they were in the old cemetery behind the chapel site. One of the tombstones was tipped over to show the exit of the passageway.

"Don Luis was a cautious man," Michael murmured

into Molly's ear.

Don Jabal gave harsh whispered orders, driving the men onward.

"We had better stay with them," Michael whispered.

"What about Jaime and Dolores?" Molly asked. "They will be wondering what is happening and might return to the hacienda to look for me."

Michael shook his head. "Gunshots can be heard for a very long distance. They will surely have heard them. Dolores will not be so foolish as to endanger Don Jaime."

"I hope you're right," Molly said.

"We will need horses and Don Carillo has a full *remuda* at his rancho—more than the *defensarios* will need," Michael said. "We'll wait until Jabal leads the men away, then take our pick. Then we can go to the cave."

He looked at Molly and the fear on her face was plain to see. "Don Carillo's mother is at the rancho. Nothing will harm you while she is there." Rising, he helped Molly to her feet. "What is the matter, Molly? Did Jabal harm you in some way? He acts like a madman during every battle, but when the fighting is done, he calms down."

"Let's go before we lose them," Molly said, pulling away from his hand. She was ashamed of her momentary panic at the thought of facing Jabal again. The pistol still bumped against her thigh when she walked and she fully intended to make use of it at the first opportunity.

Jabal was not *acting* like a madman—he *was* one! He must be completely insane to be so callous toward his beloved Condesa Magnifica. He must have forgotten Molly, probably grouping her with the nameless faces of the Indian girls he had used in the past. Well, she would make sure that he harmed no more of them in future.

Molly and Michael trudged after the men through the

foggy night. The noise the Americans made died away as distance and the deadening fog stifled all sound. When Molly's legs trembled from exhaustion and her steps faltered, Michael swung her up in his arms and carried her for a distance. When Molly regained her strength, she struggled from his grasp. Dawn poked cautious fingers into the sky by the time they reached the Carillo rancho and hacienda.

"Where are the horses, Don Carillo?" Jabal demanded.

Don Carillo gave orders to a servant before answering him. "Don Jabal, we had better eat and rest for the day," he said courteously. "American patrols will be scouring the countryside for us. Tonight we can ride out. The Mexican army is to the south and we can join them."

"I join no Mexican army," Jabal growled. "I will own this land by myself. We shall rest, as you suggest, but tonight we attack. This time we will wipe the Americanos off the face of my land!"

Don Carillo gave him a curious look, then politely bowed his head. *"Mi casa, su casa,"* he murmured.

After the men had refreshed themselves as best they could at the well in the courtyard, a servant announced the readiness of food. Don Carillo led the men to the dining salon, then returned to where Molly stood with Michael.

"Senorita," he said with a slight bow. *"Mi madre* will welcome you herself when she rises. Until then, may a servant show you to quarters where you can rest and refresh yourself? A maid will bring you food. You look weary."

"I am, Don Carillo," Molly said, managing a smile. "Thank you for your hospitality."

322

Another bow answered her before he turned to Michael. "Shall we join the others, Don Michael? When you have eaten there is something of which we must speak in private."

Molly followed the waiting servant up a flight of stairs to a room on the second floor.

"Would you like a bath first, or food, senorita?" the maid asked.

"A bath, please."

Wearily, Molly sank to the edge of the bed, wondering if she looked as dreadful as she felt. The battering she had taken from Jabal had weakened her. The long hike across country had done nothing to restore her strength. The gown she wore was soiled and rumpled. Perhaps the maid could clean it for her while she slept.

With a sigh, she removed the pistol from the gown pocket and slipped it under a pillow. Then she undressed. This time she retained her underwear, remembering the horror of her nakedness the night Jabal attacked her.

The maid returned with other maids bearing a tub and buckets of hot water. Over her arm was a voluminous nightgown and robe.

"Senorita, may I help you?" she asked.

Molly let her take her undergarments before she slid gratefully into the warmth of the bath. A soft groan came as the soothing heat took hold and removed some of the aches from her body. The maid went to work with soap and a cloth, removing the grime Molly had accumulated. Then she wrapped a big towel around Molly when she rose from the water and dried her with gentle pats. When Molly was dry, the maid slipped the gown over her head.

By the time Molly sat between the covers and propped by a pillow, another maid appeared with a tray emitting smells that made Molly ravenous. She was glad when the servants left her to eat in solitude. While she gobbled the food, her thoughts turned to Jaime and Dolores. They had supplies enough not to starve, but their food was nowhere near so tasty as this. That Jaime might get bored with the cave and venture outside was her worst fear. Dolores could not control the small Conde when he was being a monarch. Would they remain in the cave as Molly had bade them, or would they try to return to the hacienda?

There was no hacienda now. Neither was there much of the rest of Costa Cordillera left after Jabal's so-clever explosion. Would the Americans demolish Casa Grande in their anger? It seemed only fitting. The Americans had suffered grievous hurts at the hands of the Spaniards.

Dona Espicia's words about the cruelty and dark passions of the Spaniards returned to haunt her. Perhaps, as the Padre said, it was a blessing his stepmother hadn't lived to see what Jabal had done. The Padre! What had happened to him?

Padre Rodriguez had been blessing Condesa Magnifica the last time she remembered seeing him. Since he hadn't come with them, he must still be at Casa Grande. Would the Americans treat him kindly? Surely they would not harm a member of the clergy, for he had never harmed them.

The old Condesa was another matter entirely. Her own venom strangled her in the end. The evil old woman was dead, and that was all to the good. Had Noyo remained at his post beside his mistress? He had shot at the Americans and probably wounded or killed some of them, so perhaps he would be dealt with accordingly. Molly shuddered, remembering his hood-eyed stare that had turned her blood to ice. She would like never to see him again.

The cry of a bird outside stopped Molly's eating. She sat frozen by the sound. Was it Huk again?

Slipping from the bed, she walked quickly to the draped window and pushed the covering aside. Dawn had lightened the wispy fog. She peered hither and yon, straining her eyes to see through the mist, and then she saw a bird! It sailed high, then swooped down past her window with the shriek of a hunter. Culebra searching for his morning meal? Or had Condesa Magnifica sent him to find Molly even after her death?

The drapery fell into place as she backed away from the window. Her trembling legs carried her as far as the bed, then buckled. She pulled herself between the covers. Would this nightmare of death and destruction never end? Was she destined to spend her entire life in fear and trembling?

She wanted to be angry, but she was too tired. Even her fear dissolved before her weariness as she slipped gratefully into sleep.

The dark of her slumber was peopled this time. She relived Jabal's attack, only this time Condesa Magnifica was there urging him on. Her harsh voice dinned in Molly's ears while she fought Jabal's advances. He had six hands, and each time she broke free from two, two others grasped her. She tried to scream, but she had no voice.

Jabal did. He threw back his head in a wild triumphant laugh while all six hands fastened on her. Then his laughter died and the glint of madness was in his eyes.

"Your father never told me his daughter was a breed!" he sneered. "Indian! Indian! Indian!" he repeated and repeated and repeated.

Molly clapped both hands over her ears, but the sound of Jabal's words still rang in her head. She felt his bruising lips on her mouth and his greedy hands on her body, but there was nothing she could do.

Jaime entered the room and stood watching them, his eyes grave. Molly froze in horror, lying still so he would not notice what his father was trying to do. He must not know what an animal Don Jabal had become.

"Come, Jaime, it is time for your lessons," Dona Espicia said calmly.

Molly watched her lead him away, taking no notice of Molly and Jabal. When had she entered the room? The door hadn't opened. Then Dona Espicia and Jaime walked through the closed door and left Molly to her fate.

Jabal's voice droned the same phrase over and over while Molly stared at him in horror. She looked toward the spot where Condesa Magnifica had stood, but she was gone.

Suddenly Molly found her voice. She screamed and screamed, then screamed again as Jabal's face melted into runny torrents that shriveled down to nothingness. She woke bathed in sweat as the door burst open to let the maid enter.

"Senorita, senorita, what is wrong?" she asked, glancing around the room. "Are you hurt?"

Behind her Molly saw Don Jabal enter with Michael close on his heels and several of the *defensarios* behind them.

"What is all this shouting about?" Jabal asked. "Have the Americanos breeched your walls, Don Carillo?"

"Of course not," Don Carillo said irritably. "What is wrong here?" he asked the maid.

She looked frightened and shrank back as Jabal came to Molly's bed. Jabal looked down at her, and this time his eyes were those of a hunter instead of the madman she had seen before, but his manners were in place.

"Ah, it is the rose of the Sierra," he said jovially. "Gentlemen, you will please leave my fiancee's room." The dimple showed briefly. "Are you all right, my dear? Why were you screaming so loudly?"

Molly clutched the covers, her heart hammering in her ears. "I had a bad dream," she said weakly.

"Of course, my dear," he murmured. "Something in your supper, perhaps . . ."

He turned to the others. "Gentlemen, I asked you to leave," he said sternly. "My fiancee does not receive gentlemen in her bedchamber!"

Don Carillo shot a sharp glance toward Jabal, then herded the other men out before him. "Don Jabal, are you coming?" he asked, waiting at the door.

"Certainly," Jabal answered. "I trust you will now be all right, little rose?"

Molly nodded.

When the men had gone, the maid returned to smooth the covers on Molly's bed and plump the pillows. "Is there anything I can do for you, senorita?" she asked.

"No, thank you," Molly said with a wan smile. "I am very sorry I disturbed the household."

"It is nothing," she said, then left the room.

Molly lay trembling while her perspiration slowly dried. What had returned Don Jabal to such a semblance of normalcy? Had he forgotten she was half Indian? If he hadn't, he would never have referred to her as his fiancee. Or was he just playing a part for his audience?

A light rap on her door startled her. Before she could

say anything, the door opened to admit a stout white-haired lady who could only have been the mother of Don Carillo.

"*Buenas días*, Senorita O'Bannion," she said with a smile. "Please forgive my intrusion, my dear. I am Dona Carillo. I beg your forgiveness for not being awake when you arrived."

"*Buenas días*," Molly murmured.

"Were you brought enough to eat, my dear?" Dona Carillo asked.

"Oh, yes," Molly answered. "I do thank you for your hospitality, for I was in dire need of everything. The fighting at Costa Cordillera was dreadful."

"That is what my son said," she said. "He is sending me to Santa Rosa for safety," she continued. "There is room in the carriage for you, if you would care to accompany me."

"Thank you, Dona Carillo, but I cannot do that. I left the young Conde in a safe hiding place with a servant, and I must return for him as soon as I can."

"I see," she said thoughtfully. "Surely, you are not going to attempt this alone?"

Molly shook her head. "Don Michael will accompany me. He will take horses from those the army leaves."

A sigh shook her bosom. "This terrible war must end! It is disastrous for us to fight the Americans in this way. I have told my son this, but he is as hotheaded as his companions and will not listen."

"I did not even know there was a war, or what a war was, until Don Jabal's life was saved by my father. In return, when my father died, Don Jabal brought me to Costa Cordillera to be companion to Dona Espicia,"

Molly said. Tears welled in her eyes. "Life was so peaceful before that . . ."

Dona Carillo looked embarrassed. "Oh, what was I saying? You are an American, are you not?"

"Yes, I am an American."

Amatil was more American than any of these Spaniards. Why was their regard for Indians so low? The Indians inhabited this land long before anyone else.

"Forgive me if I said anything to insult you and your countrymen, Miss O'Bannion," Dona Carillo.

"You didn't," Molly answered. "You have been more than kind."

"Then you will be all right?" Dona Carillo asked. "You are sure you do not wish to go with me?"

"I'm sure."

"Then I must be on my way," she said. "Again, please forgive my intrusion. You need more sleep if you are to travel tonight. *Mi casa, su casa,*" she said politely, and left.

She was right, of course. Resolutely, Molly closed her eyes and willed herself to sleep. This time there were no dreams or nightmares.

She woke hours later to a hand clamped tightly over her mouth. Above the hand she saw Jabal's glittering eyes.

"Sh-h, *querida,*" he murmured, withdrawing his muffling fingers from her lips.

The black mustache drew close to rub against her nose while his lips covered hers. Her heart began its usual trip-hammer beat, but not from desire. This time her emotion was fear. She was frozen by it!

When there was no response to his kiss, Jabal drew

away, looking at her with hurt brown eyes. "What is it, *querida?* It is a long time since our last embrace. Are you too tired?"

Molly struggled to a sitting position. "You shouldn't be here, Jabal. It isn't proper."

He looked amazed. "Our host knows of our engagement," he said. "Spaniards have hotter blood than Americans. Once they have said their intention to marry, it is the same as though they were."

He pulled her to him and kissed her again.

Molly averted her face from his after she jerked away. "It is not the same with me, Jabal." His eyes looked sane, so she ventured a gamble. "Your word to my father should make you protect me, not harm me."

"Your father is dead, my dear," he said. "I have waited until everyone is sleeping to come to you. I might be dead after tonight's battle. In time of war one does not wait for the signing of contracts to make love."

"I do," she said stubbornly. She looked longingly at the closed door, wondering if she could escape without him catching her.

He rose and paced to the window and back, watching her as he did so. Then he stood over her gazing sternly down with a frown on his face.

"Do you not love me?" he asked. "Can you bear to make me suffer when my life may be so short? War is a dangerous game, my love." He sat on the bed and ran his hands over her bosom, but gently.

"Stop that, Jabal!"

Puzzlement grew in his eyes while he stared at her. He rubbed his hand across them as though trying to remember something. "There is an event . . ." he muttered.

"Leave my room at once, Don Jabal," Molly ordered, hoping he would not call her bluff.

Terror filled her when his hand left his eyes and she saw madness reappear. His mouth twisted in a sneer as he said, "Squaw! I had forgotten that fact for a moment. You are a breed, and as such, I have ownership of you."

His hand gripped the top of her nightgown and wrenched. The material parted with a tearing noise. Molly screamed at the top of her lungs.

"Scream, little Indian," he said as he fell across her.

The door burst open while she groped frantically for the pistol beneath her pillow.

"Get away from her, Jabal," Michael roared.

Over Jabal's shoulder she saw Michael brandishing a pistol as he came in the door. She squirmed away from Jabal's hands, still searching beneath the pillow.

Suddenly a dark shape materialized behind Michael. Light flashed on steel. She saw the hooded eyes of Noyo as he raised a knife above Michael's back.

With a cry of despair, her fingers closed on the gun. She pulled it from under the pillow, firing as she leveled it at Noyo. Blood spurted from a hole in his throat. He clutched at his neck while red liquid gurgled through his fingers, then crumpled to the floor.

The blast beside Jabal's ear threw him away from Molly. He winced, cursing a stream of obscenities that ran together like hot lava.

Michael's startled look over his shoulder took only an instant. Then his eyes returned to Jabal and he advanced toward him.

"Get up from there, Jabal," he said grimly. "This is not one of the girls from the quarters, you know. Miss O'Bannion is our guest."

"Get out of here, Michael," Jabal rasped. "This is my breed. Go find your own."

Don Carillo and some of the other *defensarios* appeared at the open door.

"What is happening here?" Don Carillo asked.

Jabal turned to face them. His hands knotted into fists and saliva ran from one corner of his mouth. "Go!" he shouted. "Leave us alone."

Michael leveled his gun at Jabal's waist. "Come away from there, Jabal. You do not know what you are doing."

With a cry of rage, Jabal swung at his brother's head, but missed. Michael ducked, but then Jabal's hands fastened on his throat. Michael gagged as the pressure on his throat increased. He clawed at the strangling hold with one hand while he tried to swing the gun barrel against Jabal's head with the other.

Jabal ducked the blow, removing his hands from Michael's throat to grab at the pistol. He caught it, wrenching the weapon from his brother's hand. A blast from the gun filled the room and the smell of gunpowder spread. Jabal looked incredulously at his shirt and the black hole spurting blood in the center of his body.

"*Madre de Dios* . . ." he gasped.

Michael stepped forward to help, but Jabal backed away.

The red blossom on Jabal's shirt grew larger. He looked down at it again and then his eyes returned to Michael. A sneer replaced the look of incredulity. "You . . . mongrel," he said, with a shower of spittle.

For an instant he looked like Condesa Magnifica at her worst. Then, slowly, his knees buckled, and he sank to the carpet while the crimson flood of life drained from him. He twitched once, then was still.

Michael's shocked face turned to Molly. "Are you all right, Molly?"

She stared stupidly, still holding the pistol and unable to comprehend what she had seen.

Michael grasped her shoulders, giving them a gentle shake. "Molly, say something . . . please?" he said.

Her eyelids refused to close as she stared at the scene with dry eyes.

"She is in shock, Don Michael," Don Carillo said. He had come to stand beside Michael, and now he motioned to the men. "Carry Don Jabal to another room, gentlemen. The Indian, too."

"Yes, get them out of here," Michael agreed.

"It would seem the senorita saved your life, Don Michael," Don Carillo said. "The Indian had a knife in his hand. Was he not Condesa Magnifica's manservant?"

"He was," Michael answered.

With a gesture of helplessness, Don Carillo followed the bodies being carried from the room.

Then Michael reached to take the gun from Molly's hand. The tips of his fingers gently pressed her eyelids closed before he drew her back into his arms.

"There, there," he said soothingly.

Tears came to ease the ache in her eyes. Michael's gentle hands rubbed her back, much as her mother had done when she was small. The tightness inside her dissolved so she could cry. She sobbed her misery against Michael's chest while he murmured soothing little sounds meant to comfort her. When hiccups replaced sobs, she drew away from him, sniffling.

He pulled a handkerchief from his pocket and wiped her eyes. Then he handed it to her. "Blow," he ordered.

She blew her nose and dabbed again at her eyes.

"Say something," he said. "Please tell me you are all right."

A hiccup came from Molly's mouth when she opened it. Tears still trickled down her face.

He pulled her head back to his chest. "You and I are the only ones left to take care of Jaime," he said. "I love you, *gringa*. The night I mistook you for Feliciana, I was glad you weren't. I loved Feliciana in the same way I do Jaime . . . they were two little children who needed me. You are a woman and I want you for my wife."

Molly lay listening to his quiet words, trying to grasp their meaning. Gradually, her mind cleared as the cobwebs of shock drifted away. Michael's heart throbbed in a steady beat against her ear to reassure her. With a sigh, Molly sat up.

"I am a breed," she said stubbornly. "My mother was a Cheyenne princess and I am proud of it!"

"Thank God!" he murmured. "I was afraid you had been struck dumb." Then he grinned. "I'm a breed, too, you know. My mother was an Irish lass, a fact of which I am very proud."

Chapter Twenty

Padre Rodriguez came puffing into the room. "May God preserve us," he gasped. "I tried to get here ahead of Noyo, but I didn't." He dropped into a chair and tried to catch his breath.

Michael rose from the bed. "I was afraid you would be harmed when we left you behind, Padre," he said, "but I thought it more necessary to get Molly away. I hope you will forgive me."

The priest waved away the apology. When he was again breathing normally, he sat straighter, saying, "The Americans were quite kind to me. They even supplied me with a horse so I could be on my way."

"Did they also give Noyo a mount so he could come here to kill me?" Molly asked.

"No, my child. If they had caught Noyo, they would have stretched his neck, for he killed some of their men," Padre Rodriguez answered. "Noyo made his escape after placing Condesa Magnifica in her bed." He shook his head. "How he did this, I do not know. Perhaps he lowered himself from a window, but whatever he did, the Americans did not see him do it."

"Noyo is dead now, so it no longer matters," Michael

said, "Jabal is also dead and he and the Condesa must be buried."

"May God forgive both of them for their actions on this earth," the priest said sadly. "Costa Cordillera has been demoralized and my Indian children have scattered into the hills. I'm afraid they will never return, Don Michael."

"They should be free," Michael said. "If they need my help, it will be given, but they must never submit to slavery as they did under Don Jabal."

Padre Rodriguez hauled himself from the chair and came to the bedside. "Are you all right now, my child?" he asked. "You, too, were grievously harmed by Don Jabal and his grandmother . . . and most especially by Don Jabal. When I have finished with the dead, I shall be most happy to take you with me to the mission. It will be your home as long as you have need of it. The children I have there will most surely benefit from your attentions."

"No, Padre Rodriguez," Molly said. "I must go with Don Michael to find Don Jaime and my maid, but I thank you from the bottom of my heart for your offer."

"Will you return to the castle to bury the Condesa, Don Michael?" the priest asked.

"I think not, Padre," Michael answered. "I will have men take Don Jabal back so he and his grandmother can be buried in the family plot. If you can accompany them, it will be greatly appreciated. Before you leave, however, I must speak with you."

Padre Rodriguez nodded. "Then if there is nothing I can do here, I had better go organize our funeral cortege," he said, then left.

When he had gone, Michael again sat on the edge of

the bed. "When there is war, there is no time for courting," he said gently. "But I have loved you for a long time, so will you marry me?"

She stared at him, wide-eyed, but said nothing.

He groaned. "Most men complain their wives talk too much, but I seem to have found a woman who will not talk at all! Please answer me, Molly. Will you marry me?"

"I don't know," she whispered.

"Do you love me?"

Did she love him? He was her rock and her savior—of course she loved him! It took her breath away as she realized it.

"Well?" he demanded.

"Yes, I love you, Michael," she said softly, "but I am ashamed. I was naked the night Jabal came and his hands pawed me while we were fighting."

She had dropped her eyes as she spoke and now the silence lasted so long her shame mounted. She would never be able to marry anyone. She would wander the earth until she grew old and wrinkled—a spinster!

And then Michael's hand lifted her chin so she would look at him. "There is nothing for you to be ashamed of, my darling. You . . . a guest in our home . . . were attacked. Mama would die of shame if she were still alive!"

He gathered her back to him. "If Jabal hadn't killed himself, I would do it now," he said savagely.

They sat in silence while Molly listened to his heart beneath her cheek. Then he stirred, sighing as he bent his head to hers.

"A savage pawing will not harm you permanently, Molly. I will make you forget it ever happened," he said.

His mouth met hers in a gentle kiss that soon became a

337

blend of love and desire that shook Molly to the depths of her being. Her arms went around him and she clung to Michael, drowning in the warmth of his embrace.

At last he straightened and his eyes were grave. "Do you really love me, Molly?"

"Oh, yes, Michael. Jabal was just . . . well, just Jabal, I guess, and I was a silly child. My father saved Jabal's life and so I was given into his keeping." She sighed. "My father didn't know what he was, and neither did I."

"If you are ashamed because he saw you naked, remember he is dead and cannot see anything," Michael said. "I will tell you a secret, *gringo*. There is a woman or two who has seen me naked, too, and I am not exactly proud of that now."

"You're making fun of me," she said indignantly.

"No, my darling—perhaps teasing a little," he conceded. "If I let myself grow angry it would serve no purpose, so I try to make light of the terrible thing that almost happened."

Molly studied the face before her. It was strong and handsome, the chin firm, the eyes steady. It was a face of which her mother would approve.

"I would like to stay here, but we have work to do, my darling," he said.

"Oh?" she asked, hoping her disappointment didn't show.

"You must get dressed for your wedding and I must go ask Padre Rodriguez if he will marry us."

"Oh, Michael . . . so soon after deaths? It hardly seems . . . appropriate," she said slowly.

"I told you there was no time for the amenities when war is raging," he said. "We had better seal our future while a priest is still available."

"Yes, Michael."

With a groan he pulled her to him. This time his kiss was fiery and demanding, bringing a melting sensation she had never felt before. Not even with Jabal. His mouth covered hers until she thought she would smother. Then he moved away.

"I had better leave before I become an even bigger jackass than my brother," he said despairingly. "I love you, Molly O'Bannion."

When he had gone, Molly sat for a time in thought. Was the brutal pawing that Jabal had done—was that part of the act of love that had bound her parents together? It couldn't be! No woman could love a man who rutted like an animal. Amatil would have told her about something so horrible, so therefore it was different. Gentle. Like Michael.

She rose and discovered that her soiled clothing had been laundered and returned while she slept. A knock on the door preceded maids carrying a tub and hot water for Molly to bathe. At least she would be a clean bride, she decided as she stepped into the tub. Her gown would not be white and flowing, but that was as it should be. She wriggled luxuriously in the steaming water with its invigorating effects.

When Michael came for her, Molly was dressed and ready. He led her to where Padre Rodriguez and several of his friends were waiting, all with grave faces, for the sadness of the day's events could not be wiped out with the joy of a wedding.

The ceremony was brief, but when it was over, Michael and Molly were husband and wife. Their delight with each other was plain for all to see, but other matters needed tending.

"And now, my children, I wish to speak to all of you," the priest said. "The Americans wish to end hostilities now that your savage leader is gone. Before I left Casa Grande I spoke with them. They would not rest while Don Jabal del Valle lived, but now he is dead, which makes a very different matter. This war has taken its toll on both sides and should be ended, so I hope you brave young men will now consider a truce."

Voices rose as the young Spaniards discussed Jabal's death and the course of the war. Padre Rodriguez left them to decide while he spoke to Michael.

"Now I shall go with the bodies to Costa Cordillera and bless the dead before they are buried," he said. "I hope you and your bride have a long and happy life, Don Michael. I also hope the young Conde is safe. *Vaya con Dios.*"

Don Carillo remained behind after the *defensarios* had gone from the room. "Dona Mollee, you are a lovely bride," he said. "However, perhaps you would like to change into clothing more suitable for riding a horse. I will have a maid show you to my mother's room, for I am sure there is something that will suit you." With a bow, he was gone.

Soon a maid came for Molly and escorted her to where she could change into a riding habit. Michael went as far as the door.

"While you are getting dressed, I will arrange for our horses," he said. "It is time we went to the cave for Jaime and Dolores."

"I won't be long," Molly said.

Soon they were mounted and on their way. Now that all the commotion had passed, Molly worried anew about the young Conde. She would have liked to kick the horses into a gallop, but Michael stopped her.

"Our horses will last long if we do not hurry them too much, Molly," he said.

"I know." She sighed. "We must be sensible about everything, I suppose." Then she glanced at him and frowned. "What about the *defensarios*, Michael? Are you not their leader now?"

"I could never be their leader, Molly," he said. "Although they are my friends, they still look down on me because my blood is not pure Spanish. Besides, I don't want to lead them. I want no part of this war with the Americans and never did. I am not a Spaniard. Since my mother is no longer on Costa Cordillera, there is nothing to keep me there."

"What about Jaime?"

A frown wrinkled his brow. "Jaime will grow up as a little boy should," he said. "When things have settled down, I will put in a claim for his grant which will probably be honored. He can be a Conde when he is grown, if he so wishes."

They rode for a while, then rested the horses beside a spring where all could drink.

"Where will you take us, Michael?" Molly asked.

"Somewhere to forget the madness of these past days," he said grimly.

"Is there such a place?"

"Oh, yes," he said, then laughed. "Sure and I'll build ye a castle, my fine lass, the likes of which ye've never before seen."

Molly stared at him. "You sound just like my father," she said wonderingly.

"Sure, and don't be thinkin' Bridget Shaughnessy didn't show me how a true Irisher would speak! There's no castle in the land fine enough for you, but I'll build one that will be," he said.

They mounted again and continued on their way while Molly hugged to herself the happiness Michael would bring. Then a thought occurred to her. "Michael, is Chia still alive?"

He nodded. "Chia is one of the funeral cortege," he said. "He will do his master one last service, then he is free. He and Dolores can be married if they wish."

The ride seemed endless as they rode toward the cave. Night overtook them, making their journey more hazardous, but still they pushed on. It was nearing midnight before they reached the glen in front of the cavern.

"I'm glad we are here," Molly said with a sigh of relief. "Let's let them sleep until morning, Michael."

"We'll be quiet so we don't wake them up," he said as he helped her from the saddle. "These horses can use some rest, too, for they'll have to carry double tomorrow."

Molly entered the cave while her new husband was settling the horses for the night. She stood just inside the entrance until her eyes grew accustomed to the gloom, then tried to see where Jaime and Dolores were sleeping. It was too dark. She inched her way into the cavern, touching the Madonna and feeling on the ground for blankets, but none were spread out.

"Dolores? Jaime?" she said softly. "Are you here?"

There was no answer, neither was there any sound of sleeping when she held her breath to listen. The cave was unoccupied! Panic-stricken, she ran from the cave.

"Michael, there's no one here!" she said.

"Are you sure? *Madre de Dios* help them if they

returned to the hacienda before the Americans left," he said, pulling her with him as he went inside to make sure.

"Jaime!" he shouted, but there was no answer.

"We have to look for them," Molly said. "We must find them, Michael."

He thought for a moment, then groaned before he said, "We can't find them in the dark, Molly, and if we don't let the horses rest, we'll find ourselves afoot. We could do with a little sleep, too, so we'll wait until first light and then head for Casa Grande."

Molly found the blankets neatly folded against the wall. She spread them before the statue while Michael folded the saddle blankets to serve as pillows. They stretched out on the makeshift bed with sighs of weariness.

Michael kissed her. "Tonight we must sleep, wife, but if ever this damnable nightmare ceases, then I will show you how much I love you."

"Yes, Michael," she said contentedly, and closed her eyes. She worried the question of where Jaime and Dolores had gone and if they were safe, but only for a short time. Then she slept the deep sleep of a tired human.

Michael woke her just as the birds in the trees were waking with sleepy chirps. "Wake up, Molly. It's time we were leaving," he said.

"Michael . . . did you get any sleep at all?"

"As much as I needed, sleepyhead. There's nothing here to eat, so we'll have to ride for breakfast."

She rose, stretching as she tried to remove the kinks from her back. Now she could see the dim interior and her worries about her two charges returned. She followed Michael outside and saw he had already saddled the horses.

"Perhaps we should search in the brush around here. They could be hiding." She shuddered, remembering the dying man she had found in the bushes.

"I have already looked," Michael said. "I walked in ever-widening circles for an hour. If they were around here, I would have discovered them."

He helped her onto the saddle, then mounted his own horse. They rode to the spring where Molly had filled her boot and drank their fill, watering the horses after them. Then they were off, pushing the horses into a faster pace as they drew nearer to where the hacienda had been.

Molly prayed silently to her father's God for the safety of Jaime and Dolores. She had not heard the cry of Huk so surely they were still alive. A merciful God could not have it otherwise.

The sun was high in the sky when they reached the courtyard of Costa Cordillera. It was deserted. They looked around the ruins, shocked anew at what they saw. The hacienda and the sheds and barns had burned to the ground. The stones of Michael's house still stood, but the building had been gutted. Casa Grande was still intact, but the front door had been torn from its hinges.

Michael led the way as they rode to Casa Grande. He dismounted and helped Molly down. The silence was appalling.

"Let's look inside," Michael said grimly.

Inside Casa Grande the results of the wrath of the Americans could be seen everywhere. Draperies were torn down, shutters wrenched from windows, carpets ripped into shreds. The once proud bastion was in tatters.

Molly slipped her hand into Michael's. "Let's go upstairs and see what's there," she whispered.

"Why are you whispering?" he asked. "There's no one here." He rubbed his forehead and closed his eyes. "Oh, God, what went on here after we left?"

They went up the stairs and began their search of the many rooms. The body of Condesa Magnifica had disappeared and no sound save their footsteps broke the quiet of Casa Grande. They returned to the stairway and sat on the top step.

"Now what?" Molly asked. "Where do we go from here? Oh, Michael, they have to be somewhere . . . God would not let such a small boy die."

"I hope you are right," he said with a sigh. "God seems to have deserted all his children at this moment."

Suddenly he straightened. "Did you hear that, Molly?"

"What?"

"Voices! Somebody is coming."

Now Molly could hear the sounds, too. Then through the doorway Jaime bounded in with Chia close behind. The men who had accompanied the bodies of Jabal and Noyo trailed after them, with Padre Rodriguez puffing in last. Dolores walked beside him.

Before Michael and Molly could make themselves seen, Jaime turned to face the assembly. "Now that Don Jabal and Condesa Magnifica lie in the cemetery, I am Conde of Costa Cordillera," he said. "Chia, you will saddle Garanon for me. I wish to see to my rancho."

Michael rose. "Chia will do nothing of the kind, Don Jaime," he said loudly.

Startled eyes were turned upward to where Molly and Michael stood.

"Aunt Molly!" Jaime exclaimed. "Tio Michael! You were not here for the funeral."

345

"We went to the cave to find you and Dolores, Jaime," Michael said. "Why did you not wait there as you were told to do?"

"I am now the Conde and no one tells me what to do!" he said, much as his father before had stated.

"What are you the conde of, Jaime?" his uncle asked. "There is not much left on Costa Cordillera save a castle in ruins."

Molly shook her head at her husband and went down the steps to where Jaime stood. She took him in her arms. "Oh, Jaime, we were so worried about you, and we're so glad you are safe."

The Conde del Valle became again a small boy who had been frightened almost out of his wits. Tears filled his eyes as he hugged her. "Oh, Aunt Molly—we heard shooting and saw flames in the sky! I could not hide any longer. Papa had need of me, so we returned. Only everything was burned and the Condesa was dead and we hid in the cellar."

He buried his head in Molly's clothing while she rubbed his small back and uttered soothing sounds to calm him.

"You are safe now, Jaime. Your uncle and I will take care of you and everything will be all right," she said.

He raised his head and brushed angrily at the tears rolling down his cheeks. "But I am Conde! I must rule Costa Cordillera like Papa did."

"You are a little boy, Jaime," Molly said gently. "There is no need to be Conde until you are grown, and then only if you wish. It is time you were allowed to be what you are, and not a seven-year-old adult."

Michael had come to stand beside them, and now Jaime looked from one to the other.

346

"Tio Michael, that is so?" Jaime asked.

"That is so," Michael agreed. Then he looked at the *defensarios* and said, "Thank you, my friends, for bringing my brother and the Indian home. *Vaya con Dios.* Chia, will you stay a moment?"

When the men had gone, Michael motioned to Padre Rodriguez and Dolores. "You look worn, Padre," he said. "Sit here on the steps, for the chairs seem to have been used in a crusher."

The priest sat down with a grunt of relief. "I shall sleep for a week when I get back to the mission," he said.

"Perhaps there is one more duty for you to perform before you leave us," Michael said. "Dolores . . . Chia . . . you are both free to go where you will. There will be no more bondage on Costa Cordillera."

Chia put his arms around Dolores and murmured into her ear. Dolores nodded, her face ashine with joy.

"Will you marry us, Padre?" Chia asked.

"Of course, my children," the priest answered. He struggled to rise, then accepted the help of Michael when he put out his hand to pull the priest to his feet.

Although he had no Bible, Padre Rodriguez performed the brief ceremony to everyone's satisfaction. The del Valles congratulated the newlyweds, wishing them prosperity and health.

Dolores hugged Molly, saying, "Mollee, we thank you and Don Michael for everything. We want to help you build your house and stay with you until you no longer need us."

"May I kiss your bride, Chia?" Michael asked. "It would seem she has volunteered you into a lot of work."

"*Si*, Don Michael," Chia answered.

Michael kissed Dolores on the cheek, then said, "I am

no longer a don. Now I am Michael del Valle, and you are my friends."

"I am no longer a don, either," Jaime said. "I am a small boy who would like to kiss the bride also."

Laughing, Dolores bent for his kiss.

Suddenly Molly thought of Jaime's pet. "Where is Mouse, Jaime?" she asked, hoping against hope that the tiny animal had not been killed.

"We left him in the cellar where we stayed, Aunt Molly. He does not like funerals, and neither do I. I will get him now," Jaime said, heading for the cellars.

Chia and Michael had gotten into a discussion of future plans, so Molly turned to Dolores. "We shall have to stay here tonight, I think, so we had better see if we can put together three of the bedrooms, Dolores."

"*Si,* Mollee."

They mounted the stairs together and searched the bedrooms that had been turned into shambles by the wrathful Americans. It took some time to manage, but they put beds together and found enough bedding to cover them. Even the pillows had been attacked and goosedown was scattered everywhere. They gathered handfuls until the pillows were filled, then sewed them closed with the sewing supplies that had been overlooked in Condesa Magnifica's room.

"With the Condesa's body in there, even the Americans would not have entered," Molly said. She sighed. "Condesa Magnifica did more good after she was dead than during her lifetime."

The room was as it always had been, but neither Molly nor Dolores wanted to sleep in the old woman's bed or stay in the room where she lived. Even though she was no longer there, a miasma of evil seemed to fill the room to bursting. The two women were glad to escape to join their husbands in the front hall.

Jaime had returned with Mouse and they were playing as a normal small boy and his dog should play. "We're hungry," he announced. "Now can we eat?"

Dolores nodded. "The kitchen is still supplied. The Americanos did not think to destroy the cellars, or perhaps one look was enough to send them on their way," she said. "I will bring food."

"I'll come with you," Molly said.

It did not take them long to prepare supper. When they brought it to the hall, it took even less time for it to be eaten.

Then Jaime yawned. "I think it is time Mouse and I went to bed," he said.

"I think it is time we all went to bed," Michael echoed. He offered his arm to Molly. "Help me up the stairs, wife."

She giggled, then said, "I have married an old man!"

"We shall see."

When they were alone in their room, Michael took her into his arms and kissed her, gently at first, then urgent and demanding. Molly responded, and a desire she had never before felt arose inside her. Then Michael ended the embrace.

"I shall be glad to be rid of these garments," he said, taking off his shirt and then the rest of his clothing.

Molly stood uncertain, shy at the thought of being naked. Then Amatil's soft voice sounded in her mind. "This is your husband, my child. Soon you will be as one." Molly nodded, then slowly undressed, sliding quickly beneath the covers to hide her nakedness. Desire and fear were mixed in her emotions. She wanted

Michael . . . but not if he hurt her.

Michael slid in beside her and again took her in his arms. "I love you, wife," he said huskily. "I will always love you."

"I love you, too, husband, only . . ."

"Only what?"

She hesitated, then whispered, "Will it hurt?"

"Oh, my darling!" Michael said, then kissed her until her toes tingled and she was filled with desire. Then he pulled away to look at her. "You must not be afraid, especially of me. I will never hurt you, Molly. I am not like the animal who ravaged you. I am the man who loves you desperately."

A twinkle came into his eyes as he bunched a pillow behind his head and lay apart from Molly. "In fact, I will not touch you unless you ask that I do so, wife."

Molly sat up with a startled look on her face. Then it changed to indignation. "Is this a way to treat a bride, Michael? You will not touch me unless I ask you? How do I know what to ask for? I am not as experienced as you in these matters!"

Michael chuckled as Molly grew irate. "Ah, that is more like the Molly I know—fire and fight like a good Irisher should."

"Don't you laugh at me!"

He pulled her beside him and closed her mouth with his. The kiss lasted longer this time, but had to end so they could breathe. Then Michael was atop her and she welcomed his weight. When they mated it was gentle and exciting and almost more pleasure than Molly could bear.

"Oh, Michael . . ."

He lay panting, bathed in sweat. When he regained his breath, he rose and opened a window wide. The cool

California night breezes came into the room. Wispy fog accompanied them. Then he returned to lie beside Molly.

His familiar grin flashed at her before he asked, "Are you all right, wife?"

"Oh, yes . . ." Then she sat up. "Are you laughing at me again?"

"Never! I would never laugh at you, Molly, only with you," he said gently. "If a husband and wife cannot laugh together, there is no chance their marriage will be successful."

She pushed him back on the pillow and kissed him soundly before she raised her head. "Sure and I love to laugh, husband. I love being your wife, too."

The scream of a bird of prey sounded outside the open window and with a cry of fear, Molly covered her head with the quilt.

"That is only Culebra," Michael said, trying to comfort her.

"It's Huk," she wailed, "and when he cries in the night someone I love dies."

"We'll see about that," Michael said grimly. He rose and got his pistol, then went to the window and peered into the mist outside. When Culebra again dived at the open window, Michael shot him. An eerie death cry marked the bird's passage to the ground. Then Michael returned to dress himself.

"Wh-where are you g-going?" Molly asked.

"I am going to bury Culebra so you will never hear or see him again," he said, and there was determination in his voice as he added, "I don't know who this Huk is, but I will do the same to him if he bothers you."

Molly hugged her knees as he left the room. Michael . . . strong-willed . . . capable . . . unbending

351

as iron.

She had been so stubborn and it had brought her
nothing but grief, so she would dispense with it in future.

Images of her parents came to mind. Amatil . . .
Colin . . . mother and father she had lost. Huk had taken
them from her. Would he follow her to take Michael?

Then she laughed. Don Michael del Valle was a
grandee of both Spain and Ireland. He would be more
than a match for the evil Huk. She looked into a future of
love and happiness, sure she would never hear the
frightening cry of Huk again.